JUSTICE

CURTIS CHRONICLES #3
JOSEPH BADAL

SUSPENSE PUBLISHING

JUSTICE
THE CURTIS CHRONICLES #3
by
Joseph Badal

GALLEY EDITION
* * * * *
PUBLISHED BY:
Suspense Publishing

Joseph Badal
Copyright 2019 Joseph Badal

PUBLISHING HISTORY:
Suspense Publishing, Paperback and Digital Copy, November 2019

Cover Design: Shannon Raab
Cover Photographer: iStockphoto.com/ HubCam
Cover Photographer: iStockphoto.com/ filrom

JOSEPH BADAL'S BOOKS & SHORT STORIES

THE DANFORTH SAGA
EVIL DEEDS (#1)
TERROR CELL (#2)
THE NOSTRADAMUS SECRET (#3)
THE LONE WOLF AGENDA (#4)
DEATH SHIP (#5)
SINS OF THE FATHERS (#6)

THE CURTIS CHRONICLES
THE MOTIVE (#1)
OBSESSED (#2)
JUSTICE (#3)

LASSITER/MARTINEZ CASE FILES
BORDERLINE (#1)
DARK ANGEL (#2)
NATURAL CAUSES (#3)

STAND-ALONE THRILLERS
THE PYTHAGOREAN SOLUTION
SHELL GAME
ULTIMATE BETRAYAL

SHORT STORIES
FIRE & ICE (UNCOMMON ASSASSINS ANTHOLOGY)
ULTIMATE BETRAYAL (SOMEONE WICKED ANTHOLOGY)
THE ROCK (INSIDIOUS ASSASSINS ANTHOLOGY)

This book is dedicated to three authors, Tony Hillerman, Parris Afton Bonds, and Steve Brewer, who at the beginning of my writing career generously provided priceless advice and invaluable encouragement and introduced me to people in the literary world who have made a huge difference in my career.
Thank you, Tony, Parris, and Steve.

PRAISE FOR
JOSEPH BADAL

TK

JUSTICE

THE CURTIS CHRONICLES
#3

JOSEPH BADAL

DAY 1

CHAPTER 1

The pounding rhythm of her heartbeat affirmed that she was still alive. But it no longer gave Miranda Sánchez comfort. It seemed to have evolved into an alien creature that invaded her being; drummed in her chest, neck, and ears; and screamed to get out.

She gripped the crucifix on the delicate silver chain around her neck and once again prayed for salvation. Not for the deliverance of her soul—for which she had prayed thousands of times in the cathedral in Ocotal—but for the rescue of her body . . . and mind.

The sickening, pale-yellow, muted light from a naked bulb provided just enough illumination to see her hands. She stared down at her shadowed fist wrapped around the cross, opened her fingers, and cringed at the filth under her fingernails and on the back of her hand. The stench of human waste assailed her nostrils, and even breathing through her mouth did little to allay the putrid odors.

Three days had passed since she'd been allowed to bathe. Three days of hunger, threats, and beatings because she resisted the man named Carlos.

She released the symbol of her faith and dropped it between her breasts, beneath the coarse, homespun fabric of her plain, soiled, once-white dress. The rag had fit tightly on her full figure just one week earlier. It now draped over her like a hand-me-down from an older, larger sister.

Miranda shifted on the pallet set against the wall opposite the cell door, pressed her back against the damp cement wall, and shivered. Despite the August heat and humidity, the wall chilled her.

It took a magnificent force of will to laugh under the circumstances, but she forced out a curt, cough-like chuckle, mocking herself for leaving her home in Nicaragua. *Why didn't I listen to Mama?*

"Miranda, only harm will come to you for trying to better yourself," Mama had said. But she couldn't stand the thought of looking like her mother—a worn-out drudge, a slave to a system that offered no hope to poor women.

A sudden *tap-tap-tap* interrupted her thoughts. Miranda cocked an ear. This was something new. She tried to quiet her heart and still her breathing. There it was again—*tap-tap-tap*. It seemed to come from the wall on her right.

She moved to all fours, pushed off with her hands, and rose from the pallet. Suddenly lightheaded, she leaned against the back wall. When the dizziness lessened, she moved to her right, touched the cell's side wall, and waited for the tapping sounds to come again. "Tap-tap-tap," she whispered, thinking for a moment IA Agent was playing a game with her, mocking her, teasing the last of her sanity from her terrified brain.

Maybe ten minutes had gone by when she wailed a mournful, toneless hymn that careened off the cell's hard surfaces and drifted like morning mist through the small, barred opening in the cell door. Miranda's legs turned rubbery and she slid down the wall to the floor. Tears flowed onto her crossed arms. Then she slowly rolled to her side and scrunched herself into a fetal ball, making herself as small as possible.

Tap-tap-tap-tap-tap. More rapid this time. Frantic.

Miranda uncurled herself and scooted to face the side wall. She removed a sandal and banged the wall three times.

Ten seconds passed, then the *tap-tap-tap* came again. The faint, feathery sound of a female voice carried to her. The words were indecipherable, but not the tone. There was no mistaking the high-pitched tone of fear.

Miranda felt a momentary exhilaration. She wasn't alone. But then reality struck and she felt more desperate than ever. Being here wasn't an isolated incident. The man had brought at least one other woman here. There could be dozens more. What did he intend to do with her? To them?

CHAPTER 2

Carlos Salgado stood on the other side of Señor José Rosales Lorca's desk and stared down at the floor. He felt perspiration roll from his head and down across his brow. He tried to blink away drops that stung his eyes. He wanted to wipe them away but his hands felt weighted, glued to the sides of his legs.

"Look at me!" Lorca barked.

Salgado bounced his eyes at Lorca, but again dropped his gaze to the floor. He was afraid that if he looked into Lorca's amber-colored eyes he would lose control of his bladder. He'd never seen eyes like *El Jefe's* eyes—cat's eyes. And there was . . . he didn't know. Something lurked behind those eyes. Anger. Hate. Madness. Evil.

For Salgado, this was only business. That's what he kept reminding himself. He took no pride in what he did, even feeling conscience-stricken at times and sometimes praying to God for forgiveness. But he knew no other way to make this kind of money. However, for *El Jefe*, it seemed somehow different. It wasn't that the boss reaped pleasure from the business. *El Jefe* seemed to gain pleasure from nothing. The big man functioned like an automaton—absent most feeling and relationships.

Señor Lorca had only one emotion that Salgado was aware of: anger. And he was scared shitless of being the cause of his boss's anger. He'd seen the man furious a few times. And he'd seen the pain he'd inflicted on the focus of that fury.

Salgado swallowed and slowly sucked in a deep breath. *Come on, maricón, act like a man*, he told himself. *You're bigger and stronger than the boss. Don't let him see your fear.* But the admonishment did no good. He attempted to put steel in his voice, despite the fact his knees felt like Jell-O and his stomach was filled with acid.

"You need something, *Jefe*?"

Lorca blew out a stream of cigar smoke and squinted while the smoke dissipated toward the ceiling. He leaned back in his chair and swiveled halfway around so he could look out at the lush jungle that bordered his Nicaraguan hacienda.

"Any progress with the Sánchez girl?"

Salgado cleared his throat and wiped the palms of his hands on the sides of his jeans. "No, *Jefe*. She is very stubborn. She has had only bread and water for three days, but she refuses to submit."

"You realize I have orders I must fill?"

"*Sí, Jefe*. But she is not ready yet. The customer will be upset if we send him someone who is injured and is not . . . *manejable*."

Lorca again drew on his cigar and expelled smoke. "*Manejable*—pliable. Yes, she must be pliable. And I don't want her bruised or cut. When do you anticipate that she will be . . . pliable?"

"Perhaps another two or three days without food." He paused a beat and added, "Lack of food and daily beatings with a belt . . ." Salgado shrugged, shifted his feet, and stared at Lorca's back.

Lorca suddenly swiveled around, and Salgado quickly dropped his gaze back to the floor.

Lorca threw his cigar at the middle of Salgado's chest where it exploded in a shower of sparks. Salgado yelped and stepped back. Lorca leaned forward and pointed a hand. "You've got one hour. Break her now. These *putas* do what I say. This isn't a fucking democracy. You understand?"

Salgado half-turned and sidled toward the door. "*Sí, sí, Jefe*."

"Carlos," Lorca said before Salgado escaped the room.

"*Sí, Jefe*?"

"If this girl doesn't cooperate, we'll take her down to the pond. Make an example of her."

Salgado slinked from the room, then rushed down the hall to a bathroom. His bladder felt suddenly weak. And nausea had come over him like a panther attack, without warning, without remorse. He didn't dare fail Lorca. Even if it meant doing things that would condemn his soul to Purgatory.

CHAPTER 3

"Are you up for another one of these dinners?" Matt Curtis asked while he stared at his image in the mirror on the back of the hotel room's closet door. He tried to fix the black bowtie, but couldn't balance both sides.

His wife, Renee, laughed and looked over at him. "It's not the dinners I mind, nor the speeches; it's remembering what city I'm in at any one time. Tell me again," she teased. "Are we in Cleveland or Honolulu?" She rose from the easy chair, crossed the room, and stepped between Matt and the mirror. After she straightened his tie, she said, "Why don't you buy one of those clip-on things? It would make your life a lot easier."

"Nag, nag, nag. I told you I never take the easy way out. And, by the way, we're in Honolulu."

Renee giggled and pinched Matt's arm. "I guess the palm trees outside should have been a clue."

"You could probably give my speech, word for word, by now," he said in an apologetic tone. "You don't have to go to dinner, you know."

"Yeah, you're right. I probably could give your speech, and I know I could skip another one of these rubber chicken dinners. But, if you think I'm about to leave you alone and let some woman on the make hit on you, you're nuts."

It was Matt's turn to laugh. He swept a hand through his thick, gray hair and said, "I think I'm past the point where I'm hit-on-able material."

Renee gave Matt her Mona Lisa smile and wrapped her arms around his neck. Between her five feet, eight-inch height and high heels, she barely had to stretch to place her lips on his. "Don't kid yourself, Matthew Curtis; you're as handsome today as you ever were."

Matt put his hands around her upper arms and gently pushed her back so he could look into her eyes. They were so damn intoxicating—cobalt blue, with an ever-present sparkle. "You've got nothing to worry about, Mrs. Curtis."

She laughed again, made the sound that reminded Matt of wind chimes, and pinched him on the same spot on his arm.

Matt pulled her to him and kissed her passionately. He felt trembly, like a teenager kissed for the first time.

When they broke away, Renee walked to the bathroom and came back with a tissue. "You might want to wipe the lipstick from your mouth," she said. "Wouldn't want to scandalize the members of the International Society of Orthopedic Surgeons."

Matt took the tissue and rubbed it over his lips. "I'll have a tough time concentrating on my speech, with you next to me on the podium."

Renee made a dismissive gesture with her hand. "You'll do what you always do—knock their socks off." She smiled. "Let's go downstairs and get this over with, so we can come back up here and make wild, passionate love."

Matt watched Renee move to the bureau and pick up her beaded evening bag and silk organza wrap. She looked stunning in her black, strapless gown and sequined heels. He wondered at the serendipity of how they'd met, fell in love, and married. It had taken his sister's murder—ordered by that psychopath, Lonnie Jackson—to bring them together in Honolulu a little more than two years ago.

And now Lonnie Jackson had caused them to turn their lives upside-down. The threat of him coming after them once again had been too real, more probable than possible. Jackson blamed Matt and Renee for the destruction of his criminal empire, his mother's suicide, and his brother's murder. *How out of touch with reality could one man be?* Matt wondered. If Jackson hadn't ordered that dirty cop, Dennis Callahan, to murder Matt's sister, Matt would never have gone to Hawaii when he did, would never have heard Jackson's name, would never have met Renee.

A sudden melancholia struck Matt. He'd given up a lot. But Renee had given up even more. A pedophile client of Jackson's had murdered her son, David. Her first husband had committed suicide over the death of their son. Matt and Renee had left their New Mexico home after Jackson tried to kill them there. But they'd had no choice. Lonnie Jackson's ghost haunted their home on the east side of Albuquerque's Sandia Mountains. Since Jackson had come after them the previous New Years, Renee had been like a rabbit in the middle of coyote country. She couldn't relax. And he knew she couldn't purge the thought that Jackson might return.

Jackson's trip to New Mexico had been the act of an irrational man. He had everything to lose and nothing to gain—except maybe to expel his own demons. The fact he'd failed in his mission to murder them left Matt with the unassailable belief that Jackson was more obsessed than ever with revenge. His instincts told him Jackson would return.

Matt had now been on the lecture circuit for three months, since selling his medical practice. Renee had been with him for the entire tour. Their home base continued to be New Mexico. But they'd only been there a total of ten days in the last ninety. The arrangement with Placer Medical had been a godsend. They had offered a generous salary and royalties from all sales, plus reimbursement of travel expenses, to promote the company's line of orthotics products to physicians all over the world. For Placer, Matt was the logical choice to be their corporate spokesman. The surgical procedure he'd developed for the emplacement of orthopedic appliances had reduced the rate of rejection by fifty percent. His twenty years as an orthopedic surgeon gave him and Placer credibility.

It had been difficult for Matt to give up his practice . . . and his patients. He'd treated three generations of some families, and these people had become a major part of his reason for being. And then there were the couple's dogs, Latifah and Dooney. He'd left them with an Army veteran who house-sat at their place.

Traveling for Placer was no guarantee Jackson wouldn't find them, but at least they were on the move. Matt thought being a moving target was better than being a sitting duck.

CHAPTER 4

Lonnie Jackson had no doubts about Carlos Salgado *now* taking care of business. But that's what bothered him about the man. He always did what he was told, but never took any initiative. Salgado wasn't tough enough. This Miranda Sánchez girl should have been disciplined from the moment she arrived. Instead, Salgado had treated her as though she had a choice. He placed both fists on the desk blotter and clenched his jaw. The little bitch has no choice. "It's my way, or no way," he said aloud.

Jackson pushed back from his desk, moved from his chair to the window behind him, and peered out at the lush green jungle. It took one full-time flunky armed with a machete to keep the vegetation from encroaching on the lawn that stretched for fifty yards from the back of the house. The electrified chain-link fence that surrounded the five-acre homestead did more than provide security against two-legged intruders; it also kept out reptiles, huge rodents, and jaguars that inhabited the one thousand acres of virgin jungle that Jackson had purchased, along with the one-story, eighteen-room hacienda, stables, and three outbuildings. The deed to the property was assigned to the new owner, José Rosales Lorca, Jackson's latest alias.

The closest town of any size was San Juan del Norte, a picturesque, seaside community on the Nicaraguan border with Costa Rica. Nicaragua offered a more flexible environment for someone who didn't want to live his life by the letter of the law. Proximity to Costa Rica gave Jackson access to the sophisticated pleasures of the country's capital city, San José—and an easy escape to another country should he need to flee. It was only a one-hour helicopter ride from his hacienda northwest of San Juan del Norte, over Volcán Irazú in Costa Rica, to San José.

Salgado crossed himself while he moved down the concrete walkway that divided the two rows of cells. Five cells on each side; heavy wood doors with a metal bar grate in each. He snorted at the faint odor of straw and horses. He'd been here when Lorca had the stables converted into a cellblock shortly after he bought the place six months ago.

He hesitated outside the locked door of the next to the last room on the right, ran a hand through his thick, black hair, then wiped the hand on the side of his jeans. The summer had been unusually mild, with unseasonable rains and temperatures in the eighties. The humidity was high, as usual, but he was used to it. He knew it wasn't the weather or the temperature that made him perspire now.

He had a fleeting thought about the circumstances of his life. Raised as a Catholic, he had considered the priesthood as a teenager. But that thought had disappeared with the first girl he'd slept with. For an instant, he wondered what that girl was doing today. He'd worked for a gangster in Managua for a few years until Lorca had recruited him. Then he jerked at a movement off to his right and saw a gecko spread-eagled on the wall. *Story of my life*, Carlos thought. *Like a chameleon. Change colors—allegiances—to survive.* His job with Lorca had been just one more such change.

Salgado took a deep breath and looked through the foot-square opening in the top of the door. The girl huddled against the back wall of the cell. He inserted a key in the lock and pushed down on the large metal handle. The three-inch thick, solid oak door creaked open. He stood in the doorway to allow his eyes to become accustomed to the meager light. The girl scurried off the pallet to the nearest corner. He coughed when the stench from the waste bucket by the door hit him.

"Stand up," he ordered.

Miranda Sánchez whimpered.

"Stand up!" Salgado shouted, spittle erupting from his mouth. He wiped a hand across his lips and yelled again: "Stand up, girl!"

Miranda's eyes were as wide as those of a nocturnal animal's as she struggled to stand. She swayed as though dizzy, then leaned against the wall for support.

"Come here," he ordered.

"Why am I here?" she cried.

Salgado quickly removed his belt and shouted, "I told you to come here!"

The girl took two tentative steps forward.

Salgado closed the distance between them. He walked around her, eyed her long black hair and imagined the curves of her body under her loose-fitting, soiled dress. *She's lost a lot of weight,* he thought. *Another week of this and no man will want her.*

He gripped her upper arm, dragged her from the cell, across the hall, and into the cell on the opposite side. At least this one had been cleaned. He threw her to the floor and watched her move crab-like toward the rear wall. She pressed into a corner, her arms wrapped tightly around her knees.

He pointed a finger at the girl and hoarsely, flatly said, "You want to die?"

Even in the poor light, Carlos saw the girl's eyes round into miniature saucers.

"No . . . no," she said.

"Then listen. You've got two options. You've been sold to a very wealthy man in Miami. You will take care of his . . . needs. For that simple duty, you will live very well. But you will do exactly what he says. No argument. You understand?"

"But the paper said I would get a job as a nanny," Miranda said. Her tears flowed. "Please, let me go back home."

Salgado walked two paces to the girl, bent down, and viciously swung his belt across her legs. The force of the blow knocked her from her sitting position. She curled into a fetal position on the rough concrete surface and sobbed hysterically.

He swallowed the guilty lump in his throat. "I said, no argument. You will live a better life than you ever imagined in your family's hovel in Ocotal. And all you'll have to do is sleep with some man who probably can't get it up more than once a month. You cooperate, or you die."

The girl pushed herself upright and glared at him. "*Nunca! Es un pecado. Yo soy una virgen,*" she cried, her voice brittle.

Salgado's heart sank. The girl's use of the words "sin" and "virgin" made him want to cross himself. *This niña has bigger cojones than most men I know*, he thought. He couldn't help but admire the way she stood up to him, despite her fear. A thought crossed his mind—*perhaps I can arrange for her escape*—when a sound startled him. He wheeled around and felt a sudden weakness in his bowels. *El Jefe* stood in the hall outside the cell.

For the briefest moment, Salgado saw the anger in Lorca's eyes. In that split second, before he averted his eyes from his boss's face, he thought he'd seen *El Diablo*. He mentally crossed himself and opened his mouth to say something. But Lorca cut him off.

"Take her outside to the pond."

The meaning of Lorca's words hung over the room like a poison gas cloud. Salgado already felt the heart sickness that was about to become even worse. But before he could react, Lorca added in a supernaturally quiet voice, "And bring the others, too. It's time we put an end to this bullshit." *El Jefe* spun around and, like a wraith, disappeared.

After he left the cells, Jackson walked to his office in the hacienda and called the motor pool.

"*Sí, Jefe?*" a man answered.

"Bring up the Land Rover."

Jackson drove to the gate at the back of his lawn, unlocked it, and then took the rutted dirt road that ran from the back of his yard into the jungle. After a half-mile, he stopped fifty feet from a pond. He observed Salgado herding six young women to a tree-shaded area twenty yards from the edge of a pond that was almost the size of a football field. *They look like homeless urchins: dirty, torn dresses; matted, filthy hair; wide, frightened eyes; and rigid postures.* He laughed. *Huddled against one another as though for protection.*

He donned a white Panama hat and sunglasses. In his white linen slacks and light-blue cotton shirt, with his *café-au-lait*-colored skin, he knew he made a strong impression on the women. He casually walked from the Land Rover to a spot halfway between the women and the water's edge and waved Salgado over to him.

"*Sí, Jefe?*" the man said.

"Besides the Sánchez woman, are the others . . . compliant?"

"Three have been cooperative from the start." Salgado shrugged. "There are always some who resist . . . indoctrination. There are only two who have been . . . resistant."

"You're too easy on them, Salgado. If you treat them as sexual objects and force them to learn all forms of sexual perversion, they almost always come around. Those that don't, you beat them. Reward the ones who follow the rules; beat the others." Lorca sighed. "Our clients want pliable, sexually-adept playthings who serve their needs in ways their wives can't or won't."

"I understand, *Jefe*."

Jackson slowly shook his head as he moved toward the pond. Salgado followed. When they reached the ledge of dry, dusty ground above the murky water, he pulled down the brim of his hat and whispered to Salgado, "Bring the bitch here."

Salgado licked his lips and opened his mouth as though to say something, but quickly wheeled around and fast-walked toward where the huddled, quivering group of women waited.

Jackson turned a bit in order to watch Salgado put on his tough-guy act as he roughly grabbed the Sánchez woman's arm. She immediately dropped to the ground and dug her heels into the soft, mulch-covered jungle floor. He backhanded her, pulled her up, bear-hugged her, and carried her over to where Jackson waited. He threw her to the ground two feet from Jackson, who smiled down at the woman, stooped slightly, and extended a hand to her. She shrank back from him, but he persisted, saying in Spanish, "It's okay, girl. Stand with me."

Miranda took the man's hand and, with his help, stood.

"You see this pond, my dear?"

She mumbled something unintelligible.

"You wouldn't think that anything other than green scum,

dragonflies, and long-legged water bugs could live in this water." He squatted and picked up a baseball-sized rock, which he lobbed into the water, fifty feet from the bank. The rock hit the murky surface and sent out concentric ripples that broke the calm, green plane. He watched the ripples radiate out from the spot where the rock sank. Everything seemed so peaceful . . . for three seconds. Then the water erupted with thrashing, leathery tails and great gnashing teeth. Quickly, the surface became a Dante-esque maelstrom of caimans that fought for position. Like Jackson and Salgado, the reptiles knew what would come next.

Jackson pointed at a spot ten feet away, on the edge of the five foot drop-off over the pond. In a subdued, almost regretful voice, he said, "Stand her over there."

The girl struggled, kicked, flailed her arms, and screamed. She fought violently for over a minute, still clutched in Salgado's arms, until she seemed spent. Salgado deposited her on the spot his boss had indicated and stepped back.

Jackson turned to face the now-transfixed group of five women. "I hear some of you have resisted my men," he said. "Not cooperating. Who do you think you are? You all come from barrios where you were lucky to have one shitty meal a day. I give you the chance to better your lives. It's time you learned there is a price for disobedience." He looked over his shoulder at Salgado and nodded.

Salgado stepped toward Miranda, his arms extended. Jackson smiled at her round-eyed, open-mouthed, shocked expression as the caimans glided forward, now just a few yards from the bank.

Salgado was still one pace away, a second from pushing the girl into the pond, when Jackson suddenly spun around and lowered his shoulder. He slammed into the man's side and drove him head over heels into the pond. He surfaced a second after he hit the water and frantically yelled, "No! No! *Madre de Dios*, help me!"

The women's shrieks provided a sinister chorus, which seemed to increase Salgado's hysterics.

Jackson stared down at the man and looked impassively into his eyes. It took less than ten seconds for the caimans to drag him below the surface. Jackson then moved to where Miranda now crouched like a frightened child. "You know what the animals are now doing to him?" Without waiting for a response, he added, "They'll drown him and then tear his flesh to pieces. They'll devour every bit of him—skin, flesh, bone. Is that what you want for yourself?"

She shook her head, frantically whipping it back and forth.

"Will you be a good little girl now?" he said in a raspy whisper.

She moved her head up and down in a rapid, mechanical motion.

"I expected so," he said. He pointed at the tight ball of shuddering, terrified women and ordered her to join them. Then he walked over to the Land Rover. Before he opened the vehicle's door, he waved at the women and said, "Follow me."

Like sheep behind a Judas ram, all six fell in behind the vehicle and shuffled up the road.

Jackson parked outside the cellblock and watched the women catatonically return to their cells, even close the doors behind them. He didn't bother to lock the doors. He knew this crop of women wouldn't go anywhere he didn't want them to go.

He walked to a wall telephone at the end of the cellblock and dialed the two-digit number for the front guard post. When one of the guards answered, Jackson said, "The cell doors will be unlocked all night. Pass the word to the men. You may all enjoy the women in whatever way you wish."

"*Sí, Jefe,*" the man said. "*Muchas gracias.*"

"But, Edilberto . . ."

"*Si, Jefe?*"

"I find one bruise on any of them and I will throw every one of you in the pond."

"*Comprendo, Jefe.*"

"One more thing, Edilberto—I want every man to . . . taste the Sánchez girl."

DAY 2

CHAPTER 5

Matt woke at 8:00 a.m. He felt rested as he slipped out of bed as quietly as possible and walked to the bathroom. After he showered and shaved, he put on one of the hotel's white terrycloth robes and padded back to the bedroom. The bed was now empty.

He moved to the sitting room where he found Renee at the Queen Anne desk, a telephone receiver pressed against her ear. She wore nothing but a short, black negligee.

Matt mouthed, "Who?"

Renee covered the mouthpiece, smiled, and whispered, "Alani."

Matt sat down on the couch and watched Renee. It seemed to him that she became more beautiful, more desirable with each day. He thought about their having lunch with his old friend and Army buddy, Esteban Maldonado, and Esteban's young Hawaiian wife, Alani. One of the benefits of his position with Placer was the opportunity to contact old friends and associates all over the world. There was no one he'd rather see than Esteban.

One of his oldest friends, Esteban had served with Matt in a U.S. Army Special Forces unit in the Balkans, when Matt was nineteen years old and Esteban twenty-two—nearly two decades ago. Matt had saved Esteban's life there. Esteban had risked his own life when Matt had gone to Hawaii nearly a year ago, after Matt's sister, Susan, had been murdered. With two of his friends, Angelo and Richie Caruso, Esteban had protected Matt and Renee when Lonnie

Jackson's men had tried to kill them. And he and the Carusos had put themselves at risk again when Jackson traveled to New Mexico from Brazil late last year to kill Matt and Renee.

Matt and Esteban had a history together and, despite their disparate backgrounds and careers—Matt was a physician; Esteban owned a string of surf shops in the Hawaiian Islands—they were best friends.

The sound of the telephone receiver placed in its cradle brought Matt out of his daydreaming.

"What time is it?" Renee asked.

"Almost eight-thirty. What time is lunch?"

"Noon. Esteban and Alani will meet us here."

"What do you want to do in the meantime?" Matt asked.

Renee gave him a coy look, tilted her head to the side, and smiled demurely. She slowly lifted the negligee over her head and allowed it to dangle from her fingers.

Matt felt an electric jolt as he looked at her naked in front of him. He shed his robe and walked to her. "I assume I didn't misunderstand your body language," he said.

She moved against him. "No, Dr. Curtis. You read me loud and clear."

Esteban groaned and rolled over onto his back. He noticed Alani tiptoeing toward the bathroom. "*Qué pasó?*" he said.

She stopped, turned, walked to his side of the bed, and sat. "Hey, sleepyhead. That was Renee on the phone. We'll pick them up at the Hyatt at noon."

He stretched his six-foot, five-inch frame and groaned again. "Did you get hold of Ange and Richie? Can they join us?"

Alani giggled. "Yeah. And what was most impressive was they were both coherent. Sunday morning and neither one seemed to be hungover."

"I told you they'd cleaned up their act."

Alani smiled, which made her look fifteen, instead of thirty. "I'll believe that when they've both been on the wagon for at least six months."

Esteban wagged a finger at his wife and scolded, "That's what happens when a man gets tangled with a good woman. No more carousing, no more late nights. Just boredom, peace, and harmony."

Alani shifted, as if to get up off the bed. "That's what you think? Marrying me made your life boring?"

Esteban shot a bearpaw of a hand around her wrist. He gently pulled her on top of him and said in a soft, tender voice, "Exciting, honey. That's what I said. Exciting, not boring."

Alani chuckled. "You're a big liar."

Esteban kissed her mouth. "You didn't have anything pressing to do right this moment, did you?"

Alani purred contentedly as she crawled under the sheet.

CHAPTER 6

"Man, you look good, *cuate*," Esteban told Matt while he lifted him off the ground and squeezed him so hard Matt couldn't breathe. The big man's loud voice and exuberant greeting caused heads to turn among the dozen or so people outside the Hyatt Hotel entrance.

"Unh, you want to put me down before you kill me?" Matt gasped.

Esteban's laugh resonated from his chest like the deep rumblings of a kettledrum. "Sorry," he said. Then he turned on Renee and opened his arms toward her. She stepped forward and hugged him.

Matt hugged Alani, then turned, an arm draped over her shoulder, and looked at his giant-of-a-friend. "You both look wonderful," he said.

Alani smiled at her husband, then looked up at Matt. In a low voice, she said, "Couldn't be better. I'm married to the biggest pussycat in America and he treats me like I'm the best thing that ever happened to him. What else could a woman want?"

Matt nodded his understanding.

"Okay guys," Esteban shouted, "let's climb aboard and go have lunch."

Matt noticed a white Ford Expedition parked a few feet away on the paver stone driveway. "Don't tell me that's yours?" Matt said. "I thought you'd never get rid of that beat up pickup."

Esteban suddenly blushed. A toothy grin creased his face and his eyes twinkled.

Alani moved to Esteban and put an arm around his waist. While she looked up at him, she said, "Oh, he didn't get rid of the pickup. He still drives that wreck around. It's part of his image. He bought the Expedition for me. Isn't that right, honey?"

Esteban tipped his head sheepishly and said, "Yeah."

"You want to tell them why you bought the SUV, or should I?"

Esteban seemed to grow even taller. He gave Alani a glowing smile. "I'll do it." He looked at Renee, then at Matt, and announced in a voice loud enough for everyone within fifty yards to hear, "I'm going to be a father. Alani's pregnant. I didn't want her driving around in some small—"

Renee's shouts and Matt's congratulations drowned out the end of Esteban's sentence.

After hugs all around, Matt and Renee climbed into the Expedition's back seat.

"We'll meet Angelo and Richie at Mori's," Esteban said. "We figured you both needed some real food for a change."

"God, I haven't had one of Mori's omelets in ages," Renee said.

"Where do you go next?" Esteban asked.

Matt didn't hear his friend as the memory of his first visit to Mori's flashed through his mind. It was the crooked cop, Dennis Callahan, who'd taken him there. Callahan—the bastard who'd drugged his sister; who'd tried to kill him and Renee. All on Lonnie Jackson's orders.

Renee placed a hand on his arm. "Matt, are you okay?"

Matt wiped a hand over his face and smiled reassuringly. "Sure, babe. I guess I was daydreaming."

With furrowed brow and narrowed eyes, she looked as though she didn't quite buy his explanation. "Esteban asked you a question."

"Sorry. What was that, Esteban?"

"I asked where you go next. Renee said you've been in more than twenty cities in the past three months."

"Costa Rica," Matt said. "An orthopedic conference in San José next month. It'll be our first trip outside the States."

CHAPTER 7

The overseas connection was poor. Static made it difficult to concentrate on the conversation, especially with the added confusion of talking through an interpreter. Jackson had to continually ask the translator to repeat his part of the conversation.

"How many did Mister Tarnovsky say he could supply?" Jackson asked.

In his heavy Slavic accent, the translator said, "Mister Tarnovsky can commit one dozen of womans each month."

"And he understands," Jackson continued, "that I want them tall? Blondes and redheads. None of those Russian broads with soccer player legs. No bleach jobs. And, my clients want them slim and light-skinned. You got it?"

With an irritated edge to his voice, the translator responded, "Yes, he understands, Mister Lorca. He understands quite clearly."

Jackson heard the guttural strains of a voice speaking in what he assumed was Bulgarian come from the other end of the line. *Now he'll ask about the money*, he thought. *Try to hike the price.*

The translator's voice came back on the line. "Mister Tarnovsky says the Bulgarian government has become more and more difficult. He is forced to pay many bribes to the officials. He says five thousand dollars for each womans is no longer enough monies."

Jackson paused; quietly and slowly he released the air in his lungs. He took in a shallow breath and said, "I can get all the

Chinese, South American, and Filipino women I want for five hundred bucks a piece. Tell Mister Tarnovsky to go fuck himself."

Jackson then lowered the phone to the cradle. He knew the Bulgarian would agree to take the usual price. He also knew he could get anywhere from twenty-five to fifty thousand dollars from any one of a hundred of his male clients for a long-legged, light-skinned Bulgarian, Russian, or any other woman from one of the former Soviet republics—depending on her looks. The last shipment of four young women from Georgia had been particularly profitable. One hundred seventy thousand dollars in total from a Miami drug dealer.

Jackson could afford to pay Tarnovsky more than five thousand dollars per girl. But there was a principle to the matter. He wouldn't allow some former communist asshole to hold him up. Besides, he was the one who had to train the women, to break them down. He had to take the risks and cover transportation costs. When they arrived in Nicaragua they were innocent and naïve, full of hope about the fake jobs they'd been promised.

He turned his attention to the files on his desk. These contained the visas and travel documents for the six Nicaraguan girls currently in the cells. He'd bought the girls from a trafficker in Managua. With varying amounts of "encouragement," most of them had quickly become pliant and obedient, pleasant little things who would make their new masters feel like feudal lords. Even Miranda Sánchez had finally come around. Jackson knew his client Rodrigo Mascarenas would be extremely satisfied with each of the girls in this shipment. Sweet, innocent virgins when they'd arrived, they were now schooled in the ways of delivering sexual pleasure to men with unorthodox appetites. Or men who just wanted women they could master. An alternative to wives who were never satisfied, always wanted more and more things, and who thought they performed their wifely duties if they serviced their husbands once a month.

This shipment would go via fishing boat and rendezvous with Mascarenas's yacht. Jackson had learned that the drug kingpin would use the girls for his own enjoyment, or to entertain clients. When he tired of them, he'd sell them to a pimp to turn out on the street. Jackson couldn't have cared less what happened to them.

He moved the files aside and re-read the paper copy of the email he'd received from Thailand five days earlier. Siriwa Pratikan wanted four white women for his exclusive whorehouse in Samut Songkhram, a little more than an hour's drive southwest of Bangkok, on the Gulf of Thailand. If Tarnovsky came through, Jackson knew he'd be able to deliver the women to Pratikan by the middle of next month.

White Eastern European women were very popular in Thailand. Pratikan would sell time with them to men who wanted something different. Jackson ran a quick mental calculation and estimated Pratikan should be able to turn three quarters of a million to a million dollars per woman over a three-year period. By then, the women would be worn out and used up . . . and probably infected with AIDS.

Hang-ups and frustrations, Jackson thought. He made a fortune because the world was full of hang-ups and frustrations. He knew some of the men to whom he sold girls were perverts. Guys who got off on rape, torture, and even murder. Some of the girls would be used only once—in a "snuff flick." He didn't lose one second's sleep about such things. There were predators and prey. He was just lucky enough to be part of the former group.

Yevgeni Tarnovsky felt the heat rise from his neck to the top of his head. He squeezed his bulbous nose, then ran a hand through his coarse, salt and pepper hair. He stared at the faces of the men around him. There was fear there. They stared back at him like children who waited for a stern father to explode with anger. Tarnovsky suppressed a laugh. His interpreter looked as though he might piss his pants at any moment. The little twig-of-a-man visibly trembled.

Fear in other men was a condition with which Tarnovsky was familiar. He knew he engendered it with a mere look. And he'd learned decades before that his features—large nose; bushy, black eyebrows; and almond-shaped eyes which spoke of ancestors from the Steppes—gave him a sinister appearance. The apoplectic rage he had unleashed in the room a moment ago had probably reduced the life spans of each of the four men there. The thought of the fear-induced scars he might have caused on their hearts gave him a moment of respite from his outburst.

That mongrel in Nicaragua had insulted him, had told him to go fuck himself. And he'd done it through an interpreter.

Tarnovsky pointed a sausage-sized finger at one of his men. "*Rakir*," he demanded.

The man rushed to a cabinet below a floor-to-ceiling, built-in bookcase and removed a bottle of the strong licorice flavored liquor, poured a generous portion into a glass, then added water from a pitcher. The concoction turned milky-white. He placed the glass in front of Tarnovsky, in the middle of the *mafiya* boss's desk, and quickly scuttled backward to a far corner of the room.

Tarnovsky lifted the glass in his ham hock-sized hand, making it disappear, and raised it to his lips. He drank half the contents, then released a great sigh, smacked his lips, and wiped his shirt sleeve over his mouth.

"That's better," he exclaimed. He detected some lessening of tension in the room, but he suspected if he said, "BOO!" at least a couple of the men would faint straight away. He considered trying it, just for the hell of it, but decided this was neither the time nor the place. He needed these men to do their jobs. As long as they were scared shitless, they were worthless to him. He had to lighten the mood.

He turned toward his interpreter, who cowered against the bookcase behind two other men who screened him from Tarnovsky. "Did I hear you correctly? That *peesda*, José Lorca, told me to go fuck myself?"

The interpreter peeked out from behind one of the men in front of him and visibly cringed. His throat muscles danced as though he tried to speak, but nothing came out. Finally, the man just nodded.

Tarnovsky grunted. Then he laughed, softly at first, then in great rumbling guffaws. He watched the men turn to one another, as though wondering how to react, then slowly, one by one, they laughed along with him.

After a minute passed, Tarnovsky shouted in a jovial tone at one of his men, "Sergei, *rakir* for everyone. We should toast Señor

Lorca. For the money he'll pay us." After a slight pause, he added, "And for the size of his balls."

While Sergei filled four more glasses, Tarnovsky glanced around at the rich furnishings of his office—the damask wallpaper, the seven meter by seven meter Persian Bokhara carpet, the wide crown moldings, the czarist-era icons—and considered how much money he'd made doing business with José Rosales Lorca. But the fire of anger still raged inside his gut. *No one insults Yevgeni Tarnovsky . . . and lives.*

CHAPTER 8

Renee leaned back in her chair and felt a warm, comforting rush. Mori's was her kind of place. Good, simple food, big portions, and the chatter of people all around. Her life with her first husband had been a whirlwind of social events at expensive residences, exclusive country clubs, and fine restaurants attended by the muckety-mucks of Hawaii. She'd held her own with that crowd, but she'd never felt a part of it.

The short time she'd spent in New Mexico had been different. The social scene there—even among the most successful members of society—tended toward understatement. A lot of people in the state were newcomers. No blue bloods. Very few pretensions.

The daughter of a career Army officer, she'd traveled the globe. Her friends had been middle class. She'd never been exposed to people like the Caruso brothers and Esteban, who'd grown up poor in tough neighborhoods. Angelo and Richie in South Philadelphia; Esteban in El Paso, on the Mexican border. She suspected Matt would never have met anyone like Esteban if he hadn't served in the Army—the ultimate melting pot.

Renee reflected on the friends and acquaintances she'd had over her thirty-nine years and concluded that she'd never been more at ease, never felt more affection for anyone—besides Matt's sister, Susan—than she felt for these people. The teasing that went on between the men, the stories they shared, the way Esteban doted on Alani, the affection Angelo and Richie had for their dog Max, all made Renee happy to have met them. These were good people.

The conversation stopped when their waitress refilled their coffee cups. Renee looked around and sighed. Mori's was still a dump. But her omelet was as good as any she'd ever had. She smiled across the table at Alani and was about to ask her if she wanted a boy or a girl, when Esteban said something that diverted her attention.

"You know," he said to Matt, "there's a large expatriate community of former Green Berets in Costa Rica."

Renee had come to know Esteban well enough to sense there was something behind this tidbit of information.

Matt shrugged. "I didn't know that," he said. "What's the magic about Costa Rica?"

Esteban rubbed his hands together and placed his elbows on the table. "From what I hear, several things. It's safe. They don't even have an army there. Just a well-armed police force. And it's cheap to live down there. Great health care. You can do okay on just a U.S. Army pension. But I suspect a lot of the guys just feel at home there. There were probably more Berets assigned to Fort Gulick and Fort Randolph in the Canal Zone over the years than to just about any other place in the world, besides Bragg. They learned to appreciate Latin America."

"I'm looking forward to the trip there," Matt said. He looked over at Renee and grinned. "Maybe we can do some sightseeing."

She smiled back. "Sounds good."

"You remember that crazy sonof . . . oops, sorry ladies," Richie said. "That crazy SF-guy we worked with in the Sudan? The one who hired out for a while after he retired?"

Renee shot Richie a querulous look, then turned toward Matt. She recalled the stories Matt had told her. About how Esteban and the Carusos had been "mercs" for a time after they separated from the Army. She couldn't imagine these sweet men ever being mercenaries.

Angelo swung his arms around like a windmill, a broad smile on his face. "You mean Quince Hansen?"

Richie clapped his hands together. "That's the one! Crazy as a Saturday night drunk."

"Crazy like a fox," Esteban said. "That guy had an IQ off the charts. And guts. Never afraid of anything." Then Esteban rubbed an eyebrow with one of his cigar-sized fingers and added, "He did act irrationally at times."

The Carusos simultaneously erupted in laughter. "Irrationally?" Richie said. "Quince Hansen was three eggs shy of a dozen."

"But boy could he make me laugh," Angelo said.

Renee noticed Esteban's pursed lips and his hooded eyes. He appeared melancholy. Her sixth sense told her Esteban was considering something that Alani wouldn't care for.

CHAPTER 9

United States Senator Peter Driscoll felt torn. Two emotions battled for supremacy: his lifelong compulsion to "do the right thing" and his political survivor's instinct to keep his head down when confronted with an open-ended issue. Just the presence of the others in his office was enough to rev up that instinct into hyperdrive.

Driscoll looked around at the three men and two women who represented the Central Intelligence Agency, the State Department, the National Security Agency, the Federal Bureau of Investigation, and Army Intelligence. *And they're all here because of me*, he thought.

The others had finished helping themselves to coffee. With no small amount of anxiety, Driscoll announced, "Perhaps we should get started. I know you're all busy and I've got a roll call vote in thirty minutes."

The others took seats around the ancient, scarred table, a relic passed down through two previous occupants of this large office in the Hart Senate Office Building.

"I appreciate you coming here today," Driscoll said. "I assume you all read the contents of the file we sent you." He paused and noted that each of the men and women either nodded or said yes. "Good. I have to admit I'm way out of my league in this matter. One of my staffers received a letter from a man in Salina. She contacted the man, researched the matter, and passed it on to my administrative aide, who dumped it in my lap."

Driscoll waited for one of the bureaucrats to respond. He was met with stone cold stares. *No one wants to pick up the ball and run with it,* he thought. *I can't say I blame them, but that's not the way this thing will go down. I need to jack up these government flacks.*

"This may be a constituent matter for me, ladies and gentlemen, but this is a time bomb for your agencies, your bosses . . . hell, the administration itself. Which of you wants to tell the President you were aware that trafficking in women was occurring, that the daughter of an American citizen was a possible victim, and you did nothing about it?" He smiled, then said, "Just imagine the headlines."

Driscoll was answered with a chorus of coughs and shifting glances. Finally, the female FBI agent spoke up.

"Senator Driscoll, we haven't been able to confirm Mr. Petrashvili's claims about his daughter. We do know he and the girl's mother divorced years ago, when the girl was three years old. He emigrated to the U.S.; the wife and child remained in Georgia. There is no evidence his daughter was sold or is being held captive."

The man from the State Department said, "We used every source available to us in Georgia. Our people in Tbilisi pulled out all the stops. They verified that Katrina Petrashvili is a Georgian citizen; lives with her mother; works as a clerk in a department store; and—"

Driscoll interrupted the man. "Katrina Petrashvili was born in the U.S. She was an American citizen before she became a Georgian citizen." He paused and then said, "Did your people talk with the young woman?"

The State Department guy averted his gaze and said, "No. She seems to have disappeared."

Driscoll's heart felt as though it took a swan dive into the pool of acid in his stomach. "So there's at least circumstantial evidence her father's claims are true."

"Yeah, but it's a giant leap from the girl's disappearance to making her a victim of human trafficking," the woman from the NSA said.

Driscoll turned to the NSA employee, nodded in agreement,

then said, "But her father thinks she's being held captive in the U.S. Not in some third world country, but right here in the goddamn U.S. of A." He knew his voice had risen in volume and anger tainted his tone. "The father flew to Georgia and learned from his former wife that their daughter told her mother she would be sent to a training center in Nicaragua, then placed in a job in the States. I can believe the Nicaragua business, but I'll give you all ten to one odds she wound up somewhere other than the U.S. But if we blow this whole thing off, and six months or a year from now *60 Minutes* entertains fifty million Americans with a story about trafficking women to America, and he interviews one Katrina Petrashvili and her father and . . . ." He intentionally let the unfinished statement hang over the others' heads.

Driscoll rocked back in his chair and stared at the ceiling. "It'll go something like this: Tell us, Mr. Petrashvili, what you told Senator Driscoll about your daughter's disappearance." After he looked at the others in the room, Driscoll continued: "Then *60 Minutes* comes to visit me and, guess what? I tell them about when I alerted all of you to the problem."

The senator rocked forward, elbows on his desk, and lasered his eyes at the others. "You boys and girls get the picture?"

The CIA man, Eddie Parnell, pushed back from the table and stood. He gave Driscoll a neutral look. "The Company will consider your points, Senator."

Driscoll and the four bureaucrats rose too. The senator said, "I'll look forward to progress reports, Parnell." He pronounced the agent's name correctly, with the emphasis on the first syllable, but it came across in a demeaning tone, as one might pronounce "po-lice."

Eddie Parnell shed his suit jacket as soon as he walked out of Driscoll's office. He swiped a hand over his forehead and wiped away perspiration. *Oh my God*, he thought. *I'm way too old for this bullshit.*

That morning, he'd noticed it wouldn't do him any good to pull out the gray hairs anymore. There were too many to mess with. The meeting he'd just left had the potential, he knew, to make him go completely gray.

He was disgusted that female trafficking had become an enormous international business. It made him violently ill to think the CIA had gotten in bed with one of the world's biggest traffickers. He sweated now as though he'd just finished a marathon and he knew the D.C. summer heat and humidity outside the building would only make it worse. This was turning into a clusterfuck of major proportions. He didn't know for sure, but the Petrashvili girl's disappearance had all the markings of another trafficking transaction. And the geography—the countries of Georgia and Nicaragua—gave Parnell an ache in his chest that made him want to throw up his hands, take early retirement, and go to work as a security guard in a Baltimore bank. *I'd do just that*, he thought, *if I didn't have to pay alimony to my goddamn ex.* Then the ache in his chest got worse. *This has got the smell of Tarnovsky all over it.*

"Yevgeni Tarnovsky, you prick," Parnell cursed under his breath while he fast-walked to his car. "You lying sonofabitch; you promised me."

CHAPTER 10

Lonnie Jackson sent half his eight-man crew into town. He only needed a scaled-back guard force because he was between shipments. He checked on the status of incoming shipments, went over his investment portfolio, and arranged for wire transfers to pay for the last two orders. He tried to keep busy, to keep his mind occupied, to avoid the emotional craziness that came with idle thoughts. He forced himself to concentrate on the news reports he pulled up on the Internet. But that only worked for a few minutes. His face felt warm and his pulse hammered in his throat, and he knew the feeling was about to come over him again. It wasn't that he didn't like some of the thoughts that accompanied the feeling. On the contrary, he loved them. It was the madness that seemed to come over him that distressed him. He'd always been so in control. He hated when his emotions overwhelmed reason.

Jackson released the mouse, slumped in his high-backed, plush leather chair, and sighed. The internal heat overwhelmed him. A red haze seemed to cover everything in the room. Even his hands glowed crimson. And, then, Matt and Renee Curtis's faces loomed before him like holograms. He felt his body tremble, but he couldn't seem to make it stop. Sweat soaked his shirt and his head felt foggy.

The thought of killing the Curtises was what gave him strength to go on. Revenge was the motivation for his existence. It was that manic need for revenge that had helped him survive the injuries

48

the cartel guy had inflicted on him in Mexico and that had led him to flee to Nicaragua. He'd hidden his Lawrence "Lonnie" Jackson persona behind his new alias: José Rosales Lorca.

The red haze slowly dissipated and Jackson felt cooler. He stared at the photographs on his desk: Mama and Johnny. The only family he'd had. The mother and brother who were dead. Because of Matt and Renee Curtis. "I'll make them pay, Mama," he said.

He pushed up from his chair. A thought struck: *What will motivate me once I kill the Curtises?* He let that thought go. *I'll figure that out when the Curtises are gone*, he told himself.

Jackson called the main guard post and alerted the guards that he would jog around the grounds. He ordered the guard to relay the information down the line. He didn't want to get shot by some trigger-happy sentry. After he tied his running shoes and donned a fanny pack in which he carried a small .32 caliber pistol and a cell phone, Jackson went to the kennels and released his two Rottweilers. He petted and rough-housed with the animals for a minute. They bounced and whined with excitement.

"Hey, Thor. Zeus," he said. "You boys want to go for a run?"

The two dogs groaned happily. Their cropped tails wagged; their heads and rumps bumped against his legs.

He rubbed their heads. "Okay, okay," he said, as he ran across the wide expanse of lawn to a gate where he used a key to unlock a padlock. Then he let the dogs run through the opening, secured the gate behind him, and jogged along the path through the jungle. The dogs tore off into the trees. Jackson knew he was safe from jaguars as long as the dogs were along.

He fell into a steady eight mile-a-minute pace as he followed the dirt road past the utility shed and the caiman pond to where the road petered out and became a three-foot wide path where dense jungle began. The path remained flat for a mile, then rose and fell in a series of shallow dips and rises for the next two miles. After it flattened out once again for about a mile, the path suddenly sloped downward and, after a couple hundred yards, ended at a precipice that gave way to a pounding, roaring river two hundred feet below.

Jackson checked the supports on the footbridge he'd had erected above the river six months earlier, then walked across the hundred-foot ravine. He'd just reached the other side and resumed jogging when his cell phone rang. He stopped, unzipped the fanny pack, took out the phone, and pressed the "Send" button. "Go!" he said breathlessly.

"Hi, am I interrupting something?" a man's voice said in a Brooklyn accent.

"Yeah, Moretti, you are. But it isn't what you think." Jackson felt his pulse rate shoot up even higher than it was already. He'd hired the man only three weeks earlier to track down the Curtises. "What you got?"

"I stopped by their old house in New Mexico and pretended to be an old friend. The caretaker wouldn't tell me shit. Then I called his old medical office. The gal who answered the phone told me Curtis had gone to work for some drug company. Placer Medical."

"Yeah?" Jackson said impatiently.

"They been on the move for months. His job takes him all over the country. They're both in Hawaii now . . . ."

The mention of Hawaii conjured up images of his mother and brother.

"You there, Mr. Lorca?"

"Yeah. Yeah, I'm here."

"Like I was saying, I thought it might raise a red flag if I called his employer; so, I pulled up Placer Medical on the Internet." Moretti blurted a short burst of laughter. "Curtis travels all over the place. From Miami to Honolulu, from Minneapolis to Dallas. You won't believe it."

"Skip the travelogue. All I want to know is where they'll be next."

"You're gonna love this," Moretti said. "They'll be in Costa Rica in two weeks. Curtis will speak at some medical conference in San José."

"You shittin' me?" Jackson exclaimed, the words sounding like a loud sigh. "You sure?"

Moretti laughed. "As sure as I'm gonna get laid tonight. And I'd say that's a sure thing. All you gotta do is check out the Placer Medical website. They've plastered Curtis's speaking schedule on the Internet. You'll be able to find out where he'll be on any given day for the next six months. How's that for convenience?"

CHAPTER 11

After lunch at Mori's, Matt, Esteban, Angelo, and Richie went to the Carusos' home; Renee and Alani went back to the hotel to sit around the pool.

Angelo went to fetch beers while Richie checked the phone machine for messages. Alone with Matt in the living room, Esteban asked, "How do you like your new job?"

"Actually, it's been great," Matt said. "I've been able to see parts of the United States I'd never been to before, and Renee and I can spend time together that wouldn't have been possible if I still worked twelve-hour days seeing patients." Matt paused, then said, "But, to be honest, the traveling's getting tiresome. I miss our home, I miss Latifah and Dooney, and I miss our friends in New Mexico."

"Too bad you couldn't bring Latifah and Dooney with you over here. Angelo fell in love with your dogs when we were all in New Mexico last winter."

Matt chuckled. "I don't know how long it'll be before Renee will have had enough of twenty-four hour togetherness. She needs a thing of her own. Tagging after me isn't the most stimulating activity in the world."

Esteban nodded. "How's she doing since . . .?"

Matt knew exactly what his friend referred to. "Okay, considering. I would never have left my practice in Albuquerque if it hadn't been for Lonnie Jackson. She couldn't relax in our home

51

anymore. Not since Jackson broke in. The best thing about my job with Placer is that we're on the move so much it's difficult for Jackson to track us down."

Esteban tapped his fingers on the ends of the chair arms. He stared menacingly into space and released a giant breath.

Angelo returned and handed beers to Esteban and Matt. In an effort to lighten the mood, Matt said, "Ange, you got a computer with Internet access?"

Angelo frowned at Matt. "What do you think I am, backward?" He walked over to a corner desk and removed a newspaper that covered a laptop computer. He booted up the machine, punched in his password, then told Matt, "It's all yours."

Matt stood and moved to the desk. "Let me show you my company's website," Matt said. "They've spent a fortune on its development. They continually upgrade it. And you won't believe the products. Talk about space age! If the technology had been available a few years earlier, a lot of young men who lost legs in Iraq and Afghanistan would be walking again—a whole lot sooner, with much less pain."

He sat down in front of the desk and pulled up the Placer website. Esteban looked over Matt's shoulder. Matt rose from the desk chair and let Esteban sit.

"Go ahead; play around with the site."

Esteban gave Matt a thumbs up.

Matt returned to his chair and nursed his beer. A minute passed, then Esteban turned in his chair and faced him.

"Old Placer Medical sure didn't do you any favors, *amigo*."

Matt scrunched up his brow. He gave Esteban an open arm gesture.

Esteban swiveled back to the computer and pointed a finger at the screen. "You're now in the public domain, my friend."

Matt walked up behind Esteban and looked down at the Placer home page. Along the left margin were a series of colored boxes that indicated links within the site. Inside one of the boxes were the words: "DON'T MISS DR. MATTHEW CURTIS."

Esteban looked back over his shoulder at Matt and said, "From the look on your face, I'd guess this is one of the recent updates your employer made to its website."

Matt shook his head. Fear and disbelief grappled inside his head.

Esteban turned back to the screen and clicked on the link. Matt's photograph and a short bio popped up. Below that was a list of each of the cities Matt would visit, along with the dates and specific venues, over the next six months.

Esteban stood and placed a hand on Matt's shoulder. "If Jackson found out where you work . . . I think you just went from being a moving target to a sitting duck."

CHAPTER 12

Westcliffe "Cliff" Reginald Moreland sat across the table from Eddie Parnell in 1789 Restaurant. Moreland liked the place, located on 36th Street in Georgetown, for its semi-private dining rooms and the quality of its clientele. And it was located three blocks from his townhouse. As always, he maintained a professional demeanor that had earned him the reputation of being a good man to have around when circumstances threatened to go out of control. Every hair in place; his white mustache impeccably trimmed. His blue cashmere blazer, Versace tie, and gold cufflinks accurately sent the message that Cliff Moreland was not dependent on his CIA salary.

He prided himself on his reputation, having patterned himself after his English forebears. Stiff upper lip and all that, you know. But he found what Parnell had told him so troubling he had difficulty remaining calm. A U.S. Senator had blundered into something that could jeopardize Moreland's career with the Company, terribly embarrass the CIA, and ruin the President's re-election bid. *Shit,* Moreland thought, *the guy in the White House can't stand another public relations disaster.*

He quickly dabbed his forehead with his napkin when Parnell glanced away for a moment, appearing to admire the ass of a woman in a black cocktail dress and heels. *This is a disaster about to happen,* he thought. *I should never have trusted Yevgeni Tarnovsky. The man's word is shit.*

Parnell looked evenly at Moreland, leaned forward, and whispered, "The Company has paid millions to Tarnovsky, since the fall of the Iron Curtain, to be its eyes and ears in Bulgaria. The guy's been invaluable."

Moreland shook his head, hoping his face wasn't as red as it felt. He, too, leaned forward. "Yeah, yeah, I know. He's given us critical intelligence as to which members of the former communist regime might be positioning themselves to take the country back into totalitarianism. As a former senior member of the old Bulgarian GRU, the guy's singularly placed to assist us. But, if he's trading in women again, that sixty-five-year-old bastard could be a severe problem."

Moreland suddenly shuddered. He sat back, picked up his glass of scotch, and considered how much worse the problem was than he'd just stated it to be. *Tarnovsky's role with the CIA goes well beyond information gathering. The man is, plain and simple, a CIA assassin. He's eliminated half-a-dozen Bolsheviks in the Bulgarian government who threatened the status quo.* All six sanctions were on orders from the Company. Specifically, on orders from Cliff Moreland through Eddie Parnell to Yevgeni Tarnovsky. U.S. law forbade any agency of the government to assassinate foreign leaders. Violating this law—and getting caught—could cost Moreland a great deal more than just his job.

Moreland noticed Parnell staring at him, a quizzical expression on his face. *Gotta get control of myself,* he thought. He leaned forward again and whispered, "You think that sonofabitch, Tarnovsky, has gotten greedy? That he's back in the trafficking business?"

Parnell rubbed his face with his hands, then nodded. "It's got all the signs of a Tarnovsky operation. Women are recruited from the former Soviet republics via advertisements in newspapers and on the radio for secretarial, *au pair*, and teacher positions in the West. The women are anxious to leave their dreary lives behind for something better. Tarnovsky's people answer the women's inquiries with fantastic promises of great salaries, benefits, travel, and tales of clients who had found not only careers, but also marriages to wealthy Westerners. They send off employment applications to the women. At the bottom of the application is an innocent-looking instruction that tells the applicant to include a recent full-length photograph. It's the photographs that ultimately determine the women's futures. The plain-looking women never hear from Tarnovsky's people again. The pretty ones are destined for a short life in hell."

"I told you months ago to order Tarnovsky to close down his trafficking business," Moreland said.

"I did. You know that."

"How do you propose to fix this?"

Parnell's face looked ten years older in an instant. "I . . . ."

Moreland could tell from the way Parnell's face had sagged and turned pale, that his message had gotten through. He'd passed this disaster on to Parnell; therefore it was Parnell's responsibility.

"I would guess Tarnovsky ships women through intermediaries," Parnell said. "If we can identify the brokers, we should be able to choke off Tarnovsky's operation."

"Yes," Moreland said, "but Tarnovsky will just find another conduit. We need to terminate our relationship with him."

"We've got a ton of money invested in the guy," Parnell said. "Are you really ready to shut him down?"

Moreland picked up his glass and sipped the scotch. Then he rattled the ice cubes around while he stared into Parnell's eyes. "Do you believe Tarnovsky can be trusted, after he lied to you once already?"

Parnell pressed his lips together and slowly shook his head.

CHAPTER 13

Miranda Sánchez guessed they'd been at sea, locked below deck in a forty-two-foot fishing vessel, for at least two days and nights. She periodically heard men grunt and shout and curse, and the crash of what must have been fish that the men dumped into the storage area above the hold where she and the other girls were.

She concentrated most of her energy on maintaining her sanity. She wanted to erase the memories of what had been done to her at José Lorca's place in Nicaragua. But every breath she took, or the slightest movement caused her pain. Each jolt of pain brought horrific memories of what the men had done to her and how they'd demanded she smile and tell them how much she enjoyed the experience. She shivered so violently that her teeth chattered. Even huddled with the five other girls, the cold in the boat's dark hold was bone chilling. She gagged and heaved, but her stomach was empty. The odors of vomit, human waste, and mold, mixed with the foul stench of fish, soiled the air. The hold was dark as pitch. Water leaked from above on and around them.

Miranda clutched her crucifix and once again prayed. She begged for rescue and she prayed for forgiveness for giving up and no longer resisting the men.

The girl next to her had cried for hours now. Miranda pulled her close, patted her shoulder. "Have faith," she told the girl. But she found her words hypocritical, hollow. How could she ask this girl to have faith when she felt her own faith lessen day by day? She fell asleep with that thought inside her head.

A loud noise jarred Miranda out of sleep. The boat seemed to have stopped. The *thump-thump-thump* of footsteps boomed. The other women stirred. A couple mewled like frightened kittens.

"What's going on?" one asked.

"Have we stopped?" another said.

The girl who leaned against Miranda burrowed against her as if to become invisible.

Suddenly, the door to the hold burst open and the startlingly bright beam of a flashlight exploded inside the hold. Miranda covered her eyes with an arm.

"Stand up," a rough male voice shouted.

Miranda felt a large, callused hand grab her upper arm and jerk her upright. She moved automaton-like when she was pushed toward the ladder that led up to the hold door. She stumbled and went down on her hands and knees. The man slapped her on the buttocks and laughed. She scrambled to her feet and climbed.

When she crested the ladder, the fish smell was overpowering. She moved to the right until she banged against a bulkhead. Then a flashlight beam hit her and another man shouted, "This way, *puta*."

The man moved the beam of light to another ladder. Miranda followed the light and climbed again. She pushed up from the cargo hold into the blackness of night. A blast of cool sea air struck her face. The clean smell of the air, after the fetid atmosphere below, seemed like a gift from God. Then someone on the deck snatched her arm again and she was sent sprawling against the gunwale.

When all six women were on deck, they hugged one another as though each was a lifeline for the next. A man came forward and inspected them. Flashlight in hand, he looked at their faces, forced their lips open, checked their teeth. Then he shined the flashlight beam on their bodies and slowly, carefully looked at them from head to toe.

The man grunted and said in Spanish, "Get them aboard the yacht."

Miranda was the first off the fishing boat. She descended a

ladder to a small platform about a foot above the roiling water. The platform rocked violently. With both hands, she grabbed a course rope that was strung on the platform's corner poles. Opposite the platform was a set of steps up to the deck of a white-hulled yacht. Even on the ebony-inked sea and under the dark shroud of a starless sky, the boat seemed to gleam. She'd only seen such boats from the shore when her family went to visit her grandmother near León, Nicaragua. How she'd fantasized about sailing on such a glorious craft.

By the time the other girls were on the pitching platform, Miranda was again retching. A man off the fishing boat jumped onto the platform, opened one part of the rope barrier, and yelled at her, "You! Get over here!"

She removed one hand from the rope and stretched it to the man. He gripped her hand and yanked her to him. He then pointed at a ladder that led to the yacht deck. She climbed the ladder. A sailor in a white uniform met her at the top and, without a word, led her to a room the likes of which Miranda had never seen: light wood trim, rich blue bedding, and shiny brass fixtures. The room was clean, warm, and otherworldly.

The man pointed to the bathroom and, in a monotone, said, "Take a shower. You will find clothes in the closet." Then he left.

Miranda waited to hear the sound of the door lock and was momentarily shocked when it didn't happen. But then she thought: *Where could I go?*

She walked around the room and ran her fingers over the soft fabric of the bedspread and the decorative pillows propped against the headboard. She crossed to a built-in desk, pulled out a chair, and sat, marveling at the softness of the plush seat under her. Then she stood, moved to the closet, and slid open one side of the mirrored door. The sight of a collection of garments—pants suits, sun dresses, cocktail dresses, and a sequined gown—literally took her breath away. A shoe rack covered one side of the closet from floor to ceiling and a dozen drawers held undergarments and casual clothes. She extended a hand to touch one of the dresses, but quickly pulled back. Her hands were black with dirt.

The sour odor of her own body suddenly disgusted her. She

turned and stepped to the bathroom. She unbuttoned the top button—the other three had long since disappeared—on the front of her soiled dress and let the stained and tattered garment slip to the floor. She removed her torn, blood-spotted cotton panties and placed them on top of the dress. After she rolled both items into a tight ball, she dropped them in a wastebasket.

It took Miranda a minute to solve the mystery of how to work the shower controls. She'd never seen anything like them before. The only shower she'd ever used had been an old galvanized tub, with holes punched in the bottom, suspended by brackets and boards affixed to the outside of her family's shack. When it rained, they had water. Otherwise, weeks could go by without properly washing. When she discovered that hot water came from the shower, she had the momentary thought she'd been transported to another planet.

For a beat, she considered the possibility this might be worth whatever price she might have to pay . . . that she'd already paid. But then she felt the touch of the silver crucifix between her breasts.

Tears sprang to her eyes while the water cascaded over her and warmed her skin and then eased the soreness in her muscles and bones. She stepped forward and let the water run over her face, erase her tears, and tried not to think about what would come next. She knew there would be a heavy price to pay for this sort of luxury.

She rubbed her body with a bar of soap that reminded her of rain forest flowers and that didn't scratch her skin like the soap her mother made. The bottles on a shelf inside the shower had labels printed with English words. She recognized the one that had SHAMPOO on it. The other one with the letters C-O-N-D-I-T-I-O-N-E-R made no sense to her. She looked down at the ivory-colored shower floor and saw circular streams of shampoo suds tainted brown with the dirt from her hair and body run around the drain, then vanish. She stood under the shower's flow well beyond the point that all the filth and smells from the cell in Nicaragua, from the men there, and from the fishing boat had disappeared from her body.

She shut off the water, exited the shower, and reached for a towel on a nearby rack. She stood there and dripped water on the bathroom floor, then pressed the thick cotton material against her face. She'd never felt anything so soft or that smelled so good. Finally, she wrapped herself in the towel, walked to the bedroom closet, and selected panties, a bra, a pant suit, and a pair of leather thong sandals. She dried her hair with another towel, then moved to the desk chair.

While she wondered what would happen next, she listened to the throaty sounds of the yacht's engines and the occasional murmur of voices. *When will they come for me?* She shuddered at the thought of what might await her. She suspected it would be terrible, sinful. But, she thought, it couldn't possibly be as bad as it had been at the place in the jungle. So many men had used her there. One after the other. Made her do things she'd never even heard of. Terrible things. Degrading things. But those were crude, dirty men. Worse than animals. The man who owned this boat must be a different sort. Wealthy . . . of course. Perhaps educated . . . cultured . . . maybe?

The yacht's rolling motion sedated Miranda. She hadn't slept well in weeks, and suddenly felt bone-weary. She slipped out of the chair and moved to the bed. *I'll just close my eyes for a minute,* she thought.

A metallic sound woke Miranda with a start. She raised her head and saw movement at the bottom of the bed. Her hand shot to her mouth; she gasped. Someone moved beside the bed, to the bulkhead. She crawled to the other side of the bed and curled into a ball. Then the curtains that concealed a porthole were drawn back and sunlight streamed through the porthole's glass; dust motes danced in its ray. Miranda squinted against the light.

She recognized the man who had escorted her to this cabin the night before. He closed the closet door, went to the bathroom, and returned with the wastebasket in one hand and towels in the other. He was dark-skinned and had a prominent, hooked nose. He moved as though he were in the jungle, on cat's paws. He turned toward the door, stopped, and said, "You'd better freshen up. There are toothbrushes and toothpaste in the drawer by the sink. Hair brushes, too. Señor Mascarenas will ask for you soon."

"What does he—?" But the man had already left.

CHAPTER 14

"What the hell was that all about at lunch today?" Alani asked Esteban as they drove to their home. "You looked like a kid who'd lost his dog."

"What are you talking about?"

Alani turned to look at Esteban. He looked straight ahead at the road.

"Don't play games with me, Esteban," Alani said. "What's on your mind? You had that same look in your eyes at Mori's that you get every time you have itchy feet."

"My itchy-feet-days are long gone," he said. "I've got a pregnant wife, a successful business, and I'm fifty-three years old. Give me a break."

"That's it, isn't it?" she said. "My being pregnant. You're upset about being tied down."

Esteban glanced in the rearview mirror then suddenly veered to the right and pulled the big SUV into a fast food restaurant parking lot. He slammed the transmission into "Park" and twisted in his seat.

"Don't you ever say anything like that again. The best thing in my life is you. I never thought I'd be a father. You've made that possible. I'm the happiest guy in the world."

Tears in her eyes, Alani reached over and placed a hand on Esteban's arm and said, "Then what's going on? I know something's bothering you. I saw it on your face; heard it in your voice."

Esteban sighed. "I guess . . . I don't know. Maybe it's being fifty-three. I've always loved living on the edge. Listening to Ange and Richie talk about Quince Hansen in Costa Rica and some of the other guys from our past made me feel old."

Alani rubbed his arm. "You *aren't* twenty-five anymore," she said. "That's a fact of life."

"I know, I know."

"Marriage changes things, Esteban. Once the baby comes along, things will change even more."

He nodded, but didn't respond.

Alani paused. "You're thinking about going to Costa Rica, aren't you? Being with Matt, seeing some of your old Special Forces buddies?"

"Well, to be honest, the thought had crossed my mind. But I've already put it away. It's not practical."

"Bull!" Alani said. She glared at him. "Why not? We can afford it. The shops run themselves. I can keep an eye on things while you're gone. Go! But, Esteban," she added as she wagged her finger at him, "get it out of your system. Once our son comes along, you'll have to play daddy. Our child won't be ignored the way your father ignored you."

Esteban stared out through the windshield; his hands now rested on the steering wheel. Finally, he turned his head back toward her and said, "Okay, I'll go, but on one condition. You have to go, too."

CHAPTER 15

Cliff Moreland hadn't told him in so many words, but Eddie Parnell knew he was dog meat if he didn't resolve the situation in Bulgaria. The Senate Subcommittee on Human Rights had sent out a bill just that afternoon with a "Do Pass" recommendation that could potentially embarrass the CIA. *All the work we've done in Bulgaria will go up in smoke*, he thought.

The legislation requested a special appropriation to fund an FBI fact-finding mission to Bulgaria, with the goal of gathering information about human trafficking. Parnell knew Senator Driscoll's staff had worked on the legislation for months. The meeting in his conference room yesterday was another part of the senator's campaign. Driscoll was a bulldog. When he sank his teeth into an issue, he never let go until it was resolved.

"Can I help you, Eddie? Yo, Eddie! Earth to Eddie."

"Oh, sorry, Aggie. I must have been daydreaming."

Agnes McIntire had been in the agency's accounting department for thirty-two years. Now accounting supervisor, she managed fifty-two men and women who cranked out paychecks, expense reimbursements, vendor checks, and payments to contract employees. Her department also handled disbursement of foreign currency to agents about to go into the field. Agnes took care of these currency distributions personally. She didn't want "just anybody" to know where CIA personnel were sent. It didn't take a rocket scientist to figure out that an agent who requested ten thousand Argentine pesos was probably on his or her way to Argentina. Agnes felt that this information was too sensitive. She was, for all intents and purposes, wed to the agency, and she considered the men and women dispatched to the field—in harm's way—her kids. She was old enough to be their mother, after all.

Agnes stood and slipped around her desk. She took Parnell's arm and gave it a motherly squeeze. "Come on, my boy. I'll get you a cup of coffee and"—she looked at him conspiratorially and lowered her voice—"one of my homemade cinnamon buns."

Parnell smiled down at Agnes and wondered why this wonderful woman had never married. *Probably never had time to meet someone, considering she put in fourteen-hour days at the goddamn CIA.*

"You're a jewel, Aggie. I should take you away from here and marry you."

She blushed and playfully punched Parnell's arm. "You boys will say anything to get one of my cinnamon buns." She lowered her voice once again and asked, "Where are you off to now?"

Parnell looked left, right, and over a shoulder, as he played along with Agnes, and said, "I need Levs."

She raised her eyebrows and frowned. "Bulgaria. Why don't they ever send you to the Caribbean or the Amalfi Coast? Always these godforsaken places! How many Levs?"

"Five thousand dollars worth," Parnell answered.

"Eighty-six hundred Levs, then," Agnes said, with less than a five second hesitation.

"How the heck do you do that, Aggie?"

She shrugged and blushed again. Parnell could see she was pleased with his compliment. He also knew deep down that Aggie wasn't playing around when she showed concern about his trip to Bulgaria.

Parnell nervously shook the keys in his pants pocket and thought about what would happen if—no, when—the Senate approved the special appropriation and investigators hit the ground in Bulgaria. With perseverance, and a little luck, they'd uncover Yevgeni Tarnovsky's role in the trafficking trade. And then what if one of the Senate investigators somehow tied the Tarnovsky name to *the* Yevgeni Tarnovsky included in the CIA's report to the Senate Select Committee on Intelligence. Parnell imagined the headline: "CIA Involved in Female Trafficking Trade. President Denies Knowledge." Parnell knew no one would care or believe him when he testified that Tarnovsky had been ordered to close down his side business, or that he had sworn to Parnell that he had done so.

He climbed the ten steps to the front entrance of his apartment building, unlocked the door, and walked wearily to the elevator. He hated Eastern Europe. Compared to the United States and Western Europe, much of it was still in the Dark Ages. Telephone and Internet services were erratic at best, the food was bad, and hotels reminded him of those in decrepit backwater American towns that had been bypassed by the interstate years earlier. Parnell knew all about such places. He'd grown up in Arkansas and screwed many a girl on the sagging mattresses and worn bedding of rundown rooms in broken-down motels. While a teenager, he'd sworn to do anything to get out of the pissant town he grew up in. But, right now, compared to Bulgaria, the memory of Podunk, U.S.A., seemed pretty damned good.

Parnell entered his fifth-floor unit and went directly to the wall safe. He dialed the combination, opened the steel door, and extracted the folio with his American passport. His travel arrangements would be made by the agency. Flight to Athens, Greece, in his own name, quick trip by taxi to the safe-house apartment in Glyfada, pick up his fake Bulgarian ID—passport, drivers license, government employee identification card, Bulgarian Army Officer's card, and then a flight from Athens to Varna, with a layover in Istanbul. Customs officials would see entry stamps on his Bulgarian passport that Petrov Ulanoff—his alias—had spent five weeks in Greece. Parnell briefly cursed the day he'd accepted the assignment to the Defense Language Institute, West Coast, where he'd spent forty-seven weeks learning Bulgarian. He'd honed his language skills over six years as an agency deep cover man in Bulgaria. He should have held out for the class in French, or Greek, or Spanish.

Varna, Parnell thought, *is a perfect location for Tarnovsky's operation. Located on the Black Sea, it offers easy access to ships that ply Black Sea ports.* Parnell guessed Tarnovsky had enslaved women from Bulgaria, Rumania, the Ukraine, and even the Caucasus, and had spirited them to their ultimate destinations via a first leg through the Black Sea to Varna.

Immediately reverting to role, Parnell whispered to himself in perfect Bulgarian, "Let's get this over with, Petrov Ulanoff."

Parnell thought: *This will be a very hairy mission. There's a lot of money involved. It will be difficult to reason with Tarnovsky.* He knew he might have to make the Bulgarian crime boss "disappear." It wouldn't be his first "wet" assignment. He would then have to find someone well-placed within the Bulgarian hierarchy who would agree to work for the CIA. It wouldn't be easy to take Tarnovsky's place.

DAY 3

CHAPTER 16

Yevgeni Tarnovsky fingered the worry beads he held behind his back and strolled in his English garden. The red roses were his favorite. Although they grew in nearly every part of the two acres around his twenty-two-room mansion, this was his favorite spot surrounded by one hundred rose bushes. His mansard-roofed home, with its wrought iron-enclosed balconies and three-meter high shuttered windows sat fifty meters on the far side of the rose garden. The hedgerow maze lay behind him.

Tarnovsky breathed deeply and imagined what the air would smell like when the roses bloomed. He smiled. Life was good. The Communist Party had been his ticket out of poverty. He waved an arm in a slow half-circle, as though to take in his property, and thought about how far he'd come.

Suddenly, his smile disappeared and he spat out, "Fucking communism! If I'd had any idea how much more profitable it was to be a capitalist, I would have gone over to the other side long ago." He laughed boisterously, while he considered how little one really can dictate one's life path.

"What's so funny, Comrade Tarnovsky?"

Tarnovsky felt his heart leap at the sound of the woman's voice. Tatiana Borodvic always had that effect upon him. He turned around and stared as she approached. *How the hell did she get behind me?* he wondered. *There are guards all over the place!* But then he put thoughts of security breaches out of his mind and drank her in with his eyes: an inch shorter than him at five foot, ten inches; brown hair swept her shoulders; eyes that varied between hazel and green, depending on her mood; a marvelous body—not thin enough to be runway model-perfect, but voluptuous enough to be statuesque.

"You really should stop with the *comrade*, you know. That's ancient history."

Borodvic stopped in front of him and offered first her right cheek, then her left.

Tarnovsky kissed each cheek in turn, then stepped back. He stuck his hands in his pants pockets and ran his eyes over the woman. "It doesn't seem possible, Tatiana, but you get more beautiful every time I see you."

"Men," she exclaimed. "You are so easy to fool. A little makeup here and there, a visit to a skilled surgeon, and we look young again."

Tarnovsky laughed. He knew Tatiana, for some reason, had always been self-conscious about her looks. Maybe she'd wanted to think her advancement in Bulgarian Intelligence had been due to her brains, not her looks. Whatever. Tarnovsky could detect almost no makeup on her face, and if she'd had plastic surgery he would have known about it. There was nothing Tatiana Borodvic, or any of his operatives did that he wasn't aware of.

"Come walk with me," Tarnovsky said.

She stepped up next to him. He put an arm around her waist and drew her close. Tarnovsky led her into the hedgerow maze, away from others' eyes and ears. He lowered his voice. "I have a mission for you."

Borodvic leaned her head away from him and stared into his eyes. "It has been a long time, Yevgeni. I have a position with the French Embassy. I . . . ."

Tarnovsky interrupted her. "This job pays one hundred thousand American dollars." He knew it would take her two years to make that kind of money in her current position. He saw the sparkle in her eyes and the sudden flush of her skin and guessed the money was only part of the reason she seemed excited. Tatiana had always been an adrenaline freak. The more dangerous the assignment, the more she liked it.

"What do I have to do to earn this money?"

Tarnovsky wanted to smile but forced himself to keep his expression flat. He'd anticipated the question and had rehearsed this part many times. He bit his upper lip, took a deep breath through his bulbous nose, and said, "You have to agree to be sold into slavery. Sexual slavery." He couldn't control himself any longer and laughed so hard that he doubled over and tears flowed down his cheeks.

He saw Borodvic's brow crease and her eyes narrow. She glared at him. But his laughs continued unabated. Irritation showed on her face, but that only made him laugh harder. A minute passed. When he'd laughed himself out, he took her arm in his and turned back toward the residence. "You must tell me, dear, how you were able to get onto my property without alerting the guards."

Borodvic winked at Tarnovsky and sensually pursed her lips at him. "I'll be happy to, comrade. After you explain about this great adventure you have planned for me."

CHAPTER 17

The man in the white sailor uniform had not returned since he'd wakened her. It was now 8 p.m., according to the bedside clock. Other than a man who twice brought Miranda a tray of food during the day, she hadn't seen another person. She wondered about the other girls who'd been with her. Especially the teenager she'd comforted on the fishing boat.

Miranda attempted to guess what went on outside, but gave up after a while. She'd heard the sounds of motors and twice had heard and felt the bumps of what she assumed were other boats that came alongside. The noise of men's voices and occasional laughter carried down to her through the open porthole in her room, but she couldn't make out their words.

She tried to take her mind off what might lie ahead for her. She kept herself busy by trying on one of the outfits in the closet. It fit her almost perfectly. This surprised her; but then she thought about the other women on the fishing boat. They'd all been almost identical in age—approximately twenty, height, weight, and body type: five foot, five inches, one hundred ten pounds, and heavy-breasted.

She surveyed every foot of the stateroom—the closets, the drawers, even under the bed. Now tired and sleepy, she undressed, lay on the bed, pulled the sheet over her, and had just closed her eyes, when the door to the room opened. The sailor stood there, his face expressionless.

The man walked to the closet and removed a slinky black dress from the clothes bar. He took the dress from its hanger and placed it on the bottom of the bed. Then he lifted a pair of black high heels from the shoe rack and put them on the floor at the foot of the bed. "Get dressed," he ordered. "Señor Mascarenas wants you upstairs."

The man spoke the words without emotion, but Miranda saw something in his eyes. Maybe sympathy? Then she reconsidered and wondered if it was disgust.

She quickly slid off the bed to the carpeted floor and moved to the bottom. The sailor averted his eyes while she slipped into the dress. The dress hem stopped six inches above her knees. *Only whores wear such things back home,* she thought. *But that's what I am now: a whore. That's what the men in the jungle made me.*

Miranda inspected herself in the mirrored closet door. She pulled down on the sides of the dress, then swept her long, ebony hair from her neck and onto her back. She sat on the bed and pointed her toes into the heels, which were a bit narrow for her. She pushed off the bed and wobbled badly. She took a step and staggered forward. She would have collided with the closet had the sailor not grabbed her arm and righted her. She inhaled and let the air out slowly, then looked up at the man. "*Gracias.* I . . . I'm ready."

The man's mouth dropped open for an instant, then slammed shut.

She'd seen that look on boys' faces before. *He likes the way I look. Perhaps this man can help me.* "Do I look okay?" she asked.

She saw the man's Adams apple bob and the muscles in his throat flex as though he had difficulty swallowing.

"Ye . . . yes," he said. Then he walked to the dresser on the far side of the bed and opened a leather-clad box.

Miranda knew the box held jewelry. When she'd seen it during her room search, she'd been astonished at how beautiful the things were. She hadn't had the nerve to try on any of them.

The sailor removed several items from the box and, palm outstretched, said, "Put these on."

Miranda took one piece of jewelry at a time from the man's hand. First, one diamond bangle earring, then the other. When she picked up the last item, a diamond necklace, she put it around her neck and turned around. "Would you mind fastening it for me?"

She felt the man's hands tremble on the back of her neck. He fumbled with the clasp for several seconds, then finally said, "There."

Miranda turned to face him once again, looked into his eyes, and said, "Thank you. Do you have any other suggestions?"

"Señor Mascarenas likes his women to wear perfume. I recommend the lacquered bottle with the black cap," he said through a clenched-jaw grimace.

She again found the heels difficult to walk in as she moved awkwardly to the bathroom. After she removed the bottle cap, she pointed the plunger at her hand and depressed it six times. She heard the man chuckle behind her.

"You'd better go easy with that stuff," he said. He showed her how to put a small amount of the fragrance on a finger and to dab the backs of her ears, her neck, her wrists and shoulders. He looked at her reflection in the bathroom mirror and said, "I think the boss will like what he sees. Maybe you'll get lucky and wind up with . . . ." But he didn't finish. His mouth clamped shut and the muscles in his cheeks twitched.

Miranda felt an icy fist grab her abdomen and she shuddered as though a blast of Arctic wind had invaded the stateroom. This was her moment of truth. She reached out an arm and said, "Would you hold my arm? I don't think I'll be able to climb the stairs in these shoes."

The man came close and slipped his hand between her arm and her waist. She leaned into him as he held her close.

"What's your name?" she asked.

"Guillermo. Guillermo Ayala."

"Thank you, Guillermo."

When he didn't respond, she said, "Tell me about this man Mascarenas."

The sailor stopped at the bottom of the staircase, looked up as though to ensure no one could overhear him, then said, "Rodrigo Mascarenas is Cuban. Very powerful and rich. He's tall and handsome. That's all I should say."

He led Miranda to the first step, then stopped again. "I

understand it helps if you are able to detach your mind from your body," he whispered.

Rodrigo Mascarenas always took time to ensure he made the best possible impression. He knew his white silk shirt set off his light mocha complexion and his pale blue eyes. He sat on a white cushioned banco with another man. Two men sat in deck chairs on the other side of a heavy, low, round wood table.

Mascarenas had completed his business with these men. They had already paid him five million dollars—confirmed by wire to his account in Geneva. He'd been on a high since they'd closed the deal. These were new clients—coarse, rough men from Quebec, Canada. Based on their agreement, Mascarenas would provide five million dollars a month in raw heroin to them. This meant he would now bring in over twenty-five million dollars per month through his drug smuggling business.

He'd promised these men entertainment. Four of the women who'd come aboard the previous night were ready, he'd been told. Two of them still hadn't recovered from seasickness.

Mascarenas felt a stirring in his groin when he heard the sound of spiked heels strike the deck halfway down the port side of the yacht. He excitedly ran a hand over his mustache and goatee. He'd been more than satisfied with the "goods" José Rosales Lorca had provided in the past. He expected this crop to be at least as good. He'd pick out one of the women, share a little cocaine with her, and then go crazy. He loved these women—girls, really—from little towns in Central America. He didn't have to buy them presents or take them out to dinner. If they acted up, he'd just dump their sorry asses into the sea. If they performed, he'd take them into Miami and sell them to that depraved pimp, Hugo Echeveria.

He raised a hand to signal the steward for another round of drinks, when one of the crew members led a single file of four women into the deck lounge. When the crewman stepped aside and Mascarenas saw the first woman in line, he thought his heart had stopped. He couldn't believe how beautiful this little village girl was. And the fear in her innocent, rounded eyes only made her more desirable.

A movement to Mascarenas's left made him turn. One of the Canadians had left his deck chair and moved toward the women. He stopped in front of the first one, who wore a black dress and diamonds and announced, "This one's mine." The man grabbed her wrist and tugged her down the deck.

Mascarenas felt a momentary rush of anger at the Canadian, but suppressed it. No point in disappointing a customer over some ignorant *puta*. He decided to wait for the other two men to select their "dates" for the evening. Like the good host, he'd take whichever girl remained.

Then an angry curse came from the side of the yacht, where the first Canadian had gone off with the woman. Mascarenas heard another curse, then a slapping sound. The Canadian dragged the girl by the wrist into the deck lounge and screamed, "Look what this bitch did to me!"

Mascarenas wanted to laugh, but he knew that wouldn't do. He rose from his place on the banco and pointed at the sailor who'd led the girls on deck. "Take that one back to her room. And get our guest some clean clothes." Mascarenas moved to the Canadian and put a placating hand on the man's back.

"I'll see that she's punished for this insult," he said. "Pick out whichever of the other girls you want and I'll have her sent down to your room."

The Canadian's face had turned so red Mascarenas thought he might explode. But then the man seemed to calm down. He pointed at one of the other women and said, "She'll do."

"Good," Mascarenas said.

When the three men had selected their "dates," Mascarenas grabbed a bottle of champagne from the bar and descended the stairs to the staterooms. He grinned and quietly said, "I can't believe it. She puked all over the sonofabitch." Then he laughed out loud while he entered the girl's stateroom and locked the door behind him.

DAY 4

CHAPTER 18

"This has been a great visit," Matt groaned, barely able to get the words out through Esteban's crushing bear hug.

Alani giggled. "Put him down, Esteban. You're embarrassing Matt in front of all these people." She hugged Renee and said, "We'll see you in Costa Rica on September 10th."

Renee smiled at Alani. "You know, while our husbands tell war stories and drink beer down in Costa Rica, you and I will have a blast. I hear the leather shops down there are spectacular."

Alani laughed. "I can't wait."

Matt, finally free of Esteban's exuberant bear hug, squinted at Renee. "Sounds like you two are plotting something," he said.

Renee turned her head at an angle and smiled demurely. "Why, sugar, what would make you say such a thing?"

Matt embraced Alani and shook Esteban's hand. "Thanks for everything, *cuate*," he said. "See you soon."

"You can count on it," Esteban said.

"Come on, sweetheart," Matt said to Renee. "Time to board the plane."

"God, it's been months since we've been in New Mexico," Renee said.

"Two months, three weeks, and seven days, to be exact," Matt said.

"I have to admit I missed it," she said.

Matt moved to the couch in their Eldorado Hotel suite in Santa Fe.

Renee walked over to him and stuck out her arm. A Hopi turquoise and silver bracelet rested across her wrist. "Would you fasten this for me?"

Matt closed the clasp on the bracelet, then looked up at her.

"I hope we'll be able to return to our home soon. Settle down for good," Renee said.

Matt didn't want to spoil the evening by saying what he was thinking. He wanted tonight to be special—drinks in the Old House, then dinner at SantaCafé. No business conversation; nothing but time spent with and for each other. But a surge of heat struck the back of his neck while Lonnie Jackson's image seemed to project from Matt's brain to the space between him and Renee. Just like that. The sonofabitch was never far from mind.

Renee grabbed Matt's hand and pulled to help him off the couch.

The concerned look in her eyes told Matt she had sensed the change in his mood.

"Come on Matthew," she said. "Let's go downstairs and have a drink."

Matt kissed Renee's cheek. "Have I told you lately how much I love you?"

She smiled and said, "Not in the last five minutes."

CHAPTER 19

Lonnie Jackson checked his wristwatch and estimated that Luis Reyes's man would be at Managua International Airport by now. Three days after picking Nicaragua for his new base of operations, he'd hired the slick Costa Rican lawyer to handle legal and political matters . . . and most other things that might arise. Reyes had a stable of "gofers" who could do anything for him and his clients. It was Reyes who'd acquired his Lorca alias for him, along with documentation.

Reyes was a diminutive forty-year-old who couldn't have weighed more than one hundred twenty pounds, soaking wet. He had a smooth olive complexion and a black mustache that stopped just short of qualifying as a Fu Manchu. He was a gutsy little guy, who seemed able to handle any exigency. Lonnie was pleased with the way Reyes had kept the legal and political wolves at bay.

Jackson had picked Reyes because of the lawyer's ability to operate equally efficiently in Costa Rica and Nicaragua. Reyes made certain the appropriate government officials' palms were greased. He'd arranged for a physician to take care of any health problems the trafficked women might have. And he managed the transportation of the women—into Managua, then on to Jackson's place in the jungle.

Whether they came from Central America, Eastern Europe, or the Orient, Nicaragua was where the women were told they would receive their "training." They came to Managua expecting to receive education in their new profession—secretary, maid, nanny, or whatever. They thought Nicaragua was merely a stopover before they went on to the Promised Land. Each woman who arrived in Managua believed she would find a new life in the United States. That's what the recruiting advertisement had told them.

Gustavo Albemarle, Luis Reyes's man, had arrived at Managua International Airport an hour before Señor Lorca's "cargo" was due to arrive. Albemarle checked in with the security and Customs personnel. They'd all been bribed in advance; he wanted to make certain they stayed bribed.

When he was satisfied that all was well, Albemarle went out to the gate assigned to the flight from Europe, took a seat on a bench in the shade of a building overhang, and lit a cigarette. He reflected on the fact that this was the second inbound flight this week. Two women came in on Monday. Now four more today: Saturday. He smiled at the thought of the money accumulating in his Bahamian bank account. He tried to estimate how much money Reyes and Lorca would make off these four women, but he quickly put the thought out of mind. Without Lorca and Reyes, he knew he'd be committing petty crimes and scraping for a meager living. He wouldn't begrudge the big *jefes* their cut.

The sudden screech of tires and the roar of engines caused Albemarle to look across the grassy fields to the runway. The blue and white jet gleamed in the afternoon sun. He took a last drag from his cigarette and flicked the butt at the pavement. He exhaled smoke from his nostrils and watched the aircraft taxi toward the terminal. He understood that the women aboard the plane were from the Balkans. There had been four other flights over the last three months from Eastern Europe. He'd never seen women like the ones who flew in from that part of the world. He scratched his crotch and thought once again about his plan: save enough money to retire, find one of these tall, long-legged Eastern European women, and screw his brains out.

Tatiana Borodvic wore a smug smile while she watched the other three women move down the aisle toward the plane's exit door. She'd listened to their saccharine-sweet conversations on board and tried to guess how they would react when they discovered they'd been duped. Their dreams about a better life were nothing but fantasies.

She waited until all other passengers had debarked, then she walked down the aisle, and stopped in the plane's doorway. As she looked toward the terminal building, she used a hand to shield her eyes from the glaring sun and felt a wave of heat and humidity sweep over her. She saw a short, slightly overweight man, dressed in a *guayavera* and tan slacks, step out from under an overhang at the back of the terminal and walk briskly toward the three women, who were now twenty meters from the plane. He bowed ceremoniously and spoke to them. Borodvic knew one of the Bulgarians spoke a bit of Spanish.

While a guy in overalls deposited passengers' bags on the tarmac next to the aircraft, the man in the *guayabera* moved toward the steps and waved benignly at Borodvic. "Don't be shy," he said in Spanish. "Come, come. There's nothing to be afraid of."

Borodvic noticed the lecherous look in the man's eyes. He seemed to undress her with that look. A confident smile played on his lips. She demurely dropped her gaze, then half-raised her head and gave the man an embarrassed smile. "You're damned right I've got nothing to be afraid of, you sleaze," she mumbled to herself. She took the stairs down to the tarmac and considered how much she'd make the bastard suffer before she killed him.

Tatiana Borodvic was the only one of the four women who knew they hadn't flown to Nicaragua for training prior to placement in jobs in the United States. She smiled at the stupidity of the other three. That they would leave their families, friends, and communities for economic opportunity was perfectly understandable. People had done the same thing for thousands of years. But to do so without doing their homework was incomprehensible. And why would they be so gullible as to believe the road to the United States went through Nicaragua, of all places. *The greater fool theory is alive and well*, she thought. *These dupas are living proof.*

Borodvic carefully observed everything on the ride from the

Managua Airport. She actually giggled when Gustavo, the guy who'd met them at the airport, told them when they'd arrived in the jungle, "Come on, ladies. I'll show you to your rooms." It was as though they'd arrived at a resort.

They followed the man across a manicured lawn, under giant trees with leaves the size of elephants' ears, and headed toward what appeared to be a stable.

"Please place your suitcases on the ground," Gustavo said. "I'll have them brought to your rooms."

Borodvic detected horsey odors. She saw no horses and guessed their "rooms" were nothing more than converted stables. They moved onto a cement floor that ran between rows of cells.

Apparently used to unquestioningly taking orders, the women dropped their bags and followed Gustavo.

Borodvic followed suit, playing the role of the submissive female. She lowered her head slightly, her eyes hooded; but she noticed everything. She spied a camera mounted at the top of the wall across from where they stood. Big brother was watching.

The women suddenly seemed confused. They huddled together and whispered to one another.

Two burly Latino men appeared from the far end of the path between the cells and moved forward.

Borodvic sneered at them. She entered the nearest cell and quickly surveyed the interior. It was beyond Spartan, but no worse than she'd anticipated. The bed was nothing more than a thin, filthy mattress placed on the floor. The toilet and sink were exposed and had obviously not been cleaned in a very long time. Dark yellow, almost orange-colored stains covered nearly every inch of the plumbing fixtures.

She noticed another stain on the floor in front of the mattress. *Blood*, she thought. She turned to look at the door to her cell, just when it was slammed shut.

Then women's cries carried to her, followed by the clanging sounds of slammed doors. She heard whimpers come from the rooms down the hall. It wasn't long before the whimpers turned to sobs.

Gustavo Albemarle checked to make sure all four cell doors were locked, then, more out of curiosity than concern for security, he peered through the iron-grated openings in the other eight doors along the corridor. Three of the other rooms were occupied—one by a Filipino girl who couldn't have been more than sixteen. He remembered her from an earlier shipment and knew she was scheduled to be sent to Thailand that very day. She cowered in a corner. Her eyes looked too big for her face. The girls in two other rooms appeared to be Latinas. They were also teenagers. Despite their dirty clothing and unwashed bodies, all of them were obviously beautiful. But none of them interested him the way the Bulgarian brunette did. He'd felt a tremor in his groin from the thought of spending time with that one. Sometimes Lorca let him take part in a woman's indoctrination. Maybe he'd get lucky and be able to spend a little quality time with that one.

CHAPTER 20

CIA Agent Eddie Parnell, under the guise of Petrov Ulanoff, had wound his way by airplane from the United States to Varna, Bulgaria. He didn't inform Tarnovsky of his trip—this wasn't a social visit. But he suspected, with Tarnovsky's connections, the man would somehow know that his old friend Petrov was in Bulgaria. After he secured his suitcase and cleared customs in Varna, Parnell walked outside the terminal toward the taxi queue. He smiled when he recognized one of Tarnovsky's men seated on the right front fender of what looked like a twenty-year-old, black Mercedes sedan parked by the curb in front of the terminal entrance. The car's finish shone as though it had just come off a showroom floor.

Parnell racked his brain and tried to come up with the man's name. The guy pushed off the car and came toward him. *Think,* Parnell told himself. The guy had reached for Parnell's bag when the name finally came to him: Metin Osmanoglu, a Turk who had worked for Tarnovsky for as long as Parnell had known the Bulgarian. Osmanoglu resembled the picture of Goliath in a book Parnell had as a child. He was tall, big muscled, and bearded. His jet-black hair hung past his collar and the dark skin on his face seemed to be imbedded with minute specks of gunpowder.

Although Parnell had a reputation within the CIA for being fearless—except maybe for his fear of politicians and senatorial investigations—this Osmanoglu guy gave him the creeps. The Turk was completely dedicated to Tarnovsky. Neither money, nor women, nor power could corrupt the man. And he had that daunting, ebony-eyed, unsmiling look that seemed to be common among many Turks. His hair, eyebrows, and mustache were pitch-black and seemed to have a natural sheen about them. There was a foreboding, ominous sense of power about Osmanoglu. His poorly made brown wool suit and clumpy brown shoes appeared out of place on the man. Parnell had a momentary vision of the Turk, scimitar in hand, riding a battle-clad stallion. He was the ultimate mysterious creature from the East, in a region where nearly everyone seemed to carry a similar aura.

Parnell tried to smile at the Turk, but he sensed that all he conveyed was a half-assed smirk that probably made him appear weak. In any case, all he got in return was the same expression that always seemed to be on Osmanoglu's face: a serpent's stare, a grim set to his mouth, and a jutted jaw. The guy might as well have been cast in bronze.

Osmanoglu tossed Parnell's bag in the back seat of the Mercedes, then held the front passenger side door open. Parnell got in. Osmanoglu closed the door, then made his way around the front of the car to the driver side. Once behind the wheel, he drove away from the terminal. After they cleared airport grounds, he reached inside his jacket pocket and handed Parnell an envelope.

Parnell ripped open the envelope, extracted a single piece of paper, and dropped the empty envelope on his lap. The note was handwritten. Parnell recognized Tarnovsky's flowery script:

My Dear Petrov:

You can imagine my distress when I learned of your return to Varna. And no advance notice from you. Shame on you. Is this any way to treat a friend?

Before I begin to sound like a scolding mother, I want to welcome you home. Metin has instructions to bring you straight to the compound. No hotels for such a dear friend.

It was signed: *Your humble servant, Yevgeni.*

Humble servant, my ass, Parnell thought. He knew he had no choice but to sit back and try to enjoy the ride. He didn't like this development at all. Being the guest of Yevgeni Tarnovsky was akin to being his prisoner. A guest ate better and was better treated. But, like a prisoner, a guest left Tarnovsky's compound only when it suited his host.

The drive to Tarnovsky's compound took fifty minutes. The landscape changed from urban to rural. Nothing had changed since his last visit. He noted the security that would have gone unnoticed by the untrained eye. Two miles from the compound, men stood in fields on both sides of the road. As usual, they weren't doing anything agrarian. They just stood there, watched the road, automatic weapons—Parnell knew—hidden under their long coats.

The closer they came to the compound, the more serious security became. A guard shack stood beside the road a mile from the estate. Two armed guards eyed the car, but immediately raised the arm of a metal bar that blocked the road. Before they moved away from the checkpoint, Parnell saw one of the guards move to the shack and pick up a telephone receiver.

An eight-foot high chain-link fence, topped by razor wire, surrounded the estate. Inside the fence was a ten-foot stone wall. Without the chain-link fence, Parnell reflected, the place would look medieval. The fence and wall were separated by ten yards of grass. This was where Tarnovsky's dog pack roamed after dark.

Parnell spied four armed guards at the main gate. There was nothing perfunctory about their inspection of the car and its passengers. It apparently made no difference that they knew Osmanoglu. Everyone who went through the entrance was treated with suspicion. Parnell knew that paranoia was one of the reasons for Tarnovsky's longevity.

The guards finally passed them through, after they telephoned the big house. Osmanoglu drove through the now-open gates. Parnell noted that heavy bunches of pale green grapes weighed the vines that covered the grounds on either side of the eighteen-foot wide paved driveway. Towering cypress trees, planted fifteen feet apart, bordered the drive. Straight ahead, under a tree canopy, was Tarnovsky's spectacular residence. A king's castle in a land where the only kings were entrepreneurs who would have made an old American railroad baron look like Mother Teresa.

The driveway branched at a raised hillock covered with thorn holly bushes intersected by a walking path. The car half-circled the hill and stopped twenty feet from the front entrance of the mansion, which was separated from the driveway by a twenty-step stone staircase. A liveried butler stood at the bottom of the steps.

"Welcome back, Mister Ulanoff," the man said. He took Parnell's suitcase and led the way inside. "Mr. Tarnovsky knew you would be tired after your flight. He told me to tell you to relax tonight. He will meet you for breakfast tomorrow at 9 a.m. I'll show you to your room."

Parnell looked at his watch: 3 p.m. He actually was exhausted after the long flight, but he would have preferred to meet with Tarnovsky today. However, he had no choice. If the oligarch wanted to wait until tomorrow to meet, then he'd have to wait until then.

After the butler showed him to his room, deposited his bag on the floor against the foot of the bed, and left, Parnell unbuttoned his shirt on the way to the bathroom. He stripped down to his shorts, turned on the shower, and played with the hot and cold shower knobs. Once he was satisfied with the water temperature, he slipped out of his shorts and stepped under the stream of water. He let it pummel him. When he felt human again, he shut off the water, toweled dry, and walked naked into the bedroom. He hefted his bag onto the bed and removed his toiletry kit and a clean change of clothes. He placed the clothes on the bed and turned back to the bathroom, toiletry kit in hand. A movement from the side made his heart seem to jump up into his throat. He prepared to toss the leather kit in the direction of the movement, and then to roll onto the carpet, when he realized it was only his reflection in an old fashioned, freestanding mirror.

"Jeez," Parnell sighed, as he willed his breathing and heart rate back to normal. "I'm too damned old for this work."

Parnell took pride in the knowledge that he was in better shape than nearly any other forty-two-year-old man he knew. His body was still hard and his mind sharp. But there was nothing he could do about maintaining twenty-year-old reflexes. His experience gave him the advantage of anticipation. But he would love to have those youthful reflexes again. He sighed as he moved to the bathroom sink. It was probably time to put in his papers. He was too old to be in the field, and there was no way he'd ever be happy behind some desk. "Time to take your pension, old boy," he said to the bathroom mirror, and thought about the dream he'd harbored for nearly a decade now: find a little place on some island, buy a boat; and set sail. But with almost no savings, thanks to a divorce, his dream was nothing more than a fairy tale.

Parnell suddenly stopped daydreaming and looked at himself with a cold, hard stare. "You've got work to do, asshole. Keep yourself centered."

CHAPTER 21

Senator Pete Driscoll stared out through the sedan's windshield and imagined the shimmering waves of heat that enveloped the district. Even at 7:45 in the evening, it was hotter than hell outside. He took a moment to redirect one of the car's air conditioner vents at his face, then turned to his administrative assistant, Francis Antonelli, and asked, "Why do you think Benedict wants to see me?"

"All he told me was that it was important," Antonelli said.

Antonelli had been Senator Driscoll's aide for the past fifteen years, ever since the good people of Kansas first sent Driscoll to the U.S. Senate. Driscoll didn't like surprises—even more than he disliked the Louisiana Democrat, Senator William Benedict. Driscoll was a straight arrow; Benedict chased every skirt that crossed his path and lived a dissolute existence, which included taking every perk he could get his hands on. And, to make matters worse, Driscoll knew he'd probably get stuck with the tab for tonight's dinner. Benedict was notorious for stiffing dinner companions.

Antonelli turned left from I Street onto 16th and then pulled up to the front of the trendy watering hole, the Lafayette Restaurant.

"And tell me why I shouldn't just ignore what that old blowhard wants?"

Driscoll was merely venting his frustration. He didn't want to spend an evening with Benedict, but he appreciated Antonelli going through the motions anyway.

"Senator," Antonelli said, "you know that despite Senator Benedict's bullshit, when he asks for a sit-down, it usually means it's important. You ignore him and you're likely to regret it later."

"I know, I know. But Jesus, did he have to pick the most expensive place in town? Some asshole correspondent's bound to see me with old Willie the Cajun and ask questions."

Antonelli laughed. "It's not like you to let your paranoia show. Hell, maybe Benedict just wants to barhop with you. You know, pick up a couple of young girls, and take them to his place in Georgetown."

"Humpf. I suppose you think that's hilarious."

As Driscoll exited the car, Antonelli said, "I can come by and take you back to your place after dinner."

Driscoll gave Antonelli a grateful smile and said, "You spend enough damned time mothering me. Go home, open a bottle of wine, and curl up with that sweet wife of yours. I'll get a taxi back to the Watergate."

"Okay. See you in the morning."

Driscoll shut the car door and entered the restaurant. He'd never been here before, but he'd heard plenty about it. Anybody who was anybody wanted to be seen here. Pete Driscoll couldn't have cared less about being seen here, or anywhere. He suspected that William Benedict could call at a moment's notice and get a table here or at any one of a hundred posh places around town.

Driscoll approached the *maitre d*'s stand. "I'm Pete Driscoll. I'm meeting Senator Benedict." The haughty look on the tuxedoed man's face quickly changed.

"Ah, yes, Senator Driscoll. Please follow me."

After he was shown to a table, Driscoll looked at his watch: ten minutes to eight. About the only good thing he could say about Benedict was that the man was manic about punctuality. Benedict had said eight o'clock. He would arrive early or exactly at eight. Driscoll ordered a cranberry juice and then looked around the room. He spied one of the network congressional correspondents and a *Washington Post* senior editor before he'd taken in the whole room. *Once Benedict shows up,* Driscoll thought, *some eyebrows will be raised.*

"Petey-boy! What you drinking there?" The words burst over the room like 4th of July fireworks. All other conversation seemed to stop, and all eyes seemed to focus on Benedict as he crossed to a momentarily flustered Driscoll.

Driscoll shook his head in disbelief. The sonofabitch had a way of disintegrating any feeling of self-importance one might have. Petey-boy! Jeez! Driscoll knew any possibility he would go unnoticed had dissipated. He felt his face warm.

Benedict shook his hand and took a seat across from him while he performed a quick reconnaissance of the restaurant. "Looks like the press is here in force tonight," he said. "Guess we better keep our voices down." He said all this in a boisterous tone that no one in the room could possibly have missed.

Driscoll saw Benedict wink at someone at another table. He couldn't be certain if it was one of the members of the press or the teenage girl dining with a man and woman who he guessed were probably her parents.

Driscoll had a momentary thought about Louisiana politics. Here was this florid-faced man with the telltale swelling around the eyes that came with high alcohol consumption. His eyes were piggy—small and beady. Despite his six foot height, Benedict had tiny feet—seemingly too small to support his body. His only redeeming physical quality was a sweeping shock of white hair. Every voter in Louisiana had to know about Benedict's extracurricular activities and his reputation as the junket king of the U.S. Senate. And he talked like a throwback to Huey Long. *How the hell does this man get reelected?*

"So, what's happening, Petey-boy? Gettin' any?"

Driscoll stared at Benedict. "Okay, Willie, you've done your little routine for the spectators. Now get down to business. You called this meeting."

The corners of Benedict's mouth turned down and his eyes squinted to the point they disappeared in his bloated face. Then he laughed. The humor quickly left his face and his gaze lasered in on Driscoll. "It's no secret you don't like me, Petey. So I'll dispense with the pleasantries." Benedict waved to a waiter who immediately scurried over. Without taking his eyes off Driscoll, Benedict said,

"Get me a bourbon on the rocks. Make it a double. And I want them lamb chops and the best bottle of Merlot you got in the joint. Senator, I recommend you order the chops, too." Benedict then added, to the waiter, "And skip the rabbit food. Don't need no salad."

Driscoll shrugged his shoulders.

After the waiter walked away, Benedict leaned forward and whispered, "I hear you got a burr under your saddle about something to do with white slavery."

Driscoll's internal alarm went off. The last topic he'd anticipated the Louisianan would bring up was trafficking.

"The correct term today is human trafficking. And that's right. I have a burr under my saddle. A constituent of mine claims his daughter was duped with the promise of an overseas job and has disappeared. Rumors have it that she, and other young women from her city, have vanished after they applied for jobs through some agency in Bulgaria."

"Bulgaria. You got to be shittin' me."

"Crazy as it sounds, our research shows that women from all over Eastern Europe have gone missing. The common element is they have all responded to ads about jobs in the West."

"Well, ain't that the shits," Benedict said. He leaned back in his chair and stared quizzically at Driscoll.

Driscoll gave Benedict a fifteen-minute briefing on what his staff had learned about human trafficking. The way Benedict paid attention, without interruption, leaning on his elbows, their faces just two feet apart, told Driscoll he had the man's interest and that much of what he said was new to him.

When Driscoll finished, interrupted only when the waiter served their meals, Benedict again leaned back from the table. He rubbed his hands over his face, then ran them through his hair. He stared for a moment at the untouched lamb chops on the plate he'd pushed to the side. Then he looked at the plate in front of Driscoll. He waved a hand at the waiter, got his attention, then made a motion indicating he wanted the check. After Benedict settled the tab—to Driscoll's surprise—he said solemnly, "Let's get out of here."

Outside the restaurant, Benedict asked, "You have a car here?"

"No, I'll get a taxi."

As though Driscoll had no right to object, Benedict declared, "I'll drive you." He gave his claim check to the parking attendant. The two senators waited in silence. When the attendant returned with the vehicle, the two men got in, and Benedict pulled away from the curb.

Driscoll knew something weighed on Benedict's mind. He'd seen it many times before. The senator from Louisiana normally talked incessantly. It was when he remained silent that you had to keep an eye on him. Despite his behavioral idiosyncrasies, the man had a steel trap mind. Finally, six blocks from the Watergate Apartments, Benedict said, "What do you think the CIA's interest is in this trafficking business?"

Driscoll's head jerked toward Benedict. He considered the question for a moment, then said, "I put the bureaucrats on notice I wanted them to look into it. I had a meeting in my office with representatives from several departments and agencies. A guy from Central Intelligence was there. Agent named Parnell. Why do you ask?"

"Huh," Benedict said absentmindedly. "Some guy named Moreland, Westcliffe Moreland, paid a call on me at my home last night. Now, I want to tell you, I found that somewhat unusual. But my being the chairman of the Intelligence Oversight Committee, I figured it was no big deal. Then he spouts a bunch of bullshit about national security and your crusade against trafficking."

"National security, my ass," Driscoll said. "That's the defense of scoundrels." He felt his heart rate accelerate. It always pissed him off when some agency asshole tried to cover something up under the cloak of national security. "What do you think is going on, Willie?"

Benedict inhaled noisily, then blew air out through his nose. He glanced at Driscoll. "I think the CIA got caught with its pecker hanging out and wants me to put pressure on you to back off your investigation into this trafficking business."

"And what will you do?" Driscoll asked. "Put pressure on me?"

Benedict laughed. "Since when can I put pressure on you, Petey-boy? Nah, I think I'll see if I can whack off the CIA's weenie before they figure out how to put it back in their jeans."

DAY 5

CHAPTER 22

"Man, just the smell of this place takes me back years."

Quince Hansen chuckled. "Esteban, I guess I've been in Costa Rica too long to notice it. But I remember when I first came down here fifteen years ago; it was the same for me. The smells of the city: the sulfur odor from cars without catalytic converters, the dampness and mold, the smell of food cooking on street vendors' grills. Nothing has changed since we were young bucks."

Esteban swigged some of his beer and said, "We were kids, weren't we?"

"Wet behind the ears and full of piss and vinegar. More testosterone than brains."

"You remember when they sent us out of Bragg to track down drug runners in Colombia? Dropped us in on a night jump."

Hansen's pale blue eyes seemed to cloud over for a second, then he chuckled again and said, "How could I forget. Your chute did a Mae West. You were falling way too fast."

"If I hadn't hit the top of that damned tree, I would probably have broken my back."

"Fun and games, Estee," Hansen said. "And, just think, Uncle Sam actually paid us to have that much fun."

Esteban laughed. "No one's called me Estee in years. Makes me feel like a kid again."

Hansen squinted at his old friend and said, "Don't get carried away, buddy. You ain't no kid."

"Tell me about it."

"When will I meet the missus?" Hansen asked.

"Tonight at dinner. And you'll get a chance to meet the guy who pulled my ass out of the fire in the Balkans. He and his wife are down here for some medical convention."

Hansen consulted his wristwatch. "It's only 10:00 a.m. Let's take a ride. I got lunch arranged with a bunch of old SF types."

Esteban gave Hansen a toothy grin. "Sounds dangerous," he said. "I can't show up for dinner tonight three sheets to the wind."

"Hah!" Hansen exclaimed. "Would I do that to you?"

"Esteban getting caught up on old times?" Renee said to Alani as she held the front door of the leather goods shop on Calle Bonifacia in San José's shopping district.

"Yeah, hopefully he'll get it out of his system."

Renee caught the worried expression on Alani's face. This wasn't the first time she'd noticed that a little tension existed between Esteban and Alani. She didn't pry, figuring Alani would open up when and if she wanted to. To change the subject, and hopefully Alani's mood, she said, "Will you look at this place." She meandered over to a wall with leather handbags displayed on glass shelves.

Alani followed her and fingered one of the bags. "So soft. And look at the price. This would cost twice as much back in the States."

Renee met Alani's gaze and said with a hint of mischief in her voice, her eyes twinkling, "Then we should both buy something. Just think how much money we'll save."

Alani laughed. "My thought exactly."

Luis Reyes, seated at a San José sidewalk café under the shade of a large red umbrella, watched a leather goods shop from across the street. He sipped his lemonade and then removed his cell phone from his suit jacket pocket and dialed Lorca's number.

"Yeah?"

Reyes said, "The woman's across the street in a shop."

"Is she alone?"

"No. She's with another woman. Polynesian beauty."

97

That stopped Jackson for a moment. "Are you sure it's Renee Curtis?"

Reyes pumped out his chest and felt a slight quiver in the pit of his stomach. He was as sure as he could be that the woman he'd followed was Renee Curtis. The desk clerk at Curtis's hotel had confirmed her identity. But with Lorca he knew there was never any room for error. He'd heard rumors about what Lorca had done to employees who'd disappointed him. Reyes shuddered, then said, "I confirmed her identity with the desk clerk."

"Okay. Describe her to me."

Reyes grudgingly admired Lorca's caution. "She's about five, eight. Maybe a little taller. Athletically built. Shoulder-length, reddish-brown hair. Could be thirty-five or so. She's a beautiful woman, *señor*." He paused a beat and added, "But a bit older than usual."

"Stay with her. I'll call you when I get into San José. Don't lose her, Reyes. You hear me?"

"*Sí . . . sí, señor.*"

Jackson slowly, softly replaced the receiver in its cradle and breathed a sigh that released months of built up tension. Renee Curtis was his. He had a special plan for that bitch. Then he'd take down her meddling husband. Life would be good again. Or, at least, better than it had been since Mama and Johnny had died.

He pressed an intercom button and shouted, "Julio, get the chopper ready!"

CHAPTER 23

Yevgeni Tarnovsky raised a glass of orange juice in salute to his guest. "Ah, Petrov," he said in Bulgarian, "how was your flight?"

"Same as usual, Yevgeni. Long and tiring. But it's worth it, being able to visit you and to see this wonderful home again."

"As always, my silver-tongued friend, you are welcome. Come—let me pour you some juice." He smiled and added, "I assume it's a bit early for single malt scotch?"

Parnell nodded and paced the room. He inspected the antique books and ornate icons that he knew were worth a fortune. How Tarnovsky spirited them from Russia was a mystery. But Parnell was no longer surprised at anything Yevgeni Tarnovsky did.

"Please sit; join me," Tarnovsky said. He placed a glass of juice in front of Parnell as the man sat across from him. Then he scooted forward to the edge of his chair, leaned forward, and in a lowered voice, said, "So, tell me, Petrov, how are things with our employer?"

Parnell smiled. He had to give Tarnovsky credit. The man always played his part perfectly. He knew Parnell's real name, but always stayed in role. As far as Tarnovsky's staff and crew were concerned, Petrov Ulanoff was a Bulgarian military officer who did business with their boss. Not a CIA agent named Parnell.

Parnell let his smile fade. "Our employer is quite distressed, my friend. Rumors have reached the wrong ears." He paused to watch Tarnovsky's reaction, but the man merely sat back, crossed his legs, and adjusted the crease of a pant leg.

"I'm sure these rumors have been exaggerated, Yevgeni. But I have been sent to clear things up. You know. Make sure our information is not . . . distorted."

Tarnovsky uncrossed his legs and leaned forward again. Elbows on his knees, hands akimbo, he said, "What is it that has our employer so concerned?"

"Trafficking in women. We've heard that women are being transported from several countries and are being sold into bondage." Parnell met Tarnovsky's stare. He looked for any sign of dissembling. He expected the *mafiya* chief to deny the accusation.

"It's too lucrative to pass up, Petrov," Tarnovsky said. He shrugged. "If I don't do it, someone else will."

Parnell was amazed at Tarnovsky's candor. He glared at the Bulgarian and said in an acid tone, "Yes, Yevgeni, that's probably true. But *someone else* doesn't work for our employer like you do. *Someone else* wouldn't put our employer's ass in a crack if it was discovered they were indirectly involved in this business."

Tarnovsky rose from his chair and crossed over to his desk. He raised the lid on his humidor and removed two Cuban Montecristos. He neatly cut a quarter inch off the ends of each cigar and returned to the table. After he passed one to Parnell, he made a big production of lighting his own.

Parnell ignored the cigar Tarnovsky had handed him and watched the Bulgarian fiddle with his cigar. He suspected the man was using the time to think. Tarnovsky was a devious sonofabitch. He warily watched the man puff on his cigar. Great clouds of smoke circled his face, then rose toward the fourteen foot ceiling.

Finally, Tarnovsky, seemingly satisfied with the condition of the cigar, turned his attention again to Parnell. "I presume your comment about our employer's vulnerability is not an exaggeration."

Parnell nodded, his eyes cold and penetrating. "There's a U.S. senator holding committee hearings on female trafficking. Another Senate committee oversees intelligence matters. Three senators sit on both those committees. What if one of those men or a committee staffer comes across your name in both committees, and makes the connection between your role as a CIA informant and as a trafficker?"

"Ah," Tarnovsky said. "Then I must do something about it."

"I remind you, Yevgeni, we had a similar conversation about this subject several months ago. You swore then you would get out of the trafficking business."

Tarnovsky waved a hand dismissively. "Yes, I remember. But this time I understand the stakes. I give you my word that things will change."

Parnell suspected his face gave away his skepticism, but he decided to take the man's promise at face value. *Again, what choice do I have? Tarnovsky's the best operative the Agency has ever had inside Bulgaria, either before or since the fall of the Iron Curtain. I don't want to have to replace him.*

"Enough on that subject," Tarnovsky said. "I'll take care of everything. Now, let's have breakfast. I have fresh Beluga caviar in honor of your visit."

Tarnovsky picked up a bell from the table and rang it once. A liveried servant appeared at the study door. "We are ready to eat," Tarnovsky said. The servant turned and waved to someone behind him. Two absolutely stunning young women entered the room. One pushed a cart; the other carried a silver carafe. They moved to the table and served Parnell and then Tarnovsky. When Parnell and Tarnovsky were alone again, the Bulgarian thumped the edge of the table, which caused the dishes, glasses, and cups to bounce. He laughed boisterously. "You look like a haggard old crone, Petrov. I gave you my word. Don't worry about a thing."

CHAPTER 24

After breakfast, Tarnovsky called Metin Osmanoglu to show Parnell around the grounds. Parnell tried to beg off, but Tarnovsky insisted. Then Tarnovsky went to his office. He paced the room; considered his options. He could close down his trafficking business, which would cost him millions. It's not that he needed the money. That wasn't the point. It was a matter of control. Power. The minute he created a vacuum, some asshole would fill it. If he allowed someone to get their hooks into the trafficking business, they might use the profits to branch out into other areas. The next thing he knew he'd have competitors in narcotics, counterfeiting, black marketing, and who knew what else. Shuttering his trafficking business would be a sign of weakness.

He could tell the CIA to go screw itself, but much of his operation was dependent on the doors the CIA opened for him. The intelligence the Agency shared with him made it possible to make timely investments in currency and international stock exchanges. It also warned him in advance of Interpol raids. That intelligence gave him a huge advantage over his competitors. The CIA's signal intelligence had once warned him of an attempt on his life by the head of the Chechen crime organization. He'd arranged for an ambush and assassinated the Chechen chieftain before the man could put his plan into action. No, he needed the agency.

Tarnovsky had a sudden inspiration. He knew what he'd do. It only required a slight tweak of the organization he already had in place. *Tatiana Borodvic should be in Nicaragua by now,* he thought. *Her job is to kill Lorca for the insult he'd committed.* What he hadn't told her was that he intended to take over Lorca's operation. Cut out the middleman. He hadn't decided who would manage the Central American site after Lorca was eliminated. That could be resolved later. Lorca must have a lieutenant or two who knew how things worked. It was the recruitment operation headquartered in Bulgaria that had to be turned over to someone else.

I'll tell Eddie Parnell a little white lie. That I assigned an assassin to terminate the conduit for the trafficking business: José Rosales Lorca. That much is true. Let the CIA think I'm being a good boy. He laughed and rubbed his hands together. *I'll break the news to Parnell this evening; send him back to his masters at Langley with good news.*

Tarnovsky then came to the conclusion that Tatiana Borodvic would be the perfect leader of the trafficking operation in Bulgaria. With her in charge, he would distance himself from the trade. The CIA was so hamstrung by Congressional committees and naïve laws, there was no way they'd discover that he hadn't actually disengaged from the business. How did the Americans put it? Oh, yes. He'd have his cake and eat it too.

CHAPTER 25

Jackson hadn't missed the look in the Bulgarian woman's eyes. She'd looked directly at the camera. This one was observant. She might be a little tougher than most of the women who went through his "school." But that thought didn't worry him. He hated to take the loss, but the recalcitrant ones couldn't be allowed to set the tone for the others. It had only happened twice before; but when a woman refused to cooperate, even after torture and rape, he'd have his men take her down to the pond. The caimans knew how to take care of the obstinate ones.

But there was something about the brunette. She gave Jackson an itch he hadn't felt in a long time. It wasn't just her long legs, tight ass, big breasts, and sculpted features. There was . . . a confidence about her. If he hadn't had to take the helicopter to San José, he would have called down to the cells and ordered Reyes to bring the woman to him. *Later,* he told himself. A wave of frustration made him feel hot and angry.

Jackson stood and looked out the window at the workers who hacked away at the lush jungle with their machetes. He turned away from the window and pulled a file from his middle desk drawer. He gently, almost reverently placed the file on his blotter and opened it. Renee Curtis's face beamed up at him. The picture had been taken five years earlier by a photographer for the *Honolulu Star Bulletin*. Something to do with Save the Kids. Jackson wagged his finger at the picture and said, "I'm coming for you, Renee."

CHAPTER 26

What Miranda had experienced back in the cell in Nicaragua had been torture, pure and simple. At first, she had resisted and fought like a tiger. She'd withstood beatings, degradation, and starvation, until the reptiles killed the man named Carlos. Then she'd surrendered. But she'd never feigned enjoyment. She'd laid there like a dead fish and let the men do with her whatever they'd wanted, at the same time making her mind find a safe place deep within herself.

She knew her hope for better treatment here on the yacht had been foolish. The expensive clothes and jewelry, the rich furnishings, the yacht itself had fooled her. Señor Mascarenas had seemed benign at first. He looked so elegant in his beautiful clothes. So handsome. And he'd been gentle with her . . . at first. But once he'd snorted cocaine, he'd turned into a wild animal.

Standing under the hot stream of water in the yacht's cabin, she moved a hand, groaned with the effort, and clutched her crucifix. She tried to pray for forgiveness, for redemption from the great sins she had committed. She remembered trying again to find her safe place; but the pain had been too great. He'd hurt her terribly. And then he made her sniff the cocaine.

"No, please," she'd begged. But he hit her. First in the stomach. Then in the face. And, when she still begged, he threatened to throw her overboard. She was so ashamed. *If I had honor, I would have let him throw me to the sharks,* she thought.

The drugs had changed things. Her skin had suddenly felt electrified. Every nerve seemed to pulse with the rhythm of her accelerated heartbeat. And then, "God forgive me," she prayed aloud, "I enjoyed the feel of him inside me."

Mascarenas had gone at her for an hour. He'd fallen asleep with his arm draped over her waist. When he woke, the rays of the early morning sun peeked through the porthole. Miranda felt sore, nauseous, and had a terrible headache. She hoped he would leave. But it started all over again. There were no drugs this time to make her believe what was happening was pleasurable. She felt as though her insides had been ripped—and still he didn't stop. He used her in ways that she was sure condemned her to hell.

Alone now, she thought about what had happened and wanted to cry, to scream her shame. But there were no tears. She felt like a dried cornhusk left in the field to whither and blow away. For a moment, she wished that was what she could be. Then a sound startled her and a jolt of panic attacked her stomach. Someone had opened the door to the bathroom. Was it possible? Was it Mascarenas again? She tensed, her body rigid. Her hands gripped the safety bar in the shower. She bowed her head and stared down at the drain, unable to gather the courage to look in the direction of the bathroom door. A knock sounded.

She tried to say "*Sí.*" Fear and shame locked the words in her throat.

The soft knock came again. Then an equally soft voice said, "*Señorita? Yo soy Guillermo.*"

Miranda recognized the voice. It was the white-uniformed man who had brought her to this room; who had taken her arm and led her up the stairs the night before.

"What is it?" she asked, her voice meek, but strained.

"Are you okay?"

She thought she was out of tears, but there was something about the gentleness in the man's voice that replenished her reservoir. First, hot tears flowed down her cheeks, dropping onto the shower floor. Then sobs wracked her body. She grabbed a washcloth and stuffed it into her mouth to stifle the sounds of her crying.

Guillermo Ayala gnashed his teeth and balled his hands into fists. *This isn't right*, he thought. He felt his short fuse burn. *I should have done something last night.* The cries and screams that came from the yacht's staterooms had nearly driven him crazy. He'd laid on his bunk, a towel pressed over his face and against his ears. But the screams had penetrated the towel and, like stray voltage, shot through his ears and bounced randomly about the inside of his head.

But he couldn't follow his instincts. He had his orders. Wait until the yacht—and the narcotics—entered U.S. territorial waters. Then the DEA and the Coast Guard would swoop down. That would be the end of this undercover assignment. Only then would he be able to help the women. If it wasn't too late.

CHAPTER 27

Matt stacked his note cards and moved to the podium. The hotel meeting room held five hundred people—physicians, researchers, pharmaceutical and medical appliance manufacturers' representatives, and a variety of sales people from companies with products or services they wanted to pitch to the doctors in attendance. He smiled while he placed the cards on the podium. As he always insisted, his presentation had been scheduled on the first day of the medical conference. He knew that, beginning on the second day, attendance at the sessions would fall off when many physicians would go off and do what the conference had given them the excuse to do tax-exempt—deep sea fishing, diving, golfing, or sunbathing. If he had to put up with travel, a different hotel every week, and hotel food, he'd at least ensure he had an audience.

Matt had a fleeting thought about Renee. She and Alani were probably power-shopping again. He would never understand the whole shopping experience. He would do almost anything, including yanking out his chest hair, one hair at a time, rather than shop. He glanced at his wristwatch and noted it was almost straight up one o'clock.

"Ladies and gentlemen . . . ."

Esteban was halfway into his fifth beer and felt as mellow as he'd felt in a long time. Somewhere in the recesses of his brain, some errant synapse said, "Don't forget, you have to meet Alani for dinner." But he silently told the synapse to go screw itself and polished off the rest of the beer in the bottle.

He returned his attention to the conversation and smiled at the grin on Quince Hansen's face. Hansen, seated across the round metal table from Esteban in the steamy bar on San José's southern boundary, stared at him, seemingly pleased with himself. Esteban looked at Fred Petrucchio to his left, then at Chris Ridgeway on his right.

Petrucchio was medium height, with a thick head of salt and pepper hair, a bushy mustache, and a great beak of a nose that had been broken so many times that the cartilage formed an "S." His soft, moist hazel eyes belied an intensity that made Fred fearless in battle.

Ridgeway looked like a severe, sharp-edged version of Robert Redford. He had the looks that could make women swoon, but there was nothing endearing about his personality. He was economical with his words and his emotions. But he had proved himself to be blindly loyal to his friends. His pale blue eyes made him look eerie. There were few men who could hold his gaze for more than a few seconds.

Esteban hadn't seen any of the men in over twenty-five years; but they picked up where they'd left off as if they'd never been separated. Their conversation was relaxed and familiar. He basked in the warmth of the reunion and remembered how close they'd been, how they'd depended on one another for life itself.

Ridgeway and Petrucchio now argued about who was the better marksman. They'd ingested so much beer, neither man made much sense. Esteban thought about how they'd all been assigned as Green Berets to the Narcotics Interdiction Task Force. Esteban had a sudden thought: I wonder what the American press would have done if they'd learned that American boys were killing *narcotrafficantes* in places like Colombia, Guatemala, El Salvador, Nicaragua, Panama, and Costa Rica? And that American boys had died in those places?

Fred Petrucchio, as though he'd penetrated Esteban's thoughts, jabbed Esteban's arm with his finger and slurred, "You remember that pissant village in El Salvador when we ran into that Cuban unit?"

"Oh shit," Esteban exclaimed. "Don't bring that up."

Petrucchio laughed his horse-laugh, sounding like a man trying to breathe after the wind's been knocked out of him. That only made the other three crack up. "Are you kidding me? That was classic," Petrucchio said between gasps.

Esteban waved dismissively at him.

"Bullshit!" Petrucchio shouted. He laughed even harder and, when he again caught his breath, said, "We were supposed to meet with the village headman. Remember? He had information about one of Castro's drug operators in the area. Castro's man just happened to send one of his teams into the village a couple hours before we were scheduled to arrive. Assassinated the village chief, raped some of the women, killed all the livestock."

Ridgeway shook his head, a frown on his face, apparently remembering the scene they'd come upon. Then he smiled. But there was no humor in his smile, Esteban noted. However, there did seem to be an aspect of satisfaction in his expression. "Those Cuban bastards were so tuckered out from raping and pillaging, they were fast asleep when we showed up."

"You know we should have just killed those sonsofbitches in their sleep and burned the drugs," Hansen offered.

"Aw, that wouldn't have been very sporting, Quince," Petrucchio said. "I think Esteban had the right idea."

Esteban felt suddenly embarrassed. He knew his face was red. It felt hot. He looked down at his empty beer bottle.

Petrucchio jabbed Esteban again and once more laughed his horse-laugh. Esteban couldn't help himself. He joined in the laughter. Hansen and Ridgeway wiped tears from their eyes.

"Esteban," Petrucchio continued, "went into a village hut and dragged out one of the guerrillas. Held a knife to the guy's throat and forced him to shout at his *compadres* to come out. We jumped them when they exited the huts, took their weapons, and made them sit on the ground in the middle of the village."

"That's when the fun began," Ridgeway said, his words barely discernible through his gasps of laughter.

Esteban shook his head and held his stomach.

"So," Petrucchio went on, "old Esteban here is so pissed off at these bastards for what they did to the villagers, he challenges them, one at a time, to a fight." Petrucchio paused long enough to catch his breath. "There we were, in this godforsaken place, watching this big maniac beat the shit out of Castro's finest."

"How many did you take on that night?" Hansen asked Esteban. Esteban hunched his shoulders.

Ridgeway now rested on his arms on the table; his back heaved. "Eight," he shouted. "He kicked the crap out of eight Cuban commies. But, if I remember correctly, the last one was a bit of a problem."

"Hell, I could barely lift my arms by that time," Esteban offered in his own defense.

The laughter had died down by this time, and abruptly ended when Hansen asked, "You ever wonder what the surviving villagers did to those guys after we left?"

Petrucchio responded by ordering another round of beers.

Renee plopped down onto a rickety cane chair and dropped stuffed shopping bags on the floor on both sides of the chair. She brushed loose strands of hair off her neck and used a paper napkin on the table to dry perspiration on her forehead.

"Whew. I haven't had so much fun in years."

Alani laughed as she moved her own shopping bags onto one of the empty chairs. "I think I spent more than I should have."

"Hey," Renee said, "how often do you get to Costa Rica? You gotta take advantage of an opportunity when it presents itself. And we saved money, remember."

Alani laughed again, then slouched in her chair. "I'm beat. Two days of shopping is too much for a woman in my condition. What time are we supposed to meet the guys?"

"Eight o'clock. Esteban's friend, Quince, and his wife are supposed to meet us in the hotel lobby."

At the mention of her husband's name, Renee noticed that creases formed at the corners of Alani's eyes and her lips compressed into a worried frown.

"Something wrong?" Renee asked.

"Oh . . . I guess I'm just concerned about Esteban. I think he's having a tough time getting used to the idea of being tied down with a baby."

Renee smiled at Alani. "It's a big change for a man who's never been married before, who has never had to answer to anyone but himself, to suddenly find himself at fifty-two about to be a father. But . . . ."

"Can I bring the *señoras* something to eat? Drink?" a waiter said, interrupting Renee.

After they placed their orders for bottled Coca-Colas and grilled fresh fish, the waiter shuffled toward the kitchen. Renee followed him with her eyes while she wondered at the slow pace of things in Central America. Then she continued what she had been about to say. "But I think Esteban's more afraid of the responsibility than he is about the commitment." She reached across the table and laid a hand on Alani's arm. "You wait. When your baby comes along, Esteban will become the biggest homebody in the world."

Alani smiled brightly. "I hope you're right."

Renee smiled back and said, "Want to bet on it?"

Alani laughed. "No thanks. That's a bet I don't want to win."

Ten minutes later, the waiter deposited their orders in front of them. The bottles of Coke were barely cool, but Renee shrugged and decided that asking for glasses of ice might not be worth the risk.

After they'd relaxed and eaten for fifteen minutes, Alani looked at her wristwatch and said, "My God, it's four o'clock! We'd better get back to the hotel. It'll take me hours to get ready."

Renee nodded her agreement. She waved the waiter over and handed him a credit card, which he ran through a hand-held device at their table. After she signed the bill, she slowly stood, arched her tired back, knelt down, and picked up her parcels. She followed Alani through the café door to the sidewalk.

"Let's grab a cab," Renee suggested. "It's too far to lug all this stuff on foot." She looked in both directions, but there were no taxis in sight.

"If I remember correctly, there's a small hotel just around the corner," Alani said. "We can probably find a cab there."

Twenty yards from the corner, Renee stopped and lowered her bags to the sidewalk. "These darn things are so heavy the handles are cutting into my fingers."

Alani said, "Seems like a small price to pay for a glorious day of shopping."

"I like your . . . ."

An early 1990s vintage Chevrolet Impala pulled up to the curb. An olive-complected man with a black mustache and wearing a jacket and tie called out through the open front passenger side window, "*Americanas, no?*"

"*Sí*, we're American," Renee answered.

"You like a taxi?" the man said through a toothy smile.

Renee paused. The car had no taxi insignia on the roof or door. *But this is Costa Rica*, she thought. *The rules for getting a taxi license here are probably less rigid than they are back home.* She shot the man a smile and said, "Your timing is perfect. Can you take us to the Intercontinental Hotel?"

"*Claro.*" The driver rushed from his seat, opened the trunk, ran around to the sidewalk, took Renee's packages and put them in the trunk, then did the same with Alani's. He opened the car's rear door and assisted the women into the back seat. He then got back behind the wheel and sped away.

The dust kicked up by the car's tires hadn't settled back in the street when the waiter from the café ran out onto the sidewalk. He held a credit card in his hand and waved it at the vehicle. "*Señoras,*" he yelled, "you forgot your . . ." The Chevy turned the corner before he could finish.

"*Mierda!*" the waiter cursed. Then his mind switched gears. He recognized the car. That damn pimpmobile was hard to miss. Jet-black paint, shiny chrome wheels, and tinted windows. He wondered what that *chingado abogado*, Luis Reyes, was doing picking up two American women.

CHAPTER 28

Eddie Parnell pressed against the back of the airplane seat and tried to get comfortable. After he flew back to Athens from Bulgaria, he'd gone to the safe house, swapped his Petrov Ulanoff credentials for his Eddie Parnell passport and other ID, and flown to Washington, D.C. He'd spent too many hours in the air over the past four days and felt the effects of changing hemispheres as often as most people changed clothes. He washed down an Ambien tablet with a drink of water and waited for it to kick in.

His mind turned like a wheel in a gerbil cage. What Tarnovsky had told him had surprised . . . no, shocked him. The bastard had secretly sent a woman to Nicaragua to pose as one of his trafficking victims, to kill some guy named José Rosales Lorca, a middleman in the trafficking business. But Parnell had learned to take nothing Tarnovsky told him at face value.

By the time his flight landed at Baltimore-Washington Airport, Parnell was exhausted. Thoughts about Tarnovsky and the potential problem he represented for the Company had apparently counteracted the Ambien pill. He thought about the king-sized bed in his apartment and wished he were there right now, but he knew he needed to call his boss and report in.

With no greeting or preamble, Westcliffe Moreland said, "What did you learn?"

Parnell related Tarnovsky's confession about his involvement in the trafficking business, his promise to close down the business once and for all, and his plot to eliminate some guy named José Rosales Lorca in Nicaragua. As he waited for Moreland to respond, Parnell thought, *I should never have checked in with my tight ass boss. It could have waited until morning.*

After a long pause, Moreland said, "I want you in Nicaragua. This guy, Lorca, has got to go. If Tarnovsky's killer fails, I want you there to finish the job."

"I have no idea where Lorca's located," Parnell said.

"I'll find that out and call you."

"I just landed at Baltimore-Washington. I'll be at my place."

"Forget it, Parnell. Take a cab to Langley. There will be a plane waiting for you to take you to Managua."

Westcliffe Moreland had been agitated since Eddie Parnell's telephone call. Instead of eliminating Tarnovsky, Parnell had demanded—once again—that Tarnovsky get out of the trafficking business. Moreland was no more convinced now that Tarnovsky would do what he promised than he was the first time the Bulgarian had given his word. *Parnell's got way too much history with Tarnovsky,* Moreland thought. *He should have found a way to terminate the mafiya chieftain.*

"Betty, no calls," Moreland snapped into the intercom. Then he rose from his desk chair and paced his office, from door to the opposite windowed wall, and back again. Over the years, he'd logged miles along that exact same course. He wasn't sure why, but he seemed to be able to think more clearly on his feet. He absentmindedly glanced down at the oriental carpet to see if he could detect any unusual wearing.

Moreland murmured, "Parnell's on his way to Nicaragua. I've got the entire Central America Department working on coming up with information about this Lorca character." He stopped at the window, stared at the trees beyond the building, then executed an about-face, and stepped toward the office door. As he moved, he said, "There's something amiss about Tarnovsky's plan to assassinate Lorca. Even if the story is true and the female assassin succeeded,

Tarnovsky will just find another conduit through which to sell women into bondage." As he turned and headed toward the window again, he thought, *At least Lorca's death will slow down Tarnovsky's trafficking business for a little while.*

Moreland paused at the window and thought about the call he'd received that morning from the Louisiana redneck, Senator William Benedict. He knew now it had been a mistake to mention trafficking to Benedict. Instead of putting pressure on Senator Pete Driscoll as Moreland had hoped would happen, Benedict had allied himself with Driscoll. *Damned good ol' boy network.*

Crisscrossing the office again, Moreland vocalized his thoughts in a cadence to match his footsteps: "Despite Tarnovsky's value as an asset inside Bulgaria, the guy has become a political liability. He has to go. With him out of the picture, the organization will be emasculated. Parnell had made that point clear in many of his reports about Tarnovsky. The Bulgarian, like most corrupt leaders, had surrounded himself with sycophants, deviants, and plenty of muscle. But there is no one in his organization with the brains and skills who can take over for the big boss. Chop off the head and the body will wither."

Moreland stopped next to his desk and stared down at his shoes. The light from a corner table lamp reflected off the shiny tips of his tasseled loafers. He closed his eyes and pinched the bridge of his nose. *It all makes sense,* he thought. *Get rid of Tarnovsky after the Bulgarian's assassin kills Lorca. If she fails, then Parnell will take care of Lorca. The CIA connection to Tarnovsky—and trafficking—will be severed.*

Moreland's heart rate accelerated as another thought hit him. He whipped around and fast-walked to the window. He looked out as though the solution to his problem was somewhere in the distance. His hands and forehead pressed against the glass, he muttered, "The worst case scenario is that some politician ties Tarnovsky to trafficking, and then dredges up Tarnovsky's name in the Senate Select Committee on Intelligence's records." He swallowed hard and tried to slow his now-rapid breathing. Then the solution came to him. "If that happens, I'll plead ignorance. Who would they ask for corroboration? Tarnovsky? Lorca? There would be absolutely no way for . . . ."

But then a sudden chill gripped his stomach. "What if that crusader, Pete Driscoll, convenes a Senate investigation and subpoenas Parnell, who has a self-righteous streak. He'd never lie under oath." Moreland knew that with a certainty. *It isn't Lorca or Tarnovsky who's my Achilles' heel. It's Eddie Parnell.*

With a resolve born of self-preservation and an ability to rationalize that whatever was good for Westcliffe Moreland was good for the Company and the United States of America, he marched to his desk, fell back into his chair, and lifted the telephone receiver. He dialed an internal agency number and, when a man answered, said, "What d'ya got on Lorca?"

"Well, get off your ass and find something," Moreland said, and slammed down the receiver.

CHAPTER 29

Jackson had timed every aspect of his plan to avoid being on the ground for more than a minute. He'd telephoned Luis Reyes from the helicopter after the aircraft crossed over the Irazú Volcano and started its descent toward San José. Reyes told him at that time that he had the two women in sight. Twenty minutes later, Jackson ordered his pilot to hover high over a *barrio bajo*—a collection of wood, tin, and tarpaper shacks—and waited for a telephone call from Reyes. His mind reeled with the anticipation of getting his hands on the woman who he blamed for so much of the torment he'd suffered since the suicide death of his beloved mother, and his brother Johnny's murder. He'd rehearsed in his mind a thousand times what he would do to Renee Curtis. Each time, the imagery had become more vivid and the pleasure he'd foreseen heightened to the point of eroticism.

Jackson's head snapped up at the *brrring* sound of his cell phone. In a forced, exaggerated show of calm and confidence, he took the phone from his shirt pocket.

"Yeah," he hissed.

"I have two passengers going to the Hotel Intercontinental. I am two minutes away."

That was the prearranged signal. Jackson clicked off the telephone and tapped the pilot on the shoulder. He shouted above the sound of the rotors, "Put her down."

As the chopper descended toward the center of a parking lot adjacent to a minor league soccer stadium, Jackson spied Reyes's black sedan.

"What is this?" Renee demanded. "Where are we?" She felt Alani's hand on her arm. Her friend's touch was cold and shaky.

The driver skidded to a stop in a dirt lot, then turned halfway around and smiled at her. "*Lo siento, señora.* I am sorry. I think maybe there is something wrong with one of the tires."

Renee, for the briefest moment, relaxed, willing to take the man's explanation at face value. But, then she looked off to the west and saw the familiar shape of the high-rise Intercontinental Hotel in the distance—at least a mile away, in the opposite direction from which they'd traveled. Her blood seemed to go cold and butterflies fluttered in her stomach.

"I don't know what you're up to, mister, but you'd better—"

A roaring noise stopped her. She noticed dirt and paper spin in the air and pepper the car; then the skids of a helicopter showed through the car's windshield.

After years of work on the streets of Honolulu, and then Albuquerque, trying to save runaways from pimps and drug dealers, Renee had learned to trust her instincts. She pulled at the door lock, yanked the handle, slammed her shoulder into the door, and flung it open. Perched on the edge of the seat, she screamed, "Come on, Alani, we've got to get out of here."

Renee saw Alani jerk her hand toward the door lock on her side. But the plastic cover on the lock was missing. Only about a quarter inch of the threaded metal stud showed. Alani tried unsuccessfully to get purchase on it.

"Come this way," Renee screamed.

Alani quickly slid across the seat. Renee grabbed her wrist, pulled her from the car, and turned to run. She slammed into the hard, broad chest of a tall man who put his hands on her shoulders and smiled down at her. Her heart seemed to stop and she felt her bladder weaken. Recognition sent spasms through her intestines and her body shook as though it had suddenly been encased in ice.

"It's good to see you again, Renee," Lonnie Jackson purred. One of his hands squeezed a shoulder; the other caressed her hair.

CHAPTER 30

It was 5 p.m. by the time Matt had completed his speech, conducted a question and answer session, schmoozed with attendees at the conference, and met with representatives from some of the largest managed healthcare organizations in the world. Matt understood his real role: he was a super salesman for Placer Medical. Managed care outfits could make or break Placer. If they approved the company's products for use by their physicians, the company's sales would soar.

Matt slow-walked into his hotel room and promised himself he would get serious about an exercise program. His travel schedule had wreaked havoc with the exercise discipline he'd started in Albuquerque. And the high fat, high cholesterol diet he maintained in hotels and fancy restaurants had only made things worse. He tossed his folio on the couch in the suite's sitting room and called out, "Renee." No answer.

Matt went to the minibar and took out a bottle of mineral water. "That will be one hell of a credit card bill," he said jokingly, as he thought about Renee in power-shopping mode. He really didn't mind. A little shopping was a small price to pay for what he'd put Renee through, uprooting her, moving from one hotel to another.

He removed his suit and stripped down to his undershorts. The thought of a hot shower felt almost erotic. Even with the air-conditioning on in the huge hotel meeting room, there was a stale, dank feel to the air.

After he showered and shaved, Matt selected a brown silk shirt, eggplant-colored gabardine slacks, and dark-brown loafers. He moved to the sitting room, sat in a plush armchair, and turned on the television. Sometime later, the telephone rang and shocked him awake. He rubbed his face with his hands and looked at his wristwatch. *Jeez*, he thought. *Six-thirty. Where the hell's Renee?* He snatched up the telephone receiver from the table next to his chair. "Hello?"

"Matt, it's Esteban. I just got back to my room. Alani's not here. Is she with you guys?"

"No, they're not here." Matt chuckled. "You know how women are when they're shopping."

"Yeah, I know." Esteban's voice sounded strained. "Except Alani promised me she'd be back no later than five. She's never late. I don't have a good feeling about this."

"I'll call Renee's cell. Give me a minute. I'll get right back to you."

Matt felt confident when he heard ringing on the other end . . . until a man's voice came on the line.

"Hello?"

"Who's this?" Matt demanded, more tension in his voice than he intended.

"Dr. Curtis, is that you?"

What the hell, Matt thought. "This is Matt Curtis. Who's this?"

"Of course, you don't know my voice. But I assure you, you will before this is over. This is Lonnie Jackson, Curtis. I have the pleasure of your wife and her friend's company." The man paused, then said, "And I promise you that they will bring me a great deal of pleasure very soon."

"You sonofabitch!" Matt shouted. "You hurt . . . ."

Jackson interrupted Matt. His voice changed from a deep, resonant, mocking tone to a high-pitched, angry screech. "Don't threaten me, Curtis. There's nothing you can do. I will finish with your sweet Renee, then I will return for you. In the meantime, I want you to imagine what I will do to your wife. It won't be pretty."

The connection was cut. Matt was awash in terror. The thought of Renee in Jackson's hands sent icy daggers of pain into his brain.

He tried to focus on saving Renee, not on what Jackson would do to her. But his mind wouldn't respond in so disciplined a fashion. A sudden vision of his sister's twisted and broken body came to mind. That, too, had been Jackson's handiwork. Jackson hadn't pushed his sister off that balcony, but he might as well have. He was ultimately responsible for Susan's death. And now he had Renee.

Matt still held the telephone receiver in his hand, pressed hard against the center of his chest. He barely heard the dial tone. Then he remembered Esteban waited in his hotel room two floors down. Matt sucked in an immense rush of air and steeled himself.

"Esteban, you'd better get up here." He hung up before his friend could ask questions. Then he dialed the hotel operator and told her to call the police.

CHAPTER 31

Guillermo Ayala didn't know how far the yacht was from U.S territorial waters, but he had a feeling they were close. While he mopped the deck, he glanced over the gunwale to the west and hoped to see the sharp prow of a U.S. Coast Guard cutter bearing down on Rodrigo Mascarenas's boat. The sun perched on the edge of the horizon. Visibility would be almost zero in another thirty minutes. His thoughts shifted to the six girls below decks. He'd seen a couple of them, in addition to Miranda, during the afternoon. Each appeared bruised, dazed, and distraught.

Ayala could only imagine what the men had done to them; the images that came to his mind made him nauseous and angry. These men were worse than rabid animals. He squeezed his eyes shut for a moment and tried to erase the terrified looks he'd seen on the girls' faces.

Hate filled Ayala's brain as his entire body felt momentarily feverish. He bunched a fist and told himself yet again that his orders were to wait. He wanted to murder the drug dealers on board the yacht and feed their corpses to the sharks.

He'd almost finished swabbing the deck when he heard whimpers on the far side of the boat. He moved behind the outside of the bulkhead and spied one of Rodrigo Mascarenas's bodyguards lead all six women toward the bow lounge. Mascarenas and the Canadians were either sitting or standing under the royal blue canvas canopy.

The heat of anger rekindled itself, rose from Ayala's gut, made his head feel as though it would explode. The women were now lined up in front of the men.

Mascarenas laughed as he looked from one Canadian to the next. "Have you enjoyed yourselves, gentlemen?"

The Canadians all seemed to respond at once. Their expressions and comments indicated they appreciated Mascarenas's hospitality.

"Anybody feel like an encore?" Mascarenas asked, his tone as casual as though he'd offered his guests a drink.

One of the men pointed at one of the girls. "Shit! I just finished with that one."

"Don't mind if I do," another man said as he pushed out of his chair and walked to Miranda. "This one looks good to me."

One of the other men shook a scolding finger and said, "Watch out she doesn't puke all over you."

The men laughed. The man in front of Miranda put a hand on one of her breasts. "What do you think, sweetie?" he asked. "You feel like spending some time with me?"

Ayala saw the girl's hand jerk to her throat. One of the last rays of sunlight reflected off a crucifix that hung on a delicate chain around her neck. She smothered the cross in her hand. Even from thirty feet away, Ayala saw the despair on the girl's face, her eyes dull, lifeless.

Mascarenas suddenly leaped from his deck chair and slapped the girl's face. "None of that religious crap," he shouted. "If God cared about you, you wouldn't be here in the first place."

The men laughed again.

The drug lord viciously snared the girl's wrist in his hand and pried her fingers open. He then grabbed the pendant with his other hand, yanked it from her neck, and tossed it into the sea.

Ayala didn't think it possible that the girl's expression could appear any more despondent. But her features sagged and her posture went from rigid to almost rubbery. Then, without a sound, the girl moved with surprising speed and leaped over the gunwale into the sea.

The men crowded at the gunwale and looked down at the

floundering girl.

Ayala moved to a spot twenty feet from where the men stood. He assumed Mascarenas would toss a life buoy to her. After all, he'd surely paid good money for her. But Mascarenas did nothing. Nor did any of the other men. They merely stared down at her as she thrashed in the water.

Then one of the Canadians said, "I'll bet ten thousand dollars that it takes her seven minutes to drown."

This seemed to energize the men and they all played along and guessed times. A couple of the men yelled curses at the girl.

The top half of the setting sun shone brightly in the distance, backlighting Miranda. Mascarenas shouted to no one in particular, "Get a light on that *puta*."

A flood light popped on and scanned the sea's surface until it landed on Miranda.

Ayala had seen and heard enough. Undercover assignment, or not, he couldn't stand here and let the girl drown. He kicked off his canvas shoes and dove into the sea. He went under the surface, then came up a short distance from the girl. He swam toward her. "I'll take you back to the boat," he said in Spanish.

She looked at him with dead eyes. Then she raised her arms straight above her head and slipped beneath the surface.

Ayala could hear the men aboard the yacht yelling at him. He picked out Mascarenas's voice.

"*Pendejo*, what are you doing?"

Ayala jackknifed his body, scissored his legs, and dove after the girl. He spotted her below him and kicked with power fed by his anger and desperation. Air bubbles from her lungs drifted up toward him. His own lungs ached as he swam deeper. He slowly gained on her. He knew he was just seconds from having to return to the surface or drown, when he snatched a handful of her hair that floated eerily with the underwater current. He pulled her to him and slashed at the water with one arm and his legs, as he worked his way back to the surface.

Ayala gulped a mouthful of salt water just before he broke the plane of the sea. He gasped for air, then vomited up the seawater. The girl seemed lifeless in his arms. "Throw . . . a . . . rope," he cried out to the men on the yacht.

Mascarenas spit down into the water. "Fuck you, *pendejo!*" he cursed. The drug lord then grabbed a fifteen-foot aluminum pole and jabbed it at Ayala's chest, pushing him beneath the surface. Ayala tried to grab the end of the pole, but Mascarenas pulled it back. Every time Ayala moved closer to the yacht, Mascarenas poked the pole into him.

You dumbshit, Ayala thought. *You couldn't stay out of it. So now you'll drown.* His legs and arms felt leaden; he was tiring fast. The girl's body was a dead weight he knew he wouldn't be able to support for more than another minute. The men laughed and cheered him on as though he were an athlete competing for some grand prize.

He'd reached the point where he had accepted his fate. He sucked in a breath and felt himself sink. Everything seemed quiet and peaceful. He held the breath as long as he could, then let it leak out as slowly as possible. His lungs were empty of air when he suddenly heard a thunderous sound.

Ayala felt a surge of adrenaline and dredged up a reservoir of strength. He kicked toward the surface and gulped air. The sound of engines from a distance carried to him and he looked to his left. A huge light illuminated the yacht.

CHAPTER 32

Francis Antonelli knocked on the door to Senator Pete Driscoll's inner sanctum and walked in. "You wanted to see me, Senator?"

"Yeah, sit down Frank."

Antonelli had a sinking feeling. He'd been Senator Driscoll's administrative aide—his right hand man—for six years. He could tell from the senator's somber tone that something important was on his mind. That usually meant he had something for him to do. This, in turn, meant that he would have to call his wife and cancel their dinner date. He'd already called her once to change the time from 7:30 p.m. to 8:30 p.m. He sighed with frustration. He thought, *This job is killing my marriage—not to mention my sex life.*

"How's your Spanish?" Driscoll asked.

The question surprised Antonelli and he realized his surprise must have shown on his face by the way the senator laughed. "A little rusty," he said, "but good enough to get by. Why? What's up, Senator?"

Driscoll picked up a file folder from the middle of his desk and handed it to Antonelli. "A friend of mine at the DEA sent this to me. He thought I might be interested. I want you to take a short trip, Frank."

Antonelli opened the file and recognized the United States Customs Service's logo on the cover sheet. He scanned the document, then returned his attention to his boss. "I don't get it.

Some narcotrafficker, his Canadian clients, and a bunch of party girls got arrested off the Florida Keys. What's that got to do with us?" Antonelli said as he closed the file.

Driscoll shifted in his chair and propped his feet on the corner of his desk. His expression became severe, his eyes squinted, and his nostrils flared. "Read the last paragraph carefully."

Antonelli reopened the file and looked at the final paragraph on the back sheet of the transmission: *All the young women on board the yacht appear to be from Central America. None of them speaks English. They claim to have been kidnapped and sold to the boat's owner. The DEA undercover agent on board the yacht corroborates their stories—at least the part about being sold to Mascarenas.*

When Antonelli lifted his head and met Driscoll's eyes, the senator said, "I have a gut feeling about this, Frank. I think the story those women told is legitimate. This could be the lead we need to identify a major trafficker in this hemisphere. But I don't want the story buried. These women will be considered small potatoes by the media and by law enforcement compared to the arrest of the drug runner. I want you to find out if these women are the proverbial tip of the iceberg."

CHAPTER 33

Matt had never seen Esteban so frightened. He'd expected the big man to be angry, even violent. But he hadn't anticipated tears. Esteban seemed inconsolable. Over and over, he said it was his fault that Alani had been kidnapped. It was he who had wanted her to come with him to Costa Rica.

"Come on, Esteban," Matt said. "What are you talking about?"

Esteban stopped pacing and looked across the room at Matt. "We shouldn't have come here. If I hadn't been such an asshole about being tied down, about losing my freedom . . ."

Matt walked over to Esteban. "That's bullshit and you know it. And it's beside the point. We have to find them. Fast. I need you angry, Esteban, and I need you thinking clearly. That sonofabitch, Lonnie Jackson, declared war on us a long time ago. He's dictated the rules of the game for too long. It's time we changed those rules."

Matt knew his words and his tone didn't reflect the panic he felt inside. The thought of life without Renee would be like hell on earth. But as long as there was the possibility of saving her, he would force himself to think positive thoughts.

A knock sounded on the hotel room door and Matt did a quick about-face and fast-walked to open it. Three men stood in the hallway. The first man was dressed in a light brown suit and introduced himself as Otto Castillo, the hotel security chief. Castillo then introduced the two men with him. They were with the San

José Police Department. Captain Carlos Gaston, dressed in a dark green uniform with gold braid on his epaulets and hat brim, headed up the violent crimes division of the local police. The other man, Gilbert Miera, dressed in a suit and tie, was a detective.

After he led the men into the sitting room and introduced them to Esteban, Matt and the police sat. Esteban stood with his back to the room and stared out the window.

The cops went through a litany of questions: When was the last time you saw your wives? What were they wearing? Do you know where they went? What time were they expected back? Matt answered their questions and, with each one, looked over at Esteban to see if he had anything to add. But Esteban just stood statue-like.

Matt explained their history with Lonnie Jackson and provided as much information as he could about where Jackson had run to after he fled Hawaii and about the aliases he'd used. Then he added, "When Jackson answered my call to my wife's cell phone, I heard the distinct noise of rotor blades. I think they were on a helicopter."

A momentary dark cloud seemed to cross Gaston's face. Then he said, "So, they could be just about anywhere by now."

Matt stared back at the man but couldn't think of anything to say.

"Do you have photographs of your wives?" Captain Gaston asked.

Matt took his wallet from his pants pocket and slipped out a photograph of Renee taken less than six months earlier. He glanced at her image for a moment and felt a stab in his heart. Then he handed it to the captain. He turned in his chair and softly said, "Esteban."

Esteban turned to face Matt, removed his cell phone from a pocket, and opened up his photo app. He scrolled through pictures for a few seconds, then stopped and looked at the phone screen. Then his body suddenly sagged. Great wrenching sobs shook his shoulders.

Matt left his chair and went over to his friend. Esteban looked down at Matt and extended his phone to him. As Matt reached for the phone, Esteban gripped his wrist with his free hand. Tears streamed down his face. His breathing stuttered. He cleared his throat, then said in a voice seemingly too tender for a man his size, "What am I going to do, Matt?"

After a few seconds, Captain Gaston asked, "Did your wives mention where they intended to shop?"

"Renee told me she and Alani were going to the leather goods district."

"You mentioned that this man, Lonnie Jackson, answered your wife's cell phone," Gaston said.

"That's right."

"Why don't you call it again?"

"I tried several times but no one answered." Matt dialed the number, but again there was no answer.

"He's probably destroyed the phone by now," Gaston said. "We'll try to track the signal, anyway. Maybe we'll get lucky."

"What will you do?" Esteban asked from his place by the window.

"We'll release the photographs and descriptions of your wives to the local media and put out a plea for help. We'll contact your banks to see if there were any credit card transactions on your wives' cards." He shrugged and, after a long beat, said, "We'll do all we can to find them."

Matt thanked the policemen when they left the suite at 8:30 and then went to the couch and collapsed. Now that he and Esteban were alone in the hotel room, with no idea where Jackson had taken Renee and Alani, Matt felt absolutely useless. After a minute, he stood and paced the floor; wracked his brain for some idea, some brainstorm that would free Renee and Alani. After ten minutes, he felt even more frustrated and useless. Then the room telephone rang.

"Hello," Matt said, his voice angry, but urgent.

"Dr. Curtis?"

"Yes," Matt said.

"This is Quince Hansen. I've tried to get hold of Esteban, but he's not in his room. We were supposed to meet in the lobby at eight. Do you know where—?"

"Maybe you ought to come up to my room, Quince. Esteban's here with me. Room 1612."

"What's going on?" Quince asked.

"Just come on up."

CHAPTER 34

It was dark out when the helicopter descended. Its rail and belly lights lit up the landing zone and immediate area around it: a lush green lawn bordered by jungle on two sides, and a large one-story house and outbuildings on the other two sides. Renee observed the layout of the property through the open side door of the chopper. Her heart sank. Jungle as far as the eye could see.

No one had said a word to her or Alani since the aircraft had taken off from the soccer field parking lot in San José two hours earlier. The two of them had been thrown into the aircraft, where they'd huddled together. Ricardo, a very large Latin man, watched them like a vulture stares at a dying man in the desert. The guy looked every bit of two hundred and fifty pounds and had the conditioning of a linebacker. But more than the man's size, it was the look in his eyes that sent a bone-deep chill through Renee. A jagged, white scar ran from his forehead, through an eyebrow, and halfway down his left cheek. He was foreboding. He reeked of sour sweat and tobacco, which made Renee want to wretch. The man never seemed to blink. He just glared at them as though she and Alani were prey. Lonnie Jackson, seated in the co-pilot's chair, never once looked back at them.

The aircraft landed in the middle of a lawn. Jackson exited and shouted above the drumming noise of the decelerating rotors, "Ricardo, put them in separate cells. No food or water."

The big man now stood on the ground beside the chopper's cargo door. He reached inside and snatched Renee by an ankle. With one swift, powerful jerk, he pulled her to the lawn. She landed on her back, the air knocked out of her lungs. While he dragged Alani from the aircraft, Renee wheezed and tried to catch her breath. The man reached down, gripped her wrist, and pulled her to her feet. He half dragged, half led them toward the outbuildings.

Alani lost her footing and fell to the grass. Renee tried to reach for her, but Ricardo yanked her back with such force that she collided with his chest. He held her in a vice-like grip and she thought he might crush the bones in her wrist. She looked up at his face and winced at the smile she saw there. His teeth were crooked and yellow. His breath smelled fetid. She tried to wrench free, but he was too strong. He held her as though she were a rag doll.

Ricardo bent at the waist, grabbed Alani by the neck, and lifted her off the ground. He shifted his hand to her hair. Then he snagged a handful of Renee's hair, too. He marched them to the front of one of the buildings, where he dumped them on the ground and walked over to a man armed with a rifle.

"Are you okay?" Renee whispered to Alani.

Alani shook her head, her eyes as big as golf balls.

Renee clasped Alani's hand and huddled against her.

The big man stepped between them, again grasped handfuls of their hair, and forced them to stand. He led them along a concrete path between two sides of a building.

Despite the tropical heat and humidity, Renee felt cold. She tried to breathe evenly, to get her heart to slow down. But it thumped in her chest like an animal trying to escape from a cage. Her body shivered and bile bubbled into the back of her throat. But, as frightened as she was, she was even more concerned about Alani. Her friend had trembled during the entire time in the helicopter. She worried about Alani and her unborn child.

The building they were in reminded Renee of jail cellblocks she'd seen in movies filmed in developing countries: cells lined up on both sides of a cement corridor, tiny barred openings set high in heavy wooden doors, the only light provided by naked lightbulbs set in the ceiling above the corridor.

Ricardo stopped in front of an open cell door and shoved Renee inside, sending her sprawling to the filthy, damp floor. The door slammed shut behind her before she'd righted herself. A moment later she heard the sound of another door closing. What she realized was that when she'd watched movies that showed third world prisons, she'd never thought about how those prisons might have smelled. The odors here were terrible. Added to Ricardo's stink was the almost overpowering reek of human waste, mildew, and horses.

She moved to the barred opening in the door, stood on her tiptoes, and called out, "Alani, are you all right?"

"O-o-o-h, Renee, what's going on?"

Renee had no answer. She had never been more afraid. Just thoughts about Jackson hunting her had sent spasms of dread through her body. Being his captive caused fear beyond what she thought she could endure.

She didn't know what to say to Alani, but she wanted to say something to reassure her, no matter how vacuous it might sound. But before she could come up with an answer, another voice sounded in the cellblock.

"Who are you?" a woman said.

My God! Renee thought. *There's another woman here.* She detected an accent that sounded Russian. She paused a moment to catch her breath, then shouted, "Renee. My name is Renee Curtis." She heard Alani cry out in a squeaky voice, "I'm Alani Maldonado."

"Where are you from?" the woman called out. "You sound American."

"We *are* Americans," Renee said. "Lonnie Jackson kidnapped us in San José."

"Who's Lonnie Jackson?" the woman asked.

"He's the one in charge here. What's your name?"

"Tatiana." Then, after a beat, the woman said, "You're wrong. The man in charge here is José Lorca."

Renee opened her mouth to respond, but a man she hadn't seen before rapped the bars in her door with what looked like a wooden club. She fell back.

The man shouted, "Shut up, *putas.*"

Renee retreated to the back of the cell where a tiny window was set in the wall a foot below the ceiling. A small aura of moonlight entered the cell there. She sat against the wall on a pallet and brought her knees to her chest, circled her knees with her arms, and lowered her head. As much as she wanted to be strong, she couldn't fight off the fear that seemed to invade her every pore. Tears started first, then sobs. The mournful cries of what sounded like at least three other women provided accompaniment.

DAY 6

CHAPTER 35

The jet landed at Managua's Augusto C. Sandino Airport two hours late. By the time Eddie Parnell arrived at his hotel, it was nearly 2 a.m. The place was on a side street, away from the bustle of the high rent district. He checked in and demanded a room at the back of the building, away from street noises. He slipped the desk clerk a fifty-dollar bill. From the round-eyed look the man gave him, Parnell guessed he wasn't used to such large tips.

"I need you to arrange for a private plane."

"*Sí, señor*. Eez no *problema*. My cousin eez a pilot."

"I want a wakeup call at seven sharp," Parnell said. "And I want a private plane ready to take off at eight."

"*Sí, señor*. Where should I tell the pilot you want to fly?"

"San Juan del Norte. Oh, and I want a four wheel drive vehicle there." Parnell watched the clerk write down his instructions. Then he said, "If you take care of everything exactly as I asked, you'll get another fifty dollars when I return."

The man smiled and tapped the counter with his pen, like a judge rapping a gavel. "Don't you worry, *señor*. I will take care of everything."

Parnell moved toward the elevator, but before he was halfway there, the clerk called out, "*Lo siento, señor, pero el ascensor está roto*. Eez broken."

Welcome to Nicaragua, Parnell thought.

He took the stairs to the third floor, then roamed the halls for a minute. He noted the location of the fire escape and listened for unusual sounds. His favorite emotion, paranoia, had kept him alive during his CIA career. He found his room and tossed his bag on a green, cracked, plastic-covered armchair. After he dragged a desk chair over to the door and propped it under the doorknob, he removed his clothes and dropped them on top of his bag. Then he cranked up the air conditioner to full blast, which caused the window unit to vibrate as though it might separate itself from its brackets. He wondered when he might hear from Moreland. His boss had told him that he'd dredged up rumors about a trafficking operation headquartered near San Juan del Norte. A flight on a puddle jumper from Managua to San Juan del Norte would take a couple hours. Then he'd have to contact an agency man in Managua. Somebody in this godforsaken country had to know about Lorca. Parnell rolled over and tucked the sheet under his chin. After he closed his eyes, he had a momentary thought about the woman Tarnovsky had sent to Nicaragua to murder Lorca. If she did her job, he'd be able to return to the States with clean hands.

CHAPTER 36

Westcliffe Moreland sat on his back patio and admired the gardens that bordered his three-quarter acre expanse of lawn in Chevy Chase. He rolled a cup of coffee between his hands and considered planting two dogwood trees at the far end of the yard. He'd just decided that would be a good plan when his cell phone rang.

"Moreland here," he said in his crisp, professional voice.

A man on the other end of the line said, "The contract team's in place. It will be done tonight." The line went dead.

Moreland slouched in his chair and crossed his legs at the ankles. He sipped from his cup and let out an exaggerated "aah," as if the coffee was the best he'd ever tasted. But it wasn't the drink that made Moreland feel at peace. The call had done that. The CIA deep cover agent in Bulgaria had arranged to solve part of Moreland's problem.

Andrei Ostraski, the Russian Special Forces—SPETSNAZ—captain had seen to it that all seven of his men had synchronized their watches. He looked at his own wristwatch: 11 p.m. The night couldn't have been better for their purposes: a crescent moon hidden by clouds. He stared up at the sky and wondered if they'd get the job done before the rain started.

Ostraski stopped his team's progress at the final staging area outside Tarnovsky's estate and slowly glanced from one man to the next. They all wore black combat uniforms and their exposed skin had been blackened. They were equipped with grappling hooks; ropes; flashlights; wire cutters; fresh, narcotic-laced chunks of meat; and weapons. Their weapons included double-bladed knives, suppressed 9mm Beretta pistols, and modified AK-47 assault rifles with flash suppressors.

He was proud of these men. He'd worked with them for ten years, from basic training, through the demanding SPETSNAZ regimen, and on many clandestine assignments. He hated that they'd been forced to become mercenaries. But they really had few other choices, none of which paid as well.

"Your rifles are a last resort. Remember that. We need to sanitize the target with a minimum of noise. In and out in a matter of minutes. We must avoid alerting the perimeter guards or the men in the barracks at the back of the estate."

He paused a beat, then added, "Malenkoff and Suriatin are already positioned on the road."

The corn field was situated across the road from two of Tarnovsky's guards who manned a road block one mile from the estate's main gate. Chain-link fences extended from the gate in front of the guard shack, on both sides of the road, all the way to the main entrance.

Other than a slight brushing sound caused by his men as they made contact with the corn plants, the team moved silently. They stopped at the base of the chain-link fence and waited.

Ostraski cupped a hand over the face of his wristwatch and pressed a finger against the illumination button. Twenty-five minutes had passed since they started. They were three minutes ahead of schedule.

At 11:45 p.m., a panel van bounced down the road, four miles from the Tarnovsky estate. The two men in the van, in their early twenties and friends since they were little boys, delivered provisions to the Tarnovsky compound twice a week.

"I'm sick of delivering shit to high-and-mighty Tarnovsky so late," Uri, the driver said.

Oleg punched his friend's arm and said, "How many times do

I have to tell you that old *Komisar* doesn't want lowly deliverymen near his palace during daylight hours."

"Screw him," Uri said.

After a thirty second pause, in an effort to change the subject, Oleg said, "You know, *Botev* could win it all this year."

Uri shouted back, "What are you talking about? *Botev* doesn't have a prayer of staying in the first division. They are a mediocre football team on their best day. They'll be relegated and *Vitosha* will go up to take their place."

Oleg laughed. "Bullshit," he said. "*Vitosha* has nothing but bums playing for them. They'll be lucky to not be relegated to the third division."

"I'll bet you a month's pay," Uri yelled.

"What the hell are you shouting for? You get so damned excited about football. It's nothing but a game."

"A game? A game? It's everything. It's life."

"My ass," Oleg said. He laughed again, but something on the road ahead cut his laugh short. "What the fuck is that?"

Uri slowed the truck and leaned forward over the steering wheel. "Maybe a deer, or some stupid dog." He brought the vehicle to a stop just feet from what Uri now realized was a man's body.

"What the hell," Oleg said. "Maybe we should call the police."

Uri looked at Oleg and said, "Let's check it out first. Maybe there's money in the guy's pockets. We call the police, what do you think they'll do? They'll strip the guy of anything valuable. We might as well get our share."

The two men scrambled from the van and walked to the body in the road. The man lay on his right side. Uri pulled on the man's arm to roll him over. In that instant, two muffled sounds cut through the still night air. Uri gasped as though he'd been poleaxed and collapsed to the road.

Oleg leaped back and rasped, "Uri, what the fuck are you doing. Stop messing—"

Then two more muffled sounds. Oleg dropped to the road.

The two SPETSNAZ soldiers, Malenkoff and Suriatin, dressed like working class Bulgarians—blue jeans, t-shirts, work boots—quickly dragged the two deliverymen's bodies from the road into the brush. They climbed into the van—Suriatin behind the wheel—and drove toward Tarnovsky's place.

"Let's hope the captain knows what he's doing," Malenkoff said.

Suriatin blew out a derisive blast of air. "You should know better than to second guess the captain."

"Yeah, but what if the guards stop us?"

"Remember what the captain told us. Regularly scheduled activities cause even the most disciplined security people to become careless."

Malenkoff said, "There's the road block."

Suriatin peered through the windshield. "Remember, wait until they clear us through."

"Yeah, yeah, yeah."

Suriatin pulled up next to the guard shack. One of the guards stepped to the driver's side door and motioned for him to lower the window.

"Nice night," Suriatin said.

The guard frowned and barked, "Where the hell are the usual guys?"

"The boss fired them. He caught them stealing."

The guard laughed. "He should have paid them better so they wouldn't need to steal."

Malenkoff laughed too. "He's a cheap old bastard."

The guard waved them through. "Keep your speed down. You'll have to stop at the main entrance."

"Yeah, we know," Malenkoff said. "The boss told us."

Suriatin waited for one of the guards to call ahead to the main gate, then he watched the other guard raise the bar that blocked the road. He drove the van forward, but stopped it as soon as he had cleared the blocking bar. "Oh, one question," he shouted.

The two guards stepped toward Suriatin while Malenkoff leaped from the vehicle and ran around behind it.

"What is it?" one of the guards asked.

Malenkoff shot both men in the head with his silenced pistol. He and Suriatin moved their bodies into the guard shack.

"The muffler," Suriatin said.

"Right," Malenkoff answered as he crawled under the van and used his knife to punch a hole in the muffler.

Captain Andrei Ostraski saw the distant gleam of headlights to his left. The noise of a vehicle engine could now be heard. He looked to the right and again calculated the distance from where he lay by the side of the road to the front gate. Twenty-five meters.

The deep-throated barking of dogs suddenly started. Ostraski worried that the dogs had detected his team's scent. He hoped the guards would attribute the animals' agitation to the noise and headlights of the oncoming vehicle.

The van's headlights illuminated the estate's front entrance, as well as the four guards and a pack of leaping, snarling dogs behind the entrance gate. The van sounded as loud as a tank. Ostraski whispered, "Good job, Malenkoff." The van's highlights were effectively ruining the guards' night vision. The vehicle's noise would cover for any noise his men might make as they cut a section out of the chain-link fence and moved from their positions.

Ostraski rose to a crouch and tapped two men's shoulders. The two men immediately went to work on the fence with their wire cutters. When Ostraski saw that the guards at the main gate were engaged in conversation with Suriatin and Malenkoff, he slowly removed the cut-out section of fence and placed it on the ground. Then he and his men crawled through the opening in the fence, got to their feet, crouched, and rushed forward.

Like musicians in a finely-trained orchestra, all eight members of the team were in perfect harmony, attuned to one another. The two men in the van pulled their pistols and shot the two guards on either side of their vehicle. The remaining members of the team took out the other two guards before they had the time to react. The *pfft-pfft-pfft* sounds of silenced pistols were barely discernible. Four men pulled the guards' bodies to the side of the road. Another man, canvas sack in hand, ran to the main gate. He lobbed chunks of treated meat over the razor wire that topped the chain-link barrier. Ostraski ran to the guard shack and pulled the plug on the security camera. He said a silent prayer that whoever monitored the video screen inside the residence had lost his focus for just a moment.

Once it was noticed the camera no longer operated, some action would have to be taken by personnel inside; but, by then, the captain hoped he and his team would have accomplished their mission.

Ostraski raised the barrier that blocked the way to the entrance gate in the perimeter chain-link fence. He peered into the exclusion area between the fence and the stone wall seven meters beyond the fence and saw the dogs were already wobbly. One animal was down and whimpering. The captain pressed a buzzer that opened the electrified outer gate while the rest of the team gathered in front of the van.

Malenkoff moved to the guard shack where he would wait. Suriatin got back behind the wheel of the van while two other team members pulled open one side of the massive interior wood gate. Only one of the dogs seemed to have any of its senses and launched itself at Ostraski, who easily sidestepped the attack and clubbed the dog with his rifle butt. The animal went down and stayed down.

Suriatin drove through the gate and stopped while Ostraski and the rest of the team climbed into the back of the van. Then he drove down the long gravel drive toward the residence.

Ostraski looked at his watch. Eight minutes since the last time he'd checked the time. This was going better than he'd anticipated. He allowed himself the luxury of confidence. The Americans had paid big for this job. Spending the fee would be almost as much fun as doing the job.

Yevgeni Tarnovsky groaned and cursed his inability to sleep. It had been like this since he'd become a bigshot. "I'd give everything I own for one good night's sleep," he exclaimed as he slid out of bed and donned his bathrobe. But, even as he said the words, he knew he was full of shit.

He padded to the hall outside his bedroom, shuffled down the long marble corridor to the curved staircase, and descended the stairs to the security room off the vestibule. He felt his pulse quicken in contemplation of the possibility that he might catch the guard there asleep. He was in a pissy mood and would love to vent his bile on someone.

The security room near the entrance to the mansion was the

electronic command and control center of his estate. Cameras were mounted on walls and trees all over the property and projected video images to the security room. Tarnovsky slowly turned the door handle and pushed the door open a few inches until he spied the guard seated at the video console. The bastard had his feet up on the table that supported the electronics in the room. He snored like a hibernating bear.

Tarnovsky threw the door open, crashing it against the file cabinet behind the door. The guard jolted at the sound and toppled from his chair. The *mafiya* chief roared as he stormed into the room. He lashed out with a foot and connected with the guard's thigh. The man grunted, but Tarnovsky yelled from the pain the kick had caused him. He'd forgotten he wore slippers, not shoes.

"You lazy bastard. Get off my property. You'll never . . . ." Then Tarnovsky had a sudden sinking feeling. There were a dozen video screens on the table—one for each outdoor camera. The one that should have shown the front gate and the entrance road to the estate was dark. Tarnovsky felt as though two birds went at each other inside his stomach. He switched his gaze to the other screens. The three that covered the back part of the property showed nothing but dark images of trees, bushes, and lawn. The same was the case with the four cameras on the sides of the residence. But when he looked at the front of the property, inside the front gate, he saw a van pull up to the bottom of the steps outside the front door. He recognized the vehicle and remembered this was one of the nights deliveries were made.

He took a deep breath. Everything looked all right. He glared at the guard who had gotten off the floor and now stood in a corner looking like a frightened child. "You shit!" Tarnovsky screamed. "How long has the front camera been out?"

The guard looked down at his feet and shrugged his shoulders. His mouth opened as though he was about to say something, but it suddenly closed.

Something moved in Tarnovsky's peripheral vision. He looked down at the video screens and saw men climb out of the van. Armed men dressed in black. He grabbed a handful of the guard's uniform shirt and pushed him out into the vestibule. "Watch the front door," he ordered. "You let anyone in and I'll shoot you myself."

Tarnovsky pressed a button on the wall next to the arms rack and felt a small measure of relief when the emergency siren went off. It would take about two minutes for his guards in the barracks to react. He removed two automatic rifles with magazines from the arms rack. He snatched two extra magazines from a shelf below the rack and then ran from the office. He rammed one of the rifles and a magazine in the guard's chest. "Hold your ground!" he hissed. "You may save your job after all."

Tarnovsky sprinted up the stairs to his bedroom and shed his bathrobe on the run. He yanked a pillowcase off the bed and jammed a pair of pants, a zippered jacket, running shoes, and the weapon magazine into the case. Stuffed pillowcase in one hand and rifle in the other, he moved along the corridor to the back staircase down to the kitchen.

The crash of broken glass carried to him as he started down the steps. Then the *brrp-brrp-brrp* of automatic weapons fire sounded from inside the house. Tarnovsky knew the guard wouldn't be able to hold off the invaders for very long. But all he needed was a minute or two. Tatiana Borodvic had told him about the weakness in his security system. She'd found a blind spot between two of the cameras that watched over the rear of the property. He'd ordered the problem fixed, but his men hadn't finished the job. She'd explained that an intruder could use the ivy to climb the back wall and walk along a seam that traced a line of trees. The seam was out of range of all the cameras. That's how she'd sneaked up on him the other day.

Tarnovsky followed the seam from the woodshed behind the kitchen, along a line of four oak trees that ended at a spot where two parts of the exterior wall joined at a ninety-degree angle. How the hell Tatiana had scaled the chain-link fence with its razor wire and avoided the dogs was a mystery. He'd have to deal with those problems when—*if*—he got over the stone wall.

Ostraski moved his men up opposite sides of the thirty-foot wide stone steps. They used three-foot-tall concrete planters for cover. Shots from inside the mansion had been erratic. So far, none of his team had been hit. But his desire for a silent assault had been obliterated. Between the noise of the assault weapons and the piercing noise of the siren, all hell had broken loose. He wished he'd come armed with grenades. One well-placed grenade would take out whoever fired at them. He guessed he had no more than one minute to eliminate the opposition inside the residence and to find Tarnovsky. If he waited any longer, he and his men would be trapped between perimeter guards collapsing toward the front entrance and the reserve guards in the barracks on the far side of the estate.

One of his men reached the front portico. The leader watched him creep forward on his stomach until he could look inside the building through an opening where a smoked glass sidelight had been a minute earlier. The man raised his head. An automatic weapons burst erupted and an explosion of red and gray matter replaced what had been his man's head.

"Go! Go! Go!" Ostraski yelled.

His team surged forward while they raked the front entrance with a tremendous fusillade of bullets. Return fire came from inside the house for a few seconds, then abruptly ended.

"Cease fire," Ostraski ordered. The front door had collapsed into the entry. A man lay sprawled on the marble floor at the base of an ornate staircase. The team rushed inside and made certain there was no one else near the entry. Ostraski then ordered his men to fan out through the building. "Thirty seconds," he shouted.

About to follow two of his men up the stairs, he saw a glow from a small room off the entry and went in that direction. He peeked inside and saw a bank of video screens. He scanned each screen, in turn, for movement, but there was nothing. He was about to turn back to the vestibule when he saw something move on one of the screens. He leaned in and peered at the shadowy images. Trees, bushes, and a high stone wall shrouded in darkness showed on the screen. He squinted at the screen. He knew he'd seen something move.

The screen didn't change for another ten seconds. Then Ostraski spied a man run between two large trees. He was visible on the screen for only a split second. *Tarnovsky*, the captain thought. Then the images of many men showed on the screen. They moved quickly toward the rear of the residence.

Ostraski knew time was up. The group of men he'd just seen advancing on the residence outnumbered his team by at least two to one. He shouted into his headset, "Retreat! Retreat!" and ran from the room. He ran down the outside steps to where they'd left the van. "Meet at the van," he ordered. "We'll spread out on both sides of the drive and go for the gate."

The members of his team poured through the front entrance in an orderly retreat. The last man had just gone past the door when a burst of automatic weapons fire erupted from inside the mansion. The man screamed, went down on his knees, then collapsed face down on the marble porch. The remaining five members of his team sprinted past him. The captain leaped back onto the staircase. If the man who had just been shot wasn't too badly wounded, he'd help him to escape. If the man was incapable of fleeing, then Ostraski would put a bullet in the man's brain. He couldn't afford to leave a prisoner behind. He knew Tarnovsky would make the man talk.

He'd run halfway up the steps when a man showed himself in the open doorway. Ostraski raised his pistol, fired two rounds, and dropped the man where he'd stood. He climbed up another step, when the pounding of footsteps echoed from within the mansion. He had no time to check on his man's condition and, instead, turned and ran.

He holstered his pistol as he ran back down the steps. Before he reached the driveway, he fired a full magazine from his automatic rifle into the rear end of the van to puncture the vehicle's gas tank. On the run, he fired rounds at the concrete pad under the van and saw sparks leap. Then a *whoosh* sounded as the sparks ignited the gas. He followed his men down the driveway.

Ostraski cursed as he ran. He'd botched the job. All he could salvage from it were the lives of his remaining men.

Yevgeni Tarnovsky shook. Between adrenaline, the cold temperature, fear, and anger, he was a wreck. He'd made it over the wall, but there was no way to scale the chain-link fence. He stopped and put on the clothes he'd stuffed in the pillowcase.

Then, he crept along the outside of the stone wall and made his way toward the front entrance gate and guard shack. He spotted the bodies of three guard dogs lying on the ground and cursed the men who had attacked his estate. Then the sounds of fired weapons further unnerved him. He dropped to the grass, listened for voices, and waited. When the shooting stopped, he heard men's voices. He recognized Metin Osmanoglu's voice and pushed to a kneeling position. He was in the process of standing when a brilliant burst of light lit up the tree canopies toward the front of his mansion.

After a minute, Tarnovsky stood, hugged the stone wall, and continued slowly through the exclusion area between the wall and the fence. When he reached a part of the exclusion area that gave him a view of the guard shack, he froze. Fifty meters up the access road, he thought he saw movement—wraith-like shadows ran into the corn fields and disappeared. He moved cautiously toward the front gate.

The sound of boots thumping on the driveway diverted his attention. He turned to the left and saw some of his men racing toward him. He recognized Metin Osmanoglu in the front.

"Are you all right, *Effendi*?" Osmanoglu asked in a voice that never seemed to change. Flat, without emotion.

Tarnovsky ignored the question and shouted, "Who were they?"

Osmanoglu shrugged and said, "I don't know yet. But I'll find out soon enough."

Tarnovsky could feel himself coming down off his fear-driven adrenaline high. Now his principal emotion was anger. "How the hell will you discover who these guys were?" he yelled.

Just a hint of a smile creased Osmanoglu's lips and his eyes sparkled. "They left a wounded man behind."

DAY 7

CHAPTER 37

The good news, Frances Antonelli thought, *is that the flight from Baltimore-Washington Airport landed in Miami right on schedule.* "The bad news is that it was scheduled to arrive at 2 a.m.," he muttered. "No point in checking in at a hotel. I'd be lucky to get a few hours sleep before going to the U.S. Customs building to interview the women from the boat."

He walked outside the terminal and signaled to the first of three cabs in line. When the car moved forward and Antonelli got in the back seat, he pulled a piece of paper from his shirt pocket and read off the address his boss, Senator Driscoll, had given him.

The ride to the Customs building took twenty minutes. The trip took him through progressively poorer sections of the city. He wasn't sure what he had expected, but this wasn't it. The route the cabbie followed traversed street after street of rundown houses, then segued to half a mile of brightly lit signs outside Latin clubs and all night fast food joints. The string of clubs and restaurants gave way to a dark, brooding area of rundown industrial and warehouse buildings that lined both sides of the street for over a mile. Some of the yards beside and behind the buildings were floodlit and surrounded by chain-link fences capped with concertina wire. Sandwiched between two looming, three-story warehouses was the concrete, windowless U.S. Customs building. The building looked new. "Wow," Antonelli said when he noticed that hundreds of pleasure boats, cars, trucks, and RVs crammed the acres of ground around the building. "The asset confiscation program is alive and well in southern Florida."

"You say something?" the driver said.

"Nah," Antonelli answered. "Just talkin' to myself."

The cabbie stopped outside a gate, then sped away as soon as Antonelli paid him.

Antonelli lugged his overnight bag and briefcase to the gate and dropped them on the pavement. A uniformed guard stepped from a shack.

"Can I help you, sir?"

Antonelli pulled out his wallet and showed the guard his U.S. Senate ID card. "I have an appointment with Agent Kosorofsky."

The guard turned and disappeared in the shack. Antonelli heard him talk with someone. After a long minute, he returned and opened the gate. "Go over to that door and ring the bell. Someone will let you in."

Antonelli followed the guard's instructions. A professionally painted sign had instructions to ring the bell. He pressed the bell and waited.

Antonelli looked over his left, then his right shoulder. Even inside the perimeter fence, standing outside this building, in the middle of the night, in a neighborhood that gave him the creeps, made his stomach feel like it was full of writhing snakes. He placed his briefcase between his legs on the pavement and pounded on the door with his fist. Still no answer. Now thinking he had made a terrible mistake, and feeling more than a little panicked, he dropped his suitcase on the ground and pounded on the door with both fists.

The guard from the shack by the gate stepped out and shouted, "Hey, take it easy, man."

The door suddenly opened. A large, fortyish man with a world class beer belly and a W.C. Fields nose stared down at Antonelli. He had to be six feet four and weigh at least two hundred sixty pounds.

"Keep your shirt on, buddy," he growled in a gravelly voice. He looked at Antonelli, then slowly moved his gaze down to Antonelli's feet, then back to his face. "You're that senator's errand boy. Well, I guess I have no choice. You might as well come in."

Antonelli was the senior aide of a very senior U.S. Senator. As such, he wasn't used to being talked down to. He licked his lips and cleared his throat. "My name's Francis Antonelli." He reached into his suit coat pocket and extracted his wallet. He flipped it open to his ID card. "I work for—"

The big guy just turned around and walked away.

Antonelli barely snatched his bag off the pavement and leaped inside the building before the door closed.

Jeez, what an asshole, Antonelli thought, as he followed the man down a thirty-yard-long corridor to a bullpen with six gray metal desks and two additional cubicles separated by six-foot high partitions. He was surprised to find all the desks occupied at this hour. The place was a beehive of activity, with men and women who talked on telephones, tapped at computer keyboards, and pored over files. He heard voices come from the two cubicles.

Antonelli nodded at a woman who merely glanced at him. No one else in the room appeared to pay any attention to him. His enormous guide walked through another hallway at the far end of the bullpen and disappeared. Antonelli wasn't sure what he was supposed to do next. He was tired from the flight and from lack of sleep, frustrated over having to make this trip—which he considered a waste of time—on a moment's notice, and pissed off about his reception. He wasn't about to stand in the middle of this room like some rube and be ignored.

"I'm with Senator Peter Driscoll's office. Would someone have the courtesy to answer some questions?"

He might as well have talked to a wall. No one in the room even acknowledged that he'd spoken. Then the big guy reappeared, poked his head around the corner where the far hallway began, and shouted, "You gonna stand there all night?"

Antonelli blew out an exasperated sigh and moved to the hallway. The man led him to what looked like an interrogation room. The only furnishings inside the room were pieces of ubiquitous gray metal, government furniture: a table with four chairs in the center of the room and a small side table stuck up against a wall. Stained paper coffee cups and an empty donut box rested on the side table. Antonelli looked at the glass in the wall adjacent to the hallway.

He couldn't see out.

The big man turned around one of the chairs, mounted it, and rested his arms on the top of the chair back.

Antonelli dropped his overnight bag on the floor and placed his briefcase on the table. He sat across from the man and met his gaze. There was coldness there . . . and intelligence. He sensed he was being sized up and just continued to stare back at the guy. He was pretty damned good at holding his own in staring contests. Even against a guy who looked like World Wrestling Entertainment material.

Finally, the guy said, "How do you want to work this?"

Antonelli assumed the man referred to how he wanted to interview the women. But before he responded, he wanted to clear the air. "What's with the attitude? Or do you treat everyone like they're the enemy?"

The question seemed to unsettle the guy. He broke eye contact for a second and cleared his throat.

"Look," Antonelli continued, "I have a job to do. I sure as hell don't want to be here. I should be waking up in a couple hours next to the finest looking woman in D.C. Instead, I'm in some shithole building in a broken-down neighborhood being treated like a deadbeat brother-in-law by a guy who looks like Haystacks Calhoun. How about slipping me a little slack? I'll finish my business and get the hell out of here. You'll never see me again."

The guy glared and, for a beat, Antonelli thought he'd only made things worse. But, then the guy blurted out a burp of a laugh, which changed into a rolling series of thunderous guffaws. When he stopped laughing, he reached across the table and stuck out his hand. "Rollie Kosorofsky," he said.

Antonelli took his hand, which was the size of a baseball glove. His grip was rock-hard. "Listen," he said to Kosorofsky, "I'm not some three-piece suit from D.C. looking to mess with you down here. My boss, Senator Driscoll, already had a burr under his saddle about human trafficking when he learned that the daughter of one of his constituents was kidnapped and sold into slavery by a criminal outfit. Driscoll's got his teeth into this issue, and I assure you whenever he does that he'll worry the issue to death before he'll give up on it."

Kosorofsky nodded his understanding. "I apologize for the way I acted. It's no excuse, but you need to understand that every time some wing-tipped bureaucrat sticks his nose in our business, one of our cases goes down the tubes. We work our asses off. My guys put their lives on the line every day. There's so much money floating around here, what with drug smuggling, arms running, illegal immigration, and money laundering, that the bad guys will put a cap in a federal agent's ass as soon as look at him. So we don't take kindly to guys with Harvard degrees who think that D.C. is the real world."

"Okay," Antonelli said, "we both know where the other stands." He paused, then said, "By the way, I graduated from San Diego State University. That's about as far away from Harvard as you can get."

Kosorofsky raised both his enormous hands in surrender and laughed again. "Okay, okay," he said. "What do you want from me?"

"I want to interview the girls you took off that drug dealer's yacht. I understand they claim to have been kidnapped, taken through Nicaragua, and sold. We have information that there's a major trafficking center working out of Nicaragua. I hope the girls can give me information about that operation."

"We've put those girls from the drug dealer's yacht in secure rooms in a U.S. Marshall's medical facility about fifteen minutes from here," Kosorofsky said. "Although the DEA was the lead organization on the raid on the yacht, they turned the women over to Customs because they didn't want to mess with them. It was Rodrigo Mascarenas, the dealer, and his Canadian clients the DEA wanted." Kosorofsky scrunched up his features in a sour look and said, "The girls will ultimately be turned over to Immigration and sent back home."

"When can I see them?" Antonelli asked.

Kosorofsky consulted his wristwatch. "It's three now. I've got phone calls to make. Then we'll go grab breakfast. By that time, the women should be up. I'll drive you over there."

Antonelli had hoped he could see the women right away, but he decided he'd better humor Kosorofsky and let him set the agenda. Besides, the women had already been through enough without having to be wakened in the middle of the night. "Sounds good to me," he said.

"You have any idea what those girls have been through?" Kosorofsky asked, then forked half a fried egg into his mouth.

Antonelli shook his head.

Kosorofsky continued to chew, but his eyebrows drooped and his fleshy cheeks sagged. "An interpreter tried to talk with them. He told me he's never seen anyone as frightened and traumatized as those young women."

Antonelli put down his fork, swiped his napkin over his mouth, and pushed his plate away. He ignored his eggs and bacon. He sensed he was about to hear something that would probably ruin his appetite anyway. It surprised him that someone with Kosorofsky's experience wouldn't be so jaded that he could no longer be shocked.

"These women—girls, really—were terrorized beyond any victims I've seen in twenty years with Immigration. And you know why?"

Antonelli gave a half shake of his head and stared at Kosorofsky.

"It was the shame. They were forced to perform sexual acts. Forced! Yet, *they* feel ashamed. Like there was something they could have done to prevent it. One girl won't say a word. All she does is cry. Another girl explained that the reason the girl cries is because she was planning to become a nun. The church was her entire life, her calling. She was kidnapped right off the street. Now she's defiled. That's the way they all feel. That they've been soiled, ruined. One girl thinks the church won't want her and the others believe no man will ever want to marry them. Not that wanting any man at this time is very high on any of their wish lists."

"What are you talking about here?" Antonelli asked. "Were they raped? Even if they were, their reactions seem a little extreme."

A brief flash of anger showed in Kosorofsky's eyes, in the rigid set to his jaw, but it passed. "These girls were innocents. They knew nothing of the ways of the world. The people in their villages will consider them tainted. And you need to be clear about something. Calling what happened to these poor girls "rape" is the understatement of the year."

JOSEPH BADAL

"How so?" Antonelli asked, not quite successful in keeping skepticism from his voice.

Kosorofsky held up a hand and counted off on his fingers. "First, other than the one who wanted to become a nun, they were induced to leave their families with promises of jobs in the U.S. Two, they were all virgins when they arrived at the "training center" somewhere in Nicaragua, but that didn't last very long. Three, their "training" consisted of rape, sodomy, and oral sex. And, four, not only were they starved and beaten into submission, they were made to pretend they enjoyed what they were forced to do. Sex with a half dozen men, one right after the other, wasn't enough. They had to show the men how lucky they felt to be able to service them."

Antonelli's instincts had been correct. His appetite was gone. His stomach felt like a volcano ready to erupt.

Kosorofsky continued. "You starting to understand?"

Antonelli nodded.

"The physical depravity these girls were forced to endure was bad enough, but they think they're condemned to perdition. And try to imagine being terrified every minute of every day for weeks. There's no doubt in my mind these Central American girls would have been sold into sexual bondage. What would have happened to them if we hadn't raided that yacht, I . . . ." He let the question hang.

"What happens next?" Antonelli asked.

"We'll get help for them. Counseling. Then, I'll pull out all stops to get them papers so they can stay here legally." He lowered his gaze and rubbed his hands together. Then he looked back at Antonelli. "But, I gotta tell ya, I don't hold out much hope. These gals don't have a bit of influence. The government will probably send them back to their villages before the month is out."

Antonelli smiled. "You know, Agent Kosorofsky, I bet I know a U.S. senator who would help."

Kosorofsky leaned over the table and playfully punched Antonelli on the arm, sending a shockwave of pain all the way down to Antonelli's fingers. "I'm sure glad you're not one of those Harvard boys," he said.

Antonelli smiled at Kosorofsky, feeling good about being able to do something for the girls. Then an idea came to mind. "What did you learn from the women about this training center? Were they able to locate it for you? Did they know any names?" Before Kosorofsky could respond, Antonelli had a sinking feeling. "How many women have gone through this center in Nicaragua? My God! There could have been hundreds."

"Or thousands," Kosorofsky said. "There are hundreds of similar operations around the world."

"Jeez. What can we do about this?"

Kosorofsky squinted. "That, my good man, sounds like a job for a sharp, young San Diego State graduate who happens to work for a very influential U.S. senator."

CHAPTER 38

At 6 a.m., Kosorofsky and Antonelli arrived at the U.S. Marshall's medical facility where the girls were housed. After they signed in at the security desk and Kosorofsky surrendered his pistol, they were escorted by a female security officer to a second floor lockup.

Antonelli peered through the wired-glass pane in the ward's entry door. Other than the security procedures, the white walls and the white-clad men and women who hurried every which way in the hallway reminded him of a hospital.

Their escort picked up a telephone receiver outside the ward and dialed a four-digit number. "Agent Kosorofsky is out here with a guest," she said.

Kosorofsky slouched against a wall and closed his eyes. Antonelli thought Kosorofsky had gone into hibernation-mode. He'd seen longtime government employees do the same thing on numerous occasions. It seemed to be an effective defense mechanism against long waits. Ten minutes passed before a fifty-something woman in a white lab coat opened the door.

"Hey, Rollie," the woman said. "How they hangin'?"

Kosorofsky pushed away from the wall and walked to the woman. He shook her hand, then put an arm around her shoulder and guided her to Antonelli. "Francis Antonelli, meet Amy Thompson."

Antonelli took Thompson's hand and was surprised at the iron in her grip. He tried not to grimace. Thompson seemed to be about two-thirds Kosorofsky's height and one-third his weight. She wasn't just small; she looked delicate. The reading glasses perched on the end of her long, thin nose only made her appear frailer.

"Mr. Antonelli works for U.S. Senator Driscoll," Kosorofsky said. "His boss sent him down here to talk to the girls we took off that yacht."

"I don't know if that's possible," Thompson said. "We've sedated all six of them and the lead psychiatrist hovers over those poor kids like a guardian angel."

Antonelli felt desperate urgency. His conversation with Kosorofsky had left him with the terrible conviction that the man who'd sold the girls to Rodrigo Mascarenas had a long string of victims. Antonelli didn't think there was anything he could do for any women who'd already gone through this monster's system. But he could try to prevent others from falling prey. Any delay could translate into more victims. He had the sudden feeling this trip might turn into a wild goose chase.

"Do you think you could at least ask the psychiatrist to talk with me?" Antonelli said. "If he's still here."

Thompson seemed to contemplate Antonelli's request, then spread her arms. "Come on," she said. "I'll show you to a conference room. You can wait there. I'll go talk to the doctor. For your information, the doc's a she."

Five minutes passed, then a tall, lithe, African-American woman dressed in a severe, dark blue suit under an unbuttoned white smock, threw open the conference room door. With her black eyebrows, hair pulled back into a chignon, and white blouse buttoned up to her neck, she looked to Antonelli like the prototypical evil nanny in a Dickens novel. The scowl on her face and the rigid way she clutched a file to her chest only enhanced the impression.

"You Antonelli?" she demanded.

Antonelli stood, walked around the table, and, hand extended, approached the woman. "Francis Antonelli," he said.

The woman still clutched the file as though it was a breastplate. She ignored his outstretched hand. "What can I do for you?" Then, before Antonelli could respond, added, "You took me away from some very ill patients."

Antonelli felt unloved and unwanted; but he also felt anger brew inside. *What is it with Florida? Do I have to get in a pissing match with everyone before they'll help?* He balled his fists down by his side, exhaled a calming breath, and said, "I'm sorry to inconvenience you, Doctor . . . I didn't catch your name."

The woman silently held Antonelli's gaze for a full five seconds, then finally relented. "Dr. Grace Butler," she said.

Antonelli nodded, then continued. "I assure you I am sympathetic about your patients. And I have no desire to interfere or keep you away from them. But you obviously know what they've been through."

He paused to get an acknowledgment from her. It came in the form of an angry look—her lips curled, eyes blazing. It struck Antonelli that perhaps the doctor blamed all men for the plight of her patients and he just happened to be the closest male target of opportunity.

She squinted. "Oh, I have a perfect understanding of what those poor girls have been through."

"Good," Antonelli said. "Then you must have an opinion about the man who trafficked them."

Dr. Butler's jaw clenched for a second, then she swallowed. "It would be unprofessional for me to describe that man with the language necessary to do so."

Antonelli nodded several times. "I understand. What I want to do, Doctor, is bring the full weight of the U.S. government down on the sonofabitch who put these girls through hell. Maybe one of them overheard something—a name, a place. I need to talk to at least one of them. I promise I'll go easy and I would appreciate it if you would stay in the room with me while I talk with her."

Butler removed one hand from her file and rubbed her fingers back and forth over her forehead, her head lowered, her eyes closed. She then raised her head and met Antonelli's gaze. "You've got ten minutes . . . with one of the girls. That's it." She glanced over at Kosorofsky and said, "Just one of you."

Kosorofsky raised his hands in surrender and looked at Antonelli. "I'll wait right here for you, Francis," he said.

CHAPTER 39

Francis Antonelli stared across the hospital room at a young woman named Miranda Sánchez. She appeared to have suffered a lifetime of abuse. The sight of the scabbed cuts and purple and black bruises on her face and arms caused his breath to catch in his chest. Doctor Butler explained that the girl had been in the trafficker's "system" for less than three weeks, yet she had the deer-in-the-headlights look and the defeated posture of someone who'd suffered physical abuse for a lifetime. Her injuries gave evidence of abuse, but the lifelessness in her eyes spoke volumes about her emotional state.

Antonelli raised his eyebrows and opened his hands toward Butler, as though to ask: *Is it all right to approach the girl?*

The doctor nodded once and she and Antonelli slowly moved to the corner of the room. The girl lay curled in a fetal position against a wall; her arms hugged her legs so tightly that Antonelli wondered how long it would take her to uncoil—if she ever would.

"This is not uncommon," Butler whispered. "Patients traumatized like this girl will often find a safe corner, where their back is protected, where no one can come up behind them. The bed in the center of the room makes them feel vulnerable."

Antonelli wanted to say something to the girl, but backed off for a moment. He wanted his words to be comforting, his tone gentle; but the anger he felt about the way this poor girl had been abused made it difficult to speak calmly. He moved to within five feet of the girl; breathed slowly, deeply; knelt on one knee; and whispered, "You're safe now. We won't let anyone hurt you."

"She doesn't speak English," Butler said.

"Of course," Antonelli said. "I forgot. *Estás bien ahora. No dejamos que nadie te haga daño.*"

He didn't think it possible, but the girl seemed to tighten even further into a ball. *What the hell do I say to her now?* He felt like a fool. *First, I cajole the psychiatrist to allow me to meet with one of the girls, now I don't have a clue about what to do or say.* He looked over his shoulder at the doctor, about to ask for her help, when a blood-chilling scream came from somewhere down the hall.

"My God," Antonelli said as he stood and turned to look at Butler, who was already rushing from the room. Antonelli wasn't sure what to do. He was afraid to be alone with Miranda Sánchez. What if she freaked out? How would he calm her? He suspected that the last thing she would want was to be touched by a man.

Then the screams came again. He moved to the door and reached for the handle, when he heard a shuffling noise behind him. He spun around and found the Sánchez girl had unfolded herself and now moved to stand up.

"*Por favor,*" she pleaded, almost childlike. "*Yo tengo ayudo Rosa.*" She moved toward the door, but when Antonelli didn't move, the girl's eyes widened and her hands shot to the center of her hospital gown and kneaded the material.

Antonelli quickly moved out of the way. He watched while she opened the door and, after she hesitated in the hallway, walked in the direction from which the screams had come. Antonelli followed close behind her and heard Doctor Butler speaking Spanish in a soothing voice from the next room.

Miranda Sánchez entered that room.

Antonelli watched Miranda rush to a young woman who stood against a wall, arms hugging her body, head shaking back and forth, hair covering her lowered face.

Butler glared at Antonelli. Her eyes looked fierce, her mouth a cruel slash. "What do you think you're . . .?"

But Antonelli put a finger to his lips and pointed his chin at the two girls. Miranda and the other girl now held each other. Miranda made cooing sounds, her voice almost dove-like. Rosa had stopped screaming.

Butler's angry expression melted. She came over to where Antonelli stood and touched his arm. She tipped her head toward the door and walked into the hall.

Antonelli interpreted the touch as an apology and followed her.

Butler said, "The DEA undercover agent on the yacht told me the Sánchez girl had tried to protect the other girls. Perhaps Rosa's screams brought out her protective nature."

Antonelli nodded and then turned toward the open doorway and watched Miranda help Rosa to her bed. She sat beside Rosa, stroked the girl's hair, held her hand. Fifteen minutes later, Rosa fell asleep. Miranda slipped off the side of the bed, straightened her gown, and, without a word, marched back to her own room. Butler and Antonelli trailed her. Miranda climbed into her bed and pulled the covers up to her chin.

The doctor went to the side of the bed and took Miranda's hand. She smiled down at the girl. "Thank you for helping Rosa," she said in Spanish.

Miranda looked at the doctor through unblinking eyes.

"Perhaps," the doctor continued, "you would assist me with the other girls."

Miranda nodded. "*Sí*," she said, in a meek, child-like voice. Then she glanced over at Antonelli and squinted. Her mouth turned down.

Butler patted Miranda's arm. "He's okay," she said. "He wants to find the man who did this to you. The man who sent you to the drug dealer."

Miranda seemed to process the doctor's words for a few seconds. Then, in a surprisingly strong voice, "His men called him Señor Lorca," she said in a surprisingly strong voice. "José Lorca. He has a hacienda in Nicaragua. I think it was near San Juan del Norte." Then her face seemed to glow with a sudden radiance and, despite the cuts and bruises, Antonelli saw how beautiful she was. Whether it was the sedative she'd been given or just plain exhaustion, or both, she closed her eyes and her breathing settled into a soft snore.

She looks like a battered angel, Antonelli thought. *What sort of monster could do the things that have been done to this girl?*

CHAPTER 40

Renee rubbed her eyes and thought, for a moment, she'd had a bad dream. But when the stench of the cell hit her and she opened her eyes, she knew no nightmare could come close to her present reality. How long had she slept? What time was it now? It was still dark out. She was amazed she'd been able to fall asleep, as frightened as she had been.

Renee looked down at her hands, then remembered that one of the guards had taken her watch, bracelet, and wedding ring. She ran her thumb over her ring finger and moaned at the loss of the ring Matt had given her.

She stood and stretched her shoulders and tried to think good thoughts. She thought about Matt, but that only depressed her. She was worried about him. She knew he would be sick with fear and filled with rage. Matt would suppress those emotions; bottle them up inside like timebombs that could go off at any moment. But there was one thing she'd learned about Matt—he was at his best when under pressure. He'd keep his head about him. It was that quality that gave her hope. But how many years would come off his life span because of the strain? Especially if they were never reunited.

She stood by the cell door and listened. Groans and whimpers carried to her. Even in their sleep, Jackson's prisoners could get no relief, no respite from their fear. Then she heard Alani's husky voice.

"Renee . . . Renee. Are you awake?"

"Yes. You okay?"

"O . . . Okay . . . . What's going to happen?"

Renee wanted to reassure Alani, to say something to chase away her fear. But Alani wasn't stupid. Renee knew they were in grave danger. "I don't know, honey. Say a prayer, and don't give up hope. Esteban and Matt will do everything they can to find us."

Alani released a mournful "O-o-o-h. They took my pocketbook, Renee."

That's the least of our problems, Renee thought.

"My medicine is in my pocketbook," Alani said.

"What medicine, Alani?"

"For my epilepsy."

Wearing nothing but bra and panties, Tatiana Borodvic crossed to her cell's far wall and, for the three hundred seventy-third time since she'd awakened, did an about-face and walked back to the opposite wall, five meters away. She would do everything possible to stay in good physical condition. While she crossed the cell, she considered her situation. She couldn't figure out what was going on. She and the three women who'd traveled with her had been left alone since their arrival, two days ago. She'd expected some sort of harassment by now. Actually, that's what she wanted. The only way she could get out of the cell and go after José Lorca was by overcoming one of the guards and breaking out. The longer she stayed in this godforsaken cell, eating mush and drinking water that came from who knows where, the more likely she'd become weak, if not sick.

And now, two women had showed up who didn't fit the mold. She'd heard them talk during the night. These weren't two ignorant peasants looking for a way out of poverty. They sounded educated, even refined. And there seemed to be some sort of history between them and someone named Lonnie Jackson.

Borodvic hated surprises. Surprises could undermine a mission. She questioned whether the one hundred thousand dollars Tarnovsky had promised her for killing Lorca was enough.

"Four hundred," she whispered, as she completed her morning walk. She dropped to the floor to perform her strength routine. One hundred push-ups, then two hundred sit-ups. She reached fifty-three push-ups when a singsong male voice startled her.

"Eh, *chi-qui-ta*, that's good, you stay in shape. I like my women tight."

Borodvic looked toward the cell door while she continued to pump out push-ups and saw a scruffy-bearded face through the barred opening. The man showed her a yellow-toothed smile. *I can't wait to get my hands on your balls*, she thought. *You've never been with a woman like me, Pedro.*

The guy continued to leer, while he made lewd comments and kissing sounds.

Borodvic finished her push-ups and crawled to the sleeping pallet. She rolled to her back to do sit-ups. Apparently, the sight of her breasts straining against her bra had stunned the sonofabitch into momentary silence. But then the guy got his second wind.

"I got a dick here for you, baby. You gonna get some of this before long, when Señor Lorca lets us play with you."

She raised her upper body and stopped, hands behind her neck, elbows out to the sides. She offered the man a gleaming smile. "I heard the other guards talk about you," she said. "They say your pee-pee is so small you couldn't make a chicken happy." Then she dropped back down and ground out rapid-fire sit-ups to the accompaniment of the man's curses. *This is the guard I'll work on.*

CHAPTER 41

Lonnie Jackson woke up feeling rested. He stretched, then jumped out of bed, excited, full of anticipation. He remembered feeling like this on Christmas Eve when he was a little boy, before his father was killed. It had been a long time since he'd been this happy. He'd waited for this day for almost two years. Except he felt even more exhilarated than he thought he would. He'd fantasized over and over about the pleasure he would get from killing Renee Curtis. But now that she was in his hands, other ideas had come to mind. He now had another plan for her. Killing her would be too easy. What he now planned sent chills down his spine.

Jackson showered and shaved and spent more time than usual brushing his hair. He dabbed cologne on his face and looked at himself in the mirror. This was akin to preparing for a date. It seemed like every nerve ending tingled.

He took his time dressing, choosing a rich, blue, silk shirt; gray linen slacks; and black, tasseled Ferragamo loafers. No socks. He turned to the bedroom mirror. "Not bad," he said as he ran a hand over his hair.

Jackson moved from the bedroom to his rarely used living room. The dark reds and blues of the oriental carpets and the ivory-colored upholstery complemented one another. The paintings on the walls were valuable originals—Goya, Titian, and Rembrandt. Jackson didn't know anything about the paintings or the artists.

But he knew they must be damned good. He'd paid a fortune to an art thief.

He pressed the intercom button by the room entry. "Consuela, breakfast in one hour," he said. "And tell Lupe to bring a bottle of champagne and a couple cans of Bud to the living room."

Then Jackson moved to the telephone on a small corner desk and punched in a number.

"*Sí, Jefe,*" Ricardo answered.

"Bring the woman to me. The brunette we brought in last night."

Renee shook her arm loose from the man's grasp. She couldn't stand his touch. He smelled even worse than he had the day before. She expected him to grab her again, but he merely waved a hand toward the house at the end of the path. "This way," he said, and walked ahead of her.

The man led her along a hardpacked dirt walkway bordered by flowers and lush ferns. They walked past the expanse of lawn where the helicopter had landed yesterday. She noticed again that it ended in jungle at the back end of the property.

The man opened a door for her. "Go down the hall to the last room," he said.

Renee passed several closed doors and then an open formal dining room. The place reminded her of Spanish colonial mansions, with wooden *vigas* and *latillas* in the ceilings and carved corbels at the room entries. The walls were thick, like New Mexico adobe structures, with smooth, plastered surfaces with an Old World patina. Despite the tropical heat outside, the interior was cool.

Renee shuffled slowly down the corridor. She felt weak and exhausted. Knife-like hunger pains stabbed her stomach and she trembled as she thought about what might await her. She stopped at the open entrance to a large room furnished with expensive-looking furniture, art, and carpets. Two steps led down to the room. A door set into the wall on the left suddenly opened and Lonnie Jackson entered.

"Join me, Renee," he said, a smirk on his lips, arrogance in his voice. "Were you comfortable last night? You don't look too bad for the experience." He tilted his head one way, then the other. "In fact, I think you look pretty damn nice."

"My friend needs her medicine," she blurted. "She's an epileptic. Her medicine was in her purse."

Jackson's eyebrows went up for just a second. This information seemed to surprise him. He turned, walked toward a sideboard, and reached for a bottle in a wine bucket.

"She's pregnant, you know?" Renee said.

Jackson's hand closed just inches from the bottle. He spun around and glared at her. "That's too bad for her," he said. "She might have at least lived, otherwise."

"She's got nothing to do with this," Renee cried out. "She was an innocent bystander." She wasn't about to tell Jackson that Alani's husband had helped kill some of Jackson's men in Hawaii two years ago. And Esteban had tried to kill Jackson in New Mexico six months earlier.

Jackson turned away again. "She's not an innocent bystander anymore," he said, while he lifted the bottle from the wine bucket. "Care for a glass of champagne?" he asked as he turned back to face her.

Renee stared at him. *What kind of creature is this man?* She turned her eyes from his and noticed a platter of rolls and fruit next to the wine bucket. She hadn't eaten since being snatched off the street in San José.

"Hungry?" Jackson asked—the smirk again.

Renee watched him carry the tray to a large coffee table in the center of the room.

"Come, sit down," he said. He pointed at a plush chair in front of where he'd placed the food. He crossed the room to a bar sink, filled a glass with water from the faucet, and carried the glass to the coffee table. He set it down in front of the chair.

Renee wanted to fight Jackson, to take nothing from him, to give him no satisfaction. But she was parched and hungry and knew it was important to keep up her strength. She moved to the table, sat in the chair, and picked up the glass of water. She downed the contents, then went to work on the food. Jackson took her glass back to the sink, refilled it, and returned it. He sat across from her, crossed his legs at the ankles, and silently watched.

Once the edge was off her hunger, Renee sat back. "What do want with me?" she asked.

Jackson smiled. After a beat, he said, "Revenge. That's all I want."

Renee detected a change in his eyes. The amber color turned almost yellow. She'd never seen anything like the man's eyes. Catlike. No, demon-like. She shuddered. Perspiration dripped between her breasts.

He uncrossed his legs, moved forward in his chair, and stabbed a finger at her. "I've wanted you and your husband dead for what you did to my mother and brother. But now I have a better idea. Killing you would be an easy way out for you. Too final. I want you both to suffer."

"What do you mean? Matt and I did nothing to your family. We didn't even know them."

Jackson shot out of his chair as though from a cannon. He came around the coffee table, leaned forward, and wrapped a hand around Renee's neck. His mouth no more than a few inches from her. Spittle sprayed her face as he screamed, "It was your meddling. You and your fucking husband's. You had to stick your noses in my business. You'll pay for what you did to my family."

The man's hand cut off the air to her lungs. She grasped his wrist with both hands and tried to break his hold. But he was too strong. Renee stared at Jackson's eyes and knew in an instant the true face of evil. She struggled for air. Her vision blurred.

Jackson suddenly released her. He dragged her by the hair out of her chair and threw her on the floor. Her head struck the side of the coffee table, leaving her foggy-headed. But she was lucid enough to realize Jackson now tore at her clothes like a raging animal. She felt disoriented; her vision clouded. She stared into Jackson's eyes and what she saw there seemed impossible. His pupils seemed to go from amber to red. He unbuckled his belt and let his pants drop around his ankles.

She screamed and fought with all the strength she could muster. She kicked at him, tried to scratch his eyes out, and hit him with her fists. But Jackson sloughed off her blows and laughed. He ripped away her blouse, then her skirt. He broke the catch on the front of her bra, then tore away her panties as though they were made

175

of paper.

Jackson pinned her wrists to the floor with his hands and spread her legs with his knees. He was propped above her and said in a voice that seemed to emanate from the caverns of hell, "Now it begins." He released one of her hands and punched her in the side of her head. Starbursts exploded inside her head and then all went dark.

Renee didn't know how much time had passed. She lay on the pallet in her cell and vaguely remembered that someone brought her back here. Her head throbbed. Her fingers touched a tender lump just above her left ear. Her body felt bruised and sore.

She struggled to sit up and waited for her vision to clear. She fixated on a cockroach on the wall across from her, removed a sandal, and hurled it at the insect. It was the only living thing she could vent her anger on. The shoe struck the bug, which fell to the floor, apparently unhurt, and scurried into a shadowy corner.

A battle began inside her head. She had an almost overpowering need to cry, but the anger she felt seemed pathological. That anger made her think things she'd never thought herself capable of before. She wanted terrible pain inflicted on Lonnie Jackson and she wanted to inflict that pain herself. The anger momentarily overwhelmed her need to cry. Then she conjured up an image of Matt and her tears flowed. Shuddering sobs echoed off the cell walls.

"Renee, can you hear me?"

Renee lowered her head between her knees. She couldn't seem to make her throat work.

"Renee," Alani shouted. "It's okay. You don't have to worry. They brought me my medicine."

CHAPTER 42

Davide Rodriguez loved Rosella Baca. She was so beautiful, so sweet. Like a gift from heaven. *What she sees in me, I'll never know,* he thought, while he stared at his acne-scarred face in the bathroom mirror. He brushed his hair and thanked God for his dark blue eyes. Rosella loved his eyes.

Davide had worked at the little coffee shop for three years. It was the best job he could find with only six years of formal education. He barely earned enough to take Rosella out to dinner and a movie once a month. At this rate, he thought, they'd never be able to get married.

He didn't have to go to work today until noon. That gave him a couple hours to watch two of the *Norte Americano* shows dubbed into Spanish: *Bonanza* and *The Beverly Hillbillies.* He turned on the television, then vented a sigh as he plopped down onto the threadbare, saggy-cushioned chair in the living room of his parent's home. *Maybe I should try to get a visa to the United States,* he thought. *At least I could make real money there.*

The TV picture went from gray to fuzzy black and white. "This damned thing won't last much longer," he mumbled, while he looked at the snowy screen. The news commentator's face blurred. "*Mierda!*" he said. "What is this crap? Where the hell is *Bonanza*?"

He pushed up to switch the channel, when a woman's photograph filled the screen. Even with the grainy picture, Davide recognized her. Then a second photograph popped up. The other woman who'd come into the café yesterday. The women who'd left the credit card on the table. The ones who drove off in Luis Reyes's car.

"The police have asked us to broadcast the missing women's faces in case any of our viewers happened to see anything," the commentator said. "The authorities haven't disclosed why they believe the women were abducted."

The picture then changed to a male reporter who stood outside the Intercontinental Hotel. He held a microphone and was bracketed by two men. He raised his voice to be heard over the thunderous vehicle noise.

"I'm here with the husbands of the two missing women. Doctor Curtis, can you tell us what the police have told you so far?"

Davide leaned forward to get a better look at the men with the reporter. They looked very tired and worried. The one named Curtis said, "The police are working diligently to try to find our wives. We appreciate everything they are doing."

The reporter switched to the second man. "Is it true that your wife, Alani, is pregnant?"

The big man looked at the camera. "Yes. If the people who took my wife are listening, you need to know she's an epileptic. If she doesn't take her medicine, both her life and our baby's life will be in jeopardy."

Davide heard the reporter ask something else, but he no longer paid attention. An idea had germinated in his brain. Opportunity had just struck.

CHAPTER 43

Esteban couldn't sit. He paced the hotel room, one hand in his pocket fingering a pill container. He always carried an extra supply of Alani's medicine—Dilantin—in case she forgot hers, or just ran out. Esteban's old Special Forces buddies, Quince Hansen and Chris Ridgeway, sat next to one another on the couch, a map of Central America spread out before them on the coffee table. Quince's wife had gone to their home a couple hours earlier. Fred Petrucchio, another former Green Beret, made calls to police friends to see if they'd come up with anything. Matt bounced from one man to another as he tried to keep on top of things, hoping they'd discovered something important, but basically feeling purposeless.

Hansen looked up from the map. "Matt, you said it sounded as though this guy Jackson was on a helicopter when he talked to you on your wife's cell phone."

Matt walked over to the couch. "That's right."

Hansen placed a forefinger over San José on the map and drew an imaginary line south through Costa Rica to Panama. "A helicopter won't give him much range. I'd bet he's either still in Costa Rica, went south to Panama, or north to Nicaragua." He ran his finger to Nicaragua. "If I had to guess, I'd say Nicaragua."

"Why?" Esteban asked.

"It has the most corrupt government of the three. A guy like Jackson would need a corrupt environment to work in if he's

179

involved in criminal activity."

"I agree," Ridgeway said.

"And," Hansen added, "Costa Rica may not have an army, but it's got one of the largest, most efficient police forces in the hemisphere. Nicaragua sounds right. But that's still a whole lot of territory to cover. We need a break."

The telephone rang. All five men in the room went silent. Matt picked up the receiver. "Hello."

"I want to talk to Doctor Curtis," a man said in heavily accented English, his voice high and shrill.

"This is Matt Curtis."

"I know who took your wife."

Matt's breath caught in his throat. "Have you talked to the police?" he asked.

"No police," the man yelled. "You hear me? No police."

"All right," Matt said. "No police." He looked across the room at Esteban and saw the curiosity in his friend's widened eyes and arched eyebrows.

Esteban mouthed the words, "Who is it?"

Matt held up a hand. "Tell me what you know about my wife's disappearance."

The man's voice cracked, then he laughed. "Oh no, Doctor Curtis. You must pay for such valuable information."

"How do I know you're not some shyster?"

"Shyster?" the man said. "What is this?"

"Crook," Matt said. "A shyster's a crook."

"*Bandito?*" the man said. "Like *bandito*?"

"Yes, like *bandito*," Matt answered.

"I promise I am no *bandito*, Doctor Curtis. I saw the automobile that drove away with the two American women. For five thousand dollars I will tell you the name of the owner of the car."

Matt thought about what the man had told him. He knew this could be a hoax, some bastard trying to extort money from the "rich American." But something told him this guy was on the level.

Maybe his pause made the man nervous. Whatever the reason, the man's voice turned plaintive. "Look, Doctor Curtis, I am sorry to do this. I need the money. I can help you."

Matt sighed. "You know, you don't have to do it this way."

"What do you mean?" the man asked.

"Call the police. I just authorized them to announce I will pay one hundred thousand dollars for information about our wives that leads to finding them."

"*Madre de Dios!*" the man said. "*Madre de Dios!*"

It took some doing, but Matt finally convinced Esteban to stay in the hotel room by the phone, while he and Quince Hansen went to meet the man who'd called. Matt was convinced Esteban would beat the informant to death. He took Hansen along because of his knowledge of the local community and his fluency in Spanish.

Hansen drove to the address the man had given to Matt. "I'll need to call the police as soon as we talk to this guy," Matt said after he climbed out of the car.

Hansen stroked his chin. "Let's hold off on that, Matt. Depending on what this guy tells us, we might want to keep the police out of this. We'll have more flexibility if they aren't involved."

Matt frowned. "What are you talking about?"

The front door to the little bungalow opened a crack before Hansen could respond.

"Doctor Curtis?"

"Yes," Matt said.

A skinny, black-haired man of about twenty-five opened the door.

When the man didn't introduce himself, Matt said, "This is my friend, Mister Hansen."

He can't weigh more than one hundred ten pounds, Matt thought. A quick look at the exterior condition of the house reminded Matt how lucky he was to have been born in the United States and to have had the chance to get an education. The place looked as though it had one good storm left in it. The wood siding on the shack was cracked and warped. What little paint remained on the boards had faded to a light blue. The roof was constructed of corrugated metal pieces on one side, tarpaper on the other.

The young man waved them inside and locked the door. He showed them to a small living room furnished with two chairs, a two-seater couch, and a stool. The couch and chairs were draped in brightly colored, threadbare throws that reminded Matt of Mexican serapes. The interior smelled of mildew and tortillas. The Costa Rican nervously rubbed his hands together while his eyes darted. He acted as though he was strung out on drugs, but Matt suspected he was just frightened.

"Wo . . . would you like something to drink? A . . . a lemonade, maybe?" the man asked.

Matt couldn't have cared less about something to drink, but he thought accepting the fellow's hospitality might help put him at ease. "Sure, lemonade sounds great."

Hansen nodded. "*Sí, gracias.*"

Once he served the drinks, the man sat down on the couch. Matt and Hansen had taken the chairs. They stared at each other for a moment, as though no one knew how to start. "I apologize about my telephone call," the man finally said. "It was the wrong thing to do."

Matt didn't have to look around again at the condition of the room—the walls in need of paint, the antique television set, the throws on the furniture that probably covered worn-out upholstery—to understand the man's desperation. He waved away the apology. "Just tell me what you know."

"My name is Davide Rodriguez," he said, then sighed as though he was relieved to unburden himself. "I work at the La Querencia Café. Two American women came into the shop yesterday afternoon."

"Describe the women to me," Matt interrupted. He knew Rodriguez could have gotten their descriptions from the TV or newspapers, but he wanted to see if he noticed something about Renee or Alani that hadn't been released to the press.

Rodriguez described them perfectly.

"I served them salads and iced tea," he continued. "They had many shopping bags with them." He laughed, but there was no humor in it. "They paid me with a credit card. The name on the card was Renee Curtis."

Hansen sat up straighter in his chair. "Are you sure of that?" he asked.

Rodriguez smiled slyly as he reached into his shirt pocket. "Oh, I am very sure," he said, then handed a credit card to Matt. "Your wife left her card on the table."

Matt took the card and stared down at the embossed letters. He caressed the plastic with a finger. *The last thing of hers . . . .* He swallowed hard and tried to rid his throat of the lump there.

"You told Doctor Curtis on the telephone you knew who took his wife," Hansen said.

"Yes," Rodriguez said. "I ran outside to give Señora Curtis her credit card, but was too late. I saw her and her friend get into the back seat of a black Chevrolet." He paused.

Matt, wide-eyed, watched him, hanging on his every word.

"It was Luis Reyes's car. I have seen it many times in San José. There is no question. It was Luis Reyes who took your wife, Doctor Curtis."

Matt knew it wasn't someone named Reyes who had taken Renee and Alani. It was Lonnie Jackson. What kind of bullshit was this guy throwing? He stood up, towering over the skinny kid. "What are you . . .?"

Hansen jumped up and grabbed Matt's arm. "Sit down, Matt," he said.

Matt glared at Hansen.

"Sit down," Hansen said again, in a softer tone.

Matt backed into his chair and watched Hansen sit down, too.

"Okay, Davide," Hansen said, "you say you saw Luis Reyes drive off with the women?"

Rodriguez nodded several times. His eyes were wide open and they darted back and forth between Matt and Quince

"Was Reyes driving the car?"

"I couldn't tell; the windows are . . . how do you say . . . clouded?"

"Tinted?" Hansen said.

"*Sí*, tinted."

Hansen turned to Matt. "This guy Reyes is a local con artist," he said. "A couple guys I know came down here after they retired from the Army and used Reyes to get them work permits. He's a lawyer, but he'll do anything, legal or illegal, for the highest bidder. This is just the sort of asshole a guy like Lonnie Jackson would work with."

Before Matt could respond, Hansen stood up and extended his hand. "*Gracias, Señor Rodriguez,*" he said. "*Me ha ayudado mucho.*" He turned to Matt. "Let's go."

Matt rose from his chair and thanked Rodriguez. He reached into his pants pocket and withdrew a money clip that held several one hundred-dollar bills. He slipped the bills out of the clip and handed them over. "If the information you gave us helps me find my wife, I will see that you receive the reward."

Rodriguez swallowed. "*Muchas gracias,*" he said breathlessly.

The Americans left the shack and got into Hansen's car.

Hansen gripped Matt's arm and smiled. "We just got our break, Matt," he said.

"Tell me about Reyes," Matt said.

"He's a lowlife," Hansen said, while he started the car. "But he knows how to get things done. He can lubricate the bureaucratic skids in several Central American countries. He works on zoning matters, business licenses, construction permits, immigration issues, whatever. You want to get something done down here, Reyes can make it happen. He always seems to know exactly whose palm to grease. But I'm a little surprised about his involvement in kidnapping. Jackson must have paid him big bucks."

Matt thought for a moment about their next move. "Tell me why we shouldn't go to the cops with this?"

Hansen slipped the transmission into "Drive," but kept his foot on the brake. "There's no doubt in my mind, if we bring the police in on this now, they'll find out whatever Reyes knows," he said in a low voice. "The cops here can be very persuasive. They'll have Reyes singing like a whole flock of songbirds. Or,"—Hansen paused and pointed a finger at Matt—"Reyes will bribe a police captain to let him go free. What then?"

Matt stared back at Hansen and waited for him to answer his own question.

"What if your wife was taken out of the country? The local police will be useless then. Or worse, what if some local cop or bureaucrat is on Jackson's payroll and tells him the cops are onto him?"

Matt saw the sense of Hansen's reasoning, but it didn't seem right to go around the police.

"This ain't the old U.S. of A., buddy," Hansen said, as though reading Matt's mind. "You want to get your wife back, or not?"

"You tell me what I have to do. I won't question you again."

"Okay, Matt. Let's go back to the hotel. We've got work to do."

CHAPTER 44

Matt and Quince Hansen returned to the Intercontinental Hotel. Fred Petrucchio was stretched out on the couch; Chris Ridgeway slouched in an armchair. Both sat up as soon as Matt opened the hotel room door. Esteban rushed forward from his usual place by the window and stared at Matt with haggard eyes. His face seemed to have wrinkled with age in the short time Matt had been gone.

As he reached up and placed his hands on Esteban's shoulders, Matt said, "It's good news. We know who kidnapped the girls and turned them over to Jackson. Guy named Luis Reyes."

Esteban's eyes hardened. "How's that good news?"

Hansen said, "I'll betcha Señor Reyes can tell us where Jackson took Renee and Alani."

That seemed to reinvigorate Esteban. His complexion colored and spirit seemed to return to his eyes. He poked a finger in Matt's chest. "If you think I'm staying in this damn hotel room while you two find this Reyes asshole, you're nuts. You got it?"

Matt rubbed his chest. "I got it, I got it."

"Let's sit down," Hansen said. "We've got to move quickly. This guy Reyes travels a lot. I've heard he's got clients in a half-dozen Latin American countries. Our only chance is to catch him here in San José before he takes off."

"Why don't I call his office and make an appointment for this afternoon?" Matt said. "Tell him I'm with an American company that needs help with . . . say something like, site approval for a manufacturing facility."

"That's a good idea," Hansen said to the group, now seated around the coffee table. "At least we'll find out if he's still in the city."

While Matt stood and pulled the telephone book from the desk drawer, Esteban moved from his chair and paced. He stopped suddenly and asked Quince, "You said earlier you thought Jackson might have taken Alani and Renee to Nicaragua."

"Yeah. I still think that's our best bet," Hansen said. He fell back against the couch. "I see a road trip in our future, boys."

Matt dialed Reyes's office number. A woman answered.

"This is Russell Stinchcolm calling," Matt said. "I represent a company in the United States that's interested in building a plant in Costa Rica. Is Mister Reyes available?"

"I am terribly sorry, Mister Stinchcolm, but Mister Reyes is out of the office at the moment."

Matt heard the sound of rustled paper. His heart seemed to sink into his stomach.

"However, his schedule is open this afternoon. I am sure he would be pleased to meet with you then."

"Say, one o'clock?" Matt said, awash in renewed hope.

"That would be fine. I'll contact Mister Reyes immediately and advise him you will be here at one."

After he hung up the phone, Matt looked at his watch, then collapsed into a chair. "An hour and a half from now," he said. Then he turned to Hansen. "Road trip?"

Hansen pushed off the back of the sofa and said, "Some of us worked together down here before we met you in the Balkans. Any time we were sent after a cartel military unit or a Maoist guerrilla group, we referred to it as going on a road trip."

Ridgeway chuckled. "That's right, Matt," he said. "Road trips are for finding and dealing with bad guys."

Petrucchio rose from the other end of the couch. "I think I'd better go to my place and dig out the equipment."

Hansen nodded. "Everything in good shape?"

Petrucchio scowled at Hansen. "I clean the weapons once a month, without fail. And none of the ammo is more than two years old."

"That should be all right," Ridgeway said. "Who's going with Quince to talk to Reyes?"

Hansen smiled and looked up at Esteban. "Oh, I think that's a job for Superman."

Esteban's face reddened as he scowled at Hansen.

Matt didn't realize his expression had shown his concern about Esteban going with Hansen until Esteban laughed and said, "Don't worry, Matthew, I won't poke out more than two of his eyes."

The others got a good laugh out of that.

Matt wasn't wholly sure his friend was kidding. But, after he thought about it, he decided he didn't really care one way or the other what Esteban did to Reyes, as long as they first found out where Jackson had taken Renee and Alani. He was just about to ask what was next on the agenda, when the telephone rang.

"Curtis," Matt answered.

"Doctor Curtis, this is Mike Ault at the bank. I'm terribly sorry about Missus Curtis. I—"

"What's up, Mike?"

"I checked the activity on your wife's credit card, like you asked. The last charge that ran on her card was at a restaurant in Costa Rica named La Querencia. I hope that helps."

"Immensely, Mike. Thanks."

Matt terminated the call and told the others what he'd just learned.

Hansen said, "That kind of closes the loop. We know the waiter wasn't lying about where he got Renee's credit card."

When no one else added anything, Hansen said, "All right, guys, let's get to work. Chris, you go with Fred and get the equipment ready." He scribbled something with a pen on a piece of paper, handed it to Matt, and said, "Here's the name of a pilot friend of mine. Call him and tell him I need his help. He isn't cheap, but he's reliable. You'll have to finance this operation."

Matt nodded.

"I'll call you after Esteban and I meet with Reyes," Hansen said. "Then you should call the number on that slip of paper and tell the pilot to meet at my place tonight around midnight."

CHAPTER 45

Esteban Maldonado and Quince Hansen gained entry to Reyes's office using the phony name—Stinchcolm—Matt had given Reyes's secretary over the telephone. The little lawyer stood behind his desk when Hansen entered, with Esteban close behind. He had a slick, gleaming smile. *Matt did a good job setting this up*, Esteban thought. *This weasel thinks he can soak a rich Yankee businessman in return for his political access.*

Reyes's smile changed to a frown when he focused his gaze on Esteban.

Hansen circled to the left side of the lawyer's desk, Esteban to the right. Reyes scampered backward, but he had only three feet of space before he crashed into the wall behind the desk. He threw his hands up in front of his face.

Esteban thrust his right hand between Reyes upraised hands, grabbed the lawyer's neck, and pulled him against his chest. He lifted Reyes a foot off the floor. "Do you know why we're here?" he said in a rumbling voice.

"No, no," he squeaked and shook his head as well as he could with Esteban's hand around his throat.

"Quince, why don't you keep the receptionist company," Esteban said, still holding Reyes off the ground. He stared into the lawyer's beady, black eyes. "I wouldn't want her to call the police."

Hansen moved to the office door and had just grasped the

doorknob when Esteban hurled Reyes over his desk onto a low coffee table set between two easy chairs. The glass top shattered and the table legs collapsed.

Esteban walked around the desk and lifted Reyes by the scruff of his suit jacket off the glass and wood debris. Reyes's face and hands showed bloody cuts. He seemed stunned. Esteban backhanded him.

"What do want with me?" Reyes whimpered. "I've done nothing to you."

"Wrong, *pendejo*," Esteban growled. Then, in Spanish, he said, "You did the worst thing you could ever do to me." He tossed Reyes over one of the chairs, into a wheeled brass cart that held glasses, a crystal pitcher of water, and an assortment of liquor bottles. They all crashed to the floor and drenched Reyes in alcohol and water. Shards of glass peeked out of slashes in his hands and were embedded in the fabric of his jacket and pants. They twinkled in the reflection of the overhead lights.

Like a wounded rabbit, Reyes skittered around the chair. "You're a crazy man," he shouted. "Please, what did I do?"

Esteban stepped over to where Reyes cringed in a corner next to a ceiling-high bookcase full of large legal tomes. He removed one of the books and dropped it on Reyes's head. The man grunted and rubbed the spot where the book had connected with the top of his skull. Esteban took another volume from the shelves. "Um, this looks interesting," he said. He rapped Reyes on the side of the head, making the man's eyes roll up.

Now squatted in front of Reyes, Esteban grasped the lawyer's shirtfront and jerked him forward so they were nose-to-nose.

"Listen to me, you little prick. You got two choices. You either tell me where Alani Maldonado and Renee Curtis were taken—and live, or I break every bone in your body, one by one, and leave you crippled."

The whites-of-the-eyes, trembling-chin-look Reyes gave him told Esteban the lawyer finally understood why he and Quince were there. The man gulped and his Adam's apple bobbed.

"Please, *señor*, I just gave the ladies a ride. I did nothing wrong."

Esteban was long past being patient. Every wasted second could jeopardize the lives of his wife, her unborn baby, and Renee. There was no time for this sonofabitch's bullshit. He whipped a four-inch dagger from a sheath on his ankle and inserted the point in Reyes's left nostril. "You lie to me one more time and they'll be calling you Luis No Nose." He pricked the inside of Reyes's nose with the knife. Blood seeped into his thin mustache, down his chin, and onto his shirt and jacket.

"It was José Rosales Lorca," Reyes screamed as he squeezed his nostrils between his thumb and index finger. "He made me do it. He told me to take the women to a football field on the edge of town. He picked them up with a helicopter. I swear. I have not seen them since."

Esteban cocked his head. "Lorca? Who's this Lorca?"

Reyes's brow wrinkled and his eyes squinted. "A very rich man. His place is in Nicaragua."

Esteban replaced the knife in his ankle scabbard. He stood and looked down at Reyes, then walked around the room, making crunching noises with his boots on the broken glass. He suddenly wheeled and snarled at Reyes. "Describe this guy Lorca."

"Light brown complexion, wavy hair, about forty-two, forty-three years old. Tall. Handsome."

"What about his eyes?" Esteban demanded. "What's the color of his eyes?"

Reyes visibly shuddered and crossed himself. "Scary eyes. Like *el tigre*. Yellowish brown."

"Sonofabitch!" Esteban cursed. "Jackson."

"*Qué?*" Reyes said.

Esteban walked back over to the lawyer, snagged his arm, and lifted him off the floor. "Come on, asshole, we're going for a ride."

He half dragged, half carried Reyes to the waiting room where Hansen sat on the edge of the receptionist's desk, smiling at the young woman.

She had a handkerchief bunched up in her hands and pressed against her mouth. Her eyes were the size of quarters. After she got a good look at her boss's face, with its cuts and smeared blood, she teetered in her chair.

Hansen leaped off the desk and caught her before she fell to the floor. He carried her to the reception room couch, then looked at Reyes who shook as though he had palsy. Hansen stared up at Esteban. "You get what you needed?"

"Yeah, pretty much. Why don't you call Matt at the hotel and give him directions to your place?" He looked at Reyes, who had gone rubber-legged, and pushed him into a chair. "I don't think it would be a good idea to drag this guy back through the hotel lobby."

Hansen nodded. "Did you cut off his balls like you promised?" he asked as he glanced at the traumatized attorney.

"Nope," Esteban said. "I'll let you do that."

Reyes sagged, wretched, and vomited on the reception room carpet.

"Jeez, Reyes," Esteban said. "What a mess." Then he looked at Hansen and said, "Maybe you'd better gag and tie up the woman."

"Nah, that won't be necessary," Hansen said. "I told her I knew what her boss had done and that I would tell the police that she was Reyes's accomplice. She ain't gonna say a word."

CHAPTER 46

Eddie Parnell had been superstitious most of his life. And when a day started out poorly, he'd learned over the years, it usually ended poorly, as well. So far, this day had been an unmitigated disaster. The car that took him from his Managua hotel to the airfield had a flat tire and the driver couldn't wrestle loose one of the lug nuts. Parnell got out and lent some muscle to the job. Even in the early morning hours, the heat and humidity had been oppressive and he was soaked in sweat by the time the spare had been put in place. His hands were grease stained. And he'd broken off a fingernail and scraped a couple of knuckles.

Then a pilot—probably a mule for a drug dealer, Parnell guessed—had totaled his Piper Comanche when a Brahma bull bounded onto the airstrip. The plane had flipped upside-down, smeared on the inside of the cabin with the pilot's blood and painted with bovine blood on its exterior. Raw bull burger surrounded and hung on parts of the damaged craft. Six local peons in baseball caps, jeans, and t-shirts, including one with the Dallas Cowboys logo and another that read: "There's No X in Espresso," took two hours to decide what to do about the wrecked airplane and the edible bull parts. Finally, a guy showed up with a team of horses and dragged the plane and the bull's carcass off to the side of the dirt runway.

Parnell had spent a lot of time in third world countries and knew he should take it easy, not let delays and inconveniences get to him. But the fact he got more irritated by the second told him, once again, he should put in his papers. Retirement seemed awfully good all of a sudden.

By the time his chartered plane was able to take off, it was the middle of the afternoon. The heat in the cockpit of the four-seater increased by about twenty degrees between the time they took off to the time—4 p.m.—when they approached the airport in San Juan del Norte, Nicaragua. In spite of being pissed off and frustrated, Parnell couldn't help but admire the view of the city and the expanse of ocean that stretched to the east. *I could live here*, he thought. *Find a place with a beach, within walking distance of a bar. Heaven.*

The plane bounced twice before it settled on the runway. After he deplaned twenty yards from the terminal, he told the pilot he'd call him when he was ready to return to Managua.

He cleared customs with another false ID, found a place inside the terminal where he could use his cell phone without being overheard, and dialed Westcliffe Moreland's mobile phone number. When Moreland answered, Parnell skipped the pleasantries.

"I'm at the staging location. You got anything?"

"I had one of our people in Managua fax information to one of our guys in San Juan del Norte."

Parnell detected strain in Moreland's voice. Even more so than usual. "What's up?" he asked, not expecting much of an answer. Moreland, he knew, was a tight ass who never shared his feelings or his thoughts with others. But the man surprised him.

"This thing's got all the makings of a world class screw-up. The guy you're supposed to find down there is . . . well, it's more complicated than we thought. Look for a man at the front of the terminal with the name Conte on a sign. That's your contact. He'll have the information we sent . . . and the equipment you'll need."

"Right," Parnell said, then hit the "End" button on his phone. As he walked through the terminal, his gut ached as it always did when his intuition told him he was about to stick his head in a lion's mouth. He didn't like what he'd heard in Moreland's voice. His normally indefatigable section chief had sounded worried.

Parnell searched for the man with the Conte sign. He spied him outside seated on a bench in the shade of the terminal canopy. The guy had the hard look of a warrior. Other than sporting a slight paunch, he still looked as though he could take care of himself. His blue t-shirt stretched taut across his chest. Parnell spotted the U.S. Marine Corps emblem tattooed on one of the man's muscular upper arms. He had the square jaw of men the Corps used in recruiting posters. There wasn't anything friendly about the look on the man's face.

Parnell walked over. "A friend in D.C. told me you had some information for me."

The man didn't acknowledge Parnell as he stood up and walked toward the curb. Parnell followed him to a white Toyota SUV. "What's your name?" he said.

"Parnell."

"Okay," the man said. "The information is on the front seat. The equipment's in the back." He handed Parnell a set of car keys and walked away.

After he watched the man go inside the terminal, Parnell walked around the front of the Toyota to the driver side door. He tossed his bag across to the passenger seat, on top of a large manila envelope that rested there. He hopped into the front seat and drove until he found a quiet side street. Parked under the canopy of a large tree, he yanked the envelope from under his bag and spilled its contents into his lap.

Parnell ignored the cover letter and leafed through the papers. There were copies of legal documents with José Rosales Lorca's name on them: a Brazilian passport, a real estate deed, a Nicaraguan residency visa, and a driver's license. There was also a map and a new ID in the name of Raoul Mendoza decorated with Parnell's photo.

The copies of the Lorca passport, driver's license, and visa included photographs of Lorca. Parnell then turned back to the letter.

It had been typed on plain white bond paper—no letterhead, with neither a salutation nor a signature. But Parnell recognized Moreland's work:

All we could find on Lorca were the enclosed copies. The passport shows a Nicaraguan entry stamp dated January 10 of this year. The documents are all dated within a three-day span—February 3 to February 5. He entered the country on a Brazilian passport.

You'll find a map enclosed. A red line indicates the overland route to the property shown in the deed. It's a hacienda that was owned by an old-line political family dispossessed by the Sandinistas. Apparently, all their fields and pastures have been overrun by jungle.

We learned that Lorca used a lawyer named Luis Reyes, who has offices in Managua and San José. We're trying to find Reyes. He wasn't in Managua. I've sent someone from San José to his office there. I'll call you on your cell as soon as I learn anything.

The Mendoza ID should get you into Lorca's property. You're with Nicaragua's Tax and Revenue Department and are out in the field doing assessments. Your capacity with Spanish and your wits ought to get you through the gate.

Good luck.

"Good luck, my ass," Parnell grumbled. "I look about as much like a Raoul Mendoza . . . ." He picked up the photocopy of Lorca's license and noted that Lorca was six-two and weighed two hundred twenty pounds. He'd developed a picture in his mind that wasn't close to the stats shown on the ID. *This is no soft, roly-poly Latin living a dissolute existence*, Parnell thought.

The map seemed to be pretty clear. The red line drawn on it followed a paved road from San Juan del Norte north for about twenty miles. The line veered toward the coast for about five miles along what looked like a dirt track. A spot about ten miles from the coast had been circled on the map.

Parnell figured he could recon the place, sneak in, take care of business, and get back to San Juan del Norte in no more than four hours. He'd use the tax assessor ID as a last resort. The problem was that it was already four in the afternoon. Any hitch in the operation could put him in the middle of some fairly primitive territory after dark. Besides, if he had to try to pass himself off as a public servant, he didn't think it was likely the average Nicaraguan public employee worked after 2 p.m.—*siesta* time—during the summer. He'd wait until morning.

CHAPTER 47

Yevgeni Tarnovsky's anger had steadily escalated during the twenty-four hours following the attack on his estate. He ranted at anyone who crossed his path and screamed about lax security procedures, lazy guards, and, especially, double-dealing CIA agents.

The captured wounded member of the attack force had talked. Osmanoglu had used extremely innovative methods of persuasion. Tarnovsky had not actively participated in the torture of the wounded man, but he'd enjoyed watching Osmanoglu in action. The Turk was an artist. The wounded man didn't have much to give up. He told how much money he'd been promised and that the assault team had been a Soviet Army SPETSNAZ unit—until they went freelance. But the most important item of information Osmanoglu pulled from the man's pain-wracked brain, before he disposed of him, was the identification of the team's employer: the United States of America's Central Intelligence Agency.

Some of Tarnovsky's anger had dissipated as he became more and more tired. Then, reason returned and, with the advent of reason, came renewed fear. Despite the fact that the attack had failed, he knew the CIA was a formidable adversary. *My God*, he thought, *they've toppled governments. They sure as hell ought to be able to bring down a Bulgarian crime lord.*

Alone in his office, Tarnovsky circumnavigated the spacious room and willed his mind to work on a solution. He had become more terrified by the minute. He knew with certainty the CIA would try again to eliminate him. He guessed the Agency had sent in the Russian team because of his involvement in trafficking.

He stopped pacing for a moment, went to the liquor cabinet, and poured himself a generous portion of *rakir*. The powerful drink burned his throat. He set down the glass and moved to his desk chair. He sat, swiveled the chair toward the window, and looked out at the blue sky. Then he turned back to the desk, pulled out a lower drawer, and propped up his feet.

Tarnovsky had a brainstorm while he stared at the bookcase. The CIA feared that some senator would learn that he was both a CIA operative and in the trafficking business. The Agency had sent a hit team to rub him out. Worst case, they could claim they learned about his other activities and eliminated him. Tarnovsky chuckled. *No point in eliminating me*, he thought, *if I call this self-righteous, asshole-of-a-senator and tell him exactly what I've done. Perfect payback for those CIA bastards for trying to kill me.*

"Metin!" he yelled at the top of his lungs. "Come in here!"

By the time Osmanoglu entered the office, Tarnovsky was doubled over with laughter. It took him over a minute to compose himself.

CHAPTER 48

One of Lorca's guards, Hector Argento, had fumed since the tall Bulgarian *puta* had made fun of him. He'd show her the size of his *pene* when Señor Lorca let him go into the woman's cell. The *puta* would be his. He sauntered down the concrete path between the cells and, still three cells away from the Bulgarian's door, he sang the words, "Hey, *prostituta*, your lover man is here. It will not be long now before Hector shows what he can do for you."

Tatiana Borodvic heard the guard's high-pitched, derisive tone. He announced himself the same way every time he entered the cellblock. This time, she'd give him something extra to think about. The scrape of the man's shoes on the concrete told her he was only a few meters away. She unbuttoned her blouse, reached behind her back, and unsnapped her bra. She slipped off the bra and tossed it near the cell door.

"You hear me, *puta*? I have something long and hard for you."

Borodvic slowly turned to face the guard. She brushed the sides of her blouse open and exposed her breasts. "Well, well, if it isn't Pee-dro Chickendick," she said. "You know, Pee-dro, I noticed a distinct resemblance between you and the chickens running around here. Are you screwing the hens, Chickendick?"

The man choked. Then he screamed a long string of curses. She knew she'd accomplished her mission. The guard was apoplectic.

"Why don't you come in here, Chickendick?" She moved her hands to her breasts, cupped them, and shook them at the man. "Or are these too big for you? Of course," she cackled, "you like chicken breasts. You wouldn't know what to do with a real woman, would you, Pee-dro Chickendick?"

Argento cursed Tatiana for half-a-minute. His ever-reddening face showed clearly through the bars. "Tomorrow, *puta!*" he shouted. "One way or the other, you will pay tomorrow."

"Chickendick, Chickendick," Borodvic sang. Her breasts bounced as she danced around the cell. She sang until Argento apparently couldn't take it any longer and walked away.

A chorus of shouts filled the cellblock after the man left. The other Bulgarian women cheered Tatiana.

Then a voice in American English said, "You make that guy mad enough, you'll be sorry."

Borodvic was already sorry she'd agreed to take this assignment; but one thing she was sure about was that chickendick couldn't make her sorry, even in his dreams.

CHAPTER 49

Quince Hansen's wife came out to the screened porch where her husband, Matt, Esteban, Petrucchio, and Ridgeway sat around maps. "So, Robin Hood," she said, "what are you and your Merrie Men up to?"

"Nothing much," Hansen said.

His wife stared at him with pinched features. Matt thought he saw both worry and anger on her face.

"Humpf," she muttered. "I'm going into town to buy some food. Will you be here when I return?"

Hansen shrugged.

She looked around at the men and wagged a finger at each of them. "You bring my husband back to me safe and sound, or you'll be sorry." She turned and stomped from the porch back into the house.

It appeared none of the men knew what to say at that moment, but Matt figured they all probably thought the same thing: Poor Quince will pay big.

Hansen broke the silence. "Okay, guys. Looks like we've got a plan." He looked at each man in turn and received a nod.

"Good," Quince said. "Fred, why don't you get another beer for everyone? I don't think my bride would take it too kindly if I asked her to provide a little hospitality. I'll go out to the shed and bring in our little friend."

Petrucchio went into the house while Hansen walked off the porch to a shed at the back of his property. Chris Ridgeway mumbled that he needed to take a piss. Matt and Esteban were left alone.

"You okay with all this?" Esteban asked.

Matt shot his friend a wide-eyed look. "What do you mean?"

Esteban cleared his throat. "What we're about to do is a long way from medicine . . . or speeches at medical conferences."

"You don't think I'm up to it?" Matt asked. "You think because I went to medical school I had a gonadectomy? If you weren't my—"

"Whoa, Matthew," Esteban interrupted, his hands held in front of him. "That's not what I meant. It's just that you've got more to lose . . . being a doctor, and all. You get arrested for illegally entering Nicaragua, the good life you've been living is finished."

Matt's expression softened. "The way I figure it, the only thing I've really got to lose is the woman I love. How's that any different from you?"

Esteban got up and walked over to Matt. He placed a hand on Matt's shoulder and said, "Forget I said anything."

Hansen returned with a wild-eyed Luis Reyes. The little lawyer looked scared shitless. His eyes darted from one man to another. His hands were clenched in tight fists; his shoulders hunched. He looked pale—almost gray. The effects of the beating Esteban had given Reyes back in the lawyer's office looked worse now than they had a couple hours earlier. The cuts on his hands and face had been treated with some kind of tincture that turned yellowish-brown on his skin. Purplish-black bruises showed on his arms. When Quince pushed him onto a two-seater, wicker settee next to Esteban, the lawyer scrunched into a corner of the settee and cringed. He seemed incapable of taking his eyes off Esteban. Every time Esteban moved a hand to pick up his beer or scratch his chin, Reyes would jerk as though he'd been poked with a cattle prod.

When Esteban put an arm around Reyes and hugged him, Matt almost felt sorry for the man. Almost.

"All right, Luis, my boy," Esteban said in the singsong cadence of the Hawaiian Islands, his arm still around the lawyer. "We'll go over everything you told us. One more time. Make sure everything is correct. You understand?"

Reyes nodded his head as though his neck was a Slinky. It reminded Matt of the bobbing head on one of those little toy dogs he'd seen in the back window of some *vato's* Chevy Impala back in New Mexico.

Esteban and Hansen grilled Reyes for forty-five minutes. They went over every detail they could think of: the location of Jackson's hacienda, its security setup, the number of men on site, the layout of the grounds and the buildings, the type of weapons the guards had, the closest neighbor, the closest town, and on and on. Reyes volunteered information about the dogs Jackson kept there and the caiman pond.

Esteban gave the man a bone-cracking squeeze. Reyes grimaced. His eyes were wide and unblinking.

Hansen leaned across the table toward Reyes. "If we find out even one thing you've told us is false, I'll come back here and make you sorry you were ever born," he said in a calm, venomous whisper. "You got that?"

The head bob started again.

"What will we do with him while we're gone?" Matt asked.

Hansen opened his mouth, but before he could say anything a short, wizened fellow marched onto the porch. He was about five-feet-six, slender and taut, like a piano wire. He wore his hair—what there was of it—in a gray crewcut. He had ice-cold blue eyes and a body that reminded Matt of beef jerky.

"What's with your old lady?" the guy asked. A slight smile curled the corners of his mouth. "She treated me like yesterday's dog shit."

Hansen waved a hand at the new arrival, as though to say his wife's attitude was unimportant. "To answer your question, Matt, about what we'll do with Counselor Reyes," he said, "this old fart will babysit him. Guys, meet Eric Gates, affectionately referred to by his old Army buddies as either 'that little asshole' or 'numb-nuts.' "

"There you go, trying to get on my good side again, Hansen," Gates said. "Flattery ain't gonna get you anywhere."

Matt and Esteban stood up and shook hands with Gates. Matt noticed the tattoo on the man's right hand, between his thumb and forefinger. It had faded with the years, but he recognized the sword and lightning bolts of the Special Forces emblem.

Gates looked at Reyes seated on the settee. "Is this the guy you want me to watch?" he asked.

"That's him," Hansen said.

Gates gave Reyes a big smile. "Esteban, you mind if I sit next to our guest," he said. "Might as well get to know him."

Esteban shrugged, stood, and moved away. "Be my guest."

Gates took a seat and laid a hand on Reyes's thigh. "You've been a bad boy, Luis. What do you have to say for yourself?"

"I . . . I . . . I . . . don't . . . ."

Gates looked around the room. "What did you guys do to my new friend, Luis?" he asked. "Look, he can't even talk." He put an arm around Reyes's shoulder. "Come on, Luis. Let's go for a walk. Get away from these cretins. They're nothing but a bunch of big bullies."

Reyes looked relieved. His face lost some of its pallor and he stopped clenching his fists.

Gates let the lawyer walk in front of him, then followed him to the doorway into the living room. When Reyes stepped through the doorway, he suddenly crashed to the floor.

Gates grabbed his arm and helped him stand. "You gotta watch yourself, little buddy. You know most accidents happen in the home."

Matt watched Gates and Reyes cross the living room, then move out of sight. He shook his head as he wondered what was in store for Reyes. He'd seen Gates trip the lawyer.

Hansen brought Matt's attention back to their mission. "We leave at one a.m. Jerry Estrada will be here then with his helicopter."

"Does he know where we're going?" Petrucchio asked.

"I told him Nicaragua," Matt said. "It didn't seem to bother him after I mentioned Quince's name . . . and agreed to his price."

Petrucchio chuckled. "Oh, Jerry Estrada thinks the world of Quince. But I suspect mentioning Quince's name didn't get you a discount off his charter rate. That bastard is the most money-hungry guy I've ever met."

Hansen stood. "It's five now. Fred and I will check the equipment and weapons again. The rest of you get some sleep. It'll be a long day tomorrow."

Matt and Esteban moved to the bedroom they'd been offered. Matt sat on his bed, removed his shoes, and stretched out.

"Man, am I exhausted," he said.

Esteban grunted. "Just like old times, huh?"

DAY 8

CHAPTER 50

Tarnovsky waited until 9 a.m., Washington, D.C. time, then called Senator Peter Driscoll's office. A receptionist finally answered after seven rings.

"Senator Driscoll's office. How may I help you?"

"I vant to talk to person who works on white slavery issue for the senator."

"You mean, human trafficking?"

"Vatever."

"That would be Samantha Tate. I'll connect you."

The phone line went silent and then elevator music played in Tarnovsky's ear.

He lit a cigar, rolled his chair under his desk, and tapped his feet on the floor. "Damn bureaucrats," he muttered, while the seconds turned to minutes. He was about to put down the receiver when a brusque voice said, "Samantha Tate."

Tarnovsky caught the officious tone of the woman's voice. "I have information about a white slavery operation. CIA is involved. Are you interested?"

A sigh sounded from the other end of the line. "First of all, using the term 'white slavery' is racist. We call it *trafficking*. Second, I just returned from a long trip to Thailand and I don't have time for twenty questions."

Tarnovsky had actually been in a good mood. But this bitch was rapidly spoiling it. *Thrilled with her own importance*, he thought. He tried to keep his tone even. "Listen to me. I either talk to you or newspapers. You understand?"

"Don't you threaten me. Who do you—"

Tarnovsky hung up and decided to bypass the senator's staff. He'd ask for Driscoll. If the senator wouldn't take his call, he would call the newspapers.

"Senator Pete Driscoll's office. How may—"

"I need to talk to senator. This is Russian Embassy calling. Is very important," Tarnovsky said, putting the proper balance of seriousness and weightiness in his voice. *That ought to do it*, he thought.

Again, the line went silent. Just as the elevator music kicked in, a man came on the line. "This is Francis Antonelli, senior aide to Senator Driscoll. May I help you?"

"You have one chance to listen to me before I go to American press."

"Yes sir. What is this about?"

"Your senator is holding hearings about white . . . about trafficking in women. Is that correct?"

"Yes," Antonelli said.

"Did you know that CIA works with one of biggest traffickers in vorld?"

Silence.

"How do you know that?"

"Because, Mr. Antonelli, I am on CIA payroll and I sell women all over world. I run the trafficking business."

"Wh . . . why are you telling me this?" Antonelli asked. "What do you want?"

"Nothing," Tarnovsky said. "Absolutely nothing. I will call you." Tarnovsky disconnected the call and looked across his desk at Metin Osmanoglu.

"Why didn't you tell him everything? Parnell's name. Your name."

Tarnovsky laughed. Switching to Bulgarian, he said, "I want to build the tension a bit. Let them sweat. This guy, Antonelli, will tell his senator about my call. Driscoll will immediately have visions of a press conference where he will break the news of the CIA's involvement in trafficking. Then he will think about how much press coverage he will get. My God, think about the headlines, the interviews. He might ride this thing into the White House." Tarnovsky laughed until he devolved into a coughing fit.

Osmanoglu squinted at his boss. "I still do not see how you benefit."

Tarnovsky pulled a handkerchief from his pants pocket and wiped the tears from his face. He smiled at Osmanoglu. "Once the word is out," he said, "the CIA has no reason to come after me. I will no longer be a threat to them. The threat will have already become reality."

"But what about your business? We'll have to close it down."

"Why? All we have to do is build a cushion, a shield, between the operation and me. That's where Tatiana comes in."

Osmanoglu nodded his head, but Tarnovsky could tell from the way the man's forehead creased, looking like the skin on a too-ripe tomato, that he was still confused.

"Don't worry, Metin. Everything will be fine." Tarnovsky lifted the glass in front of him and sipped the single malt scotch. While the liquor slid down his throat with a pleasing burn, he thought about the pleasure he would get from paying back the CIA.

CHAPTER 51

Senator Pete Driscoll rested his forehead against the tips of his steepled fingers. "Now, let me get this straight, Francis. You think this call was legitimate? Even though the guy didn't give you a name or a return number, and didn't mention any names at CIA?"

Antonelli leaned forward in his chair and looked across the senator's desk. "It's a gut feeling. Yeah, I think the caller was legit."

"Damn. Did he say when he'd call back?"

"Nope. But I think it'll be soon."

"Hunch again?"

"Yeah," Antonelli responded. "That's the best I can do."

Driscoll smiled. "That's good enough for me. Your hunches have always proved good. I want to use this as soon as possible."

Antonelli felt an instant of panic. "I don't think that's a good idea, Senator. Not until we have all the facts."

Driscoll waved a dismissive hand. "Budget hearings are going on all over Capitol Hill. That asshole Benedict is the swing vote I need on the Senate Budget Committee. He's been unwilling to support my budget bill amendment for the money to construct a cancer research lab at the state university. I need the money for that project. It will be a tough election coming up. I've got to show the voters I can still bring home the bacon."

Pork is more like it, Antonelli thought. "So you want to take this to Benedict and threaten to disclose information about CIA involvement with a trafficker, thereby embarrassing the Senate Oversight Committee on Intelligence, which he chairs, and the administration? That about cover it?"

"That's about it," Driscoll said, his lips compressed into a thin line.

"Which means if Benedict votes to fund the lab, you'll give him whatever information we get and let him try to deal with the problem. You won't go to the press with it. You just want to use it to blackmail Benedict?"

Driscoll looked back at Antonelli and hunched his shoulders, as if to say: That's the way the system works.

CHAPTER 52

"Petey-boy!" Senator William Benedict proclaimed, as though speaking to a crowd, when Peter Driscoll entered his office in the Russell Senate Office Building. "What brings you up here?"

"Got a minute?"

"Of course," Benedict boomed. "I always got a minute for one of my colleagues. What's on your mind?"

Driscoll related the story about the telephone call, embellishing wherever appropriate. He could tell from the way Benedict's nostrils flared that the Louisianan understood the significance of the information.

"So, you see, Bill, this could be embarrassing to the Agency and your committee, not to mention the administration," Driscoll said.

Benedict gave Driscoll a nauseous look; his face was pale, but there was fire in his eyes. "Like you care about whether this administration looks bad."

"Well," Driscoll said, "that's really neither here nor there, is it?"

"The caller didn't give his name?" Benedict asked.

"The only thing I know is the man had a Slavic accent. My aide tells me he sounded like Boris in the old Rocky and Bullwinkle cartoons." Driscoll laughed, but he cut it short when Benedict didn't join him.

The subject of the taxpayer-funded laboratory hadn't yet come up. Driscoll wanted to handle the matter gently. No crass commerce for him.

"Well, I gotta thank you, Petey-boy. Do you have anything in mind as to how I could show my appreciation? Assuming you get me Boris's real name."

"Oh, I'm sure you'll think of something," Driscoll answered.

"Do you think that la-bor-a-tory you been lobbying for might be enough?"

Driscoll smiled and waved at Benedict while he crossed the office. He hesitated for a moment at the door. "It's a start, Bill. It's a start."

Benedict pulled open his bottom desk drawer and removed a pint bottle of Wild Turkey. The bourbon went down as smooth as molasses and warmed his belly. He grinned and thought, *Damned blackmail inside a velvet glove.* He hoisted the bourbon bottle in a salute to Pete Driscoll. The Kansan had played it well. "I love this game," Benedict announced to the four walls. Then he pressed the intercom button on his phone. "Madeline, get me an appointment with Seymour Katzman. Today."

"I think the president's got Mr. Katzman tied up all day with the Middle East Summit out at Camp David," said a voice over the speaker.

"Honey," Benedict said in a low growl, "you tell Mr. Katzman's assistant that those Semites can blow each other to kingdom come, for all I care. I got something a whole lot more important for his attention."

"Yes, sir. I'll get right on it."

Benedict took another pull from the bourbon bottle and lifted his feet onto the corner of the open desk drawer. "Jeez. One more damned scandal in this administration and I'll be back to being nothing but the ranking member of my committees. The damned Bible-thumpers will take over and I'll be up shit creek without a paddle."

CHAPTER 53

Ricardo, the scar-faced man, opened the door to Renee's cell an hour after sundown. Her heart raced like it would burst from her chest. Fear turned her insides to jelly. The man led her down the row of cells, but stopped at Alani's cell door, two down from her own. He used a key to unlock that door. "Let's go. Señor Lorca does not like to be kept waiting," he said in his gravelly voice.

"Where are you taking us?" Renee asked.

Ricardo sneered. "Señor Lorca has plans for you two tonight."

As Alani stepped out of the cell, something changed inside Renee, as though a fire had erupted in her veins and ignited her blood. Heat swamped her and she jumped at Ricardo.

"You can't do this," she screamed. "She's pregnant. I won't let you do this."

The big man was momentarily caught off guard. Renee's fists beat at his chest, then her fingers reached for his face. But he recovered and easily grabbed her wrists. He held her away from him, smiled, and made a clucking sound. "*Aiee, chiquita, cálmate.* I would not want to hurt you."

Alani stared with wide open eyes at Renee. Then she must have noticed the bruises on Renee's face and arms. "Renee, what happened? What's going on? Your face . . ."

Renee slumped and the man released her.

Alani moved to Renee and hugged her.

Renee sobbed as she clutched Alani.

Ricardo pulled them apart and led them down the path to the house. Once inside, he took them to a large bedroom furnished with bulky antique wooden furniture. The four-poster bed had angels carved on its posts and headboard. The room smelled musty, unused. But it appeared to be clean. Two dresses had been neatly laid out on the four-poster bed, along with undergarments, scarves, shoes, and even handbags.

Ricardo pointed toward a door in the middle of one of the side walls. "The bathroom is in there," he said. "Clean up and put on fresh clothes. I will be back to get you in an hour." Then he left. The sound of the door being locked behind him sounded inordinately loud in the confines of the bedroom.

Alani rushed to Renee's side and gently took her hands in her own. "What happened to you?"

"It's nothing. How's your medicine situation?" she asked, changing the subject.

Alani gave Renee a look that seemed to say that she knew Renee was holding something back. "I'm okay for two days. After that . . . ." She shrugged and her chin trembled.

Alani then turned to the bed. "What do you think this is all about?" she asked. "The clothes? Who's this guy named Lorca?"

"It's Lonnie Jackson. He's using Lorca as an alias."

"What does he want with us?"

Acid attacked Renee's stomach. What could she tell Alani? What could she say to a woman four months pregnant about what might lie in store for her? She looked at the filthy shift Alani wore. Her pregnancy had barely begun to show. Despite the fact that her hair was a mess and her arms and legs were covered with dirt from the cell, she still looked beautiful. Her almond-shaped eyes, light brown skin, and delicate features, in any other situation, would be assets. Here they were negatives. She thought, *Jackson will go after her the way he attacked me.* She felt her backbone stiffen and she swore she would die before she let Jackson put his hands on Alani.

"I don't know, honey," Renee said. "Let's get cleaned up and play this thing out." It made her sick to think about getting "fixed up" for Jackson. But she could use the time to think. "Why don't you shower first?" She smiled. "It'll feel good to wash off this dirt."

Alani took in an uneven breath and nodded.

While Alani showered, Renee searched the room for something she could use as a weapon. Something she could conceal. But the room and closet had apparently been sanitized. She tried the wardrobe and looked under the bed. Nothing. Then she looked in the dresser. Like the other furniture in the room, it was bulky, dark-brown, and old. The four drawers were empty.

"Dammit," Renee whispered. Then something caught her attention. The front panels of the drawers were thick. There were two cut-glass pull knobs on the outside of each drawer. The knobs were attached to long metal screws, anchored with a nut on the inside of the drawer. Renee used one hand to twist the left knob of the top drawer while she held the nut with her other hand. But the nut and screw were rusted. When she turned the knob, the nut turned with it.

Renee tried the knob on the other end of the drawer. No luck. The same with the two knobs on the next drawer down. She closed the second drawer and opened the third one. She felt her heart hammer in her neck. Half of the nut on one of the screws was broken off. She twisted the glass knob and, using a corner of her skirt to protect her fingers, squeezed the remaining part of the nut. It, too, was corroded and wouldn't budge. She removed a sandal and struck the nut with the side of the sandal. Once—twice—three times. The nut broke free and dropped to the bottom of the drawer. Renee pulled on the knob and removed it from the drawer. She gripped the glass portion in her palm; the screw end thrusted out between her fingers.

The bathroom door opened. A cloud of steam rolled into the bedroom and quickly dissipated in the cooler air.

"Your turn," Alani said, an obviously forced smile on her lips.

Good girl, Renee thought. *Keep your chin up.*

After she showered, Renee used a hair dryer, then finished dressing, just when she heard the sound of a key in the door lock. Ricardo entered and looked them up and down as though he was a buyer at a livestock auction.

"Not bad, ladies. I think Señor Lorca will be pleased." He

stepped aside and waved an arm to indicate they should precede him through the door. When Renee stepped by him, he smirked. "The living room," he said. "You know the way."

Renee stared down the hall. She steeled herself to confront Jackson, to show no fear. But the walk toward the last room made her think of the death march of the condemned.

A male voice carried from the living room. Renee felt her resolve melt. Her stomach was in an uproar and she thought she might vomit. She concentrated on her promise to protect Alani, inhaled a long breath, and tried to stand taller.

At the end of the hall, she looked down into the living room and saw the back of Jackson's head and shoulders. He sat on a plush chair. Across from him, seated in another chair, was an Asian man in the process of saying something, when he met Renee's gaze. His mouth hung open and he stood.

"My, my," he said in a cultured English accent. "Your description of the ladies was understated, my friend."

The Asian had jet-black hair that stuck out over each ear. His nose was bulbous, his face pockmarked. A sparse, silky Fu Manchu mustache hung down to his chin. He wore gray slacks, a white dress shirt open to the middle of his chest, and a gold chain around his neck.

Jackson rose from his chair and turned around. "Ah, our dates have arrived. Come in, ladies. Join us."

Renee saw the shocked look on Alani's face. She took her hand and squeezed it.

A light seemed to go on behind Alani's eyes. She stared at Renee's face, as though she suddenly understood what had caused Renee's bruises. She jerked her hand free of Renee's grasp and backed away from the living room. She stepped back two paces and bumped up against the scar-faced man, who pushed her forward.

Renee again reached for Alani's hand and gave her a pleading look. "I won't let them hurt you," she said under her breath.

Alani hesitated, then came forward.

Renee put an arm around Alani's waist and felt the tremors that shook her friend's body. She looked past Alani at Jackson and saw a satisfied look in his eyes, in his smile. *Ultimate payback*, she thought. She guessed his plan was to use her—and Alani—until he tired of them. Then they would die.

Renee said a quick, silent prayer for strength. It seemed to give her courage. She felt the knob, with its long screw in the hand that held a scarf. She gritted her teeth and vowed to pay Jackson back for what he had done to her. The thought of revenge helped her resolve. What he had done to her was nothing compared to what Jackson had done to her son, David, or Matt's sister, Susan.

Renee squeezed Alani's waist and smiled at her. She sent her friend a telepathic message: everything will be all right.

Jackson walked up the steps to the entry, took Alani's hand, pulled her away from Renee, and led her to the couch. Without being prompted, Renee walked to a chair next to the Asian man and sat down. The Asian reclaimed his own seat.

"I think you ladies will enjoy the evening I've planned," Jackson said. "All in all, this will be a memorable night." Jackson laughed.

The Asian sniggered, reached over, and brushed Renee's hair back from her face. "You are exquisite, my dear, even with the damage done to your face. What animal did this to you?"

The man looked from Renee to Jackson, as though he expected Jackson to answer his question. The cold, narrow-eyed look on Jackson's face seemed to unnerve the man. Renee noticed his face flush and perspiration bead on his forehead.

Jackson's expression quickly softened. He walked to the bar and poured champagne into two flutes and carried them to Renee and Alani. The dregs of what looked like beer was in a glass on the table in front of Jackson's chair. The Asian sipped a blonde-colored liquid.

Jackson returned to his seat. "Ladies, let me introduce you to an important friend of mine. Siriwa Pratikan is a very successful businessman from Thailand." Jackson's demonic eyes flashed. "Renee, I have confidence you will give Mr. Pratikan at least as much pleasure as you gave me last night."

Alani sucked in a noisy breath and looked at Renee with sadness in her suddenly lusterless eyes.

Jackson put an arm around Alani. "Don't worry, dear, you don't have to feel like you've been deprived." He patted her shoulder. "Tonight it'll be your turn."

CHAPTER 54

Senator William Benedict knew Pete Driscoll was passionate about the issue of human trafficking. But, on a scale of one to ten, he guessed Driscoll rated trafficking an eight or nine, and the research facility he wanted for Kansas a ten. Driscoll would get his lab. So, now Benedict had to do something about the trafficking. He had to prevent embarrassment to the CIA and, thereby, the administration. But what?

Benedict checked his watch. His meeting with Seymour Katzman was scheduled for nine that night. He'd drop the news on him like the A-bomb on Hiroshima. Benedict chuckled. Katzman would stay cool, as he always did. The guy had a nervous system made of dry ice. Benedict knew, however, that Katzman's stomach would hemorrhage acid. Even an unsubstantiated story about CIA involvement with a contract agent who trafficked in women would tear this administration apart. One more fiasco that left the impression that this president didn't give a shit about women would, at best, generate a bunch of embarrassing investigations and, at worst, ruin the man's re-election chances. He used women on an individual basis as though they were put on earth to service his libido. It wouldn't be much of a leap for people to believe that the President condoned trafficking within his CIA.

Like Katzman, Benedict knew how to control his emotions. But this situation had gotten to him. *This thing goes public*, he thought, *and that asshole in the White House won't have a snowball's chance in hell of getting re-elected in the fall. And he'll drag down the party with him.* "I'll be damned if I'll be just a goddamn committee member again," he shouted at his office walls. He liked being a majority party member on the Budget Committee and chairman of the Intelligence Committee. The lobbyists dumped bags of cash in his lap like fucking loose slot machines.

Benedict slowly rose from his leather desk chair. He suddenly felt old and tired. A lot rode on covering up this potential scandal. He straightened his jacket and took a step toward his private bathroom. *Better brush my teeth and gargle with mouthwash. No point in offending that teetotaler, Katzman.* But his private telephone rang before he reached the bathroom. He turned back, stretched over the corner of his desk, and snatched the receiver from its cradle.

"Yeah?"

"Bill, it's Pete Driscoll."

Benedict detected raw, brittle excitement in Driscoll's voice. "What ya got, Petey-boy?"

"The guy called back a couple minutes ago."

"I assume we're talking about our friend Boris?"

Driscoll paused for a moment. "Oh yeah, Boris and Natasha. Yes, that's the one. But his name's not Boris. It's Tarnovsky. Yevgeni Tarnovsky. Ring any bells?"

Benedict thought for a minute. "I don't know why, but the name's familiar." *Think, you old fart,* he commanded himself. *Why do you know that name?*

"Well, anyway, that's the guy's name. And you'll love the reason he called. He claims the Agency tried to murder him. He figures they'll back off if he spills the beans. I hope this helps."

Benedict continued to try to come up with the connection to Tarnovsky's name. But his synapses weren't sparking.

"You still there, Bill?"

"Huh? Oh, sorry, Petey-boy. Yeah, yeah, thanks." Then Benedict forced a lighthearted tone. "You enjoy that new la-bor-a-tory, ya hear," he said. "It ought to be worth at least fifty thousand votes this November." Then he hung up.

The clock on his desk read quarter after eight. The ride to Katzman's townhouse would take thirty minutes. That gave him fifteen minutes to try to come up with why the name Tarnovsky seemed familiar. He was almost certain it had come up in the past in relationship to the CIA. The guy who called Driscoll had said he was on the CIA's payroll. A lightbulb flashed in Benedict's brain. *The Senate Select Committee on Intelligence! If the sonofabitch is on the CIA payroll, then they had to have disclosed his name to the committee.* That was the law.

Benedict jerked the phone from its cradle and pressed the buttons for the Committee on Intelligence's staff office. "Come on, come on, come on," he said, while he waited for someone to answer. "Please, someone be there."

"Danni Buchanan," a young female voice said in Benedict's ear. "You've reached the Senate Select—"

"Sweetheart, this is Senator William Benedict," he said in his most honey-sweet, Cajun accent. "I wonder if you could do me a favor."

"Uh . . . I can try, Senator."

Benedict grinned. He detected nervousness in the woman's voice. Probably thinks I'm going to ask her to come up here and get down on her knees. *Hell of a reputation you got here, Billy-boy,* he thought.

"I need you to pull up a name out of your database for me. I need to make the connection between this man's name and the committee."

The young woman breathed an audible sigh that whistled in Benedict's ear. "What's the name, sir?" she asked.

"Yevgeni Tarnovsky."

"What's this man's connection to the committee, sir?"

Benedict sighed. *Shit,* he thought. *They got so many damned databases down there, it could take days to find Tarnovsky. I'll have to take a guess and cross my fingers.* "Deep cover. Probably in Eastern Europe. Maybe the former Soviet Union."

"Uh, that could be a problem, Senator. That disk is in the Top Secret safe. It's a two-person control safe. I can't access it alone."

Benedict gripped the telephone receiver so hard his fingers

hurt. He took in a slow, controlled breath. "What'd you say your name was?"

"Danni Buchanan."

"Well, Danni Buchanan, if you want to still have your job tomorrow, you'd better find a second person with access to that safe, and you'd better find out who this Yevgeni Tarnovsky character is within the next thirty minutes." He recited his cell phone number to her, made her repeat it. "Call me at that number," he snarled, then hung up.

Benedict crossed the floor in front of his desk and walked to the bathroom. He brushed his teeth, gargled, and splashed some aftershave on his face. Then he rushed out to his car in underground parking, feeling the beginnings of a world-class headache coming on.

The closer Benedict came to Seymour Katzman's Georgetown townhouse, the worse his headache became. He promised himself that he would fire Danni Buchanan if she didn't call soon. Then his cell phone rang.

"Go," Benedict growled into the phone.

"I got it, sir. Yevgeni Tarnovsky. Bulgarian. Former Bulgarian Secret Service and current crime boss. Invaluable information source on the names of players inside Bulgaria and other former communist countries. He's been on the CIA's payroll for the past two plus decades." She paused and then blurted, "Wow!"

"What?" Benedict shouted. *What now?*

"Says here he gets five million a year."

The number surprised even Benedict. "Must be one hell of an undercover agent," he said. "Where's he located?"

"Varna, Bulgaria. Near the Black Sea."

"Thanks, honey. I'll come down there real soon and show you how much I appreciate your help." He smiled as he hung up the phone.

CHAPTER 55

Seymour Katzman looked longingly at the blackened brick of the fireplace in his townhouse's study. *It's bloody summer and it feels like ten below zero in here. Too bad I don't have any firewood.* He rubbed his hands together. He knew it was just his nerves. Late night, private meetings spelled trouble. And Katzman thought of William Benedict as trouble under normal circumstances.

He moved to the liquor cabinet and stifled a sigh. *Fucking Benedict,* he thought, while he poured a club soda. *The guy gives me the creeps.* But, all the same, he knew Benedict was no bullshit artist. When the guy said he had something important to talk about, Katzman knew it would be significant. Enough to cause him to leave the peace talks down at Camp David.

Benedict was one of the president's confidants, the commander in chief's eyes and ears in the Senate. When Benedict talked, the president listened. So, by proxy, the president's National Security Advisor, Seymour Katzman, had to listen to the Louisianan.

A spray of headlights flashed in the room. Katzman walked to the window and peered out. A silver-gray Lincoln pulled up the short driveway and stopped in front of the garage door. He watched Benedict get out of the car and straighten his suit jacket. The senator then marched up three stone steps and turned right toward the walk that led to the front door. Katzman sucked in a deep breath and put his glass on the coffee table. "Well, here goes," he said, and went and opened the door.

"Senator."

"Hey, Sey," Benedict said in a voice that was almost a shout. "How're they hangin'?"

Damn redneck, Katzman thought, all the while smiling as though he was thrilled to see the senator. He shut the door behind Benedict and then led the way back to the study. He walked to the table where he'd left his club soda, hoisted it, and said, "Care for something?"

A smile illuminated Benedict's face as though there was a built-in light bulb behind his eyes. "Bear shit in the woods?" he said. "Bourbon."

Katzman poured two shots of bourbon over ice and handed the drink to Benedict. Then he pointed at a chair. "You said this was important. Maybe we better get to it. I have to return to Camp David tonight."

Benedict took a generous swig of his drink, placed the glass on the coffee table, and rested against the high-backed leather chair. He rested his head for a moment, ran his hands through his hair, and closed his eyes. When he reopened his eyes, there was no joviality left in them.

"We got a little problem, Sey."

Katzman put on his most inscrutable expression. "I figured as much," he said. Decades of negotiations on Wall Street, and now years of sitting across the table from heads of state and foreign diplomats, had taught him how to hide his emotions.

Benedict reached inside his suit coat and removed a folded sheet of paper. He slid the paper across the table to Katzman and waited for the man to unfold and glance at it. "The name written there is a former Bulgarian intelligence chief," he said

Katzman gave him a look that said, *Yeah, so?*

"This man, Tarnovsky, is on the CIA's payroll. The sonofabitch gets five million a year to keep the Company informed of political activities inside the old Communist Bloc. And to erase people our boys over at Foggy Bottom want to get rid of."

"The price to buy a snitch sure has gone up," Katzman said. A hint of a smile played at the corners of his mouth.

"Snitch and assassin. The amount kind of surprised me, too. But that's only part of the story. This guy Tarnovsky is a world class drug smuggler."

"Oh shit," Katzman said. "The CIA's doing business with a drug dealer?"

"Oh, it gets even better," Benedict said. "He's also involved in human trafficking."

"Does the Agency know this?"

"Apparently," Benedict said. "Tarnovsky thinks the CIA sent a hit squad after him yesterday to sort of sweep the Agency's embarrassment under the rug, so to speak."

"And . . . ?"

"They botched it."

"Who else knows about this?" Katzman asked, imagining the way the press would jump all over this story. The president's reputation was already in the crapper because of his peccadilloes. Now he'd be plastered with the accusation that he condoned the CIA doing business with a criminal who sold drugs and women on the open market.

"I got this from Pete Driscoll."

Katzman screwed up his face, all pretext of hiding his emotions long gone. "Why the hell would Driscoll give you this? Why didn't he just take it to the press? That self-righteous asshole hates the president."

"Oh, it's not that he wants to help the president. He wants to help himself. It's a budget matter."

Katzman nodded his head in understanding. He didn't need or want to know what kind of bargain had been struck between the two "public servants."

A thought suddenly hit Katzman. "Isn't Driscoll the one who's railed about women's rights and female trafficking?"

Benedict smiled.

"What are you thinking?" Katzman asked.

"It will only take Tarnovsky one, maybe two days for him to figure out Driscoll's sitting on the information he gave him. The Bulgarian already threatened to go to the press with that information. He wants the CIA off his ass."

"I see," Katzman said. His eyes bored into Benedict's.

CHAPTER 56

Renee remembered what her father had told her when he'd taken her on hunting trips: "Let your nervousness seep out through your fingers and toes. Breathe slow and easy." She never liked to watch her father kill birds or deer, but she loved those times with him.

She tried to do what her father taught her. She drank a little wine, put down the glass, and rested her hands on her thighs under the dining table. Her heart thudded with a vengeance and her chest rose and fell. *Take it easy*, she told herself. *You can do this.* Slow and easy. Deep breaths. Slow release.

Her heart slowed and her breathing relaxed. She raised her gaze from her plate and stared across at Alani, who looked frightened, panicked, like an animal whose leg is caught in a trap. Her hands shook and her eyes seemed unnaturally large. Renee smiled at Alani, although her stomach ached as though she'd been punched.

Pratikan sat at the end of the table to Renee's left. Jackson sat at the opposite end. The Thai couldn't seem to take his eyes off her. He continuously gave her puppy-dog looks like a teenager in lust. The man made her feel as though slimy leeches crawled on her skin. She needed to get Pratikan away from Jackson. Maybe then she could put the dresser knob to good use. She figured she weighed only twenty pounds less than the Asian, and was two or three inches taller. She could take this guy if she had surprise on her side. But, as long as Jackson was nearby, she didn't have a chance. The trouble was, if Jackson *wasn't* with them, it would probably mean he'd taken Alani somewhere. She couldn't allow that to happen.

"Did you enjoy your salads?" Jackson asked, a toothy smile on his face.

Alani stared at her lap.

Renee bolstered her courage and looked over at Jackson. "Yes," she said.

She knew what kind of game Jackson was playing. He wanted to build up the tension. The dinner was nothing but part of a psychological warfare drama. Keep the victims off balance. Make them think their lot in life had improved. Then bring them crashing back to earth. The bigger the fall, the worse the mental and emotional damage. Renee had seen many children suffering from that sort of damage in her work with Save the Kids. She was certain Jackson would rape Alani. *She* would be Pratikan's dessert. At least, that's what she thought their plan was.

Pratikan's voice intruded on her thoughts. He leaned toward her. His foul breath came across the space between them in intermittent, nauseating waves. Up close, his acne scars looked like craters.

"You know, my dear, life for you will not be so bad. I would never allow the peasants to touch you. You will be special. Reserved for my important clients." He patted her hand and looked at her as though he waited for a thank you.

Renee felt her throat spasm. She tasted bile and nearly vomited. *So, that's what Jackson has planned for us! That's what he meant when he said he wanted revenge. He won't kill us. We'll be forced into prostitution.* She felt the composure she'd tried so hard to construct start to melt. *Don't blow it now*, she told herself.

Jackson rose from his chair and lifted the wine bottle from the cooler in the middle of the table. He refilled his and Renee's glass, then looked at Alani. "I see you haven't touched your wine. Don't you like it?" Then he grinned. "Oh, I forgot. You're pregnant."

Renee looked at Alani and saw something in her friend's eyes that scared her. Alani's face seemed to go lifeless. Her eyes lacked focus. The fear wasn't there anymore. Nothing seemed to be there. She coughed in an attempt to get Alani to look back at her.

Jackson laughed. "Are you listening to me?"

Alani sat there as though comatose.

Jackson picked up his wineglass and threw its contents in Alani's face. The shock of the liquid hitting her seemed to bring Alani back to the present. She gasped as though she'd been thrown into a pool of freezing water. But she made no other sound.

Jackson looked at Pratikan. "As I was saying," he said, "our dark-haired beauty here is with child. Why don't you tell the ladies, Siriwa, why you will pay me more for Alani than for Renee?"

Pratikan chuckled. "Oh, but that's quite simple, my friend. I have clients who will pay many dollars for a virgin child—boy or girl. Especially a child who looks different. And the lovely lady here will surely have a very exotic-looking child. We will raise her child to be strong and healthy and then, when the child is ten or eleven . . . ." He let the thought hang over the room like a sinister cloud.

Renee thought, at first, the man had to be joking. The implications of what he'd said were too monstrous to be true. It was just another way to torment them. But when she saw the look on Pratikan's face, she realized he was deadly serious. He appeared to relish the idea of the money he would earn from selling Alani and Esteban's child. She felt her temperature rise. Anger boiled inside her. She turned back toward Alani, just as the table erupted in flying glasses, plates and silverware.

Alani was on her feet, the tablecloth gripped in her hands. She screamed dementedly; tears flowed down her face. She sounded deranged as she railed incoherently at Jackson.

Ricardo burst into the room, pistol in hand.

Jackson held up a calming hand. "Take her to my room." Then he faced Pratikan. "Well, Siriwa, it looks like dinner is over. Perhaps you would like to retire to your room with your date."

Pratikan smiled. "I cannot think of anything that would give me more pleasure."

Jackson twisted around and pointed at Ricardo, who had Alani by the upper arm and was in the process of dragging her from the room. "After you lock her up, go tell the men they can have playtime tonight. Mr. Pratikan will leave the day after tomorrow and I want his shipment ready to go."

The hulking man nodded and walked from the room with Alani

under one arm, carried like a sack of grain.

Breathe easy, Renee reminded herself.

CHAPTER 57

Tatiana Borodvic awoke to the sounds of men howling like a pack of wolves with the scent of blood in their nostrils. The noise echoed off the cellblock's concrete surfaces. The creak of her cell door brought her fully alert. A shadowy presence hovered in the open doorway. The door then closed with a report like a gunshot. The shadow moved toward her. She smelled him before she was able to make out who he was.

"Hello, *chiquita*. I told you I'd come for you."

She recognized Hector's voice and sidled backward against the corner of the cell, feigning fright.

The man came forward. He pulled the tail of his t-shirt from his pants. Still four feet away, he lifted the shirt over his head.

In that instant, Tatiana launched herself off the floor and rammed the palm of her hand into the center of the spot where the t-shirt covered Hector's face. She felt a warm thrill as she heard the crunch of cartilage.

The man groaned and dropped to his knees. Tatiana stepped back, shot out a bare foot, and connected her heel with the man's throat. A muffled gasp exploded from the man's mouth as he landed face down on the concrete floor.

Borodvic leaped on the man's back and wrapped her hands around his neck. She levered his upper body backward, her knee jammed into his back. She pulled with all her strength until she heard his neck snap.

She quickly searched his pockets and came up with a switchblade knife, a set of keys, paper money, and coins, which she placed on the floor. Then she stripped off his pants, discarded her soiled skirt, and stepped into the pants. She picked up the knife and money and shoved them into the pants pockets.

The cell door creaked as she pushed on it. She opened it enough to get a view of the corridor. Screams and the sounds of grunts and slaps came from other cells. The corridor was empty. She took a step outside her cell, but the sound of footsteps from the end of the corridor stopped her.

She eased back inside the cell; closed the door behind her. The footfalls became louder. She ran to Hector's body and dragged it into the darkest corner of the room. After she lay on her back next to him, she pulled the corpse on top of her. She screamed and moved her body up and down as much as she was able to. Over the dead man's shoulder, she saw a man peer between the cell bars and laugh. The face remained there for a few seconds, then disappeared.

Borodvic shoved the body off her and ran to the cell door. She withdrew the knife from her pocket, opened the blade, and slowly pushed on the door. When it opened a crack, she looked down the hall. A large man moved from cell to cell. He stopped for a few seconds at each door to look through the bars. He would laugh or shout encouragement. This was the man they called Ricardo, she remembered, the one with the long white scar on his face.

Ricardo paused to peer into the cells on the opposite side of the corridor as he worked his way toward this end of the hall.

The women's screams were now agonizing—almost too hideous to bear, even for Borodvic. She didn't have anything invested in these women. In fact, she looked down on them as though they were stupid sheep. Pathetic creatures for being duped. But she felt a visceral hatred for these men. She waited until Ricardo stopped at the cell directly across from hers, shoved the door open, and charged across the five-meter-wide corridor. She was afraid the sound of the opening door would warn the man, but she attacked with speed.

Knife in hand, she rushed at the man and swiped the blade at his exposed neck. She thought she made contact, but couldn't be sure if she had done real damage or just nicked him. His hand shot toward his neck. She anticipated that and sliced the knife across the back of his hand to sever veins and tendons.

Ricardo bellowed like an enraged bull. He caught her by surprise when he swung his injured hand and knocked her back through the open doorway into her cell. She staggered, tried to catch her balance, but tripped on the pallet and struck her head against the floor.

Stunned, Borodvic shook her head to try to clear it. She squeezed her right hand, feeling for the comforting hardness of the knife handle. Her hand was empty.

Ricardo came through the doorway, his wounded left hand pressed against the wound in his neck. He ran at her, as he moved his right hand to his waist and came away with a long-bladed knife.

She pretended to be unconscious and peeked out through slit eyes at the man. She waited until he stopped a couple feet away and bent over her. She kicked at his knee and connected. As his left leg gave way, he leaned to his right. With a hopping step, he shifted his weight to his other leg. In that instant, she rolled to the right and came to her feet. She grunted when she felt a pain in her left foot. The knife she'd dropped had sliced into her foot.

Borodvic dodged one way, then another, as she avoided Ricardo's thrusts. She maneuvered him in a direction that would allow her to pick up her lost knife. She glanced at the floor, when Ricardo made a desperate lunge at her and swiped the blade at her chest, just above her left breast.

"Aagh!" Tatiana exclaimed.

The strike seemed to give Ricardo confidence. He charged, knife arm extended, the blade pointed at her heart.

She rolled to the side in a tight ball, narrowly avoiding the thrust. Now, near where she'd dropped the knife she'd taken from Hector, she swept her hand across the floor. She felt the hard bone of the knife handle and clasped her fingers around it. Then, she came up in a crouch and stabbed at Ricardo. She heard his surprised cry of pain as he doubled over and dropped onto his hands and knees.

Borodvic shoved him in the side with her foot and forced him over on his back. Red foam bubbled from his mouth. She came around behind him and stepped on the wrist of his knife-wielding hand. Then she sliced his throat, sending a gusher of blood spurting across the cell.

Ricardo gurgled and grasped his neck with his hands.

The noise from the other cells had covered sounds of her struggle with Ricardo. She checked on her foot, found the cut on her heel wasn't too bad. She ripped Ricardo's shirt and wrapped her foot. Then she yanked off chickendick's boots and slipped into them. They were a little tight, but would work until she found something better. She peeked into the corridor. No one. Then she noticed a jacket draped over the back of a chair about ten meters away. A pistol belt hung over the jacket.

She ran to the chair and removed the pistol from the holster. She was familiar with the Brazilian-made Taurus PT92, a double-action 9mm pistol with a 15-round magazine. She ejected the magazine, found it loaded, and reinserted it. She stood by the hinged side of the nearest cell door and peeked through a corner of the opening in the door and, in the light from a single overhead bulb, saw a naked man on top of one of the Bulgarian women. Borodvic pulled the jacket from the back of the chair and wrapped it around the pistol. She grasped the handle on the heavy wood door and pulled. Like the door to her cell, the hinges creaked as though they hadn't been oiled in years.

The noise startled the man in the cell and he looked back over his shoulder. The woman's eyes were wide. "Help me," she screamed in Bulgarian.

Borodvic rushed into the cell and pointed the pistol at the man's back. He rolled off the Bulgarian and moved to stand. But, before he could get his feet underneath him, she placed the muzzle of the jacket-muffled pistol against the man's forehead and pulled the trigger. Blood, hair, bone shards, and gray matter exploded out the back of the man's head and splattered the cell walls, the floor, and the woman he'd been raping.

The Bulgarian woman's screams were amazingly loud as they echoed off the cell's hard surfaces. Borodvic moved to cover her mouth, but decided the noise she made wouldn't come as a surprise to the other men in the cellblock and would help disguise any noise she might make as she moved to other cells.

One by one, she executed four more men. Two were in the process of raping the other Bulgarians. Two others were with a couple of Latin American girls. She had a fleeting thought about the two American women and wondered what had happened to them. But she put them out of her mind and gathered the five women together. She told the three Bulgarians to run to the back of the property, where the jungle began. She pushed the Spanish girls in the direction the other women had gone and whispered, *"Pronto! Pronto!"* They took off, too.

Now to find Lorca. She quickly but cautiously moved from one shadow to another, from the cellblock to the hacienda. She followed the right side of the wall where the house began and worked her way past an entry to the first window. Plantation shutters were closed over an open, but screened window. The first room was dark; no noise came from inside. She moved down the length of the house, from window to window. The fourth room was occupied.

An Asian man sat on the edge of a bed, stripped down to his undershorts, removing his socks. She was about to continue on to the next room when a movement stopped her. A tall woman in nothing but a bra and panties stepped out of the light of a bathroom. The woman closed the bathroom door, walked over to a table lamp, and turned it off.

The Bulgarian resisted the urge to move past this room. There had been something in the woman's face before the room went dark that froze her to the spot. She squinted into the room and tried to make out what was happening. After a couple seconds, she heard a scream. Then gurgling sounds, as though someone was drowning.

She ducked down when the light in the room came on again. She slowly rose up until she could see over the sill. The Asian man was now on the floor. A glass knob protruded from the side of his neck. He flopped around like a beached fish. Blood flowed from around the thing in his neck. The woman straddled his chest and held a pillow over his face.

What the hell? Borodvic watched with fascination. When the man finally stopped thrashing, the woman ran to the bathroom.

Although she couldn't see her anymore, she did hear running water. The woman was out of her line of sight for barely a minute, but then she reappeared in the bedroom and frantically moved around. She picked up a dress from the top of a wooden trunk and slipped it over her head. Then she fumbled with the buttons. Tatiana could see her hands shaking.

"*Pssst*," Borodvic whispered through the screen.

The woman jerked around and cried out. Her hands shot to her mouth.

"*Ssh!*"

The woman dropped her hands. "Who are you?" she whispered in English.

"American?" Tatiana asked, ignoring the other woman's question.

"Yes."

"Were you in one of the cells?"

The woman nodded as she stepped to the window. "My name is Renee Curtis," she said.

"Well, Renee, I like your style. What did you stab that guy with?"

"A knob from a dresser drawer."

"Do you know which room José Lorca is in?"

"Yes, I think so. But his name is Jackson. Lonnie Jackson. José Lorca is an alias."

Borodvic could not have cared less what the man's real name was. She waved away Renee's explanation. "Do you know which room he's in?" she asked again.

"I think it may be the last bedroom on the other side of the hall."

Borodvic stuck the pistol into her pants, removed the screen, and boosted herself through the bedroom window. She padded past Renee, went to the bedroom door, and tried the knob. Locked.

Renee pointed at the body on the floor. "He's got the key. He locked the room from the inside."

Borodvic scurried past the Asian, jumped over the spreading pool of blood that had already soaked the carpet. She lifted his trousers from the footboard and thrust her hand into a pocket. Coins, a cigarette lighter. She checked the other pocket. Nothing. "Where's his jacket?" she rasped.

"Closet," Renee said.

Borodvic moved to the closet and found a single key in a side pocket. She checked the other pockets, found a wallet, and emptied it of cash.

The key fit the lock. She carefully turned it until the mechanism rolled over with a *click,* then she cracked the door. There was no one in the hall. "Stay here, I will come back for you," she told Renee.

Borodvic had gotten what she needed from the American: the location of Lorca's . . . Jackson's room. She didn't need her tagging along. She had a tough enough situation without an amateur slowing her down. She went into the hall and closed the door behind her.

Renee felt a momentary exhilaration. She'd done what she'd planned. The pimp, Siriwa Pratikan, was dead. Now she had to find Alani. Then a sinking feeling hit her. The woman with the Slavic accent had a pistol. She'd asked about Jackson's room. She intended to go after him. *What if she shoots Alani by mistake?* Renee opened the door and tiptoed into the corridor. She saw the woman outside the last room on the other side of the hall, her ear pressed against the door.

Suddenly, the woman spun around and pointed her pistol at Renee. The sight of the weapon made Renee freeze. She threw up her hands in a defensive posture. When the woman lowered the pistol, Renee continued forward.

"I told you to stay in the room."

"My friend is in there," Renee said. "I don't want her to get hurt."

"Shit!"

CHAPTER 58

Jerry Estrada put his helicopter down on a vacant piece of ground five miles outside the San José city limits, between the fenced vegetable garden north of Quince Hansen's house and the edge of the rain forest. He was early. It was an hour before midnight. He'd landed on this same spot twice before, so he knew the area. But it helped that reflector pads had been placed in a large circle on the lawn.

After the rotors had slowed, Hansen ran over and opened the pilot's door and Estrada jumped to the ground.

"Welcome, Jerry," Hansen said as he handed the pilot a beer.

After he took a hefty pull on the bottle, Estrada gave it back to Hansen. "Got work to do tonight," he said. "I'd better take it easy."

Hansen led Estrada past stacked weapons and a pile of equipment a short distance from where the aircraft had set down. "Let's go to the barn," he said. "We'll brief you on the mission there."

"That'd be nice," Estrada said. "All I know at this point is you want me to take you into Nicaragua. We goin' after Sandinistas?" The pilot laughed as though he'd told the joke of the century.

Hansen introduced Estrada to Matt and Esteban. Estrada waved to the others—all old friends. They were gathered around a large plywood panel set on two sawhorses. Maps were spread out on the panel. A spotlight hung on an electrical cord over it.

Estrada smiled at the way the other men stared at him. He

realized what he'd done was a bit dramatic. He'd shaved his head and donned a dangly gold earring. Combined with his mustache that ended in a pointed goatee, he knew he looked like Ming the Merciless.

"What's the matter, Fred?" Estrada said.

"You auditioning for a spaghetti western, Estrada?" Petrucchio said.

Estrada shot Petrucchio his middle finger, then removed his nylon flight jacket, exposing a red and white tropical-patterned shirt. His pants were faded fatigues and his black leather boots were well worn, but spit shined.

Hansen pointed out the location of Jackson's hideaway on a map. "Matt, why don't you provide a little background information on Jackson? A little color, so to speak," he said.

Matt told Estrada enough to make sure the pilot understood this would probably not be a walk in the park. "Jackson's paranoid about security," Matt said. "He'll have plenty of well-armed guards."

"Which means I won't be able to drop you on top of the target. You'll have to hoof it in."

"There are small farms in the area," Hansen said, "including one about a mile down the dirt road that services Jackson's place. It's been abandoned for years. I think that would be the best place to drop us. Any closer, and the chopper noise would give us away."

Estrada scratched his beard and studied the map. "How many miles to the site?"

"Ninety-five," Chris Ridgeway said.

"I got plenty of fuel," Jerry said. "Assuming we don't hit any headwinds or run into a storm. But we'll be pretty damned close to max load going in."

Matt said, "What about the—"

Hansen interrupted, "Anything else you want to know before we leave?"

"Nope," the pilot said. "Let's do it. I gotta go to my kid's confirmation tomorrow afternoon."

Matt moved from the barn in the direction of the hulking dark form of the helicopter. He thought it looked like a giant prehistoric bug. He remembered thinking the same thing so many times back in the Balkans. He moved to the stacks of equipment and weapons and lifted an AR-15 rifle and a pack. He concentrated on keeping his breathing steady, his heart rate even. He knew his hatred of Lonnie Jackson had already changed him, had burned a black spot on his soul. The only thing that would prevent that blackness from consuming him was getting Renee back.

Matt watched the others pick up their things and march to the aircraft. He turned to follow, when Hansen grabbed his arm.

"Jerry's a little cautious," Hansen said. "Don't worry—we'll be able to load everyone on the chopper for the return trip."

"Okay," Matt said. "But how come you didn't tell Jerry why we're going into Nicaragua? About Renee and Alani?"

"He's just the chauffeur. No point in getting him worried any more than necessary. And, if we're intercepted, he can claim he didn't know what we were up to."

Matt stopped and let Hansen precede him to the chopper. *Well, Matt*, he thought, *this is one for the* New England Journal of Medicine.

CHAPTER 59

Jackson drummed his fingers on the desk on either side of the computer keyboard. He chuckled at the way his dinner party had ended. That little Hawaiian chick had made a shamble of things. But he'd got what he wanted. The two women were scared shitless. He'd let Alani sweat it out for a while, then go in and do her.

He scratched his stomach and adjusted his position in the chair. He felt a stirring in his groin and promised himself he'd find out what Alani had to offer in no more than another five minutes. But he had to send an email message to his banker in Switzerland. He checked the time on the bottom of the computer screen: eleven thirty. The banks were just opening in Switzerland. He wanted to get a wire transfer acknowledgment from Gunther Richter before he enjoyed Alani. One hundred thousand dollars had to be transferred to Luis Reyes by the end of the business day tomorrow. Reyes would again grease the palms of appropriate Nicaraguan government officials. Jackson knew he could remain in the country only as long as the local politicos felt it was worth their while. He had to make the payments twice each year.

Jackson booted up his computer, inserted a flash drive into the hard drive, and pulled up his "Lorca Personal" folder. Inside the folder were several files, which were, in effect, dummy files. He opened the only viable file, the one titled "Retirement," which showed a three-column list. The first column had cryptic abbreviations of his banks; the second column included dollar amounts; and the third column listed his passwords on each account. He copied the account number and password for his Swiss bank account, opened his Internet account, and opened email. He then tapped out a message to Gunther Richter at the *Banque Unite des Alpes*: *This authorizes the immediate transfer of $100,000 US to Luis Reyes account number 0001789534, Banco Cardinale de Nicaragua*. He finished the message by adding his account number and password.

He placed the cursor on the "Send Now" icon and shot the message into cyberspace. He was about to shut down the computer when a noise burst from somewhere outside his office. Jackson's breath caught in his chest. He yanked open a desk drawer, pulled out a pistol, and leaped from his chair. He opened the office door, crouched, and moved into the hall, which was empty. He held the pistol in front of him in a two-handed grip. Then his heart vaulted to his throat when he saw light spilling from his bedroom—where Ricardo had taken Alani Maldonado.

Jackson moved quickly to his bedroom. He reached around the corner of the jamb and flicked off the overhead room light. Then he dove into the room, rolled, and came up beside a dresser, gun hand extended. The room was empty. The window was open and the screen had been removed.

He ran from the room and down the hall to Pratikan's room. Light seeped from under the door. He threw it open. Pratikan's blood-drained body lay pale and ghostly on the floor, surrounded by a darkly-stained carpet.

"Sonofabitch," Jackson growled. "Ricardo," he yelled. He ran back to his bedroom, grabbed the telephone receiver and pushed "14."

"Front Gate," the guard responded. "Is that you Ricardo? I'm ready for my turn with the women. When—?"

"Fuck the women!" Jackson shrieked into the phone. "Two of them have escaped. Where the hell are the guards who are supposed to watch the house?"

When the gate guard recognized his boss's voice, he babbled, "*Lo siente, Jefe. Yo no . . . .*"

"Shut up!" Jackson howled. "Pass the word. I want every man

out on the grounds. I want those women found. Do you hear me?" Jackson slammed down the receiver and rushed from the room.

CHAPTER 60

Eddie Parnell luxuriated in the cold air from the air conditioner vents of the Toyota SUV as it cruised the paved road out of San Juan del Norte. He figured he was about twenty miles from Lorca's place. The butterflies that bounced around inside his belly were old friends. Adrenaline always gave him the same feeling. And he always had the same tingling sensation just before he went into action. But, like a professional performer, the nervousness would disappear as soon as he went into his "act."

Parnell chuckled at the ridiculous terms the desk jockeys used to describe what he was about to do—"wet work," or "eliminate with extreme prejudice." *They read too many Ian Fleming novels*, he thought. "What a bunch of assholes," he said, "sitting in their Langley offices, their Yale diplomas conspicuously displayed, experiencing vicarious testosterone rushes from the orders they give guys like me."

The *brrring* of his cell phone knocked him off his introspective soapbox. Parnell snatched his phone out of the cup holder in the Toyota's console and looked at the screen: *Moreland. The worst of the lot*, he thought. *God save me from bluebloods with hormone deficiency.*

He swiped the "Answer" icon on the phone and said, "Yeah?"

"Moreland here."

Parnell wanted to laugh. 'Moreland here!' Jesus! "Whataya got?"

He could give a rat's ass about offending Moreland.

"Something wrong?" Moreland asked.

"No, everything's hunky-dory."

"I have information which you might find interesting." Moreland's voice seemed strained. "The target is more than a flesh peddler. His real name is Lawrence Jackson. Goes by the name of Lonnie. He had to provide fingerprints when he got his passport in Brazil. We received a copy of the print card. Some clerk ran them through the NCIC computers on a lark and hit the motherlode. Jackson's been on the run for a couple years. He was an organized crime bigwig in the Hawaiian Islands. He escaped the islands as the cops were about to bust up his operation. And get this: they think he had over one hundred million dollars stashed in overseas accounts."

"I thought crime didn't pay," Parnell said.

"Yeah, right. Anyway, Jackson's a mean sonofabitch. You need to go in there with extreme prejudice."

"I'm not familiar with that term. You want to explain it to me," Parnell said in a flat tone.

"It means . . . ." Moreland stopped. The line was silent for several seconds.

Parnell waited. *Maybe Moreland's wondering if I just made fun of him. Friggin' idiot.*

Moreland apparently chose to drop it. "We still can't find Lorca's . . . Jackson's attorney, Luis Reyes. Our man in Managua says he hasn't been in his office there for a couple weeks. And his office in San José is in shambles. But his files in both locations were full of all sorts of stuff, including information on several of his large American corporate clients. Lots of payola changing hands down there for the right licenses and government approvals. That information might come in handy down the road."

Parnell suddenly felt dirty. *What a way to spend a life,* he thought. *Digging up dirt on people and organizations. A place on the beach in the tropics is sounding better by the second.*

"Anything else?" Parnell asked.

"When do you expect to finish with your . . . business . . . down there?"

"Why? Am I on a schedule?" Parnell said, not bothering to

disguise his contempt.

"This is important, Parnell. I hope you understand that," Moreland hissed. He sounded worried and pissed off at the same time.

"Yeah, I understand." Then Parnell terminated the call.

CHAPTER 61

Earlier in the evening, Seymour Katzman called the CIA, used his National Security Identifier and password to establish his ID, and asked to talk to the duty officer. He requested the name of the CIA officer who ran the Tarnovsky operation. It was almost 11 p.m. when he called again, not having heard anything. He was put through to the same duty officer.

"Where's the name I asked you for nearly three hours ago?" Katzman demanded.

"We've tried to dig up that information, sir, but so far—"

"Listen to me, you fucking obstructionist," Katzman shouted. "Don't you stonewall me. How'd you like to be assigned to Equatorial Africa? I'll plant your ass so deep in Ebola country you'll hemorrhage from your eyeballs fifteen minutes after you arrive. And, by the way, that's all the time you've got to get me the name I asked for. Fifteen minutes!" He slammed the receiver down into the cradle so hard it amazed him the telephone didn't shatter.

The call came in seven minutes later. No salutation. Just a quick statement: "The section chief is Westcliffe Moreland. The field handler is Eddie Parnell." He provided cell phone numbers for each man. The caller then hung up.

Katzman called Parnell's number first. He figured a field man would be less likely to bullshit him. When he got no answer, he called Moreland.

"Hello."

"Westcliffe Moreland?" Katzman asked.

"Yeah, who's this?"

"Shut up and listen. You know the name Tarnovsky?"

There was a pause from the other end of the line. Then Moreland said in a dry, husky voice, "Uh, who, uh, is, uh, this?"

"I'll take your hesitation and nervousness as affirmation, Mr. Moreland. This is the president's national security advisor. I want to talk to you about Tarnovsky."

"I, uh, don't think—"

"Listen to me, asshole," Katzman rasped. "I want you parked outside the Georgetown Four Seasons Hotel in one hour. And my advice is you don't notify your boss about this telephone call. We'll have a nice, private conversation, Mr. Moreland. I don't think you want this thing to escalate any more than it has already. You understand?"

"Ye . . . yes."

"What do you drive?" Katzman demanded.

"Lexus. Silver."

Moreland pulled up to the Four Seasons Hotel at a few minutes before midnight. He'd committed a dozen traffic violations on the way there. He'd told himself that if a cop had stopped him, he would have shot the bastard and ripped out the camera recorder from the patrol car. Anything to keep from showing up late for his meeting with Katzman.

He sighed as he shut off his car. He was early and he hadn't had to murder anyone. He gripped the steering wheel, pressed his head against the headrest, and closed his eyes. His heart seemed to explode in his chest when the front passenger door flew open.

"Moreland?"

Moreland stared at the man who now sat across from him. He immediately recognized Katzman from television news. "Yes, sir."

"I want to know everything about this guy Tarnovsky," Katzman said.

Moreland was relieved he was seated. He didn't think his legs would have supported him. He suppressed a groan and swallowed, hoping his voice wouldn't betray him.

"I . . . I think I ought to ask you why you want to know," Moreland said, amazed that he got the words out.

Katzman glared at him and, for a moment, Moreland thought the man would react badly. In the light from the hotel's entrance, Katzman's face appeared red and his eyes looked as though they might pop from his skull. But then the man seemed to relax. "That's probably a good idea," he said.

By the time Katzman had related everything he'd learned from "a U.S. senator who shall remain nameless," Moreland wished he'd never asked for an explanation.

"Is this all true?" Katzman demanded.

Moreland couldn't make his vocal cords work, so he nodded and stuck a finger between his collar and neck and pulled at his shirt.

Katzman sat silently for half-a-minute. "You know where Tarnovsky's headquarters is?" he finally said.

Moreland nodded. "Outside Varna, near the Black Sea."

"That's a break. You still have a general inside the Turkish Air Force?"

"How did you—"

"Cut the crap, Moreland," Katzman shouted. "I know a whole lot more than you think. I also know you sleuths have U.S. and foreign military boys on your payroll."

Moreland thought he would have a heart attack.

"I want the coordinates of Tarnovsky's headquarters given to the best Turkish pilot you got. I think we can solve this problem very quickly. A pilot flying low over the water and using electronic countermeasures ought to be able to take out Tarnovsky and get back to base without being detected by radar. One smart bomb and your problem is over." Katzman made a motion with his arm that simulated a diving bomb.

Moreland wanted to be anywhere but in his car with Katzman at that moment. Then a thought hit him like an electric shock. He saw an opportunity to solve two problems at once. The White House and unnamed parties in Congress now knew about Tarnovsky. The only way to sanitize himself was to claim Parnell had put the whole Tarnovsky operation in place without his permission. But the only way that lie would stand up was if Eddie Parnell were no longer around to deny it.

"Mr. Katzman, the problem's bigger than just Tarnovsky."

Katzman's eyebrows peaked into two upside-down "V"s.

"Explain that."

"I just discovered Tarnovsky has a middle man in Nicaragua. Guy named Parnell works for me and he's gone rogue, in cahoots with the middleman. I tried to resolve the situation without the word getting out. I can see it's too late for that now."

Katzman seemed to consider what Moreland had said. "Do you know exactly where Parnell is located?"

"Yes, sir. On the Caribbean coast of Nicaragua, near a town called San Juan del Norte."

"Well, you might as well put one of your Panamanian pilots to work, too," Katzman said.

Katzman opened the car door. The courtesy light's glare caused Moreland to squint. Katzman was halfway out of the car when he glanced back. "Mr. Moreland, I warn you. If this . . . situation isn't handled satisfactorily by the time the president takes his morning piss, I'll see that you never hold a job in this country or anywhere there are indoor toilets."

Moreland gulped and bobbed his head.

DAY 9

CHAPTER 62

Parnell couldn't be sure of the exact distance from San Juan del Norte to Jackson's place. But based on the intelligence Moreland had provided, he had to be close. The sudden warm glow of lights that bathed the treetops in the distance was his first clue that he might be closer than he'd thought. He stopped and checked the odometer. He'd gone twenty-two miles. He hid the SUV in a field of ten-foot high sugarcane stalks, then felt a little stupid for doing so. *Who the hell would drive down this rutted trail at night other than some idiot from the CIA*, he thought.

Parnell opened the driver's side door and, in the SUV's overhead light, again inspected the pistol and rifle the guy at the airport in San José had provided. Parnell admitted that Moreland was adept at logistics and he was impressed with the weapons: a Steyr rifle—a Universal Army Rifle, which could be extended from sniper mode to machinegun—and a Steyr SPP, a pistol that resembled a submachine-gun. The SPP was a double action 9mm that came with two optional 30-round magazines. The rifle came with four magazines. Both weapons looked brand new. Their serial numbers had been filed away. The weapons package also included a double bladed, nine-inch knife and two stun grenades.

Parnell left the vehicle and headed toward the lights. He estimated he was a half-mile away from something, and hoped it was Lorca's place—*Jackson's place*, he reminded himself. He hated the idea of a half-mile trek through the jungle and then possibly discovering he was in the wrong place, and having to hike all the way back to the car. The humidity was nasty and the mosquitoes were already making a meal out of his arms and neck. "Bug repellent, you dumb ass," he muttered. "You should have brought bug repellent."

The road curved near the light source and appeared to then circle a homestead surrounded by jungle. Parnell heard men's voices coming from several directions, some fairly close to where he stood. They seemed to be calling to one another and sounded as though they were searching for someone. He hid in the trees and listened. The voices now seemed to move away from him.

He shrugged his way through thick foliage and made an effort to quietly move in the direction of the nearest voice. One hundred yards from the road, he saw the roofline of a large, single-story house. He moved through the jungle to the edge of a wide expanse of manicured lawn that extended to the house. The place was lit up like a Christmas tree; security lights bathed the building's exterior and the grounds. Light poured from nearly every window.

Parnell watched a tall, well-built man with a pistol in hand move into a shadow cast by a huge tree. The man faced away from Parnell toward a security fence on the far side of the lawn. Then two armed men ran up to him. The man with the pistol shouted something at them that Parnell couldn't make out, then the man turned, moved into a cone of light from a security lamp, and pointed toward the jungle where Parnell was now crouched behind a palm-like plant; his back pressed against a tree trunk. His heart pounded as he worried that he'd been spotted. Then he thought he recognized the man giving orders: Lawrence Jackson. The photo the man at the airport had given him turned out to be a good likeness, after all.

Jackson shouted in Spanish, "They may be inside the tree line."

The two men raced toward the tree line where Parnell was. Jackson seemed to stare right at Parnell.

The two men split up as they ran. One broke through the foliage ten feet from Parnell's right; the other penetrated the jungle twenty yards further away, also to his right.

Jackson had told his men, "They may be inside the tree line." *They're not looking for me,* Parnell thought. As the two men crashed through the jungle, Parnell's gaze followed Jackson until the man rounded a corner of the house.

The two men charged through the jungle like linebackers breaking through an offensive line, and they made about as much noise, too. They grunted and swore while they banged into and trampled bushes. Parnell waited until he couldn't hear them anymore, then stepped forward toward the lawn. He moved along the edge of the jungle, always ready to fade back behind the tree line, careful to stay out of range of the security lights.

Based on the shouts he heard, it appeared the main focus of the search was on the far side of the property, near the fence. Parnell saw the tops of thirty-foot-high trees in the distance.

He crouched and crept forward, in the direction of an outbuilding. There was an open, unlit stretch of ground between where he now stood and this building. He had an idea how he might be able to get Jackson to come to him. But he'd have to race across the clearing. Even in the shadows, an observant guard might see him. He slipped the rifle from his shoulder and held it at port arms. He steeled himself for the sprint across the open lawn, when a noise behind him made his heart stop. He fell to the ground and crawled back into the trees.

"*Shhh.*"

"We've got to get out of here," a woman said.

They moved in the direction of the road, away from Parnell, but toward the two men who had just passed him. *Bad for them,* Parnell thought.

He again broke from the trees and raced across the lawn, skirting the inside wall of what he thought might be stables. He waited for his heart rate and breathing to slow, then moved down a concrete corridor. He immediately saw that this was no stable. Cells lined both sides of the structure. *This must be where Jackson keeps the women,* he thought.

The building's roof was pitched. Above the tops of the cells were wooden rafters and a deck. It looked like a barn loft. From the smell of the place, there was stale straw still there, somewhere. Parnell found a ladder around the side of the last cell and climbed to the deck. A six-inch layer of moldy, stinking straw covered the entire deck.

Parnell climbed back down and searched the building. He found what he needed in a tiny cinder block-walled room on the back side of the building; a gasoline generator. The damned thing sounded like a Hell's Angels' convention. Parnell swiped a gas can off a shelf and ran back to the cellblock. He again climbed to the deck and tipped the gas can on its side, letting the fuel flow in an ever-widening pool that soaked the straw, which turned black as it absorbed the gas. The odor of the fuel made the rotted straw smell even worse than before.

Parnell laid the rifle down on the edge of the deck, took from a pocket an aluminum container the size of a lipstick tube, and unscrewed its lid. He shook out a blue-tipped kitchen match, replaced the lid, and struck the match across the abrasive container bottom. The match sparked, then gave off a bright yellow flame. Parnell tossed it in the middle of the sopping mess of gas-saturated straw and descended the ladder. A *whoosh* sounded above his head.

He ran back outside, returned to the generator room, and yanked on the fuel line between the generator and a fifty-five gallon drum of gasoline. He returned to the tree line and waited for the gas already in the generator's feed line to run out.

"*Incendio! Incendio!*" someone shouted a couple of minutes later.

First, one man rushed to the burning building, his arms flying about his head. Then three more ran up.

Parnell hid in the jungle cover and waited for Jackson to show. The Steyr would blow a hole in the guy that no surgeon could repair—and it was a long way from here to a hospital, anyway.

He didn't have to wait long. Jackson appeared and looked at the burning building. Parnell raised the rifle, trying to place the scope's crosshairs on his target's skull. But Jackson stepped behind one of his men and shouted, "Don't worry about the cells. They're a loss. Find the women."

Jackson stepped away from his men for an instant as one of them yelled, "But, *Jefe*, don't—"

Jackson stopped, rushed to the man, grabbed him, and swung him around by the front of his shirt. "No buts. I want those . . . ."

The man's head exploded like a smashed watermelon.

Parnell saw Jackson drop to the ground and crawl behind a tree. *What the . . .?* He hadn't fired. *Someone shot at Jackson.*

Jackson's men froze in place for a second, then dropped to the ground, too.

"Over there," Jackson screamed. "In the trees!"

The three men pointed their weapons toward the tree line and let loose with a barrage.

There was nothing Parnell could do but scurry behind a tree and plant himself on the ground. Rounds from the automatic weapons singed the air above and around him and shredded leaves and branches. The guards emptied their magazines in a few seconds. Parnell raised his head in time to see Jackson escape from behind the tree and run in a crouch around the far side of the house.

"Shit! Shit! Shit!" Parnell said under his breath. He ducked down again when the three men on the lawn had reloaded and fired again in his direction. He waited for the guards to again empty their magazines. Two seconds later, he shot one of the men through the top of the head. A second man took a round in the neck. When the last man wheeled to flee, Parnell shot him in the middle of the back.

The lights still illuminated the grounds and the house. He'd hoped the generator would have run out of fuel and quit by now, but he couldn't afford to wait any longer. Allowing Jackson to escape wasn't an option. About to follow Jackson, he hesitated. *Who fired at Jackson earlier? Do I dare leave the shelter of the jungle?*

Jackson looked over his shoulder as he approached a door to his house. Bodies littered the ground. The staccato burp of automatic weapons fire echoed in his ears. He kicked in the side door and sprinted down the hall to his bedroom. After he set down his "getaway" bag in the hall outside his bedroom, he hurried to his office. He'd left the computer on when he ran from the room earlier. He would erase everything in the hard drive. The only thing he really needed was the flash drive with the numbers and passwords of his overseas accounts.

Jackson ejected the flash drive, slipped it into his shirt pocket, and began deleting files from the hard drive.

"Sort of like Nero, don't you think?" a woman said in a slightly Slavic accent. "Fiddling with the computer while your home burns." She laughed. "Hands up. Turn around."

Jackson raised his hands when he heard the metallic sound of a pistol slide slam into position. He swiveled around in his chair and saw one of the Bulgarians he'd bought from Tarnovsky. He focused on the cold look in her eyes and then the steady, confident way she held the pistol. This was no innocent woman flimflammed with the promise of a pissant overseas job. And then it hit him. *I've been set up. Fucking Tarnovsky.*

"How much did that pig Tarnovsky pay you?" Jackson asked as he slowly lowered his arms.

She smiled. "One hundred thousand dollars."

"How much to buy out his contract?"

The question didn't seem to surprise her. "What did you have in mind?" she asked.

"How about half-a-million dollars?"

Her eyes went wide, but she quickly regained her composure. "It seems to me that if your first offer is five hundred thousand, you would more than likely double that number."

Jackson smiled back at her and shook his head from side to side. "I think you drive a hard bargain. But it appears I am not in a very good bargaining position at the moment."

But then the woman's face turned hard as stone; her mouth set in a grim line. "Ah, but this is all hypothetical. You surely don't have one million in cash lying around, and I don't think I'll take a check." She raised her arm an inch and zeroed the pistol at Jackson's face.

Jackson threw up his hands, palms out. "I can send an email message to a bank right from here," he said, more than a little tension in his voice. "I'll send an order to transfer one million dollars to your account anywhere in the world."

She hesitated. "And how will I know the money is actually transferred?"

"Easy," he answered, warming to her question, seeing a chance she might not put a bullet in his brain. "My banker will send an email confirmation message back to me. Then all you have to do is call your bank and confirm the money transfer."

She tilted her head to the side and rested an index finger against her temple. After several seconds, her arm went rigid. She pointed the pistol at the computer screen. "Do it."

Parnell went from room to room along the exterior wall of the house. All the lights were on. A couple of the rooms' windows were open and the screens had been knocked out. Swarms of insects had invaded the rooms and attacked the light fixtures. But, so far, all the rooms were unoccupied.

A different glow came from a room twenty feet away, near a corner of the building. He crouched down and moved to the edge of that room's window. The bluish glow of a computer terminal generated eerie light. A woman stood with her back to the window. He recognized Jackson seated at the computer, tapping the keys. The woman moved closer to Jackson and turned slightly. Parnell saw the pistol in her hand.

Jackson pulled a red flash drive from his pocket and inserted it into the computer. He played with the mouse and the screen came alive with letters and numbers.

The scene playing out in front of him intrigued Parnell, but he'd been in this damned jungle location too long already. He didn't need to hang around to satisfy his curiosity. He pulled the Steyr SSP from the holster on his hip and lifted it to the window—just when the room was thrown into darkness. The generator had finally run out of juice.

Parnell fired the pistol at the spot where Jackson had been seated. He put five rounds into the room and prayed that he'd hit the man. Then he ran as fast as he could to the nearest door. He stepped into a hall that led to the part of the house where Jackson and the woman had been and, arms extended, pistol at the ready, moved to that room. The sound of breaking glass came from the opposite side of the house, then shots were fired.

Parnell found the room he'd shot up. He stumbled over a waste basket, but caught his balance and moved to where he thought the desk was located. The desk chair was empty. No bodies on the floor. About to leave the room, he stopped and, more from instinct than reason, felt around the face of the hard drive and yanked out the flash drive. He thought, as he pocketed the drive, *God forbid, if Jackson escapes, maybe there's something on the flash drive that will help me track down the guy.*

He found a room where it appeared someone had taken a header through a closed window. Shards of glass still hung from the window frame, but most of the glass lay outside on the grass. Parnell saw the reflection of moonlight on the broken pieces.

This has turned into the disaster of the century, he thought.

Matt watched the helicopter's altimeter from the co-pilot's seat while Jerry Estrada piloted the chopper just above the jungle canopy. He took his eyes off the instrument panel and peered through the helicopter's window. There appeared to be a large mass ahead.

"My God, what the hell is that?" he asked.

"*Volcán Irazú*," Estrada said. "The Irazú Volcano. It's dead, but it sure looks ominous."

"Can you get enough altitude out of this bird to get us over the damn thing?"

Estrada laughed. "No sweat," he said as he pulled back on the collective and gained altitude.

Matt looked out the window and tried to pick out the volcano crater, but it was too dark and they now flew inside clouds. It was like flying inside a whiffle ball. Nothing but white and a few patches of something—maybe treetops—every once in a while. When he sensed that the aircraft was descending, he looked outside. The jungle was once again visible and the moon was almost full.

Matt looked over his shoulder into the cargo bay. Esteban and Ridgeway were asleep, their heads against their packs. Petrucchio reassembled his rifle—with his eyes closed. Hansen had a flashlight pointed at a map he'd spread on the floor. Then Estrada's voice came over the speaker.

"Five minutes to drop zone."

Matt felt a flutter in his stomach. The last time he'd heard those words he was about to jump out of a perfectly good airplane over a Serbian valley on a HALO. He never liked jumping out of an airplane, but high altitude, low opening jumps terrified him. Estrada's announcement had taken him back to a time he would have just as soon forgotten. Thank God this aircraft would land. No more parachutes for him.

Matt unbuckled his seat belt and climbed between the seats to join the others.

Esteban stirred and rubbed his hands over his face, smearing the black and green camouflage grease he had put there earlier. He smiled at Matt. "Just like old times, hey Matthew?"

Matt nodded. "Better poke Chris."

The helicopter swooped down on a section of jungle that looked from the air to be impenetrable. Then Matt saw a bright light on the horizon.

"Something's on fire," he shouted over the noise of the rotors.

Estrada shouted, "I see it. It's got to be right where we're headed. Something's already happening down there boys. Better hold onto something."

The sound of the helicopter's revving engine filled the cargo space. Estrada brought his ship in fast. He found a flat landing site and set the chopper down with a thud. Matt threw open the cargo bay door and jumped into a sea of six-foot-high saw grass that undulated with the rotor wind. He gazed out at the perimeter and looked for movement, while the other men leaped from the aircraft. They waited until the rotors had died.

Hansen rasped, "On me." When they had all congregated around him, Hansen sprinted away from the chopper.

They ran to a dirt road three hundred yards from the LZ. The light in the night sky caused by the fire provided a heading and they headed in that direction. Like a ten-legged creature, the five men moved at the same steady pace and quickly covered the distance to what Matt prayed was the right location, where he'd find Renee and Alani. Alive.

Hansen raised a hand when they were close to the objective and the team stopped and spread out in the tree lines on both sides of the dirt track. They remained still for nearly a minute, allowed their breathing to settle down, and listened. Hansen moved back to the road and raised his arm. But instead of waving them forward, he jerked his hand back down and disappeared back inside the jungle.

A couple seconds passed before Matt heard what Hansen had

apparently heard: men's voices. The men, sounding agitated, were fast coming closer.

"*Es muy malo,*" one of the men said. "*Primero, las culitas se escapan, después el fuego, y ahora oímos tiros.*"

A second voice hissed, "*Cállate, pendejo! Y ojo a las culitas!*"

Two men moved down the center of the road. They wore jeans and white t-shirts. Matt put his head down; his half-closed eyes peered out from under the brim of his jungle cap. He and Esteban were on the left side of the road; Hansen, Petrucchio, and Ridgeway on the other side. When the two men passed the spot where Matt hid, he expelled a slow stream of air.

"What did those two say?" Matt asked Esteban.

Esteban leaned down and whispered, "They mentioned something about women escaping, a fire, then shooting. Apparently, those two were sent out here to try to find the women."

"Maybe Renee and Alani got away," Matt said.

"Yeah, maybe," Esteban said.

Hansen walked over to Petrucchio. "Cover our backs," he said, as he pointed at the tree line. "In case those two men return."

Petrucchio nodded and melted back into the trees.

Hansen then led the others up to a spot where the road curved. He pointed at a guard shack fifty yards further up the road and hand-signaled the others to stay put. He turned and, hugging the tree line, walked toward the guard shack.

A minute went by, then another. Finally, a low whistle sounded and the team took off at double-time. A man lay on the floor of the guard shack. He looked unconscious and was trussed up like a calf at a rodeo. His mouth was taped.

Hansen led the group down a narrow drive. They had traveled about a quarter of a mile, when the sharp report of a branch breaking on the left side of the drive stopped them.

Matt drifted into the jungle to investigate. Esteban followed. Then another sharp noise sounded. A couple seconds later, breathless female voices carried to where Matt had stopped. They sounded as though they were running, crashing through the underbrush.

He poked Esteban, crooked a finger at him, then moved to intercept the women. Esteban followed Matt in a circling movement.

They took up positions behind two trees and waited.

The women seemed to be panicked, running blindly in the darkness. The canopy was so thick that no moonlight penetrated the treetops.

Matt could hear their labored breathing from several yards away. He rested his rifle against the base of the tree.

The women ran in file. They broke from a thick grouping of bushes into the clearing between the two trees.

Matt pushed off the tree when the first woman approached him. He wrapped an arm around her chest and pressed his other hand over her mouth. "*Shhh*," he ordered as he dragged, the woman back behind the tree. He saw Esteban grab the second woman. The one Matt held seemed to relax for a moment, although her chest heaved. Then she kicked her heels at his shins, tried to stomp on his feet. Then she shot her head back against his face and connected with his mouth.

Matt slammed the woman to the jungle floor and dropped on top of her. He heard the air rush from her lungs and then she gasped for air. Matt didn't know if someone had been chasing the women, but if someone was, they would surely hear the ruckus the woman made. He put his mouth against the woman's ear and whispered, "I'm American. I'm here to find my wife."

The woman suddenly went still, but she groaned loudly while she tried to get her breath. She said something, but with Matt's hand over her mouth it just came out as gibberish. Matt slowly removed his hand.

"*Amerikanska?*" she whispered.

The woman's accent shocked Matt. *My God, she sounds Russian*, he thought. "*Russki?*" he asked.

"No," the woman took in a deep breath. "No *Russki*," she spat. "Bulgaria."

"Both of you?" Matt said.

"*Da.*"

Matt stood and pulled the woman to her feet. He retrieved his rifle, walked to where Esteban held the other woman, who now sobbed.

"Are there other women here?" Matt asked, his breath and heart beat on hold as he waited for an answer.

"*Da*," the woman said. "Much womans."

"How many?"

"Four from Bulgaria womans. Me. That one is Anna. Two more in jungle. Two Nicaragua womans, and two *Amerikanska*."

Matt felt his heart jolt and his breath come in gulps. He gripped the woman's arm. "Where are the other women?" The sudden look of pain in her face made him realize he was hurting her and quickly released her arm.

She shook her head. "I not know." She waved her arm as though to indicate they could be anywhere. "In jungle. Mans are chasing them."

CHAPTER 63

One minute, Renee and Alani ran from Jackson's house with the Bulgarian woman, Tatiana. The next minute, Tatiana had disappeared. Renee looked around the yard, but she couldn't see the woman anywhere. Then Renee took Alani's hand. "We've got to find a place to hide until it's light. Then maybe we can find a way out of here."

Renee instinctively sought out the darkest area to flee to. The fire in the cellblock lit up the front part of the property. The jungle in the back seemed to be the logical place to hide. As they skirted the back of the house, she thought she'd have a heart attack when a pair of enormous Rottweilers launched themselves at the chain-link enclosure she and Alani ran past.

"Oh my," she exhaled. She ran to the edge of the jungle where it met the end of the lawn but found a high fence all along the back of the yard. It was topped with barbed wire and too high to scale, anyway.

They followed the fence line until it turned back toward the house. Renee stopped abruptly and whispered, "We can't go back there."

But Alani gasped and whispered, "Look."

There was a gate built into the fence. Renee took off toward the gate. An open padlock lay on the ground; the gate was open about a foot. She opened the gate wide enough to slip through. When Alani had followed her, Renee shut the gate. They fast-walked down a dirt path just wide enough to allow a car to pass and followed it into the jungle. The path went straight for two hundred yards, past a large pond that reflected the thin moonlight, then suddenly narrowed and became little more than a footpath. Piles of dead plants and trees had been piled intermittently on both sides of the path.

Renee had operated on nothing but pure adrenaline for hours. She felt exhausted. She stumbled, then fell on her knees into the damp earth. Alani dropped beside her, arms clutching her stomach, her chest heaving.

"We should get off the path and hide," she said. "I can't go another step."

Renee stood and brushed dirt off her dress. She pulled dirt clogs from her sandals. "Okay," she said.

Jackson raged. Everything he'd worked for was going down the drain. He knew he should go back to his office, to retrieve the computer flash drive. *But someone shot at me? What if that person is still watching the house?* A soft, undulating rosy glow seemed to paint everything around him as a voice pounded inside his brain: *Find Renee Curtis. Kill her! She's responsible for Mama's death. For Johnny's death.*

Jackson howled like a primordial beast. The rosy glow became brighter, more intense. He heard his mother's voice again, begging him to avenge her death. He ran to the room where the two American women had dressed for dinner. He found their old clothes in a corner and snatched up a blouse. Then he sprinted down the hall, out of the house, and toward the burning cellblock. He ignored the flying embers and crashing timbers. He put the danger of being shot out of mind.

Jackson saw two of his men in the yard. "Come with me," he shouted. He didn't look to see if they obeyed. He just ran until he reached the kennel.

"Come, Thor," he said, while he opened the kennel gate latch. "Good boy, Atlas."

The dogs whimpered; their tailless rear ends gyrated. They pushed their shoulders against Jackson. It was all he could do to keep from being knocked over. After the animals settled down, Jackson took the blouse and shoved it against their noses, allowing them to pick up a scent. He rubbed it over them. "Find," he said. "Kill!"

The Rottweilers raced across the yard in serpentine patterns, their noses to the ground. They huffed and snuffled, intersecting one another's paths. Finally, one of them appeared to pick up a trail along the perimeter fence. Its howl brought over the second animal. They raced along the fence line and stopped at the closed gate.

By the time Jackson caught up to the dogs, they were leaping at the fence. He opened the gate and Thor and Atlas bounded through it. They were out of sight within seconds. But Jackson saw the direction they had taken. Straight down the dirt path into the jungle. He ran so fast after the dogs that he left his men behind. Where the path narrowed, he looked back to see how far behind his men were. "This way," he yelled.

Matt and Esteban led the two Bulgarian women to within a couple of yards of the path where they'd left Hansen and Ridgeway.

"Stay here," Matt said. "We'll be back for you."

One of the women grabbed his hand. "No, please, not leave us."

"It's okay," Matt said. "I promise. We'll be back. Stay low and don't make a sound. You'll be fine."

Matt and Esteban then broke through the tree line to the path and joined the others.

"Two women," Matt whispered. "There are six more running around in the jungle. There are armed men looking for them."

"Okay," Hansen said. "Let's go in a little farther, then we can decide who covers what."

They jogged down the drive, until they came within sight of a burning building off to the left and a large house on the right. An expanse of yard ran between the buildings and seemed to terminate where it met the jungle.

Eddie Parnell had seen enough. This thing was way beyond the point of being a screw-up. Now there were paramilitary types on the scene. He watched four men dressed in fatigues, their faces smeared with camouflage paint, run down the drive. He decided the rules of the game had changed and no one had bothered to share the new rules with him. He sighed and remembered the old saying: sometimes you take two steps forward and one step back. He felt that this mission had been more like one step forward and two steps back. He retreated into the trees on the front side of the house and became one with the jungle. He was confident he'd be able to retrace his way back to the road and the field where he'd left the SUV. He knew Moreland would give him a bunch of crap about not accomplishing his mission, but Parnell didn't give a shit. He was finished with the Agency.

The jungle now seemed almost peaceful. The fire had nearly burned out and voices no longer careened through the trees. He quietly worked his way toward the road. Just ahead, he saw the brown ribbon of moonlight-highlighted road. And then the world seemed to spin away in a confused, topsy-turvy way. He felt himself fall and his skull suddenly felt as though he'd been headbutted by a Brahma bull. Then, there was only blackness.

Tatiana Borodvic turned the man over and stepped to the side so that what little moonlight seeped through the jungle canopy could shine on his face. "*Dupa*," she said under her breath. "Not Jackson." She leaned to get a closer look at the man's face. He didn't look Hispanic. The side of his head bled where she'd hit him with the pistol. "Bad luck, *señor*," she whispered, then turned around and looked back in the direction of Jackson's house. With all the lights out, she couldn't be sure of the exact location, but the acrid odor of burned wood and wiring drifted from the west. She figured the house was in that direction. The thought crossed her mind that maybe she should cut her losses and get the hell out of there. But she knew if she didn't kill Jackson, she'd never collect the one hundred thousand dollars Tarnovsky had promised her.

She groaned at the thought of the one million dollars Jackson had offered her. But then she told herself, just be glad you're still alive. It was a miracle that whoever shot up Jackson's office hadn't hit her. Thank goodness for quick reflexes. Well, at least she'd collect from Tarnovsky . . . if she found Jackson. Without that money, she'd be just another out-of-work woman with nothing to fall back on but her looks and what pleasure she could sell to a man. She had to go on.

Parnell felt disoriented and his head throbbed as though snakes were trapped inside it and fought to get out. He opened his eyes and saw a shadowy form. He rubbed his eyes to clear his vision. A woman stood over him. A very tall woman. Had she knocked him out? Her back was turned to him. She appeared to stare back through the jungle, toward where he had come from. Then she suddenly moved away.

He got to his feet, fought off a wave of nausea, found his pistol that he'd fallen on, and followed the woman. Parnell was pissed off. It was bad enough he hadn't got Jackson, but now a damn woman had tried to take him out of the game. That just wouldn't do.

He mimicked the cadence of the woman's steps. His footfalls matched hers. He was about to rush her when she stepped inside the trees and disappeared. He followed but couldn't spot her. *Sonof—*

Something slammed into his right wrist. His pistol flew from his grip. He whipped around and ducked a fist that came at his head. The woman brought up her weapon. He chopped at her wrist, knocked the weapon from her hand, then twisted around and struck at her with his elbow. She danced away from the blow and went into a bent-knee stance. She moved slowly, cautiously toward him.

Parnell lowered his center of gravity and spread his legs just wide enough to give himself a more stable base. He anticipated that her first strike would be with her leg—probably the right one since her weight appeared to be predominantly on her left leg. This was a well-trained opponent.

The woman side-kicked at his throat, a strike intended to crush his larynx. He stepped away, then struck at the inside of her knee with the sole of his boot. Then he dropped down to his hands, and attacked her standing leg with a sweeping leg kick. Her base now destroyed, her one leg, he knew, now numb, it was a simple matter to finish the job. From a kneeling position, she attempted to rise on her one good leg. He slammed a quick punch to her stomach, then drove a fist into her head. The woman went limp and fell forward in the jungle grime.

Parnell turned her over. Her face was smudged with dirt and wet leaves stuck to it. Blood leaked from a scalp wound over her left temple, where he'd punched her. There was also blood on the front of her blouse. He pulled the blouse off her shoulder and saw a blood-soaked cloth wedged under the top of her bra. He lifted the cloth and saw a wound.

Ah, what the hell, he thought. *I can't leave her here in the jungle for the wild animals.* After he retrieved his pistol and pocketed it, he grabbed one of the woman's arms, pulled her into a sitting position, and hefted her onto his shoulder. Then he marched toward the road. *I can't wait to hear this gal's story.*

CHAPTER 64

The F-16 took off from the Turkish Air Base near Izmit, at the eastern end of the Sea of Marmara. It flew north, over the village of Agva and across the 42nd parallel, climbed to dizzying heights, then turned westward toward the Bulgarian coast. Twenty miles from the city of Varna, the pilot checked the coordinates in his missile guidance system.

He pressed the firing switch on two missiles armed with high explosive warheads. With the missiles away, the pilot leaned on the stick and brought his aircraft around on a screaming, G-pulling turn and raced back to his base.

"Just a walk in the park," he muttered.

A second jet took off from a base near Colón, Panama, headed north into the Caribbean, then made a slow turn toward land. Flying low, it skirted the territorial waters of both Costa Rica and Nicaragua. Thirty miles from San Juan del Norte, Nicaragua, the pilot unleashed two missiles, then returned to base. The entire mission took no more than thirty minutes.

Both jets' missiles had what were termed "smart systems." But, in reality, they were nothing but metal alloy spears loaded with high explosive that slaved to targets a specialist at Langley had given to two pilots on different sides of the world.

The missiles followed their inexorable paths of destruction, providing no warning to their intended victims. The two from the Turkish jet struck the roof of Yevgeni Tarnovsky's palatial residence outside Varna. One plunged through the ceiling and detonated a split second later. The other burst through the front wall, incinerating the front half of the structure. Yevgeni Tarnovsky shattered into charred pieces of flesh and bone. The *rakir* he'd just poured vaporized.

Westcliffe Moreland exhaled a sign of relief when the call came in from Izmit. Half his problem had been obliterated. He'd be in the clear once he heard from the Panamanian general in Colón. He thought about what he would do as soon as Parnell was no longer a threat. *I'll see to it that Parnell's parents receive his government insurance benefits. His retirement account will go to his ex-wife. And, of course, I'll send a letter to each survivor telling them what a hero Parnell was.*

A warm, fuzzy feeling washed over him as he wondered if Seymour Katzman would remember and reward him for his service to his country.

Renee and Alani staggered down the narrow dirt path, in search of a hiding place. But, as exhausted as they were, Renee did not relish the idea of leaving the trail and going into the jungle. Alani seemed to understand and stumbled along beside her without complaint.

They supported one another as they went along the path, deeper into the jungle. Then Renee saw something ahead and moved off the path. She and Alani knelt on the ground and peeked out from the trees. Then clouds moved away from the face of the moon and light shone on a two-foot wide, rope footbridge. The thunderous roar of fast-flowing water carried to her.

Renee helped Alani to her feet. "Come on, Alani," she said. They moved back onto the path to the bridge. Renee looked down and saw a roiling river at the bottom of a gorge.

Renee looked at Alani and saw fear in her wide-open eyes. She knew exactly how her friend felt as she watched the bridge sway in the breeze above the chasm. She was about to suggest they leave the path there and hide in the jungle, after all, when the chilling sound of barking dogs filled the night. The walls of the jungle along the path seemed to funnel the noise straight at them and Renee's fear ratcheted to a level that made her, momentarily, feel stunned and paralyzed. She looked into Alani's face and, in a weak, shaky voice, said, "We've got to do this."

She released Alani's hand and stepped onto the swaying structure. She suppressed the fear that had a moment earlier seemed to turn her insides to stone and moved forward. Her hands gripped the rope supports. She carefully stepped onto the cross boards. She stopped for a second to look back and was relieved to see that Alani followed.

Suddenly, the barking dogs seemed closer.

"Go! Go! Go!" Alani yelled.

Her lungs close to bursting, the muscles in her thighs and calves on fire, Renee knew she couldn't go much farther. Her hands felt like thorns had penetrated them. The fibers from the bridge's rope supports had bloodied her palms.

As she approached the end of the bridge, Renee noticed that the path on the far side split. One path went straight ahead; the other branched downward to the left. Renee staggered off the bridge and stopped at the juncture, her chest heaving.

"I can't go on, Renee," Alani gasped.

The dogs' deep-throated howls sounded as though they came from just across the bridge. She hoped the dogs wouldn't cross the footbridge. Renee twisted first one way then the other. She felt too frantic to think, too tired to move.

"*Aquí, señoras,*" a woman said from the left path. "*Rápido!*" the woman rasped.

"Where are you?" Renee called out in a hoarse whisper.

A short, dark-skinned young woman stepped from the cover of the tree line and reached for Renee's arm. She wrapped both her hands around Renee's wrist and pulled her back off the path. Renee snagged Alani's hand with her other hand.

The vegetation seemed to be made up of large-leafed plants that covered small areas of the jungle floor, and clusters of tall, thin trees that grew as high as sixty feet. The young woman ducked under a dead fungus and moss-covered tree that lay three feet above the ground. Renee and Alani followed her into a shelter formed by a thick canopy of foliage. Two other women huddled together in a space not much larger than a bathroom stall.

When the dogs' howls penetrated the shelter, she knew she had done these women no favors.

Alani collapsed to the ground. Renee looked at her and saw the whites of her eyes. Renee felt so tired, so defeated that, for an instant, she contemplated dropping to the jungle floor and giving up. She drew in a deep breath, let it out slowly, and steeled herself for what she had to do. She crouched under the dead tree at the shelter entrance, ran back toward the trail, and screamed as loudly as she could.

She heard Alani's plaintive, "Renee, no!" Then all she heard were the dogs. Renee ran with energy she didn't think she had. She raced down the sloping dirt path. Her legs churned like pistons as she concentrated on drawing the dogs as far from the other women as possible.

The trail paralleled the gorge they had crossed earlier. The roaring sound of rapids came from somewhere ahead. Maybe, if she could reach the water, she might be able to elude the dogs. She tried to extend her stride, but her hamstrings suddenly cramped. Sweat poured from her forehead, stung her eyes, clouded her vision.

A bright light suddenly flashed from behind her, illuminating the sky. Thunder crashed. She tried to make sense of it, but her tired mind couldn't deal with more input. It was the dogs she had to focus on.

The roar of the river was now intense. She knew she was closer to it. She glanced back over her shoulder and felt a fear so primal that an Arctic-like chill seemed to freeze her spine. Lightning split the sky and backlit four yellow eyes behind her. Not more than fifty feet away. Then pain jolted her brain. Her right leg buckled and she went down in a rolling heap, a sandal gone. She tried to come up off the ground, to prepare herself to fight off the dogs. Like two demons, they drove toward her. And then the heavens seemed to crash down.

The missiles fired by the F-16 from over the Caribbean had homed in on Lonnie Jackson's property. One hit the cells and spewed high explosive and propellant over a large area. Although the ground where the projectile impacted absorbed most of the explosion's force, enough flammable material spread to the residence and set its roof on fire. It didn't take long for the fire to spread to the structure's interior.

The second missile hit seconds after the first one landed. But this one missed the residence completely. The missile hit the target it had been programmed to hit. But the programmer had made a slight error. Instead of targeting Jackson's house, it landed fifteen feet from the footbridge. It struck with a mighty detonation, then sent a rolling fireball into the air. The fireball lifted above the bridge, then drifted with the prevailing wind down the ravine. Acres of virgin jungle were incinerated, along with several species of insects, mammals, and birds. The missile created a five-foot deep crater, spewed fire in its path, and set the bridge ablaze.

Jackson covered his head with his arms as he backed away from the bridge. He could no longer hear the dogs and looked on with growing rage while fire turned his bridge into a burning, crackling disaster. One by one, the ropes snapped and then the structure broke loose and fell below the rim of the ravine.

"Sonofa . . .!" *I had her. She was as good as dead. Maybe the dogs* . . . . He let the thought hang in the damp, smoke-filled tropical air. His ears rang from the detonation. Then he saw a movement on the far side of the chasm. He drew his pistol and glanced over his shoulder to order his men to aim their weapons across the chasm. But the men weren't there. "Bastards!" he cursed.

He returned his gaze to the far side of the chasm. Was it the dogs he'd seen? Maybe it was the Curtis woman. If it was her, he'd shoot her. He waited while a filmy cloud of smoke and the last particles of dirt and debris drifted away. His finger tensed on the trigger. It was a long shot for a pistol, but he had the weapon braced in both hands. He could do it. He had to do it.

The smoke had nearly cleared when Jackson heard a whimper. First one dog, then the other showed itself across the gorge. They approached the edge of the chasm and looked down into space.

Jackson thought, *It won't be long before the leopards make a meal of Atlas and Thor.* He walked away. He had to go back to the house for the flash drive. It was his key to accessing one hundred thirty-seven million dollars in thirteen different banks in ten different countries—his future.

Renee couldn't control her emotions any longer. The dogs had been there. Almost on top of her. Then the tremendous explosions and the fire in the sky. As frightened as she felt, the Rottweilers had appeared to be traumatized. They'd skidded to a stop and looked uncertain about what to do—kill or run. They'd circled one another, seemingly looking to the other for confidence, for direction. Then the dogs had run back the way they'd come, leaving Renee limp, an emotionally wasted husk. Sobs wracked her body and she shook as though it were ten degrees there in the jungle.

She hugged her legs to her chest and wailed one word, over and over: "Matthew! Matthew!" She cried for the solace and protection of her husband's arms. Then the sounds of movement came to her and her heart leaped. Had the dogs returned? She looked up and saw Alani running toward her, with the other women trailing close behind.

CHAPTER 65

Matt dove into a muddy depression by the side of the driveway. His heart felt as though it had grown too big for his chest. His ears felt stuffed with cotton. Sound had become less sharp. An explosion had shaken the earth and lit up the sky.

"Felt like a mortar," Ridgeway exclaimed.

"I've never seen any damn mortar create that kind of fireball, unless it had hit an ammo dump or fuel storage," Hansen said. "That was a rocket or missile."

The air was full of debris. Matt regained his feet and covered his mouth and nose with a handkerchief. The shock of the first detonation had barely passed when a second explosion occurred, this time deep in the jungle, on the far side of the property.

The second blast sent up an incredible fireball that reminded Matt of napalm bombs dropped by jets in the Balkans. The fire was red and yellow, etched with black, and it tumbled over and over while it grew bigger and bigger and backlit the jungle. Trees that had been nothing but dark, indistinct monoliths a moment earlier were now as clear as though it were daylight. Then, trees and bushes burst into flames. Matt watched the inferno build to a fiery crescendo, then begin to dissipate. After fifteen minutes, the only traces of the explosions were acrid chemical odors and burning vegetation, a fine mist of smoke and dirt, and the temporary imprint of the fireball on the lenses of his eyes. He waited for more bombs to drop.

After a minute, Hansen pushed off the ground and whispered, "Did you notice the dirt trail into the jungle on the far side of the lawn? That fireball lit it up like a searchlight."

"Yeah. Straight back through the trees," Esteban said.

"Esteban, you and Chris check out the house," Hansen said. "Matt and I will follow the trail. Meet back here in fifteen minutes. Be careful, everybody. There's got to be . . . ."

"*Sshh*—listen." Matt hissed.

The others froze.

"Did you hear that?" he said. "Did you hear a woman calling out?" He looked at Hansen who wore a sorrowful expression.

"Sorry," Hansen said, "I didn't hear anything." He patted Matt on the arm. "We'd better move."

Matt knew he'd heard something. He'd heard Renee's voice in his dreams last night. The dreams had jolted him awake. But this was no dream. He thought he'd just heard her call him.

Esteban and Ridgeway jogged off toward the residence.

Hansen set off at quick time with Matt trailing. He ran down the last twenty yards of the driveway, then cut across the lawn to where the dirt path began. They'd reached the tree line on the far side of the property, when Hansen suddenly pulled up and moved off the path, into the trees. Matt followed. They'd scarcely found cover, when two armed men wearing jeans and t-shirts charged up the trail past them, running as though the devil himself chased them.

"They looked like they'd seen a ghost," Hansen said.

"I suspect it was the explosion in the jungle that scared them," Matt said.

Hansen edged out of the tree line and took a step toward the path when the report of a pistol sounded. He clutched his right arm as he dropped to the ground.

"Dammit," he groaned. "Dammit."

Matt leaped to the path, grasped the back of Quince's fatigue shirt, and dragged him back behind the cover of the trees. Another shot, and then the crack of a branch very close behind him. Matt unslung his AR-15 from his shoulder and fired across the path, in the direction from which he thought the shots had come. He heard a few seconds of movement in the jungle on the other side of the path. Then all was quiet. Matt dropped beside Hansen and said, "You okay?"

"Yeah, as soon as I stop the bleeding."

Matt used his handkerchief to tightly bind Hansen's arm above the wound. When the bleeding slowed, he tapped Hansen's chest. "I'm going after the guy. Why don't you use the radio to contact the others?"

Hansen reached to his belt for the radio and said, "Shit. It must have fallen off when I was shot." He groaned and muttered, "I should have given everyone on the team a radio." Then he snagged Matt's arm. "Be careful," he said. "Don't forget the concussion grenades. You hear anything, open up with the 16."

Matt crawled on his belly to the edge of the trees and scanned for movement on the path. Nothing. He peered back toward the house and realized the reason the shooter got off such an accurate shot was because they were silhouetted against the glow from flames dancing on the roof of the main building. Matt moved back inside the right tree line and worked his way through the jungle. He planned to move down the tree line about fifty yards and then cross over the path to the far tree line, hoping to flank the man who had shot at them. He'd gone about twenty-five yards when he heard footfalls to his right. The shooter had apparently flanked him.

Matt lowered himself to the ground and removed a grenade from his belt. He rolled onto his back, popped the grenade's arming handle pin, and then remained perfectly still while he held the handle in place. One sound was all he needed. But no sounds came, other than insects chittering and a monkey howling. Matt knew that in this little cat and mouse game, he was both hunter and hunted.

Then Matt heard rustling in the bushes. His heart tap-danced in his chest. He lobbed the grenade, rolled over on his stomach, and covered his ears with his hands. The grenade ripped through the stillness and sent a shock wave back toward him. Then he rose to one knee and opened fire with the M-16. He quickly ejected the now-empty magazine, reloaded, and waited.

Jackson felt as though someone had clapped two big hands over his ears. His head felt like the inside of a kettledrum. He wanted to scream in agony, but the fusillade of bullets that stitched the jungle around him convinced him otherwise.

He froze in place on the jungle floor. Apparently, that's what the other guy had done, as well. Finally, he heard movement and listened as someone's footfalls faded away in the near distance.

Matt rejoined Hansen. "You okay?"

"Shit, yes," Hansen answered in a hoarse whisper, his teeth clenched, one hand over his wounded arm.

"Good. I don't know if I hit the guy, but I suspect he's lying low." Matt helped Hansen stand, then gripped his elbow.

"Don't look at me like you're my mother," Hansen said. Then he shot a smile at Matt.

Matt returned the smile, then turned and moved quietly toward the path. He looked left and right, then back to make sure Quince was with him. He moved out of the tree line and onto the side of the path. He hand-signaled Hansen to keep an eye on the left side, while he concentrated on the side the gunman had escaped into.

Matt followed the trail toward the direction from where the second explosion had come. The air carried the bitter remains of smoke and burnt chemicals. A gray haze filled the air, thickening the farther they walked. Visibility deteriorated to less than five feet.

Matt lifted his fatigue shirt and ripped off a strip of his undershirt. After he placed the piece of cloth over his nose and mouth, he slowly continued down the trail.

The haze soon transitioned into smothering smoke. Matt could no longer see Hansen across the trail, but he could hear the crunch of his boots on the dirt. Matt stopped and said, "Whatever it was that blew up around here must have had a hell of a charge."

"Yeah," Hansen agreed. "I'm glad we weren't any closer when it went off. I don't think there's anything down here. And even if there had been, the explosion probably—." He stopped in mid-sentence.

Matt felt as though a knife had penetrated his heart.

"Sorry, Matt," Hansen said. "We might as well start back."

"Just another minute or two," Matt said, his words sounding dry and brittle. He hacked when he took in another breath of smoke-clogged air.

"Okay, that's it," Hansen said. "Another minute. Then we head back."

A light breeze kicked up and blew away some of the smoke. But the breeze lingered for mere seconds, then the smoke closed in around them once again. Matt minced his steps and listened for voices or movement. The only sound he heard was the noise of fast-moving water. Hopelessness closed in on him as he realized that the roaring water would mask any other sounds. Time was running out. With each step, his heart became heavier.

He took another abbreviated step and the earth suddenly dropped away. He tossed his rifle aside to free his hands. His butt hit ground, then he slid down a steep decline. He thrust out his hands and grabbed handfuls of dirt, but continued to slide. Then his hand closed around something course and prickly. He felt as though a thousand needles had pierced his hand as it slid along the rope. He clutched it, twisted, and grasped it with both hands. The pain in his hands was excruciating. But at least he'd arrested his slide. He pulled on the rope. It held his weight. He dug the toes of his boots into the soft, shifting earth and pulled himself upward.

A sudden blast of wind lashed at him and cleansed the air. Matt looked around. He saw that the rope was secured to something ten feet above his head. Pieces of burned and smoldering wood lay scattered on the side of the slope. As he peered down, his breath caught in his chest. The dirt hillside descended to a granite cliff. The moonlight that seeped through the haze showed that the cliff extended at least two hundred feet below to a roaring river.

"Matt, you okay?" Hansen said. "Can you hear me?" Then Hansen must have spotted him. "My God, man." Hansen grabbed the rope and helped Matt climb back up to the path.

As soon as he stood on flat ground, Matt noticed Hansen's arm bleeding again.

"We'd better go find Esteban," Matt said. "He's got the first aid kit."

Hansen nodded.

Matt looked back at the ravine and felt a chill run down his spine. He knew how close he'd come to death. He gazed across at the other side of the chasm. The explosion had taken out a bridge . . . and probably every living thing around it. He felt a hand on his back.

"Come on, *compadre*," Hansen said. "It's time to go."

Matt took a step backward and turned. But then he stopped. Something had moved. He'd seen it out of the corner of his eye. *Probably just my imagination*, he thought. But he couldn't help himself. He turned back to the ravine and looked across it. Smoke danced above the chasm. The wind appeared to move in several directions at the same time. Finally, a blast of air blew straight down the gorge. Matt's heart and breathing seemed to stop and an electric current hit the back of his neck.

Across the gorge, a group of women—maybe six or seven of them—stood near the edge of the drop-off. They seemed frozen in time. Then one woman stepped forward, her hands clutched to her breasts. The breeze shifted her skirt around her legs and blew her hair. *Like an angel*, Matt thought. *Like an angel in a dream.*

The woman's mouth moved, but no sound seemed to come out. Then he heard one barely discernible word: "Matt," float across the space between them.

"Matt," Renee shouted again.

The other women with Renee—Matt now saw that there were six of them, including Alani—were apparently confused, huddled together, clutching one another. Then Alani turned and said something to them. They screamed, cried, and hugged one another.

Matt saw Alani move next to Renee and put her arm around her. He felt Hansen's hand on his back.

CHAPTER 66

Jackson's head felt as though it were twice its normal size. Blood trickled from his left ear and he felt as though he would vomit. He stumbled through the jungle, not daring to take the trail back to his house. *I'll work my way through the trees until I reach the perimeter fence. I need to get the flash drive. Without it, I'm just another hustler trying to scrape a living.* The thought of starting all over again made him feel even more nauseous. Then he gagged and spewed the contents of his stomach.

The foliage was so thick it was impossible to follow a straight line. He became more frustrated by the second. It took twenty minutes to find the fence. Smoke hung over the lawn, shrouded the trees, and obscured the moon. The fire in the cellblock had run out of fuel and was now nothing more than smoldering embers and ashes.

The ache in his chest, when his eyes swept over the remains of his hacienda, made him feel desperate. Smoke plumed from the center of the house. Flames roared from most windows and doors, and through a hole in the roof where his office used to be. His hopes of retrieving the flash drive were dashed. He felt as though he were in the middle of a nightmare from which he couldn't wake. *What the hell had happened? Armed men! Explosions! Who is behind the attack?* He knew Tarnovsky had sent the Bulgarian woman, but that didn't explain the armed men and the missiles.

Jackson moved to the lawn. He hoped he could salvage something from the burning wreck: clothes, jewelry, money and identification from his safe. *I can fly to Switzerland,* he thought. *I know the account number and passwords for my primary bank there. Maybe the account numbers and passwords for some of my other accounts will come to me.*

The crunch of boots on gravel shocked him from his thoughts. He fell to the grass, behind a gardenia bush. Two armed men dressed in camouflage gear moved around the corner of the house. They continued toward the north wing. The men were on alert, continually moving their heads from side to side, apparently scanning the grounds.

Jackson saw one man step up to a broken window through which wispy plumes of smoke spiraled. The other man swept the backyard with his eyes and his rifle. Finally, they moved on, past the next window, which spouted yellowish flames.

"If anyone survived the explosion, the fire would have taken care of them by now," Jackson heard one of the men say.

"Fried to a crisp," the other man added. "Let's wait by the path for Matt and Quince. This thing has turned into a waste of time . . . unless they found the women in the jungle."

Matt? Matt Curtis? Jackson wondered. The rosy-red aura returned, making the remains of his home, and the jungle surrounding it, look as though they were covered in blood. Even the smoky sky had gone red. Jackson's veins seemed to course with molten lava and his head ached with expanding pressure. He wanted to scream, but forced himself to stay in control as thoughts of Matt Curtis slithered through his brain like poisonous vipers.

The men who'd attacked his place came here with Curtis. He tried to wrap his mind around the missiles, but couldn't tie them into Curtis. Momentary glee overwhelmed him as he thought about what he'd done to Renee Curtis. But the feeling quickly passed. Raping her wasn't enough. He wanted to tear the Curtis's apart with his bare hands.

Jackson watched the two men move toward the north end of the property and then disappear around the corner. He rose and dashed across the lawn to the south corner, ran around it, and raced to the east side. He stopped when he found a collapsed wall. The inside of the room that had been his library was now black.

He moved inside, crossed the room, and entered a hallway. The expensive paintings he'd been so proud of had been incinerated, along with everything else in the corridor. He heard the crackles of flames devouring wood and fixtures ahead. He moved down the hall and put his hand on the door. The wood felt warm, but not hot. He placed a finger on the doorknob and found it too hot to touch. He wrapped his hand in a handkerchief and turned the knob, opened the door, and stepped inside. The room had been destroyed as the hall had been. Ashes and charred furniture were all that remained.

The blackened closet door was closed. It looked as though it might disintegrate if he touched it. Jackson nudged it with his foot. It teetered, fell into the closet, and fractured into sections of flat, black, alligator-skinned pieces. Jackson breathed a sigh of relief. The large gun safe hadn't been exposed to the fire. He twirled the dial and put in the combination. The safe didn't open. *Dammit, take your time*, he told himself, and redialed the combination. This time the handle moved and the door sprang open. He reached for the light-tan leather bag on the top shelf, dropped it to the floor, and unzipped it. The stacks of U.S. currency inside it gave him a brief moment of pleasure. He removed a bag of uncut diamonds from another shelf and pushed it into the bag on top of the currency. Finally, he took his José Rosales Lorca Brazilian passport, several credit cards—also in the Lorca name, and a black book with contact names all over the world. *If I'd only written the account numbers and passwords in the book, too*, he thought.

Jackson left the bedroom and walked toward the study. He'd seen flames column from the study window and through the roof and figured the room would be a disaster scene. But he had to check, just in case. He turned down the hall and saw a great wall of flames shoot from the study door and lick at the wall on the other side of the hall. *There's no hope. The computer's gone. The flash drive with it.*

He turned around and moved to the kitchen. In the pantry, he stepped on glass shards from broken jars and bottles. Cans had ruptured from the heat and spewed their contents on the floor. He put down his bag on a dry spot and grabbed a metal ring the size of a doorknocker set into the back of the pantry wall. He pulled on it and felt the shelved wall come toward him. He leaned back and moved the false wall. Then he tossed his bag into the space, slipped through, and pulled the wall closed behind him.

A set of stairs led to a damp concrete basement. The mouth of a tunnel gaped at the far end of the basement. *Like the devil's maw,* he thought, as he walked briskly toward it. He took a flashlight from a bracket on a wall near the tunnel entrance and switched it on. Then he followed the underground passage for fifty yards. It branched off, passed beneath what was left of the cellblock, and extended another fifty yards under the jungle.

There the escape tunnel ended and opened up into a large garage. A blood-red Humvee sat parked there. At the end of the room was a long ramp that terminated at a door. Jackson tossed his leather bag onto the front passenger seat, then removed a metal locking bar from the ramp door. He winced at the clanging sound it made when he tossed it on the cement floor. Then he pushed open both sides of the door, stepped outside, and looked around. All clear. He returned to the Humvee, got behind the wheel, and cranked the ignition. The vehicle roared to life. Jackson maneuvered it from the garage.

To the left, the road led to the airport. He could call his helicopter pilot and have him meet him there. Be out of Nicaragua within an hour. He turned in that direction, but a voice inside his head challenged him.

Escape on one side, revenge on the other. Jackson pressed his hands against the sides of his head and tried to make the voice go away. The rosy aura began to return. His head pounded. As though the voice of revenge had conquered his mind, his hands moved the steering wheel to the right. He gunned the Humvee down the jungle road.

Jackson knew exactly where to go. To the other side of the gorge. To find Renee Curtis.

The road led to a shallow spot in the river, three miles from his house, where the gorge petered out to become a two-foot-deep ditch. From there he could drive up the far side of the ravine. Where the road narrowed to a dirt trail, he'd have to walk in.

Somewhere between the head of the trail and the burned out bridge he would find Renee Curtis. He'd get justice for her part in what had happened to his mother and brother. Then he'd leave this place, get re-established somewhere else, try to get his money out of the banks, and go after Matt Curtis.

CHAPTER 67

"What was that?" Esteban whispered.

Cliff Ridgeway had already turned toward the sound. "A vehicle."

"Where the hell did it come from?" Esteban asked. "I thought there was nothing but jungle behind us."

The sound of the vehicle's engine became less and less distinct by the second.

"Sonofabitch," Esteban cursed. "Jackson!"

"What?" Ridgeway said.

"It's got to be Lonnie Jackson. That bastard's like a rat. He always leaves himself a way out."

Then another sound diverted Esteban's attention. Footsteps. He swung his rifle around. Quince Hansen and Matt appeared from a bend in the path.

"My God, what kept you? We heard shots." Then Esteban noticed the smile on Matt's greasepaint and smoke-darkened face.

"We found them," Matt said. "Alani's alive. They were hiding in the jungle with five other women."

"Are they okay?" Esteban said, his voice shaky. "My Lord, are they okay?"

"They're great," Matt said, while he helped Hansen sit on the ground. "He's been shot. Where's the first aid kit?"

"I got it," Esteban said. He dug into his pack, pulled out the kit, and worked on Hansen's arm.

Matt looked at Ridgeway and said, "You have your radio?"

Ridgeway nodded and said, "Yeah."

"Call Jerry Estrada," Matt said, "and say I'm going to him. I'll pick up Fred on the way."

Esteban looked up at Matt. "I'll go with—"

"Not a good idea," Matt said. "Jerry will have to do some pretty fancy maneuvering in the jungle. The less weight the chopper carries, the better. Besides, Jackson's men are probably still around."

Esteban reluctantly nodded. "Listen, you need to be careful. We heard a vehicle move off in that direction," he said, pointing back toward the gorge. "It could be Jackson."

Matt left his pack there and sprinted down the path to the road. He was exhilarated. His feet fairly flew over the dirt surface, then across the lawn, to the path they'd come in on through the jungle from the helicopter. He couldn't wait to hold Renee in his arms. When he arrived near the spot where they'd left Fred, he stopped and whistled. "Fred, it's me, Matt," he said in a hoarse whisper. Matt heard rustling, then Petrucchio emerged from the trees.

"Hey, Matt. I was starting to worry. What were those explosions?"

"I'll explain later. We've got to go get Jerry. We found the girls."

"Thank God," Petrucchio said. "They okay?"

"Fine. Jerry will fly us in to pick them up. All seven of them."

"You shittin' me?"

"Nope."

"How the hell will we all fly out of here?" Petrucchio asked. "There's no way that chopper will carry"—he counted on his fingers—"holy shit! Thirteen people."

"I know. We'll worry about that later. Let's go."

Petrucchio jabbed a finger toward the tree line. "What do you want me to do with the two clowns I tied to the tree back there?"

"What guys?"

Petrucchio smiled. "They ran down the road about thirty, forty minutes ago."

"Why didn't you just let them run on by?" Matt asked.

"Hell, I don't know," Petrucchio said. "I guess I was bored and needed something to do."

Matt coughed out a laugh. "They any threat?"

"Nah. I busted their weapons on a rock. I told them I would leave them for the animals. I suspect they'll run like hell if I cut them loose."

"Do it," Matt said.

Petrucchio ran back into the trees. Matt heard him talking, then two men burst from the jungle and raced down the road in the direction of the nearby town. By the time Petrucchio reappeared, the men had vanished.

"Jeez, Fred, what did you tell those guys? They looked scared to death."

Petrucchio grinned. "That I would give them a one minute head start, then I would hunt them down and drop them out of a helicopter."

Matt tilted his head to the side and looked at Petrucchio as though he was pulling his leg. The look he got back said something different. Matt turned and, with Petrucchio, ran down the road toward the helicopter.

CHAPTER 68

Jackson knew, with the footbridge out, the men he'd shot at earlier could not have crossed over the gorge. And, unless the women had yelled or shown themselves, the men would never find them. Jackson suspected the women were too afraid to come out of hiding. Especially if strange men dressed in jungle fatigues suddenly appeared.

The old familiar anger took over. His face felt hot and the drumming inside his head got worse. The jungle was red tinted. He fought to control his rage.

Renee Curtis has to be on the other side of the ravine. Hadn't the dogs run in that direction? Hadn't they picked up the scent from her clothes? "I'll finish with that bitch once and for all."

The road dropped down to the river. The first rays of sunrise cast a light glow on the water and Jackson saw the tops of rocks show above the waterline. The Humvee would easily clear them. The roar of the falls could be heard off to the right, fifty yards across the river, a two-mile ascent along the other side of the gorge, then a half-mile walk. "Renee," he whispered breathlessly, "I'm coming."

Renee's legs felt like wet strands of spaghetti. Between physical exertion, fear, and relief at seeing Matt, she was spent. Matt said he would return, but every second that passed seemed like a death sentence.

Alani leaned against her, shoulder to shoulder. They held hands. Renee wondered how soon Alani would need to take her medication, and was afraid to ask.

She tried to raise her head to look at the other women, but she didn't have the strength. The Bulgarians were clustered together, seated in the middle of the path, like three tired little girls. There was no animation in any of their faces, as though they wore stone masks. The two Latin American girls sat next to one another on a rotted log off the side of the path. One cried; the other sat with her head bowed, hands over her face.

Renee felt her backbone turn to ice when she thought about what Jackson had done to these women. Even worse, what he had *intended* to do to them. What he had already done to her, Renee knew, was nothing compared to what would have happened once he'd shipped her off to Thailand with Pratikan. She shuddered at the thought of what she'd done to the Thai.

She heard the roar of a high-powered engine and mustered the strength to stare toward the treetops on the far side of the ravine. She looked for the helicopter. Nothing. Then the engine sound stopped. Had it come from down the path below where she sat? She couldn't be sure. The noise of the water made it difficult to identify sounds or the direction they came from. Maybe it had been her imagination.

CHAPTER 69

The helicopter lifted off. Matt could tell from the speed and angle of its climb that Estrada piloted the aircraft with a sense of urgency. The chopper skirted Jackson's property and skimmed just above the jungle canopy.

The gorge showed as a long, gray slash through verdant jungle. The wind from the chopper's rotors whipped at the women, who lowered their heads and covered their faces with their hands.

"They're over there, Jerry!" Matt shouted from the cargo bay.

"What the fuck is going on, Matt?" Estrada shouted back. "My God, there's two, three . . . jeez, there's seven of them."

"I know, Jerry. Don't worry about it."

Estrada glanced back at Matt, then turned to look down at the women again. They were partially obscured by the debris tossed around in the aircraft's rotor wash. "I can take the seven women and three guys, and that's stretching it."

"Fine," Matt yelled. "Esteban and I will find another way out."

"Cliff and I will go with Matt and Esteban," Petrucchio said.

"You'd better get them on board quickly. I'll burn a lot of fuel hovering like this. Drop that damn ladder back there," he ordered. "And make sure one of the women down there holds onto the anchor rope. Otherwise, the damned thing will whip all over the place."

Estrada positioned the chopper directly above the women.

Matt leaned out the cargo door and watched Petrucchio drop the ladder. It lashed back and forth under the chopper's churning rotor. Matt watched Renee try to snatch it. Three times she tried, without success. Matt tapped Petrucchio on the shoulder, pointed him away from the bay door, then grasped the top of the ladder and lowered himself out the door.

His descent took a minute. When he jumped the last three feet to the ground, Renee rushed into his arms and nearly knocked him down. He hugged her, kissed her. When he pushed her away to look at her, he saw cuts and bruises on her face. One eye was blackened. Matt's jaw tightened. *Later*, he told himself. *I'll deal with Jackson later.*

He kissed Renee again, put an arm around her, then faced the other women. He'd never seen a more frightened group. He smiled, pointed at the rope ladder, and explained what he wanted them to do. It was immediately obvious the women were confused. He used hand gestures and pointed at the rope and then at the helicopter. One of Bulgarians seemed to get it and shouted at the two Hispanic women, who seemed even more confused.

Renee moved over to the two girls and put an arm around each one. She hugged them and then guided them to the ladder. She pointed up at the helicopter and gave each girl a smile that seemed to ease some of the tension on their faces. But neither one stepped toward the ladder.

"I'll go first," Alani yelled.

Matt hugged her. "You all right, sweetie?" he asked.

"I will be when I see Esteban," she said.

Matt smiled and patted her shoulder. He grabbed the rope at the bottom of the ladder, pulled the ladder to him, and watched Alani step on the bottom cross rope. She slowly made her way upward. Where Matt's descent had taken less than a minute, it took Alani four minutes to make it to the helicopter.

We've got to speed this up, he thought. He didn't want to get them loaded on the helicopter, then not have enough fuel left to return to Costa Rica.

He tried to get Renee to go next. He wanted her off the ground and in the safety of the chopper.

"I'll wait for the others," Renee said.

Alani's climb to the chopper seemed to have fortified the other women. They cued up. The Latin American girls went next. By the time it was Renee's turn, fifteen minutes had passed.

"Okay, honey," Matt shouted in Renee's ear. "Just like climbing up a flight of stairs!"

She raised her eyebrows. "Yeah, sure," she said.

Matt held onto the anchor line and watched Renee start up the ladder. He focused on each step she took, watching her plant her feet in the middle of the cross ropes as she grasped the sides. "That's it, Renee," he shouted. "You're doing great!"

She climbed to the fourth cross rope, her feet firmly in place ten feet above the ground, her head turned up toward the helicopter's underbelly, when something slammed into Matt's side.

Knocked to the ground, Matt felt a pain over his kidney and his lungs screamed for air. But more than the physical pain, it was the flapping ladder that caused him the most distress. He heard Renee scream. Then he saw Lonnie Jackson's angry amber eyes.

Matt rolled over to his stomach, pushed off the ground, and gathered his legs underneath him, when Jackson caught him in the ribs with a kick that turned him over onto his back. His vision clouded as pain swirled through his chest and numbed his brain. He fought through the fog, rolled again, and came to his feet. He heard Renee scream again and glanced up. She dangled from the ladder by her hands. Her legs churned as she tried to snag a cross rope with a foot. Her body whipped back and forth. Then the nightmare became even worse. Jackson had his arm extended upward, a pistol in his hand. The crack of a shot sounded cannon-like, even amidst the thunderous noise of the helicopter and Renee's piercing screams.

Matt leaped forward as though he'd been catapulted. Anger ripped through him, the pain in his side, in his ribs, in his lungs all but forgotten. Before he reached Jackson, the man fired off another round. The thud of the bullet loudly struck the helicopter's metal underbelly.

Matt's shoulder hit Jackson in the chest. He gripped the man's wrist, pulled down his arm, and fell on top of him as they crashed to the ground. He could feel Jackson's strength while they grappled for the weapon. He knew he couldn't match the man's youth and power. Jackson flipped him. His weight pressed on him with such force that Matt could barely breathe. He still held Jackson's gun hand with both of his own hands.

Jackson raised his upper body for a moment and pulled his free arm back. In that second, Matt was able to catch a quick breath—and to see Renee fall. She hit the ground with a *whoomp* and gasped. The helicopter rose slightly, still hanging in the air above the path. The rotor wash seemed to get worse, whipping dirt and torn foliage debris, creating a mini maelstrom. Matt turned his head just enough to avoid taking a blow as Jackson's fist came down. But even the glancing impact against his cheek caused an explosion of sparks behind his eyes. He felt strength ebb from his arms and he lost his hold on Jackson's wrist.

The pistol suddenly appeared before his eyes and Matt saw the muzzle pointed at the bridge of his nose. He struck out at Jackson's face with a fist and connected, snapping the man's head to the side. But Jackson merely looked back down at him and laughed. The sound of the clicking hammer told Matt he was a split second away from death. But then a shadow swept past Matt's vision, a *thud* sounded, Jackson's smile faded, as he toppled to the side.

Renee stood over him, a moss-covered tree branch in her hands. Matt scrambled to his feet and spied the pistol in the dirt. Then he saw Jackson stand, blood running down the side of his face from a deep cut in his scalp. Jackson leaped for the gun. Matt had no time to dive for the pistol. Instead, he kicked at it and sent it spinning over the side of the ravine.

Jackson touched the side of his face and looked at his bloodied hand. He licked his fingers and smiled first at Matt, then at Renee. His eyes seemed to glow like a panther's at night. "You'll pay for that. This time I'll break your neck after I fuck you."

A sound exploded from Renee's throat, as though she were being strangled. She ran at Jackson, the tree limb cocked back. She swung it at his head, but he easily sidestepped her charge and smashed a fist into the side of her head. She reeled off the path into a dense thicket of bushes. Matt heard her groan, then lay still.

"You know I fucked your wife, Curtis? You're a lucky man. But

I'll bet she doesn't fight you the way she did me." He threw his head back and laughed.

Matt took a step toward Jackson and struck him at the base of his ribcage with a flattened hand, knuckles extended. The blow seemed to take Jackson by surprise. His mouth dropped open and air escaped from his chest. But then Jackson charged.

Jackson's bull-like charge seemed to ignite a flash of a memory for Matt. The hand-to-hand combat training he'd received at Fort Bragg decades ago. Instinctively, he stepped to the side and kicked out at Jackson, tripped the bigger man, and dropped him to the ground. But Jackson came off the path in an instant, bellowing like a wounded animal. He swung an arm like a swinging gate, catching Matt in the side, where he'd kicked him a moment earlier. A shock of pain hit Matt, but he gritted his teeth and levered Jackson's arm. He bent at the waist and flipped Jackson onto the ground. Then he smashed a boot down into the man's face.

Jackson howled, chopped at Matt's leg with his arm, and threw him off balance. While Matt fell away, Jackson rose from the ground and rushed him. He kicked at Matt; but Matt was able to scissor kick Jackson's standing leg. The man fell forward and landed on Matt's legs. Matt rose to a sitting position and pummeled Jackson's face and head with his fists. He heard bone and cartilage break when he struck Jackson's nose, and more blood poured down the man's face. Where a lesser man might have been knocked cold by Matt's barrage, Jackson seemed only dazed and went after Matt with powerful blows of his own. A fist crashed into Matt's chin and he felt the bones there give way. His head felt as though it were filled with mush.

Jackson scrambled to his feet, reached down, grabbed a handful of Matt's fatigue shirt, and pulled him to his feet. He connected with another punch to Matt's head.

Matt now felt as though his brain had become detached from his body. He was operating purely on instinct and training. He blocked Jackson's next blow and brought a knee up between the man's legs. He heard Jackson grunt. Despite feeling woozy, Matt stepped back and kicked Jackson's leg with all the strength he could summon. He spread his feet apart to better balance himself and prepared to counter Jackson's next attack.

Jackson slowly struggled upright. He glared at Matt, his eyes blazing like yellow flares. In that moment, Matt saw how hatred had consumed Jackson's reason.

Jackson snapped a jab that caught Matt's left shoulder.

Matt felt the blow numb his upper arm and send electric shivers of burning pain down to his fingers. He tried to raise the arm, but it hung uselessly by his side. Jackson swung again, but Matt ducked the punch and hit Jackson with his right fist at the base of the sternum. When Jackson doubled over, Matt blasted his fist into Jackson's temple, dropping him to his knees. Matt then leaped onto the man's back, wrapped his legs around Jackson's chest and pulled back on his head with his one good arm. Jackson fought for his life. He thrashed around like a rodeo bull and it took all Matt's strength to keep from being thrown off.

Jackson's screams sounded otherworldly. They seemed to be generated by rage rather than pain. Matt squeezed with his legs and pulled back the man's head with one arm.

Jackson wheezed. His ears and the back of his thick neck reddened. His once-flailing arms dropped to his side and he stopped struggling. The thought of killing this evil man seemed to give Matt even more strength. He tightened his lock on Jackson's chest, his ankles hooked together. Jackson's arms lifted and his fingers and nails ripped at Matt's ankles, but Matt could no longer feel pain. Finally, Jackson crumpled to the side, on top of Matt's right leg. No sound came from him. He didn't seem to be breathing. But Matt didn't dare release him. He continued the pressure on the man's chest, until one of his thighs cramped.

Then Matt heard Renee moan. He untangled himself, pushed Jackson away and struggled to his feet, teetering for a few seconds. He felt limp as a blade of grass while he moved toward Renee. He fell to his knees beside her and cradled her head in his hands. She opened her eyes and looked up at him.

"Can you move?" Matt asked as he brushed hair away from her face.

"I . . . I think so," she said.

Matt helped her stand. She groaned and wobbled for a moment.

He waved at the helicopter.

"Thank God," he mumbled when Estrada lowered the chopper over them. Matt and Renee leaned against each other, a few yards away from Jackson's crumpled body.

Renee looked at Jackson. "Is he dead? Please let him be dead."

Matt glanced at Jackson. "I think so." Then the rope ladder hung a few feet away from the tops of their heads. He smiled down at Renee. "Let's see if you can make it all the way to the top this time." He grabbed the anchor line, took up the slack in the ladder, and watched her climb to the helicopter's cargo bay. When he saw Fred pull her inside, he dropped the anchor line and stepped onto the ladder. *Okay, Matthew,* he thought, *you've got two good legs and one-and-a-half arms. You can do this.* But he knew if he couldn't climb all the way to the chopper, he would hang on for dear life and let Jerry lift him out.

The ladder swung wildly as he took another step up. Petrucchio leaned out of the cargo bay and hugged his arms to his chest, signaling Matt to hold tight to the ladder.

Matt wrapped his arms around the ladder and gripped a cross rope with his hands. He circled the side ropes with his legs and then rested his feet on the cross ropes. *Daredevil Curtis,* he thought. *Now I remember why I got out of the Army and went to college.* He felt the chopper gain altitude.

Matt thought how good it would be to live the rest of his life without the threat of Lonnie Jackson. He craned his neck and looked up at the chopper. Renee smiled down at him. But the smile suddenly cracked and her eyes and mouth rounded with shock. Then Matt felt hands on his legs and he knew he'd made a terrible mistake. The Army had taught him to finish his enemy. He'd failed.

Matt looked down at Jackson. There was a demented look on his face. Blood covered one side of his face, from scalp to chin. More blood dribbled from his nose. His eyes seemed to gleam.

Jackson gripped Matt's legs with one arm; his other arm clutched the rope where Matt's feet were. Jackson struggled as though to break Matt loose from the ladder. He fought with a frenzy Matt didn't believe he would have been capable of after the damage he had done to the man.

Matt freed one of his legs and kicked at Jackson. But the man caught Matt's ankle and sank his teeth into his calf. Matt lost his footing and now hung from the ladder with one hand on a cross rope, his numb arm wrapped around the side of the ladder.

There was nothing below the helicopter now but green. They were high above the jungle floor. Matt steeled himself to hold on, but he felt his arms weakening. It would have been difficult enough to hold his own weight, without his legs to support him, but it was becoming impossible with Jackson weighing him down.

Matt knew there was no chance he could hold on long enough for the chopper to put down where Esteban, Quince, and Chris waited. His arms straightened. He looked down and saw the edge of the tree line ahead, then the chopper cleared the trees and there was water below. Jackson's weight was inexorably dragging him off the ladder. He felt the helpless sensation he'd always known when parachuting, before the chute opened. Then he slammed into the water. Sparks exploded behind his eyes and everything went dark.

CHAPTER 70

Fred Petrucchio yelled at Jerry Estrada to turn around, to drop low over the water.

"What happened?" Estrada shouted.

"Matt's in the water."

Estrada banked the chopper and zoomed down toward the pond.

"Oh my Lord," Petrucchio shouted. "There are caimans down there." He watched what he'd originally thought were old logs on the sides of the pond come to life and push off into the water. "Get as low as you can," Petrucchio said. He hoped the chopper's rotor wash would distract the reptiles, scare them away. He looked back at Renee, thinking she would be traumatized with fear. But what he saw shocked him. She had pushed off from the opposite side of the cargo bay and moved toward the door. He tackled her at the instant she leaped forward. He wrestled her to the floor of the cargo bay, pushed her back toward the other women, and yelled, "Hold her."

The chopper now hovered three yards above the churning water. The caimans had disappeared and Petrucchio feared they'd grabbed Matt and dragged him under.

Matt found himself surrounded by black goop. He knew he was underwater, but was disoriented and couldn't recall why he was there. His lungs felt as though they were about to burst. Then a bright light from above caught his attention and he saw movement. A man swam with powerful strokes across the surface of the water—*Jackson!*

Matt's feet touched the murky bottom. He bent his knees to propel himself to the surface. But before he kicked off the bottom, he noticed something else in the water. Something with a long, undulating tail. It moved across the water with speed and closed on Jackson. Then Matt saw another long-tailed creature, then another, and another. Alligators, or crocodiles, or whatever lived in the Nicaraguan jungle, converged on the man who had brought Renee and him so much pain and fear. Six, seven, then eight animals converged on Jackson. Matt lost count as his lungs shrieked for oxygen and his vision blurred.

He kicked off the bottom and slashed at the water with his arms and legs, trying to reach a stand of reeds at the pond edge. To his left, the water churned as though someone had turned on a giant blender. Red plumes billowed around the frenzied animals.

Matt kicked feverishly. The surface and the bright sunlight made the water sparkle like a thousand bursting flashbulbs. He'd nearly reached life-giving air—just feet from the surface—when he gulped a mouthful of water. The cold liquid streamed into his lungs and he felt pain spread through his chest. He knew he was drowning, but the thought of being torn apart by a pack of prehistoric reptiles—whether he was alive or dead—seemed like a fate worse than drowning. But a bright light flashed behind his eyes and all became dark.

Petrucchio leaned outside the helicopter. He gripped the cargo door handle with one hand and scanned the pond's surface. He spotted a caiman suddenly turn away from the boiling center of the pond where the animals had attacked Jackson. The eight-foot reptile whipped its tail in a lazy, serpentine fashion and moved toward a cluster of reeds by the bank. Matt had been under water for over a minute. If the caimans hadn't already found him, they would any moment now. He looked from one end of the pond to the other and tried to find Matt. When his eyes shifted back to the spot where the lone caiman cruised toward the bank, his breath froze in his chest. A body floated facedown near the reeds. The caiman drifted toward it, now just ten feet away.

Petrucchio scrambled sideways, grabbed the M-16 he'd set against the fuselage, and scuttled back to the open bay. The reptile nosed the floating body, then floated backward two feet. The animal opened its jaws, displaying rows of vicious-looking teeth. Petrucchio aimed at the caiman's tail and stitched the animal with deadly 5.56mm rounds up to its midsection. He stared at the water below him. Matt's body seemed to be caught in the reeds. The caiman rolled and thrashed, bloodying the water even more. Hoping the reptile's blood would attract the other animals, Petrucchio dropped the M-16 and jumped feet-first from the helicopter. His boots touched bottom, about six feet from the bank. He kicked into the reeds and came up next to Matt. He rolled him over and stared into his lifeless-looking, open eyes.

He dragged Matt by the wrist onto the bank. By the time he had him half out of the water, Esteban ran up and helped pull Matt to dry ground.

"Oh, Jesus," Esteban said mournfully. "Not now, Matt! Come on, Matt, don't die!" He flopped Matt onto his back, knelt, and checked for a pulse. Nothing. He lifted Matt's neck and checked his airway. It was clear. Esteban placed his hands on Matt's chest and pressed down half-a-dozen times. Then he again checked for a pulse. Still nothing. He, pinched Matt's nostrils and breathed into his mouth. Over and over, he repeated the process while Petrucchio cried out, again and again, "Come on, Matt! You can do it!"

Esteban huffed as though he'd run a marathon, as he continued to apply artificial respiration to his old friend.

Petrucchio heard a noise behind him. He glanced back and saw Renee sprint up the path toward them. She skidded to a stop next to Matt and dropped to the ground. Her eyes looked like saucers; her mouth gaped, then slammed shut. Tears leaked down her cheeks. "Don't you dare leave me, Matthew!" she shouted, while Esteban continued to work. "Don't you dare!"

Matt's body suddenly convulsed; his back heaved. A gout of cloudy liquid burst from his mouth. Esteban rolled him to his side and muttered a prayer as more fluid ran out of Matt's mouth. Then

Matt coughed as though his lungs would burst. Petrucchio helped Esteban lift Matt into a sitting position. He looked ghostly white. His eyelids fluttered. He gave Renee a weak smile, then collapsed into Esteban's arms.

"Let's get him to the chopper," Esteban said.

"The helicopter's in the yard by the house," Renee said in a brittle voice.

Petrucchio nodded, stood, and hefted Matt under the arms while Esteban took hold of his legs. They quick-walked to the path. They had almost reached the yard when the nerve-grating sounds of sirens floated down on them.

CHAPTER 71

Although he'd disarmed the woman who'd attacked him, Eddie Parnell kept a wary eye on her while he drove the SUV down the rutted dirt road. She'd surprised him. She'd obviously had hand-to-hand combat training.

He wondered if he'd done any permanent damage when he knocked her out. When she finally groaned and moved her head, he felt relieved but remained wary. It took another minute for her to gather her senses.

She suddenly sat up straighter, pushed back against the front passenger seat, and rubbed her hands over her face. She groaned again, then touched the fingers of one hand against the left side of her chest. "Ooh," she said. Then she looked at Parnell who glanced at her. "What happened?" Then her eyes went hard and the muscles in her cheeks bounced.

Parnell looked back at the road. "You okay?" he said in a flat tone.

"Yes, I am fine," she answered.

"There's a bottle of water in the side pocket of the door. You'll find some Advil in the glove compartment."

"Advil?"

"Painkillers."

"I do not need . . . ." She didn't finish the sentence, reaching for the glove box latch instead.

Parnell smiled, but stifled a laugh. He figured she felt bad enough already.

"Bulgarian?" he asked.

She swigged some of the water, washed down the pills, then said, "How do you know?"

"What are you doing here?" he said, ignoring her question.

He saw her turn her head to look through the side window. "I applied for job as nanny. But it was . . . what's the word? . . . *izmama*."

"Scam," Parnell said.

The woman jerked her gaze toward him. "How you know my language?"

"Long story," Parnell said.

Parnell didn't think there was a grain of truth in what she said. The woman didn't appear to be the nanny type. But he decided to play along. "What was the man here going to do with you?"

"Sell me to someone for sex slave."

"I see. What are you, thirty-four, thirty-five years old?"

"Twenty-five," she said, a hint of anger in her voice.

This time Parnell laughed. "Bullshit. Don't get me wrong, lady. You're about the best-looking woman I've seen in a long time, but there's no way in hell you're twenty-five. And at thirty-four, I think you're a little older than the average woman thrown into sexual slavery. So . . . why don't you cut the crap and tell me the real reason you're here?"

"*Mainata ti!*" she spat as she turned toward him.

Parnell slammed on the brakes, bringing the vehicle to a skidding stop. "You really think cursing me will help you? You got two choices. Get out of the car right here and figure out how the hell you'll get out of Nicaragua, dressed like a bum, filthy dirty, and, I suspect, without money." After a beat, he added, "I don't suppose you have a passport either?" He waited for her to say something, but she just glared at him.

"Your second option is to tell me who the hell you are and why you're here. If you tell me the truth, I'll try to help you. But if you lie about even the smallest point, I'll kick your ass out. You can take your chances with the Nicaraguan police. They'll find something real nice to do with you." He waited ten seconds for her to respond and, when she didn't, he hit the automatic door locks and reached across her to open her door. "Get out," he ordered.

"Wait . . . wait a minute," she said, her voice completely devoid of its former arrogance. She twisted in her seat and looked down at her folded hands. "My name is Tatiana Borodvic. I was sent by a man in Bulgaria to kill José Lorca."

Parnell knew his mouth dropped open, but he was too shocked by what she had said to do anything about it. "What man in Bulgaria?"

She turned her head toward him, but hesitated. Apparently the look she saw in his eyes reminded her of the options he'd given her. "Yevgeni Tarnovsky," she said.

"Holy Mother," Parnell said in a barely audible voice. He gripped the steering wheel and looked down the road, while he tried to collect his thoughts. "Well, little lady, we were both on the same assignment."

"What you mean?"

"I was sent here to kill Señor Lorca, too."

It was her turn to look shocked. "By Tarnovsky?"

He shook his head and put the car in 'Drive.'

CHAPTER 72

Cliff Moreland placed a hand on his knee and pressed down in an attempt to stop his leg from bouncing up and down like a runaway jackhammer. He felt perspiration drip from his underarms—each unanswered ring of the telephone only made him jumpier.

Seymour Katzman finally answered. "Katzman here," he said in his usual abrupt manner.

"Mr. Katzman, it's Cliff Moreland. I have—"

"I presume, Mr. Moreland, you have taken care of that matter we discussed."

"Yes, sir."

"And," Katzman continued, "may I pass on your assurances that the issue is resolved in a way so as to never be a problem in the future?"

"Yes, sir. We are the only ones who know about the . . . the issue," Moreland said.

"Good, Mr. Moreland. You've been quite helpful."

Moreland stared at the phone in his hand after he heard Katzman hang up. He slowly replaced the receiver, rose from his desk chair, and crossed to the bookcase. He opened the double doors on the cabinet below the bookshelves and found the bottle of scotch. It was barely 7 a.m.

He poured two fingers of the liquid into a glass and walked to the window. The sun came through and Moreland pressed a palm against the glass to feel the warmth of the morning rays. But the window glass was still cold. He shivered. Icy fingers gripped the back of his neck.

Moreland moved back to his desk and plopped down in his chair. He spilled some of the scotch on his pants. But he ignored it and stared glassy-eyed at the window. He'd been a good soldier. He'd covered his commander in chief's ass—and his own ass, too. The death of a lone agent was a small price to pay to protect the reputation of the current administration and to ensure his personal future. He downed the remainder of the scotch, leaned back in his chair, and closed his eyes. Maybe, with time, he told himself, he might even learn to believe that.

CHAPTER 73

Senator William Benedict turned right out of the elevator at the third floor of the Russell Senate Office Building and saw his colleague, Pete Driscoll, down the hall. He caught up with him and put an arm around the Kansan's shoulder. "Hey, Petey-boy, how they hangin'?"

Driscoll continued to walk toward his office three doors down. "Fine, Bill. What's up?"

"You seem in a hurry, buddy. You think you could spare a minute?"

Driscoll looked at his wristwatch "I got a Commerce Committee meeting in ten minutes," he said.

"I just need a minute."

Driscoll turned into his suite. "Hold my calls," he told the receptionist as he cruised past her desk. He led the way into his private office and closed the door after Benedict. While Driscoll crossed his office and took a seat behind his desk, Benedict sat on a couch on the opposite side of the room. "I got the votes for that little research facility of yours," Benedict said. "Should be funded in the next fiscal year."

Driscoll felt acid drip in his stomach. He knew his deal with Benedict had gone beyond normal deal making. He'd forsaken his principles for a laboratory. But that lab would create a thousand jobs and great prestige for his state . . . and earn him votes. Without those votes he might not get re-elected. And, if he didn't get re-elected, he couldn't do the things he wanted to do to change America. He recognized the rationalization of his argument, but . . . . He cleared his throat, then said, "I appreciate your help, Bill."

Benedict waved a dismissive hand. Then he narrowed his eyes and stared hard at Driscoll. "That little problem you told me about," he said. "You hear anything more from that Boris character?"

Driscoll shook his head. "Not a thing," he said. "May have been a hoax."

Benedict stood up and moved to the door. "I'll bet you're right, Petey-boy. It probably was a hoax." He shrugged and the corners of his mouth turned down. "I guess I just got you a nice, shiny new research lab for nothing." He opened the door and walked out without another word. After he cleared the reception area and turned to go to his office, he hummed a nondescript tune and thought about how grateful the president would be. Once again, he'd saved that skirt-chasing reprobate's ass.

After Benedict left his office, Driscoll moved from his desk and reclined on the couch. He dropped his feet and considered another problem with which he needed to deal. His constituent whose daughter in the Ukraine had disappeared had called again. The man was desperate. Of course, Driscoll understood that. But what the hell was he supposed to do? It was highly likely the girl had been transported from the Ukraine to some godforsaken place like Nicaragua. He wouldn't be surprised to learn that Yevgeni Tarnovsky had been responsible for the girl's abduction. *But how can I turn over that rock without jeopardizing my own position?*

He processed options in his mind and finally came up with a solution that made sense to him. He'd call the girl's family and tell them that the trail had dead-ended, but that he wouldn't give up trying to find their daughter. He congratulated himself on this elegant resolution, one that would require him to do nothing in the future except continue to bullshit the family.

CHAPTER 74

Esteban couldn't believe the scene inside the helicopter. It was like a riot in a phone booth. The cargo bay was crowded to the point that three of the women had to sit on top of men's laps.

Matt had been laid on his back in the center of the bay. His breathing was labored and he looked deathly pale. Hansen's arm wound had burst open again. Petrucchio now wrapped it with gauze and tape from the first aid kit. Several of the women cried. Esteban hugged Alani. But he knew he would have to do something to settle the situation down. The sound of sirens had gotten louder by the second. He wasn't sure if the smoke from the fire had attracted fire engines, or whether someone had heard the explosions and gunshots and called the local militia. Either way, he wanted out of there. The last thing they needed was to be arrested by the Sandinistas—especially in light of the fact that he, Petrucchio, and Hansen, along with the Caruso brothers from Hawaii, had helped train anti-Sandinista guerrillas for the U.S. government. Their presence in the country illegally and armed to the teeth wouldn't help their situation one bit.

"I'm telling you," Jerry Estrada screamed again from the cockpit, "I can't get this thing off the ground. We're overloaded."

Esteban gently released Alani. "I'll be right back, honey," he said. He struggled to his feet, stepping over other passengers, moved to the cockpit, and leaned over Estrada's seat.

"Listen to me," he said in a gravelly voice that vibrated with anger. "You get this damned machine off the ground. You don't want to deal with the authorities down here."

Estrada nodded. "We'll be lucky to get over the trees," he said. "Take my word for it." The chopper's rotors already created a windstorm that whipped at trees and bushes on the lawn's perimeter. Estrada revved the engine and tried to lift the overloaded aircraft. The machine rose a foot, then dropped back to the lawn.

Esteban, back on the floor next to Alani, looked at Quince Hansen and saw his concern. Hansen shook his head. "It ain't gonna work! Too much weight!"

"How 'bout dumping the weapons and other gear?" Esteban asked.

Hansen and Ridgeway immediately tossed out everything they could, but, when Estrada tried again to lift the bird off the ground, it barely rose a couple of yards before falling heavily back to earth.

Esteban happened to look at Fred Petrucchio and saw a sudden change in his expression. The man's eyes narrowed, then he glanced at Chris Ridgeway and tilted his chin at him. He jerked his head toward the open cargo door.

Esteban thought he knew what they were about to do. "Don't even think about it!" he yelled. "Jerry'll get this thing—"

Packs in hand, Petrucchio and Ridgeway leaped from the struggling chopper, raced across the lawn to the jungle, and vanished. By the time they'd entered the tree line, the helicopter had struggled to rise, but finally lifted off the ground and now approached the treetops—just as a half dozen Jeeps with "Guardia Nacional" imprinted on their doors poured down the driveway and sped toward the lawn.

Esteban vowed to come back to find Ridgeway and Petrucchio. Two guys he had just met a couple days ago had risked their lives to save Renee and Alani. Now they had again put themselves in jeopardy to help the rest of them. Band of brothers. Some things never change. He figured they'd flee south along the coast until they crossed the Nicaraguan border into Costa Rica. What he would do in their places was find a broad beach where a chopper could land. And then make a telephone call to Quince Hansen. Esteban said a silent prayer, thanking God for men like Chris Ridgeway and Fred Petrucchio, and begged Him to keep them safe.

The helicopter groaned like an old man getting up from a chair. Then it slowly gained additional altitude. But Esteban knew there was still too much weight on board for them to follow the route they'd taken when they'd entered Nicaragua. They'd never get over the Irazú Volcano.

Estrada looked back over his shoulder and crooked a finger. Esteban again tiptoed his way to the front of the aircraft. "Yeah?"

Estrada tapped a finger against the glass over the fuel indicator and said, "I'm losing fuel. Jackson must have hit the fuel line. Don't have enough gas to reach San José."

"Can you reach a hospital?" Esteban asked.

Estrada shook his head as though he wasn't entirely certain. "Maybe Puerto Limón along the coast," he said. "At least I can fly low all the way there. Conserve fuel."

Esteban patted the pilot on the shoulder and went back to his seat on the floor. *What next?* he thought.

DAYS 11-12

CHAPTER 75

Eddie Parnell tried to connect with Franco Caravelli at the U.S. Consulate in Sofia, Bulgaria. He and Caravelli had been young agents assigned to post-Communist Bulgaria right after they'd graduated from the Farm and attended the Defense Language Institute, West Coast's Bulgarian language course. It had been a heady time when the two young men had bonded.

Caravelli was now cultural attaché—just a fancy name for "spy"—at the American Embassy in Managua. On his first call, Parnell learned his old friend had signed out and wasn't expected to return for twenty-four to forty-eight hours. So, he took a room in a three-story pensionné in the city's old section. He would have preferred one of the newer places, but he knew they'd demand passports from both him and the Bulgarian woman. Since she couldn't produce one, the pensionné became the viable alternative. A twenty-dollar bill slipped to the desk clerk and Parnell's explanation that the "lady didn't want her husband to find her," cleared the way.

He grilled Tatiana Borodvic for hours about her relationship with Tarnovsky and why he'd sent her to Nicaragua. He could understand Tarnovsky wanting to eliminate Lorca in order to prove to the CIA that he was serious about ending his trafficking business. At the same time, however, he didn't believe for an instant that Tarnovsky was being truthful about his intent to get out of the business. *Tarnovsky is a greedy bastard*, Parnell thought. *Maybe he wanted Lorca killed so he could cut out the middleman.*

Parnell wondered if he could chance leaving Borodvic in the hotel room, but decided, without money or a passport, she wasn't likely to go anywhere. He walked out of the hotel, and used his cell phone to call Tarnovsky's headquarters in Varna, Bulgaria. He got a busy signal. He tried the number a dozen times over a two-hour period, with the same result. For a moment, he considered a call to Langley to see if they knew anything, but something seemed amiss. He had that old familiar feeling in his gut. It would be better to lie low.

He and Tatiana Borodvic wandered around Managua that evening and the next morning, shopped for clothes, saw the sights, took their meals in places the locals frequented, and, to Parnell's surprise, got along famously. He discovered he enjoyed her company.

In the late afternoon of their second day in Managua, Parnell again called the embassy.

"Cultural Affairs Office."

"Mr. Caravelli, please."

"Who's calling?"

"Tell him it's an old friend from Sofia."

After a pause, a man said, "This is Franco Caravelli."

"I've had car trouble in Managua and wondered if you could recommend a mechanic," Parnell said.

Caravelli hesitated a second, then answered the code words. "There are a lot of excellent mechanics in Managua, but the best is Lujan's on *Calle de la Revolución*, near *Avenida Colón*."

"Will they still be open at five?"

"Of course."

Parnell hung up and checked his wristwatch. Less than an hour until five. He walked back to the hotel.

Borodvic sat on a chair she'd dragged out to the narrow balcony. She turned and looked over her shoulder at him as he entered the room. It appeared the maid had already been there—the beds made, the bathroom neat. Tatiana's wet hair hung over the shoulders of her shirt. Parnell admired her long athletic legs propped up on the balcony railing. He exhaled quietly and wondered what it would be like rolling around in bed with her.

"Did you talk with man you have been calling?" she asked.

"Yep. I should have our papers by tonight."

She turned her head back toward the hills in the distance.

"What's on your mind?" Parnell asked.

"Nothing," she said in a too-tight, too-abrupt voice.

He walked out to the balcony and leaned on the railing. She dropped her legs to the concrete floor and shifted in her chair. He looked out over the roofs and trees to the distant hills. "Nice view." He knew that the Pacific Ocean lay about thirty miles to the west of those hills.

"It's beautiful," she answered. "I could get used to this."

Parnell looked down at her. "You know you don't have to go back to Bulgaria. I can arrange for any sort of passport you want— Italian, French, whatever."

"What will you do?" she asked.

"Put in my papers and find a beach somewhere. Lose myself."

"What is 'put in my papers'?" she asked.

"Retire."

"Oh, I see. You can do this when you are so young?"

He shrugged. "I won't live like a Politburo member, but I've got a little saved, and with my retirement pay . . . ."

"Like somewhere in the Caribbean?"

"Huh? Oh, where I want to retire?"

She nodded.

"Hah," Parnell exclaimed and looked down at her. "You read my mind. As long as it's warm, has a beach, and cold beer, that's all that matters."

She got a wistful look; her mouth opened just a crack and she sighed. Her eyes seemed suddenly sad. "Why don't you surprise me?" she said. "I don't care where I go, as long as it is not Bulgaria, or any of former communist countries. They are all . . . how do you say it? Messed up."

"Why don't you narrow down your choices? Give me a hint."

She waved her hands. "I can speak English, German, Russian, Spanish, and French."

"Okay," he said. "I'll take care of it." He turned to leave the balcony, then stopped. "I have to go out to take care of our documents. I'll leave money on the dresser, if you want to get something to eat. I'll try to get back here within a couple hours."

"I will wait here for you." She stood and smiled at him.

Parnell stopped in the middle of the room, rooted to one spot for several seconds, and stared at her. Then he turned and left the room.

CHAPTER 76

Parnell entered the open garage bay at Lujan's and looked around for Caravelli. When he didn't spot him, he walked to an office where a man in light-blue coveralls, with grease-smeared hands handed over a set of keys to a man in a suit and tie.

After the man in the suit left, Parnell handed the man in coveralls a twenty-dollar bill. "I'm meeting a man here," he said.

The man dropped his gaze to his desktop as though he didn't want to remember Parnell's face, waved an arm, and pointed toward the back of the shop.

Parnell left the office and walked past a car mounted on a hydraulic lift. He glanced left, then right. There was no place for anyone to hide in this part of the garage. He saw a metal personnel door at the back, moved to it, and pushed on it. It didn't budge. He threw his shoulder against it and it popped open with a groan. He stepped out into the brilliant sunshine and raised his arm to shield his eyes. About to turn to look left, something hard poked into his spine.

"Who the hell are you?"

Parnell recognized Franco Caravelli's gravelly voice. "Come on, Franco, is this any way to greet an old friend?"

The pistol poked even harder against Parnell's backbone. "Don't fuck with me, asshole. I asked you a question."

"It's me, Franco. What the hell's going on? I'm the guy who saved

319

your bacon on Wiesenplatz in Berlin twenty years ago."

"Turn around."

Parnell slowly turned, his hands in the air. He saw Caravelli's wide-eyed expression.

After he slipped his pistol in a holster under his suit jacket, Caravelli stepped forward and hugged Parnell. "Jeez, Eddie. I thought you were an imposter. I couldn't figure out how someone stole your code phrase when I got the call at the embassy. But I was sure it wasn't you on the phone. You're supposed to be dead."

Caravelli released Parnell and gave him the once over. "God, you look like you've been rode hard and put away wet."

Parnell laughed. "That's what comes from doing field work. Unlike *former* field agents who copped out and went the diplomatic route."

Caravelli smiled. "Some of us, my friend, figured out early on that the field was a short route to an early grave."

"Let's go find a place to talk," Parnell said. "Someplace where we can get a couple beers. Your surprise at seeing me alive tells me I'm going to need a drink."

Caravelli led Parnell back through the garage to a black Fiat.

"Why were you so surprised to see me," Parnell said, as Caravelli pulled away from the shop. "You looked like you'd seen a ghost."

Caravelli took his eyes off the road for a second. "The Agency put out a bulletin that said you were killed a couple days ago."

"News to me," Parnell said.

"I can see that."

"What made them think I was dead?"

"According to Langley, you died in an explosion while on a mission. That's about all the explanation we got. Of course, the message was loaded with a bunch of crap about what a hero you were and how much the Agency will miss you."

Parnell smiled. "Is that right? I'm a hero?"

"That's right. A bona fide hero. Gonna put up a star for you at Langley. At least that's what that asshole, Moreland, said in the communiqué he sent out."

"Moreland," Parnell spat. "I smell a rat."

Caravelli glanced at Parnell again. "I think we should go to my office and call the Agency," he suggested. "You need to talk to Moreland."

Parnell rubbed his chin while he stared out the passenger window. "I agree we should make a call to the Agency. But let's not contact Moreland just yet," he said.

"What's on your mind?" Caravelli asked.

"I want to talk to Aggie."

"Mother Agnes in Accounting? What the hell can she tell you?"

"Franco, my boy, you'd be surprised."

CHAPTER 77

Caravelli called Langley on his encrypted cell phone.

"Agnes McIntire, may I help you?"

"Aggie, it's Frank Caravelli. How are you?"

"Oh, I'm all right, Frank."

"You sound kinda down, Aggie. What's the matter? Something on your mind?"

"It's nothing, Frank. I . . . . Really, it's nothing."

"It's Eddie Parnell, isn't it?" Caravelli said.

"Yes," she said. "He was such—"

"Aggie, listen to me. I want you to leave the office and call the number I'm about to give you from a secure phone. I suggest you buy a burner."

"What the heck's going on, Franco? Is something wrong?"

"No, Aggie, everything's fine. Just do as I ask, okay? Write down this number."

Caravelli hung up and looked at Parnell who slugged back half-a-bottle of beer, placed the bottle on the café table, and put on a shit-eating grin. They shot the breeze for forty-five minutes, getting caught up on recent activities in which they'd been involved, when Caravelli's cell rang.

"Yeah," he answered.

"Okay, I'm back, Frank. What's up?"

"Aggie, Eddie Parnell isn't dead."

Caravelli heard a strangled sound come over the line. "Oh my Lord," Aggie said. "Are you sure?"

"He's right here with me in Managua. But you need to keep that between us."

"Oh, my Lord," she said again. "We'll have to change all the reports, his records." She paused for a few seconds. "And the Parnells. We contacted Eddie's parents, his former wife, and told them he'd died. This is awful." Then sobs came over the line.

Caravelli motioned with a hand toward Parnell, as if to say, "You're on."

Parnell took the phone from Caravelli. "Hi, Aggie," he said. "You okay?"

"Is it really you?" Sniffling sounds.

"Calm down, Aggie. I don't have a scratch on me. You think I'd let anything happen to me when I've got a classy dish like you waiting for me back in D.C.?"

"Oh, you are so full of baloney," she said, the tension now out of her voice.

"Listen, Aggie, I have a couple questions. I don't want anyone to know about this conversation until I'm ready. You understand?"

"No," she said. "But if that's the way you want it, I'll keep mum."

"Good. Now tell me how you learned about my untimely death?"

"Why, Mr. Moreland called down here and left a message in my voicemail. He said you had been . . . killed on a mission by an explosion. Left instructions to close out your personnel file."

"Can you tell me the date and time he called you?"

"Of course," she said, a tinge of satisfaction in her tone. "I keep a log of all my telephone calls. Been doing that for thirty years. But I don't need to check my log. I remember exactly when he called. Fifteen minutes past three on Monday morning, two nights ago. That was the time the message was left on my voicemail. I pulled it up when I came in that morning."

Parnell wrote it all down. "This may seem unusual, Aggie," he said, "but I assure you it's very important. Have you received a requisition to make a contract payment to anyone in Central American for aircraft services rendered in the past few days?"

"How did you know that?" she asked, her voice rising in pitch.

"I'll explain some other time. Just tell me as much as you can about the payment request."

Aggie lowered her voice. "It was for one hundred thousand dollars to a Panamanian general. The notation on the request indicated the service rendered by the pilot had something to do with Nicaragua." She gasped loud enough to make the phone sound as though it suddenly had static. "That's where *you* are, Eddie."

Parnell instinctively knew what her answer to his next question would be. "Who signed the requisition, Aggie?"

"Mr. Moreland."

"Okay, Aggie," Parnell said. "I appreciate your help. I'll give you a call in a day or two so you can work on correcting the misunderstanding about my death. Talk to you soo—"

"Don't you want to know about the other payment request? For the other pilot, I mean. They came in at the same time. Also from Mr. Moreland."

Parnell looked at Caravelli and frowned. "Sure. What other pilot?"

"Mr. Moreland sent down two payment requisitions. One for the Panamanian general. The other for a Turkish general for a job in Bulgaria."

Parnell felt a lightning bolt strike his heart. He tried to calm down. He handed the phone back to Caravelli and whispered, "Terminate the call."

He paced while he heard Caravelli thank Aggie, then cut the connection. Finally, Parnell stopped in front of Caravelli. "That sonofabitch! That double-crossing sonofabitch!"

DAY 13

CHAPTER 78

Matt shuffled through the entrance to the San José Intercontinental Hotel suite that his employer, Placer Medical, had booked. Renee followed him and felt a surge of warmth rush through her at the sight of their friends. It seemed that everyone spoke at the same time, tossing out questions about Matt's health.

"Whoa, everybody," Renee said. "One at a time." She laughed and suggested everyone sit. Matt and Renee sat next to one another on the couch. Esteban stood behind Alani's stuffed chair, a hovering presence that guarded against evil. Fred Petrucchio sat on a windowsill. Chris Ridgeway slouched at the other end of the couch. Quince Hansen and his wife, Irene, occupied two straight-back chairs they'd pulled up. Eric Gates, the old Green Beret who'd babysat Luis Reyes, sat on a chair he'd dragged over from the dining room.

After Renee brought them up to date about Matt's condition, explaining that his broken jaw had been wired shut and that he was on antibiotics to guard against pneumonia, Matt mumbled, "What happened to the women we pulled out of the jungle?"

"Jeez, what a nightmare," Ridgeway said. "No passports; they're in Costa Rica illegally. For a while there, I thought the local government would send them home, back to the same conditions that made them jump at a chance for an overseas job in the first place. But Esteban pulled a rabbit out of a hat and changed everything."

Ridgeway turned to Esteban. "Why don't you take it from here?"

"Heck, it was easy. While we were in Nicaragua, old Eric here pumped Luis Reyes for every bit of information the guy had on Jackson." Esteban glanced at Gates and saw the grin on the little man's face. He winked at him. "Reyes spilled the beans on every official he'd bribed, including corrupt immigration officials. It was a simple matter to approach one of those men, threaten to expose him, and get his full cooperation. The three Bulgarians and two Nicaraguans were given visas and a promise they'd be issued passports before the month is out. The immigration guy was so shook up, he even provided the women with spending money and promised to find jobs for them here in Costa Rica."

Esteban looked over his shoulder at Petrucchio on the windowsill and smiled. "From what I hear, one of the Bulgarians has spent time with one of the former Green Berets here in San José."

Petrucchio blushed. "Gee, thanks, Esteban. Remind me to tell you all of my most intimate secrets."

"What about that weasel, Luis Reyes," Matt asked.

"Who's Luis Reyes?" Renee said.

"The guy who picked up you and Alani and delivered you to Jackson," Hansen said. Then he looked at Eric Gates. "You want to tell them?"

The wiry, bald-headed Gates grinned. "No, no, let Esteban do it. He's telling it fine, so far."

Esteban looked first at Renee, then at Matt. "Maybe we could all use a little humor around here." Matt had yet to recover his normal color. He was pale and his eyes sunken. Esteban had noticed that Matt and Renee were affectionate with one another, as they always were; but there seemed to be tension between them.

"Okay," Esteban said, "you know we left Reyes with Gates here." Matt nodded.

"If I recall correctly," Ridgeway said, "Reyes looked scared to death when he learned Eric would be his baby sitter."

"Not at first," Esteban said and laughed. "Old Reyes was petrified only after Gates tripped him and knocked him to the floor." Esteban pointed at Gates. "Can you imagine anyone being frightened of that sweet, gentle man?"

Hoots and catcalls erupted.

"Little did Reyes know that Eric was the least of his worries. It was Irene he should have worried about."

All heads turned to stare at Irene Hansen. She sat up a bit straighter and crossed her arms. Her face reddened as she glared at her husband.

"Eric locked the lawyer in a shed," Esteban continued. "The next morning, before Eric went to check on him, Reyes pried open a couple boards on the back of the shed and slipped out. He sprinted along the side of the house, turned the corner to the front gate, and ran smack into Irene."

Esteban paused long enough to get someone to ask, "What happened then?" Renee obliged.

"Irene had heard Reyes working on the shed planks and saw him escape. She ran through the house and met him by the front porch . . . with a frying pan. She coldcocked the midget with one shot to the head."

The room erupted in laughter and applause. Hansen leaned over and hugged Irene, who had turned crimson, waved her arms, and said, "Stop it. Stop it."

"The police need to put that crooked lawyer away for a long time," Renee said, when the room quieted down.

"Funny you should mention that," Hansen said. "The cops reported that Reyes hung himself in his jail cell. But I'll bet you a dollar to a donut someone with the police helped him with the rope. That little bastard knew too much and he was in a talkative mood. He gave Eric the names of several high-level police officials who were on the take."

"By the way," Petrucchio said, "a Bulgarian woman I know says there was another woman with them. A fourth Bulgarian."

Esteban looked suddenly confused. "What are you talking about?" he said.

Petrucchio spread his arms and said, "I'm just telling you what Ludmila told me."

"Oh, God," Esteban said. "You mean we left a woman in the jungle?"

Petrucchio shrugged.

This news seemed to cast a pall over the room.

To change the subject, Matt said in barely discernible words because of his wired jaw, "We leave for New Mexico tomorrow." He swallowed and paused for a couple seconds. "I can't thank you all enough. I owe you so much." He hunched his shoulders as if to say, there is nothing more to add.

The men seemed embarrassed and looked away or down at their feet like schoolboys caught in the act.

"Hell, Matt," Hansen finally said, "we should be thanking *you*." He looked at Petrucchio, then at Ridgeway. "We haven't had this much fun in years."

Irene Hansen coughed and wagged a finger at her husband. Her jaw tightened and her nostrils flared.

"But, it would probably be a good idea if you call the Marines next time," Hansen added.

That elicited a laugh from everyone, then Hansen stood. "I think we'd better let these people get some rest. They've got a long flight in the morning."

"Before you go, Chris, Fred," Matt said. "How'd you get out of Nicaragua?"

Ridgeway smiled. "Esteban and Jerry picked us up on a beach just across the border in Costa Rica."

"Yeah, but how'd you reach the beach," Matt said. "That would have been a hell of a hike through the jungle."

Ridgeway looked at Petrucchio and nodded his head.

Petrucchio stood and walked to the hotel room door. He lifted a bag off the floor, carried it to the coffee table, set it on the table, and unzipped it.

"Who said anything about hiking out," Ridgeway said. "We drove all the way to the beach in a bright-red Humvee we found in the jungle."

"Yeah, can you imagine that?" Petrucchio added. He chuckled. "Someone left this perfectly good truck in the middle of the boondocks."

"And guess what we found inside the Humvee?" Ridgeway said.

On cue, Petrucchio picked up the bag, turned it upside-down, and spilled stacks of cash, a bag of diamonds, and documents on the table.

"The way we figure it," Ridgeway said, "is that we ought to split up the cash among the Bulgarian and Nicaraguan women we saved. They'll need it."

Everyone stood up and said their goodbyes. When Esteban and Alani were the only two left with Matt and Renee, they hugged one another and promised to meet in Honolulu in December.

Esteban and Alani walked to the room door. Alani turned and looked at Renee. Tears rolled down her cheeks. "You're the bravest woman I know. I hope we have a little girl so I can name her after you." Then they walked out.

Renee returned to the couch and sat a few feet away from Matt. When he tried to hold her hand, she pulled it away.

"What's going on, honey?" Matt said.

"Matt, will you . . . ?" She suddenly sobbed, sounding as though she might never stop.

"Renee, what's the matter?"

"Will you ever want to touch me again? Are you disgusted with me?"

Matt jerked around and groaned when the movement sent a dagger of pain into his jaw. He twisted in his seat so he could look into Renee's eyes. "How can you say that? You're the most important person in the world. I love you."

"I know, Matt. But—"

"No buts." He touched her cheek. "I wish I could prove how badly I want you. It's just that my jaw—"

She again dissolved into body-wracking sobs. "I was afraid you didn't want to touch me . . . because of what Jackson—"

Matt pressed a finger to her lips. "You never have to say that name again. Not ever." He pressed a finger on her lips. "You're the light of my life. Nothing can or will ever change that."

"Oh, Matt," Renee said. She rolled and put her head on his lap and cried until she had no more tears to shed.

CHAPTER 79

The president paced back and forth across the Oval Office's royal blue carpet. Senator William Benedict, seated on the sofa, wished that POTUS would sit down, but this was the way the man did his thinking—pacing, hands clasped behind his back, head down.

Suddenly, the president stopped and wheeled around, a broad, toothy smile on his handsome features, his head raised, chin pointed toward Benedict. "I understand you resolved a situation that could have become a major problem."

Benedict crossed his legs and laid an arm over the back of the sofa. "No big thing, Mr. President."

"You've been a loyal friend, Bill. Your committees have always supported our programs and you've kept your ear to the ground and saved us a lot of trouble and embarrassment."

Benedict tipped his head in acknowledgment but didn't think he needed to say anything.

"I think it's time," the leader of the land continued, "to show you our appreciation. Is there anything that would make you *extremely* happy?"

Benedict had anticipated he was about to be rewarded for managing the Bulgarian business. He also knew he might very well have enabled this womanizer-in-chief to win a second term. A female trafficking scandal at the CIA could very well have finished the man's political career. It was time for payback and he had come prepared. What he wanted would cement his own future with the voters of Louisiana. *Hell*, he thought, *I'll break old Strom Thurmond's record for longevity in the Senate. If I can live that long.*

"Well, Mr. President, there is one thing that would make me the happiest Cajun in all of Louisiana."

The president smiled at Benedict as though he enjoyed the way this good old boy from the bayou's mind worked. "I'll bet there is, Bill. I'll just bet there is."

"You know the Department of Energy has had lots of problems in recent years with that little laboratory in Los Alamos. What with the forest fire that nearly burned the place down in 2000, the security problems, and then that whole Chinese spy catastrophe. That place is a disaster waiting to happen. I think it's about time the United States of America moved that lab to another state."

"Holy jeez, Bill," the president shouted. "Why the hell don't you just ask me to move the White House to New Orleans?"

Benedict laughed. "I thought about that, Mr. President, but I didn't think it would be seemly."

The president had an exasperated look on his face. He shook his head in disbelief and paced again. After a minute, he threw up his hands. "All right, Bill. I'll talk to the energy secretary. We'll figure something out."

Benedict stood. "Thank you, Mr. President. It's always a pleasure."

The president walked him to the door. He put an arm around Benedict's shoulder. "You know the senators from New Mexico will have a fit when they lose their lab."

"Hell, they still got the big lab in Albuquerque. It ain't fair that one poor state should have two national laboratories when my poor state doesn't even have one."

The president guffawed and slapped Benedict on the back. "I like your style, Bill. I surely do."

CHAPTER 80

It didn't take Eddie Parnell long to come up with a theory about what Cliff Moreland had done. He couldn't be one hundred percent certain his theory was correct, but he figured he was close enough to the truth for government work. Moreland had sent him after José Lorca because he wanted the man dead. That was simple enough to understand—Lorca's involvement with Tarnovsky and trafficking in women were huge problems. But Parnell suspected something had happened after he'd been assigned to make the hit. Something that ratcheted up the importance of erasing Lorca. And whatever that something was had caused Moreland to take the unusual and risky step of using foreign contract pilots to blow up Lorca's place, and Tarnovsky's, too.

What really made Parnell's blood boil was that Moreland had obviously targeted him as well. He had a cell phone with him and Moreland had the number. He could have warned him off at any time. No, Moreland wanted him dead. There were to be no survivors who could implicate Moreland or the CIA in Tarnovsky's operation. His life was the price to cover Moreland's ass.

As angry as he was, Parnell had to give grudging credit to Moreland. He never would have believed the weenie had the guts to do what he'd done. *And, if he wanted me dead that badly*, Parnell thought, *he won't be happy to hear I'm still around. I can hide for a while, but not forever. Sooner or later, the Company will track me down, and then I'll be dog meat. Dead dog meat.*

Franco Caravelli had so far been a true friend; but Parnell realized he had put his old friend in jeopardy. He needed to quickly come up with a resolution.

Before he worked on it, he said to Borodvic, "Tatiana, would you try to contact people in Bulgaria? I want as much information as possible about Tarnovsky. Is he alive? Did anyone survive who might have information?" Parnell didn't think she'd come up with much of anything, but the assignment kept her busy; made her feel useful.

Parnell again met with Caravelli. He borrowed some embassy equipment, loaded it in the back of the SUV, and returned to his hotel room.

Tatiana greeted him with a big smile—he liked coming back to the room—and her. "What is this?" she asked. "You are making movie?"

"That's right. I'll be the producer, director, and star. You'll be the camerawoman."

"Good. I like movie business. My father said I should be famous Bulgarian movie star." She grinned at him as though she were joking.

Parnell smiled back. "Your father was right. You're more beautiful than any actress I've ever seen."

Tatiana looked surprised. She blushed and gave Parnell a closed-lipped, hooded-eyed smile. She walked over to him and helped him lay the equipment—a video camera, tripod, floodlight mounted on a six foot aluminum pole, and mesh bag with DVD disks inside—on one of the beds. She then moved against him and placed her hands around his neck, and drew his mouth to hers.

"What was that for?" he asked.

"For being so good to me, for saving my life, and for being so good looking."

They held each other's eyes for a long moment, and then Parnell pulled her to him and this time their kiss was long and passionate. He was out of breath by the time he broke off the kiss and his lips felt bruised. He lifted her in his arms and carried her to the second bed, where he placed her gently on top of the bedspread, and sat down next to her.

"I've wanted you from the first day."

"Yes," she said, a giggle in her voice. "You are very obvious, you know?"

He was at a loss for words. He brushed the hair out of her eyes and stared at her finely sculpted face. She had the facial structure of a runway model, with exotic, almond-shaped eyes and high cheek bones that spoke of Tartar ancestry. Parnell had never been with a woman so beautiful and had a sudden uncertain feeling.

"Are you going to keep clothes on?" she said in a husky voice. "Is that way Americans make love?"

Parnell's face felt hot. He mumbled an apology and knew he sounded like a high school kid. "I'm sorry about what . . . happened back in the jungle. Knocking you out."

She scowled, pouted, then laughed. "You are funny, Eddie Parnell. If you not knock me out, I kill you."

She reached up and pulled him to her. "You are very good man, Eddie Parnell. I cannot be finding better man than you."

Her words gave Parnell the assurance he needed. He kissed her mouth, then her forehead, chin, and neck. He wasn't quite sure when or how he removed his clothes, but he was absolutely certain he would never forget helping Tatiana out of hers.

Despite an urgency that made him tremble with excitement, and a need that made him want to take her quickly and furiously, he made love to her slowly, languorously. When they climaxed together, he felt that he'd reached a new place in his life. A place where the dirt, intrigue, and double-dealing were in the past. Where there was a future that would offer something different, something truly worthwhile. And when he held her in his arms afterward, he felt as comfortable as he had ever felt with a woman: a sensation he had never known before. This was a woman worth committing himself to.

She moaned and nestled even closer; her mouth burrowed against his neck. "That was nice, Eddie Parnell."

"Umm," he hummed. "As nice as it gets."

She suddenly extricated herself from his embrace and moved on top of him. "No, I do not think it was nice as it gets. I think it gets even nicer."

Parnell awoke spent, groggy, but as happy as he'd been in a long time. He was amazed. *I go to Nicaragua to murder a man,* he thought, *and fall in love with a Bulgarian assassin. Go figure.* She stirred next to him and opened her eyes.

"You are awake," she said.

"Barely. You okay?"

"Yes, but I think I would like to make love again. You make me . . . ."

Parnell slipped out of bed and looked down at her, his hands in front, in a protective position. "Oh no. No way. I need food and more rest before I can go again. What do you want to do, kill me?"

She laughed heartily and threw up her hands in victory. "Bulgaria one, America zero."

Parnell squinted at her, his mouth open. *What the hell have I gotten myself into?* he thought. He smiled at her and then thought, *What a way to go!*

He looked at the camera gear on the other bed. "Maybe we better get to work on our movie."

"I forgot to tell you," Borodvic said as she rolled off the bed and picked up her clothes from the floor, "I finally found someone in Bulgaria with information."

Parnell, bent over to retrieve his trousers, jerked upright. "Who?"

"That bloody Turk who worked for Tarnovsky. Metin Osmanoglu. He was pissed off. He was only one who survive explosion at Tarnovsky's estate."

"Is Tarnovsky dead?"

"Yes. There were not any pieces of him left."

"Go on," Parnell said.

She grinned. "Tarnovsky called United States senator the day before bombing. Man named Driscoll. He wanted to tell Driscoll about relationship with CIA and trafficking in women. There had been attack on his compound two days before bombing and Tarnovsky discovered CIA was behind it. He thought confessing to trafficking and saying he worked for CIA, there would no longer be reason for CIA to kill him."

Parnell nodded. He remembered the meeting with Driscoll and the other government officials . . . was it just a week ago? The senator had been righteous about trafficking. But then a light bulb flashed in Parnell's brain. If Tarnovsky had called Driscoll, then Driscoll may have told Moreland, or told someone who had passed the information on to Moreland. Tarnovsky's threat of exposure must have been the catalyst that caused Moreland to order the air strikes against Lorca and Tarnovsky. So, the U.S. senator had betrayed Tarnovsky. Parnell suddenly knew the situation was worse than he'd originally thought.

"What are you thinking?" Tatiana asked.

"That there are many people who are very happy thinking I am dead. And I am about to ruin their day."

DAY 14

CHAPTER 81

Eddie Parnell met Franco Caravelli the next morning on a side street in Managua to return the video equipment he'd borrowed from him. After they'd loaded the equipment in the trunk of the car, Parnell handed Caravelli two brown, sealed shipping envelopes.

"You think you can put these in the diplomatic pouch?"

"What's in them?"

"Better you don't know."

"Then let's forget about the pouch. Anything that goes in there has to be recorded with the name of the sender and the recipient. I'll drop them off at a FedEx office."

"I'll never be able to thank you enough, Frank," Parnell said after the gear was stowed. "You ever need me, just . . . ." Parnell didn't finish the sentence because he knew he had to disappear. He wouldn't leave a forwarding address. Caravelli would have no way to reach him.

Caravelli only half-suppressed a knowing smile. He shook Parnell's hand. "I hope you make those damn bureaucrats sweat."

Parnell grinned. "All the way down to the soles of their feet." Then he said, "Remember, deny you saw or heard from me. Don't worry about Aggie at Langley. She'll keep her mouth shut."

Caravelli nodded. "What will you do?"

"Oh, I've got something in mind. But, listen, there's another favor I have to ask."

Caravelli's eyebrows arched and his jaw tightened. Then he paused a beat and said, "Aw, hell. In for a penny, in for a pound."

"Would you call my parents and tell them I'm alive; that I'll try to make contact with them soon. But tell them not to tell a soul, including my ex. Until Moreland understands that my death will only expose him, I've got to lie low. I don't know for how long that will be."

"Sure," Caravelli said. "I have to be in D.C. next week for a meeting; I'll go see your folks personally."

"Thanks, Frank."

Caravelli waved a dismissive hand. "You need some cash?" he asked.

"Nah. I still have most of the advance I got from Aggie. I already exchanged it into dollars. It'll hold me over for a while." He pointed at one of the envelopes in Caravelli's hand. "Once Moreland gets that envelope and understands what's at stake, I should be in the clear. I'll call the Agency then and collect back pay and start drawing my retirement checks. I'll be okay."

Caravelli gave Parnell a sorrowful look, his spaniel-like brown eyes sad and moist. Parnell could tell that his friend wasn't confident about his future.

"Buck up, Frank," Parnell said. "I'll be okay." Then he turned, walked back to the SUV, and drove away. He didn't feel as confident as he'd sounded.

DAY 15

CHAPTER 82

The once-daily FedEx delivery from Managua arrived in Washington, D.C., within twenty-four hours from the time Caravelli dropped them off.

When the FedEx package was deposited on Cliff Moreland's secretary's desk, she thought nothing about it. It was just one of dozens of letters or boxes her boss received each day from a multitude of overseas locations. And this one wasn't even classified. It was marked "Personal," so she didn't open it.

Moreland returned to his office at 3 p.m. from a meeting at the State Department. He felt drained. One more damn problem in another third world country, a country that would never amount to a pile of road apples, no matter how many U.S. dollars were poured into the place.

He sat in his chair and stared at the pile of mail on his blotter. The letters had all been neatly sliced open, the envelopes stapled to the backs of the correspondence. He vented an exasperated sigh, lifted the first letter, and noticed a Post-It message on top from his secretary that advised him a "Personal" package had come in from Managua and was on the bottom of the stack. Normally, he wouldn't have thought twice about it. But recent events in Nicaragua caused him to wonder. He pushed the pile aside, exposing a FedEx package.

"Huh," he said. He ripped open the envelope with a pair of

scissors. Inside was an unlabeled disk.

He stood, walked to the far corner of his office, used the remote on the coffee table, and pressed the television "Power" button. After he switched to channel three, he inserted the disk in the machine, and punched the "Play" button.

He settled back in a chair opposite the television. *Je-e-ez*, he thought, *what kind of bullshit have they sent me now?* Then he hoped that whatever it was would be more entertaining than the boring, goddamn meeting he'd just left with that ugly, hairy-legged witch at State.

The screen rolled; there was a burst of electronic snow. Then Moreland's heart did a full gainer. Eddie Parnell sat on a chair against a wall badly in need of paint.

Scratchy sounds came from the television, then Parnell's voice boomed inside the office. Moreland reached for the remote with a frantic jerk of his hand and reduced the sound level.

"Hello, Cliffie. I'm sure you're thrilled to see I'm still alive," Parnell said. "It must have been heartbreaking for you to think I had died." Parnell glared, then continued, "You're a rotten sonofabitch, Moreland, and if I could figure out a way to take you down without risking my own life, I would. But, as usual, there just ain't no justice. So here's the deal."

Moreland whipped a handkerchief out of his trousers and wiped perspiration from his forehead. *Seymour Katzman will have my balls*, he thought. *I'm ruined.*

Parnell shifted in his chair. "There are five copies of this disk. One for you, another sent to Senator Peter Driscoll. I'll keep one with me. The remaining two are in sealed containers and are in the hands of people I trust with my life. They have been instructed to go to the media if I should disappear, or die under suspicious circumstances.

"I know Yevgeni Tarnovsky called Senator Driscoll about his relationship with the CIA and disclosed his involvement with trafficking in women and drugs. The fact that none of this information became public indicates to me that Senator Driscoll sat on it and used it for his own benefit. If the media knew this, they wouldn't need much time to figure out what the trade-off was.

I read about the laboratory that's to be built in Kansas.

"You got pen and paper handy, Moreland?" Parnell paused, as though he knew Moreland would have to return to his desk to get a pad of paper. Fifteen seconds later, he began again. "I'll keep my mouth shut, if you do what I demand. I want you to call Agnes McIntire in Accounting and tell her that when I call and give her instructions, she is authorized to do exactly what I tell her to do. Don't get nervous, I won't take anything that's not mine. I want whatever pay I have coming to me and my entire retirement fund wired to the bank of my choice. I want the present value of my retirement pay, with a three percent compounded annual cost of living adjustment over thirty-five years, sent to my bank in one lump sum. I'll give Ms. McIntire the number; you just make sure she knows you've authorized it."

Parnell leaned forward and glared again. Moreland couldn't make eye contact with him, even on the television screen. "If the money isn't in the account within one hour of my call to Agnes, I'll release a whirlwind that will ruin you and a whole lot of other assholes."

Parnell relaxed against the back of his chair and smiled. "Pay attention, Cliffie, to the facts I'm about to recite."

Moreland slumped in his chair while Parnell told a tale that, if exposed, would send him to prison for the rest of his life.

Then Parnell finished: "Take it easy, Cliffie. Pray you never run into me." Parnell chuckled, then added, "A day, a year, ten years from now, you could turn a corner and there I'll be. Stay alert. You just never know."

The screen went black and Moreland sat as though paralyzed. He ignored the humming sound from the player, not bothering to switch it off.

CHAPTER 83

What Parnell had not told Moreland, in case the perfidious bastard tried something stupid, was that the monies he asked Aggie to transfer would be wired to one of three aliases he'd set up years earlier, just in case he got crosswise with the Agency. It wouldn't have been the first time the CIA had turned on one of its own. Passports and other identification backed up each of those aliases in safety deposit boxes.

Parnell and Tatiana Borodvic flew to Aruba, where he went to one of his safety deposit boxes to pick up a set of documents. Then, he left Tatiana in Aruba, ensconced in a luxury beachside hotel room, and caught a flight to Buenos Aires. He took a cab from the airport to the bank where his money would be transferred.

At 7 a.m., D.C. time, he used his cell phone to call Aggie at her home. "Mornin' darling," Parnell said.

"Hi, Eddie. I've been waiting for your call."

"Here's what I want you to do, Aggie." After he gave her the details, she repeated them back to him, word for word.

"Perfect," he said. "After you execute the wire, try to keep the information between us for an hour."

"Don't you worry, Eddie."

"I'm not worried. I got you on my side. And, by the way, they won't do anything to you. They even breathe on you hard and I'll release what I got on them to every news service in the world."

"Since when am I afraid of a bunch of Ivy League halfcuts?"

"That's my girl."

Eddie hung up and reviewed his plan. An hour should be more than enough time to withdraw the money, stuff it in a soft-sided leather bag, and catch a flight back to Aruba, using yet another identity.

Parnell looked down at the bag on the floor between his feet and sighed. Not a lot of money after he'd risked his life for more than two decades. *Ah, well, them's the breaks*, he thought. He smiled. He used the time in the air on the return flight to Aruba to think about what he would do with the rest of his life. The money from the Agency would last four years, maybe five if he was frugal. But there wasn't enough to put in a bank and live off the interest.

Seated in the last row, he craned his neck and looked over the tops of the rows of seats in front of him. The flight was barely half full, and he was the only person seated in his row. He needed to dump a few things. Lifting the leather bag from between his feet to his lap, he opened it, removed the clothes he'd placed on top of the money, and laid them on the seat next to him. Then he rifled around in the bottom of the bag and removed the alias ID he'd shown at the bank in Buenos Aires. He also pulled out his Eddie Parnell papers. They were no good to him anymore. The CIA cell phone was next. He slipped everything under the clothes on the adjoining seat, then started to repack the clothes in the bag. He noticed something red in a corner at the bottom. He reached in and gripped it between his thumb and forefinger. And then he remembered—Jackson's flash drive. The one he'd taken out of the hard drive in Jackson's office. He started to toss it on the seat with the other junk, but thought, *it might be fun to see what the sonofabitch has on this thing*. He picked it back up and slipped it into his shirt pocket.

After he repacked the bag, Parnell carried it and the junk on the seat cushion to the restroom. There he ripped up the documents and flushed them down the toilet. It gave him enormous satisfaction to hear the pieces disposed of with a great, watery sucking sound. He broke the cell phone into pieces and stuffed them in the trash container.

He returned to his seat and tried to come up with a job plan. *Or, maybe I should open my own business.* Nothing came to mind that turned him on—other than Tatiana. He'd wait until he arrived in Aruba and talk with her. Maybe they could both get jobs, work for ten or so years, then really retire. He suddenly felt depressed.

The plane landed at 2 p.m. Parnell caught a taxi to his bank and put the money in his Aruba safety deposit box. Then he taxied to the hotel and went straight to his room. Tatiana wasn't there. Probably down at the beach. She'd become a real sun worshiper. *Who could blame her,* he thought, *after she'd lived most of her life in Bulgaria?*

"What the hell," Parnell said. "I'll get something to eat, then join her." He left the room and went to the lobby restaurant. He ordered a BLT and a beer, then reached over and took a copy of *The International Herald Tribune* off an adjoining table. The headline read "Kidnapped Americans Rescued." A photo of two couples taken at the airport in San José, Costa Rica was captioned with the words: "Renee Curtis and Alani Maldonado, pictured with their husbands at Juan Santamaría Airport, leaving for their homes in the United States."

Parnell read the article, which was full of assumptions and devoid of detail. It left the impression that the kidnapped women's husbands had been involved in their recovery and that other women had also been saved, including three from Bulgaria and two from Nicaragua. By the time he'd finished reading the article, his heart was racing. He'd read between the lines and suspected that he'd crossed paths with Curtis and Maldonado on José Lorca's estate. "I'll be damned," he muttered.

After he'd gotten over his shock from reading the article, and while he waited for his order to arrive, he glanced around the restaurant and people-watched. When he looked out at the lobby and saw a sign for the Business Office, he remembered the computer flash drive in his pocket. He pulled it out and tapped it against the edge of the table. *I probably have time to check this thing out before my order arrives.*

Parnell caught the eye of his waitress. When she came over to his table, he told her he would be back in a few minutes. He stood and walked across the lobby to the Business Office. He asked the female attendant there for a computer terminal.

"Of course, sir," she said, and led him to an alcove.

When she left him alone, he inserted the flash drive into the computer and opened the D: drive. The flash drive had five folders on it, each with innocuous titles: "Associates," "Customers," "Personal," "Shipments," and "Travel."

"Shit!" he muttered. He clicked on the first folder: "Associates." A long list of names, phone numbers, and what might have been account numbers of some kind popped up. Parnell didn't recognize any of the names, although some of the phone number country codes were familiar. He didn't bother to guess what the numbers represented. He got out of the "Associates" folder and opened the "Customers" folder. Again, there were names and phone numbers. He saw only one name he recognized: "Tarnovsky."

In the "Personal" folder, he clicked on the first file, "Assignments," but found nothing there. The same thing occurred with the next three files. He looked at the clock on the wall and realized that fifteen minutes had gone by. *My lunch has probably already been served*, he thought. He pushed back in his chair, about to return to the restaurant, when he thought: *Aw, what the hell. I'll try one more folder.*

He decided to give up on the "Personal" folder and opened the "Shipments" folder. A list popped onto the screen that, at first, confused him. But it took less than a minute to decipher the information. It was a spreadsheet of José Lorca's victims and included names, ages, descriptions, points of origin, names of customers, final destinations, and sales prices. He recognized some of the customer names from the "Customers" folder he'd opened a few minutes earlier. There were also two columns that showed the dates the women arrived and ultimately left Nicaragua. There were fifty-seven pages with the names of about twenty-five women on each page. Parnell did a quick mental calculation. "Holy shit!" he blurted. "Over fourteen hundred victims."

On a lark, he checked to see if the name Katrina Petrashvili, the daughter of Senator Peter Driscoll's constituent who had disappeared from her mother's home in the former Soviet Republic of Georgia, was on the list. He scrolled through page after page.

There it was on page twenty-three. She'd been transported to a buyer named Ronoldo Catanach in Miami Beach nearly sixty days ago.

In the price column, the numbers ranged from $8,000 to $50,000. "Hell," he muttered, "at $10,000 a head, that would come to $14,000,000." Then he recalled that there had been a "Retirement" file in the "Personal" folder. *What if Lorca recorded his trafficking earnings in that file?*

He went back to the "Personal" folder and opened the "Retirement" file. Another spreadsheet came up on the screen. The sheet showed twelve lines of data over five columns. In the first column were letters that seemed to be initials, none of which Parnell recognized: SdS, ISB, BSdeS, FBN, and so forth. The second column showed twelve lines of numbers. All the number sequences included at least nine digits. A couple had as many as thirteen. The third and fourth columns were obviously a list of email addresses and telephone numbers, respectively. The last column was as much a mystery as were the first two.

Parnell sat and stared at the screen. He was puzzled and disappointed. Breaking codes had never been his forte. He'd been a field agent his entire adult life, not a crypto guy. *Maybe this is more information about some of Lorca's underworld buddies.* On a lark, he took his cell from his jacket pocket and called the first telephone number on the list. He waited, more curious as the seconds passed. *Who will pick up? An international gangster? A corrupt government official?*

Finally, a recorded voice came on the line. Parnell recognized the Swiss German dialect and knew enough of the language to understand the words: "You have reached the twenty-four-hour service line of the Wire Transfer Department at the Sicherheitsbank der Schweiz. Please hold. A customer service representative will be with you shortly."

Surprised, Parnell took in a calming breath and then slowly released the air in his lungs. He recognized the bank's name. He'd seen their signs on a number of buildings during his frequent Agency-assigned trips to Europe. He looked back at the computer screen and wondered about the information there. He stared at the first line, first column with the initials BSdS: Sicherheitsbank der Schweiz.

A voice sounded in his ear—"*Gerhard Fiedler. Kann ich helfen Sie?*"—startling him, nearly causing him to hang up the phone. He wasn't quite sure what to do next.

What do I have to lose? he thought. He couldn't come up with the German words, so he said in English: "Number 50295116291." He read off the numbers in the second column, across from the bank's initials. He held his breath. Silence from the other end was his response—for ten seconds. Then the banker said, "Yes, sir. Your password, please."

Parnell was used to passwords. The CIA was nuts about them. But there was nothing on the drive that even resembled any password he'd ever used. The Agency used passwords like "Hector," or "Bloodlust," or "Flashpoint." Out of desperation, his eyes shot to the last column on the screen. There was nothing but numbers in this column that ranged from one line with six digits to a line that included eleven digits. Parnell rattled off the numbers on the BSdeS line.

Another short silence. "That is a valid password," the Swiss then said. "Deposit or withdrawal?"

Parnell's throat tightened. He had to swallow and lick his lips to get the words out. "Withdrawal, please."

"How much would you like transferred and to where, sir?"

Now, barely able to breathe, let alone speak, Parnell squeaked out the words, "What is the balance in the account?"

"Would you like that denominated in Swiss francs or U.S. dollars?"

"Dollars, please," Parnell responded. Despite his electrified nerves, he was beginning to have fun. "How much is in the account?"

"Including interest and dividends, credited through today," the man said, "twenty-seven million, nine hundred ninety thousand, four hundred seventy-three dollars and fourteen cents."

"Holy shit!"

"Excuse me, sir," the banker said, sounding shocked.

Parnell hadn't realized he'd spoken out loud until he heard the man's reaction. "Excuse me. Please give me a second." He pulled his wallet from his pants pocket and dumped the contents on the alcove desk. He looked for the slip of paper on which he'd jotted his Aruba bank account number. He shuffled credit cards and bits of paper around until he found it.

He cleared his throat and tried to sound dignified. "Please transfer the entire balance to the following account," he said as calmly as he could. He read off the name of his Aruba bank and account number. He expected some objection, or at least a question from the banker, but Fiedler just said, "Do you want to close the account?"

"Yes," Parnell answered.

"It was a pleasure to be of service," Fiedler said.

Parnell thanked the man. He continued to hold his cell to his ear long after the man in Switzerland had hung up, staring blindly at the brightly lit computer screen. When he finally got his wits about him, he terminated the call and put his phone back in his pocket. He looked at his wristwatch and saw it was too late to contact his bank here. Besides, the wire probably wouldn't be processed until the morning. If it was processed at all. He still couldn't believe what had just occurred. *But why wouldn't it be processed?* he thought. He considered calling the other numbers on the disk, but decided his heart wasn't strong enough to deal with it at that moment.

He stumbled out of the business office, mumbled thanks to the attendant, and returned to the restaurant. He laid a twenty-dollar bill on the table, took his beer, and ignored the sandwich that had been left there. He was afraid he would barf if he ate anything. His stomach felt as though it housed a Ferris wheel loaded with monkeys.

As he wandered back toward his room, he wondered about the discrepancy between the fourteen million dollars he'd estimated that Lorca had earned from trafficking, according to the spreadsheet he'd pulled up, and the amount of money in the man's Swiss bank. *Perhaps, the man was into other businesses, like narcotics*, Parnell thought.

Parnell entered his room, walked through to the patio, collapsed in a web chair, and looked out at the sand and the sea beyond. Then he noticed Tatiana walk from the surf. She looked like an Amazon queen. She reminded him of Ursula Andress when she came out of the water in the old James Bond movie, *Dr. No*. Her wet hair was plastered to her head. Her body sparkled with a thousand sunlit water beads. The sight of her did nothing to settle down his stomach, but it sure as hell sent his pulse racing.

She jogged across the sand, her smile so radiant it made his heart feel as though it had doubled in size, now much too large to fit inside his chest. When she reached the patio, she landed in his lap, wetting his shirt and pants. She giggled like a schoolgirl and kissed him as though his being there was the most wonderful thing in the world.

"You look pale," she said, her brows knitted. "Is it money you are concerned about? Don't worry. I will get job and help out. Everything will be fine." She kissed him again, then nuzzled his neck. She whispered in his ear, "It is Eddie Parnell and Tatiana Borodvic against the world." She giggled. "Watch out world!"

Parnell gently pushed her away, so he could see her face.

"What kind of job do you plan to get?"

She shot him an innocent smile and said, "We can make company that kills bad man. We have much experience with that. We will call company name like Hit Parade. You get it?"

Parnell examined her expression and couldn't tell if she was serious. "I guess you're right," he said. "Everything will be fine." Then he had a thought. "How would you feel about trying to find the women that Lorca sold?"

She looked at him quizzically. "But we would have to know where he sold women. How is that possible? Wouldn't that cost much dollars?"

Parnell smiled at her, kissed her neck, and said, "We should talk about it."

CHAPTER 84

Matt put an arm around Renee's shoulders. She seemed to hover near him more than usual. *I know she's tough*, he thought. *She'll get past the trauma of the past week—hell, the past . . . how many years had it been? Her son's murder, her husband's suicide, Susan's death, the attempts on their lives, the kidnapping, the rape. Not to mention the nightmares. All because of Lonnie Jackson.*

"What do you think, honey?" he asked.

Renee continued to stare out over the rolling Santa Fe foothills. When she finally turned to look at him, there were tears in her eyes. "It's beautiful, Matt. But are you sure this is what you want?"

He pulled her to him and kissed the top of her head. "I always wanted to live in the City Different. We can get this land for the right price and you can design your dream home."

"My dream home," she whispered pensively, "is wherever I am with you. Let's hold off building until your contract with Placer is finished. If you think I'll let you travel around the world all by yourself, you got another think coming."

"Wouldn't want it any other way. I think—" Matt's cell phone interrupted him. He didn't recognize the caller's number or name: Spencer Carlisle. He was about to ignore the call, but then changed his mind. "Hello," he answered.

"Dr. Curtis?"

"Yes?"

"My name is Spencer Carlisle. Our paths crossed recently down in Nicaragua."

Just the mention of Nicaragua made Matt's pulse race.

"I don't recall our meeting, Mr. Carlisle. What is this about?"

"I'd like to discuss a business proposition with you and Esteban Maldonado."

THE END

ACKNOWLEDGEMENTS

To my readers, thank you for your loyal support. You virtually keep alive my passion for writing. Your kind feedback and suggestions are invaluable, and your reviews make a difference.

I have been fortunate to receive reviews of and blurbs for my novels written by many successful and prolific authors, including Mark Adduci, Tom Avitabile, Parris Afton Bonds, Steve Brewer, Catherine Coulter, Philip Donlay, Robert Dugoni, Steve Havill, Anne Hillerman, Tony Hillerman, Alan Jacobson, Paul Kemprecos, Robert Kresge, Jon Land, Mark Leggatt, D. P. Lyle, Michael McGarrity, David Morrell, Michael Palmer, Dennis Palumbo, Andrew Peterson, Douglas Preston, Mark Rubinstein, Meryl Sawyer, and Sheldon Siegel. I know how busy these men and women are and it always humbles me when they graciously take time to read and praise my work.

Special thanks to John Badal for information that helped create some of my characters.

My sincere thanks go to John Byram for doing a superb job of editing *Justice*. Every author needs a top-notch editor, and John certainly is as top-notch as they come.

I want to recognize Burt Parnell who purchased the naming rights to Eddie Parnell, a key character in this story, at a Rotary Charity Auction.

Finally, my heartfelt thanks and appreciation go to John and Shannon Raab and all their staff at *Suspense Publishing* for their professionalism, support, advice, and friendship. You have all made the publishing side of writing a pleasure.

ABOUT THE AUTHOR

Joseph Badal grew up in a family where story-telling had been passed down from generation to generation.

Prior to a long business career, including a 16-year stint as a senior executive and board member of a NYSE-listed company, Joe served for six years as a commissioned officer in the U.S. Army in critical, highly classified positions in the U.S. and overseas, including tours of duty in Greece and Vietnam, and earned numerous military decorations.

Joe is an Amazon #1 Best-Selling Author, with 15 published suspense novels, including six books in the *Danforth Saga* series, two books in the *Curtis Chronicles* series, three books in the *Lassiter/Martinez Case Files* series, and three stand-alones. He has been recognized as "One of The 50 Best Writers You Should Be Reading." His books have received two Tony Hillerman Awards for Best Fiction Book of the Year, three gold medals from the Military Writers Society of America, and Finalist honors in the International Book Awards and the Eric Hoffer Awards.

Joe has written short stories which were published in the "Uncommon Assassins," "Someone Wicked," and "Insidious Assassins" anthologies. He has also written dozens of articles that have been published in various business and trade journals and is a frequent speaker at business, civic, and writers' events.

To learn more, visit his website at www.JosephBadalBooks.com.

"EVIL DEEDS"
DANFORTH SAGA (#1)

"Evil Deeds" is the first book in the *Bob Danforth* series, which includes "Terror Cell" and "The Nostradamus Secret." In this three book series, the reader can follow the lives of Bob & Liz Danforth, and of their son, Michael, from 1971 through 2011. "Evil Deeds" begins on a sunny spring day in 1971 in a quiet Athenian suburb. Bob & Liz Danforth's morning begins just like every other morning: Breakfast together, Bob roughhousing with Michael. Then Bob leaves for his U.S. Army unit and the nightmare begins, two-year-old Michael is kidnapped.

So begins a decades-long journey that takes the Danforth family from Michael's kidnapping and Bob and Liz's efforts to rescue him, to Bob's forced separation from the Army because of his unauthorized entry into Bulgaria, to his recruitment by the CIA, to Michael's commissioning in the Army, to Michael's capture by a Serb SPETSNAZ team in Macedonia, and to Michael's eventual marriage to the daughter of the man who kidnapped him as a child. It is the stops along the journey that weave an intricate series of heart-stopping events built around complex, often diabolical characters. The reader experiences CIA espionage during the Balkans War, attempted assassinations in the United States, and the grisly exploits of a psychopathic killer.

"Evil Deeds" is an adrenaline-boosting story about revenge, love, and the triumph of good over evil.

https://amzn.com/B00LXG9QIC

"TERROR CELL"
DANFORTH SAGA (#2)

"Terror Cell" pits Bob Danforth, a CIA Special Ops Officer, against Greek Spring, a vicious terrorist group that has operated in Athens, Greece for three decades. Danforth's mission in the summer of 2004 is to identify one or more of the members of the terrorists in order to bring them to justice for the assassination of the CIA's Station Chief in Athens. What Danforth does not know is that Greek Spring plans a catastrophic attack against the 2004 Summer Olympic Games.

Danforth and his CIA team are hampered by years of Congressionally mandated rules that have weakened U.S. Intelligence gathering capabilities, and by indifference and obstructionism on the part of Greek authorities. His mission becomes even more difficult when he is targeted for assassination after an informant in the Greek government tells the terrorists of Danforth's presence in Greece.

In "Terror Cell," Badal weaves a tale of international intrigue, involving players from the CIA, the Greek government, and terrorists in Greece, Libya, and Iran—all within a historical context. Anyone who keeps up with current events about terrorist activities and security issues at the Athens Olympic Games will find the premise of this book gripping, terrifying, and, most of all, plausible.

"Joe Badal takes us into a tangled puzzle of intrigue and terrorism, giving readers a tense well-told tale and a page-turning mystery."
—Tony Hillerman, *New York Times* bestselling author

https://amzn.com/B00LXG9QNC

"THE NOSTRADAMUS SECRET"
DANFORTH SAGA (#3)

This latest historical thriller in the *Bob Danforth* series builds on Nostradamus's "lost" 58 quatrains and segues to present day. These lost quatrains have surfaced in the hands of a wealthy Iranian megalomaniac who believes his rise to world power was prophesied by Nostradamus. But he sees the United States as the principal obstacle to the achievement of his goals. So, the first step he takes is to attempt to destabilize the United States through a vicious series of terrorist attacks and assassinations.

Joseph Badal offers up another action-packed story loaded with intrigue, fascinating characters and geopolitical machinations that put the reader on the front line of present-day international conflict. You will be transported from a 16th century French monastery to the CIA, to crime scenes, to the Situation Room at the White House, to Middle Eastern battlefields.

"The Nostradamus Secret" presents non-stop action in a contemporary context that will make you wonder whether the story is fact or fiction, history or prophesy.

" 'The Nostradamus Secret' is a gripping, fact-paced story filled with truly fanatical, frightening villains bent on the destruction of the USA and the modern world. Badal's characters and the situations they find themselves in are hair-raising and believable. I couldn't put the book down. Bring on the sequel!"
—Catherine Coulter, *New York Times* bestselling author of "Double Take"

https://amzn.com/B00R3GTLVI

"THE LONE WOLF AGENDA"
DANFORTH SAGA (#4)

With "The Lone Wolf Agenda," Joseph Badal returns to the world of international espionage and military action thrillers and crafts a story that is as close to the real world of spies and soldiers as a reader can find. This fourth book in the *Danforth Saga* brings Bob Danforth out of retirement to hunt down lone wolf terrorists hell bent on destroying America's oil infrastructure. Badal weaves just enough technology into his story to wow even the most a-technical reader.

"The Lone Wolf Agenda" pairs Danforth with his son Michael, a senior DELTA Force officer, as they combat an OPEC-supported terrorist group allied with a Mexican drug cartel. This story is an epic adventure that will chill readers as they discover that nothing, no matter how diabolical, is impossible.

"A real page-turner in every good sense of the term. 'The Lone Wolf Agenda' came alive for me. It is utterly believable, and as tense as any spy thriller I've read in a long time."
—Michael Palmer, *New York Times* bestselling author of "Political Suicide"

https://amzn.com/B00LXG9QMI

"DEATH SHIP"
DANFORTH SAGA (#5)

"Death Ship" is another suspense-filled thriller in the 45-year-long journey of the Danforth family. This fifth book in the *Danforth Saga*, which includes "Evil Deeds," "Terror Cell," "The Nostradamus Secret," and "The Lone Wolf Agenda," introduces Robbie Danforth, the 15-year-old son of Michael and Miriana Danforth, and the grandson of Bob and Liz Danforth.

A leisurely cruise in the Ionian Sea turns into a nightmare event when terrorists hijack a yacht with Bob, Liz, Miriana, and Robbie aboard. Although the boat's crew, with Bob and Robbie's help, eliminate the hijackers, there is evidence that something more significant may be in the works.

The CIA and the U.S. military must identify what that might be and who is behind the threat, and must operate within a politically-corrupt environment in Washington, D.C. At the same time, they must disrupt the terrorist's financing mechanism, which involves trading in securities that are highly sensitive to terrorist events.

Michael Danforth and a team of DELTA operatives are deployed from Afghanistan to Greece to assist in identifying and thwarting the threat.

"Death Ship" is another roller coaster ride of action and suspense, where good and evil battle for supremacy and everyday heroes combat evil antagonists.

"Terror doesn't take a vacation in 'Death Ship'; instead Joseph Badal masterfully takes us on a cruise to an all too frightening, yet all too real destination. Once you step on board, you are hooked."
—Tom Avitabile, #1 Bestselling Author of "The Eighth Day" and "The Devil's Quota"

https://amzn.com/B016APTJAU

"SINS OF THE FATHERS"
DANFORTH SAGA (#6)

The Danforth family returns in this sixth edition of the Danforth Saga. "Sins of the Fathers" takes the reader on a tension-filled journey from a kidnapping of Michael and Robbie Danforth in Colorado, to America's worst terrorist-sponsored attacks, to Special Ops operations in Mexico, Greece, Turkey, and Syria. This epic tale includes political intrigue, CIA and military operations, terrorist sleeper cells, drug cartels, and action scenes that will keep you pinned to the edge of your seat.

Joseph Badal's twelfth novel is complex, stimulating, and un-put-down-able. You will love his heroes and hate his villains, and you will root for the triumph of good over evil.

This is fiction as close to reality as you will ever find.

"Outstanding! Joseph Badal combines insider knowledge with taut writing and a propulsive plot to create a stellar thriller in a terrific series. Well-written, intense, timely and, at times, terrifying. Highly recommended."
—Sheldon Siegel, *New York Times* Bestselling Author of the Mike Daley/Rosie Fernandez Novels

http://a.co/eZTFJlO

"BORDERLINE"
THE LASSITER/MARTINEZ CASE FILES (#1)

In "Borderline," Joseph Badal delivers his first mystery novel with the same punch and non-stop action found in his acclaimed thrillers.

Barbara Lassiter and Susan Martinez, two New Mexico homicide detectives, are assigned to investigate the murder of a wealthy Albuquerque socialite. They soon discover that the victim, a narcissistic borderline personality, played a lifetime game of destroying people's lives. As a result, the list of suspects in her murder is extensive.

The detectives find themselves enmeshed in a helix of possible perpetrators with opportunity, means, and motive—and soon question giving their best efforts to solve the case the more they learn about the victim's hideous past.

Their job gets tougher when the victim's psychiatrist is murdered and DVDs turn up that show the doctor had serial sexual relationships with a large number of his female patients, including the murder victim.

"Borderline" presents a fascinating cast of characters, including two heroic female detective-protagonists and a diabolical villain; a rollercoaster ride of suspense; and an ending that will surprise and shock the reader.

"Think Cagney and Lacey. Think Thelma and Louise. Think murder and mayhem—and you are in the death grip of a mystery that won't let you go until it has choked the last breath of suspense from you."
—Parris Afton Bonds, author of "Tamed the Wildest Heart" and co-founder of Romance Writers of America and cofounder of Southwest Writers Workshop

https://amzn.com/B00YZSAHI8
Now Available at Audible.com: http://adbl.co/1Y4WC5H

"DARK ANGEL"
THE LASSITER/MARTINEZ CASE FILES (#2)

In "Dark Angel," the second in the Lassiter/Martinez Case Files series, Detectives Barbara Lassiter and Susan Martinez pick up where they left off in "Borderline." Assigned to a murder case, they discover that their suspect is much more than a one-off killer. In fact, the murderer appears to be a vigilante hell-bent on taking revenge against career criminals who the criminal justice system has failed to punish.

But Lassiter and Martinez are soon caught up in the middle of an FBI investigation of a monstrous home invasion gang that has murdered dozens of innocent victims across the United States. When they discover a link between their vigilante killer and the home invasion crew, they come into conflict with powerful men in the FBI who are motivated more by career self-preservation than by bringing justice to innocent victims.

Award-Winning and best-selling author Joseph Badal presents another intricate, tension-filled mystery that puts readers on the edge of their seats from the first page to the last, and will have them demanding more Lassiter/Martinez stories.

"Badal delivers a nice tight mystery and two wonderful female detectives you'll be cheering for."
—Catherine Coulter, *New York Times* bestselling author of "Nemesis"

http://a.co/5fFx9vs

"NATURAL CAUSES"
THE LASSITER/MARTINEZ CASE FILES (#3)

Homicide detective partners Barbara Lassiter and Susan Martinez return in this third edition of the *Lassiter/Martinez Case Files* series.

Called in to investigate a mysterious death in a retirement center, Lassiter and Martinez find themselves entangled in a case that might very well involve multiple murders committed by a psychopathic killer. The deeper they get into their investigation, the more complex and dangerous the case becomes, threatening the lives of the detectives and their loved ones. Political and bureaucratic machinations within the detectives' department and the involvement of organized crime only make their jobs more difficult.

Award-Winning, Amazon #1 best-selling author Joseph Badal offers up another suspenseful, *unputdownable* tale, with twists and turns that will put and keep the reader on a roller coaster ride of drama, action, and emotion from the first to the last page.

"A first-rate thriller, a powerhouse of a story that will keep you turning the pages into the wee hours. The pacing is relentless, with a sense of menace that grows almost unbearable. Lassiter and Martinez are two homicide detectives for the ages. I loved it!"
—Douglas Preston, #1 Bestselling Coauthor of the Famed *Pendergast* Series

https://amzn.to/33fXgEm

"THE MOTIVE"
THE CURTIS CHRONICLES
(#1)

In "The Motive," Joseph Badal presents the first book in his new series, *The Curtis Chronicles*. This latest addition to Badal's offering of acclaimed, best-selling thrillers delivers the same sort of action and suspense that readers have come to expect and enjoy from his previous nine novels.

Confronted with suspicious information relating to his sister Susan's supposed suicide in Honolulu, Albuquerque surgeon Matt Curtis questions whether his sister really killed herself. With the help of his sister's best friend, Renee Drummond, and his former Special Forces comrade, Esteban Maldonado, Matt investigates Susan's death. But Lonnie Jackson, the head of organized crime in Hawaii, afraid that Matt has gotten too close to the truth, sends killers after him.

This is an artfully written book that will appeal to readers who like thrillers with fully-developed characters, a big plot, and plenty of action, seasoned with friendship and romance.

"The Motive" puts the reader on a roller coaster ride of non-stop thrills and chills, propelled by realistic dialogue and a colorful cast of characters. It is another entertaining story from a master story-teller where good and evil struggle for supremacy and everyday heroes battle malevolent antagonists.

" 'The Motive' is a nail biter I couldn't put down. Joseph Badal knows how to make his legion of readers sweat to the very last paragraph. He has mastered the art of writing—and suspense. Bravo!"
—Parris Afton Bonds, Award-Winning Author of "Dream Time"

http://a.co/gAt7BtZ

"OBSESSED"
THE CURTIS CHRONICLES
(#2)

A world-class thriller with non-stop, heart-pounding tension and action, "Obsessed" brings back Matt Curtis and Renee Drummond and their villainous nemesis, Lonnie Jackson. This second installment in Joseph Badal's *The Curtis Chronicles* takes the reader from Rio de Janeiro to the mountains of New Mexico to the Mexico/United States border, following a crazed Jackson on his single-minded quest for revenge against the two people he blames for the deaths of his mother and brother and for the destruction of his criminal empire in Hawaii.

"Obsessed" is another master stroke of fiction from this Amazon #1 Best-Selling Author, two-time winner of the Tony Hillerman Award for Best Fiction Book of the Year, and three-time Military Writers Society of America Gold Medal Winner.

If you like fast-paced stories that put you on a breathless, adrenaline-filled journey, with realistic good guys and believable bad guys, "Obsessed" will have you begging for more.

"Joseph Badal's characters play on a world stage—and that world is a dark and dangerous place, seen through the pen of a master story teller."
—Steven F. Havill, Award-Winning Author of "Easy Errors"

https://amzn.to/2VCFwPL

"THE PYTHAGOREAN SOLUTION"
STAND-ALONE THRILLER

The attempt to decipher a map leads to violence and death, and a decades-long sunken treasure.

When American John Hammond arrives on the Aegean island of Samos he is unaware of events that happened six decades earlier that will embroil him in death and violence and will change his life forever.

Late one night Hammond finds Petros Vangelos lying mortally wounded in an alley. Vangelos hands off a coded map, making Hammond the link to a Turkish tramp steamer that carried a fortune in gold and jewels and sank in a storm in 1945.

On board this ship, in a waterproof safe, are documents that implicate a German SS Officer in the theft of valuables from Holocaust victims and the laundering of those valuables by the Nazi's Swiss banker partner.

"Badal is a powerful writer who quickly reels you in and doesn't let go."
—Pat Frovarp & Gary Shulze, Once Upon A Crime Mystery Bookstore

https://amzn.com/B00W4JVIYC

"ULTIMATE BETRAYAL"
STAND-ALONE THRILLER

Inspired by actual events, "Ultimate Betrayal" is a thriller that takes the reader on an action-packed, adrenaline-boosting ride, from the streets of South Philadelphia, through the Afghanistan War, to Mafia drug smuggling, to the halls of power at the CIA and the White House.

David Hood comes from the streets of South Philadelphia, is a decorated Afghanistan War hero, builds a highly successful business, marries the woman of his dreams, and has two children he adores. But there are two ghosts in David's past. One is the guilt he carries over the death of his brother. The other is a specter that will do anything to murder him.

David has long lost the belief that good will triumph over evil. The deaths of his wife and children only reinforce that cynicism. And leave him with nothing but a bone-chilling, all-consuming need for revenge.

" 'Ultimate Betrayal' provides the ultimate in riveting reading entertainment that's as well thought out as it is thought provoking. Both a stand-out thriller and modern day morality tale. Mined from the familial territory of Harlan Coben, with the seasoned action plotting of James Rollins or Steve Berry, this is fiction of the highest order. Poignant and unrelentingly powerful."
—Jon Land, bestselling and award-winning author of "The Tenth Circle"

https://amzn.com/B00LXG9QGY

"SHELL GAME"
STAND-ALONE THRILLER

"Shell Game" is a financial thriller using the economic environment created by the capital markets meltdown that began in 2007 as the backdrop for a timely, dramatic, and hair-raising tale. Badal weaves an intricate and realistic story about how a family and its business are put into jeopardy through heavy-handed, arbitrary rules set down by federal banking regulators, and by the actions of a sociopath in league with a corrupt bank regulator.

Like all of Badal's novels, "Shell Game" takes the reader on a roller coaster ride of action and intrigue carried on the shoulders of believable, often diabolical characters. Although a work of fiction, "Shell Game," through its protagonist Edward Winter, provides an understandable explanation of one of the main reasons the U.S. economy continues to languish. It is a commentary on what federal regulators are doing to the United States banking community today and, as a result, the damage they are inflicting on perfectly sound businesses and private investors across the country and on the overall U.S. economy.

"Shell Game" is inspired by actual events that have taken place as a result of poor governmental leadership and oversight, greed, corruption, stupidity, and badly conceived regulatory actions. You may be inclined to find it hard to believe what happens in this novel to both banks and bank borrowers. I encourage you to keep an open mind. "Shell Game" is a work of fiction that supports the old adage: You don't need to make this stuff up.

"Take a roller coaster ride through the maze of modern banking regulations with one of modern fiction's most terrifying sociopaths in the driver's seat. Along with its compelling, fast-paced story of a family's struggle against corruption, 'Shell Game' raises important questions about America's financial system based on well-researched facts."

—Anne Hillerman & Jean Schaumberg, WORDHARVEST
https://amzn.com/B00LXG9QFA

CPSIA information can be obtained
at www.ICGtesting.com
Printed in the USA
FFHW011046200819
54349353-60040FF

9 780578 559285